An Ashy Affair

by

Lynn Shurr

This is a work of fiction. Names, characters, places, and incidents are either the product of the author's imagination or are used fictitiously, and any resemblance to actual persons living or dead, business establishments, events, or locales, is entirely coincidental.

An Ashy Affair

COPYRIGHT © 2016 by Carla S. Hostetter

Cover Art by *Diana Carlile*

The Wild Rose Press, Inc.
PO Box 708
Adams Basin, NY 14410-0708
Visit us at www.thewildrosepress.com

Publishing History
First Champagne Rose Edition, 2016
Print ISBN 978-1-5092-0944-6
Digital ISBN 978-1-5092-0945-3

Published in the United States of America

"Don't look at me!

Remember, a dog, four pups, and now Bandit. My mom will kill me if I bring any more home. Besides, I still owe you for Jolie's BOGO and tonight's tickets. I hope you take credit cards." He'd tried to make light of the situation, but watched Leah's face. Obviously, she was having an "Aha!" moment.

Her green eyes went wide and almost glowed as if she'd discovered radium or some other deadly substance. "I knew it! You aren't perfect. You live with your mother. Ashton Blaise is a mama's boy. That's why I couldn't find your number in the phone book to cancel the kayak trip."

The bow tie that went with the tux suddenly seemed too tight around his neck. "Come on, this is the South. Lots of guys still live at home if they aren't married. If you need the number, it's under Hank Blaise. My mother didn't change it after my dad's death. But, I have my own cell. Here, I'll write the number down for you." Ash seized a pen attached to one of the clipboards, but not a single sheet of plain paper in sight and all the napkins were linen.

"I can write it on your palm!"

"Why not on my breast, oh most desired of all the firemen in Chapelle?" Leah smirked.

"That would work for me, but the competition isn't that tough. Most of the men are married. Look, I have extenuating circumstances. If you'd just give me a chance to…"

Praise for Lynn Shurr

"Shurr is a wonderful storyteller"

~The Romance Studio

~*~

"Very easy read, well written, combined with conflict, believable plots and secondary characters that make the story come alive."

~Jane Lange, Romances, Reads and Reviews

~*~

"Lynn Shurr breathes life into the characters and allows each turn of the page to lead up to a pleasurable ending."

~Cherokee, Coffee Time Romance and More

~*~

"I love the picture the author paints of the town and the way of life, and the characters are strong and interesting. Great read of this summer and for the beach."

~Joan Conning Afman, author

~*~

"Lynn Shurr stories have that distinctive Louisiana flavor…and make you eager for another taste."

~J. L. Salter, author

Dedication

For outstanding naturalist Stacey Leah Scarce,
Angel Paws Rescue Center,
and the BOM Volunteer Fire Department

Other Wild Rose Titles by Lynn Shurr

Single Titles:
A Trashy Affair
A Will of her Own
~*~

The Sinners sports romances:
Goals for a Sinner
Wish for a Sinner
Kicks for a Sinner
Paradise for a Sinner
Love Letter for a Sinner
Son of a Sinner
She's a Sinner
~*~

The Mardi Gras Series:
Queen of the Mardi Gras Ball
Mardi Gras Madness
Courir de Mardi Gras
~*~

The Roses Series:
The Convent Rose
A Wild Red Rose
Always Yellow Roses

Chapter One

Smoke, soft, gray, and deadly slipped under the sill of the old kitchen door and wrapped its tendrils around the fireman's boots before dissipating toward the ceiling. Ashton Blaise searched the downstairs rooms while a volunteer clumped up the stairs to check the bedrooms before the entire house became engaged in flames. Nothing much in the first floor bedroom— double bed, dresser, chair and desk, but no computer sitting atop it, the one object most people wanted saved.

Casting an eye at the door that might collapse at any moment and release the inferno on the other side, he moved to the living room across the hall. Same here, a worn sofa and side chairs centered about a brick fireplace, a small LED television hung over the mantel, no precious ornaments or family pictures anywhere, no Bible on the coffee table. Sometimes, homeowners wanted the holy book saved more than anything. Ashton's fellow firefighter beat it down the stairs and paused to give him an all clear sign. No one overcome by smoke lying in bed up there.

Ash finished his own survey and headed for the front entry. He nearly missed the small body sprawled by the threshold. In fact, he almost stepped on it. That would have been the end of the black and white kitten, someone's precious pet. Scooping it into his gauntlet with one smooth motion, he continued outside kicking the front door shut behind him. They found crispy critters under these raised frame cottages all the time, but this animal might have a chance. Splaying the kitten belly up in his glove, Ash gave it a whiff from his oxygen tank and compressed the tiny white chest a few times with two fingers. Nothing. He tried the oxygen again.

Pity about the house. Late nineteenth century, he guessed. It had one of those pleasing half moon windows on the second story and lots of pretty gingerbread trim hanging from the eaves and around the porch like icing on a wedding cake. He figured the house with its dry wooden frame was a goner, but not this kitten. He pumped its chest again.

"Shouldn't you be putting out the fire instead of dawdling over a stray cat? She's got dozens of them. A spinster cat lady, that's what Leah Allain is or will be in a few years." An elderly woman, her short white hair feathered around her ears, her nose sharp and pointy as a beak, her eyes black and beady as a shrike, her voice as raucous as a crow, leaned over his hand. "She lives here alone except for cats, lots of bird-killing feral cats. One more or less won't make any difference."

Ash continued his work on the kitten, but gave the woman his attention. "Are you the person who called in the fire?"

"No, I'm the next door neighbor. I'd have let the place burn to the ground and those pests with it. "

Cottages exactly like this one, some not so well kept, spread out along the crumbling, pot-holed blacktop of the rural Louisiana road. They weren't close together and left plenty of room for the trucks to park and the firemen to work in semi-peace until the curious neighbors, the looky-loos, and a reporter with photographer in tow from the *Chapelle Clarion* showed up. Ash didn't let the hostile neighbor rattle him.

"Miss Leah lives alone here, ma'am? No guests staying over?"

"Didn't I just say it's only her and the damned cats? I'm Tweedy, Mrs. Ernestine Tweedy, a Berard that was. My family once owned all this property before the War." She made a grand gesture that sent the Bingo wings of flesh under her scrawny arms waggling from the sleeves of her housedress patterned with huge hummingbirds sucking nectar from red hibiscus.

Ash had no doubt which war she referred to, the Civil War, the only war still being fought in the deep South if only verbally. "Do you know where we can contact the homeowner, Miz Tweedy?"

"She's at the animal shelter. Runs the place. Saves animals that should be put down."

"Thank you for the information. Now, please step across the road and out of the way of the firefighters."

"Why should I? You're just sitting here on the truck fooling with a dead kitten. My family farmed this land for a hundred years before the Yankees came." Her words were interrupted by a blast of shattered glass as the front windows blew out, and greedy flames reached up to gobble the gingerbread trim.

"For your own safety, ma'am." He had Ernestine Tweedy on the move now, but the kitten still failed to respond. One of his crew rounded the flame-engulfed building.

Ernestine stopped in her tracks. "That you under the big hat, Cubby?"

"Sure is, Miss Ernestine. Me and Daddy are

3

volunteer firemen. We come in our truck with the red light slapped on the top. We was working down the road fixin' up a rent house."

"Well, when you're finished here, come on over for some of my teacakes. I know you love 'em."

"I do!" Under his fireman's helmet, Cubby's round face glowed with sweat and the prospect of cookies. His innocent, round blue eyes positively shone.

"Miz Tweedy, please step back. Cubby, you have a message for me?"

"Yes, Captain Blaise. My daddy says this is arson. He could smell the gas splashed around the screen porch. We turned off the line to the house right away so it couldn't be from that. Can't do nothing more around back."

"Tell him to move the hose lines to the front."

Cubby trundled off to deliver the order. He was dim as one of those curly light bulbs just turned on, but the heavy boy added considerable weight to a hose line and took orders with complete obedience. Awww shit, Ash knew he'd have to give up on the kitten soon and break the heart of Miss Leah, the cat lover. The mobile headquarters housed in an old bookmobile would have the number of the shelter. They used the place often enough to get an assist for injured animals. Or maybe that wouldn't be needed. A white SUV breaking the speed limit veered to the side of the road nearly putting the vehicle into a deep, weed-clogged ditch. The urgency had homeowner written all over it.

A young woman emerged with her short but shapely legs already pumping in his direction. Khaki shorts covered flaring hips. A leather belt cinched in a small waist. Ample breasts wobbled beneath her Safe

Haven Animal Shelter polo shirt as she ran. Some people might say she was stocky, but Ash would have called her well-built and compact. She moved with energy and purpose, arriving before him in under a minute.

"Leah Allain?" Ash asked.

"Yes, and that's my house. It doesn't look good."

"No, sorry. We got here eight minutes after the call, pretty good for this far out in the country, but the rear of the building was fully engaged. I tried to save your kitten, but…" The ball of fur nestled in his glove opened bright green eyes set in a mask of black and squeaked a tiny cry. "I mean I saved your cat. Here he is." Ash held out the resuscitated animal and released what the guys called his panty-melting grin. Not that he thought so. Leah Allain did not accept the kitten or burst into tears as many did when a beloved pet survived the flames.

Instead, she bushed a choppy wing of thick, black hair cropped man short on the sides out of eyes as green as the cat's and said, "That's not my kitten. It's Bandit, one of the ferals I feed. The mom and four offspring were dumped out here a couple of weeks ago. The female is tame enough, but the kittens are wild, all but Bandit who aspires to be a housecat. Every time I open the door, he sneaks inside—which almost got him killed today."

"Well, um, here he is." Ash tried again to deliver the kitten into her care, but she didn't put her hands out. No panties melted today, only a side awning of plastic slats that caved in and fell to the ground. In the distance, he heard the approach of a second pumper truck from one of the substations, reliable B.O.M. or ever ready Nebo, coming to put the coup de grace to the fire. "I need to get back to work."

"You keep him."

"I, ah, have a dog."

"They'll adjust. You saved Bandit's life. Now he's yours."

Ash began to suspect Leah Allain possessed real skills in pushing abandoned animals off on other people. "Another crew is coming. I have to set up another hose line. You can wait in the command unit until the fire is out. If you have nowhere to live, we'll connect you to the Red Cross and the Salvation Army to replace some of your household items."

"Don't bother. I can live in the barn." She pointed to a sturdy structure a safe distance from the burning house. A high peaked red metal roof swept down into two wings on the sides. Window panes were set in the spaces where the tops of stall doors once hung.

"I think we can set you up better than that."

"Look, this place belonged to an artist who had a studio in its loft and converted the bottom into a tidy apartment with a shower and kitchenette. I'll be fine. A bunch of my stuff is stored in there. Been here three months, and I haven't gotten moved into the house yet. I've been using some old furniture the Miss Delta left behind. Thank God for small favors—and the home insurance required to get the mortgage."

Strong woman, no weeping, no hysteria, Ash had to admire that. He tried again. "So, if you'd take the kitten over to the mobile unit—maybe you have some folks you want to contact." Ash jerked his head in the direction of the old bookmobile now chock full of the latest communications equipment being operated by the youngest tech savvy fireman and providing an air-conditioned spot where Chief Fontenot roosted during crises. Flaking red lettering on a dirty beige background still proclaimed *Ste. Jeanne de Arc Parish Library System.*

"You mean the bookmobile?"

"The mobile command unit. The fire department ran out of funds before we got it repainted. In the summer, kids still try to flag it down to get books."

Leah quirked a little smile at him. "I loved the bookmobile as a child. I'll give you room to work." She walked off to the MCU minus the kitten, which flopped over in his glove and curled into a ball as if exhausted from all the commotion. The second pumper truck arrived, squeezed over the culvert and along the narrow gravel drive to get into place. Ash took a spare helmet from the engine and placed the kitten inside before going to organize the second hose line. Maybe, it would jump out and return to its mother once things settled down.

****

Leah climbed the three steps of the command unit and pressed the latch on the door. She stepped into its long, narrow space kept deliciously cool by a humming generator. Outside, mid-October continued to be stubbornly hot and dry, ripening the stands of ragweed, wild asters, and black-eyed Susans along the road. The farmers longed for a cold snap to make the sugar rise in the cane and got none. Regardless, grinding had started, bringing along with it a mess of stalks on the road and blue skies made hazy by the burning of the fields. Houses nearby sometimes caught fire, but hers sat well away from any plantations.

Cases of bottled water sat stacked against a wall, and a rack held spare oxygen tanks. Amidst the supplies, sitting in the comfortable driver's seat swiveled away from the wheel, Chief Fontenot enjoyed coffee and a jelly donut that had splurted across a white T-shirt covering a belly the size of a water cooler bottle. Red suspenders forced to either side of that vast gut held up the head fireman's pants and kept them from sinking over the boots on his feet. He pointed the lemon center of the donut at her and said with his blubbery, jelly-smeared lips, "You're one of Sam Allain's girls, right? Leah, the older one. I can tell by the green eyes. Must have some Irish woman hiding in your genealogy."

Lean nodded. The trouble with coming back to the small town of her birth—everyone knew her ancestry and her business. "Yes, sir, on my grandmother's side."

The Chief nodded into his treble chin. "That's right. Your granddaddy always said he fell in love with Miss Alene's eyes first and then the rest of her. She taught me in sixth grade back in the days when a teacher wasn't afraid to use a paddle. Commanded respect, she did, like one of the nuns."

Through the windshield of the van, Leah watched the beams of her home implode, sending a shower of sparks into the air. The spray from the hoses hunted them down and rained on the dry earth surrounding the house to prevent the fire from spreading. Bandit's savior, the guy with the smoky gray eyes and flash fire grin, directed the volunteers while Chief Fontenot continued to shake her family tree for conversation.

"How's the old gal doing?"

"Good enough for someone approaching ninety.

Look, I should notify my insurance agency."

"I heard you bought this old place when Miss Delta found the nerve to go back to New Orleans. She was one of those Katrina refugees, you know. Claimed she couldn't make a living from her art here and mostly survived on renting out the house and staying in the barn apartment."

"Yes, Chapelle isn't exactly a bastion of the arts, though it is getting better." Leah worked her phone from a buttoned hip pocket and hoped the Chief would shut up long enough for her to make the call.

"Bet you got great insurance coverage with your granddaddy once owning the biggest agency in town."

"Yes, my second cousin gave me a good deal." She summoned up Brock's number and hit the call button. While it rang, Fontenot started a new line of inquiry.

"You leave anything burning on the stove? Smell any gas before you left this morning?'

"No. I had cold cereal, and the place was inspected before I bought it. No problems with the gas lines. Brock," she said with great relief. "Bad news."

"Insurance agencies, even ones owned by relatives, sure don't like to pay up, especially when the cause might be suspicious. Houses don't just sit there catching fire middle of the day for nothing." Nothing got past Terrill "Tank" Fontenot, the man who had been fire chief since before she could remember, and Leah was twenty-five. Not when he played lineman in high school and college, and certainly not now when he'd become another kind of immovable object.

Leah moved away toward the rear of the vehicle where a college age kid wearing a headset appeared to be in charge of communications. She kept her voice low as she made the report and disconnected. Now, to squeeze past the Chief and make her escape no matter how cool the interior or hot the coffee. His booted feet got in her way.

"You don't seem all that broken up over your place, Leah. When I first came on as chief, I had a guy in town always burned down some of his property whenever he needed cash. I put an end to that." Though his eyes were small, dark, and piggy buried in all that flesh, they still possessed a certain shrewdness.

"I haven't been in the house long enough to get attached. Besides, most of my stuff is still in boxes in the barn, and I left my laptop at work."

"Convenient."

Leah stepped over his thick ankles and made for the door, but the Chief delayed her again. "No sense in going out there and getting in their way. Besides, Ashton Blaise got no time to flirt right now. I saw you two talking. The ladies drool all over him—handsome guy, I guess."

"I didn't have time to notice. He had a kitten he wanted me to take." Leah laid her hand on the latch to make her escape.

"Yeah, sounds like Blaise. He always tries to get the animals out. Once pulled an angry cat from under a building, and good thing he had his shield down or it would have taken out one of his pretty gray eyes. Lots of grateful ladies appreciate what he does."

"It's not my kitten!" She didn't bother to hide her exasperation.

"Okay, okay, I hear you. I'm only trying to warn you he's an odd duck." The Chief popped the stub of the donut into his mouth.

"You mean gay?"

Fontenot had the grace to swallow before answering. "No, not that." He paused as if he had something far worse to tell her. "He's one of them—vegans. Loves animals so much he won't eat 'em."

The way he pronounced the word it might as well have been Venusian, an alien from another planet. Leah gave him a minimal response. "That's admirable, I suppose."

The Chief eyed her closely. "Maybe you're one, too."

"No, not me. I'd have smaller hips if I were. I like a good burger with all the fixings."

"Nothing wrong with a woman having a nice caboose. Donut?" He offered her the box from the new shop in town giving old Pommier's Bakery a run for its money. "Fresh and warm every a.m. and not far from the firehouse."

"Another time, thanks." Leah plunged down the steps and shut the door behind her. Another thing she'd have to get used to again, sexist remarks said in a well-meaning way. She'd lived in the big city too long. No sense staying around here and wasting her time. She went directly to her SUV with the animal cages filling the rear and headed back to work. Ashton Blaise had his hands too full with a fire hose to try to foist the kitten on her again.

Chapter Two

Toting a huge burger and a ton of fries in a bag from Duffy's Diner along with her usual ironic Coke Zero, Leah returned to the scene of the crime after six p.m. Scene of the crime, that's what Chief Fontenot called her former home when she'd contacted him about getting the fire report for her insurance claim. He suspected arson and warned her to do no cleaning up until the State Fire Marshall came and had his say. She drove past the heap of blackened rubble merrily decorated with yellow crime scene tape. The old refrigerator that came with the place stood like a scorched monolith marking the kitchen area. Only warped and tangled pieces of screening remained of a once pleasant porch. A few bent wires served as crosses for the Boston ferns she'd bought on sale not too long ago, their fronds now charred to ashes.

Leah continued along the gravel drive to the barn with its red roof and gray cypress planking. Before she turned off the ignition, the cats began to appear: tabbies and grays, calicos, blacks, whites, and one with Siamese markings. They emerged from the shadows, from beneath bushes and tall clumps of weeds. Bandit's calico mother wound around her ankles while the cautious kittens, one nearly a twin to Bandit, another orange and bigger than the others, the last a calico female like the mom, immediately hid under the SUV.

She knew what they wanted and considered her here to serve them.

Delta Savage had sealed off the wide barn door and decorated the panel with a swamp scene of knobby cypress trees and wading egrets. A rather good-natured alligator laid low in the water with turtles sunning on its back. Leah went to one of the people-sized side doors. The sack of cat chow sat just inside. She heaved the large bag under her arm and poured a stream of dry food into two large tin pans sitting under the eaves. While the feral cats swarmed their free meal, she hosed out the water dishes and refilled them to the brim. As part of a very good deal on the property, she'd sworn to care for the cat colony. Miss Delta had seen to the spaying and neutering of most of the flock. As soon as Bonny, yeah, she'd named Bandit's mom, stopped nursing, Leah planned the same fate for her, freedom from constant reproduction. She'd trap the kittens, take them to the shelter to be tamed, and try to find good homes for them all.

Leah also inherited a feud with Ernestine Tweedy whose yard bore a perky wooden sign with a cardinal image proclaiming it a bird sanctuary. On the other side of a thick and hostile row of sharp-leaved pampas grass, the Tweedy live oaks were festooned with bird feeders thick as Christmas ornaments. Tubes of sugar water bedecked the rear porch with their red plastic flowers designed to draw hummingbirds, all very busy in October when the migration took place. Initially, Miss Ernestine had invited her over for teacakes, a friendly Southern gesture that soon became burnt around the edges when she learned Leah did not intend to dispose of the cats. No amount of arguing about the overcrowded no-kill shelter, the inability to place wild cats, or the fact they were feed regularly to cut down on bird depredations received any slack from Miz Tweedy. They hadn't spoken since, no great loss in Leah's opinion.

She went back to her hulking SUV, the one her father gave her when he'd bought a Corvette convertible during his mid-life crisis, and retrieved her dinner. Come morning, the interior would reek of French fries because of the delay. Dog tired, she hadn't stopped for any groceries. With the odor arousing her stomach juices, she'd pull into Mickey D's tomorrow for an egg muffin, hash browns, and coffee, breaking her diet yet again. Shaking her head, Leah moved toward the door she'd left open a crack. She half expected Bandit to be sitting in the hallway and felt a small pang when she didn't find him there. Maybe he'd died, but she hoped the fireman had taken him home. The kit was big enough to eat wet food and kitten chow, but still nursed whenever Bonny allowed it. She knew he'd partaken of a squirrel his mom killed and dragged home to her family because she'd found the little family and the remaining bushy tail on her front porch one morning. That memory killed her yen for hash browns.

Leah slung her sack onto a small table with two metal chairs that appeared to have been salvaged from a defunct ice cream parlor and comprised all the furnishings of the small kitchen, not counting a vintage fridge with ice trays, a small stove, the sink under the window, and a stacked washer-dryer combo in the corner. She took a long drag on the Coke despite its diluted quality and waited for the caffeine to kick into gear. On a day when little else could go wrong, the volunteer who hosed down the dog runs daily hadn't showed, and that chore fell to Leah since the older ladies who did come couldn't stand the heat. She heard a rumbling sound and knew it wasn't her belly.

Making her way to a window, she watched a silver Prius slowly negotiating the gravel drive. Great. Some do-gooder had gotten wind of the tragedy and already arrived with a sack of used clothes that probably wouldn't fit and a big pot of gumbo because this is how small towns worked. She'd be grateful for the gumbo at least. Maybe the person wouldn't stay long, allowing her to get a hot shower and fall into bed in one of the cleverly converted box stall rooms that lined the other side of the barn.

The vehicle parked, and she observed Ashton Blaise unfold his long, lean length from the driver's seat, not a hard view on the eyes at all. He noticed her peering at him and moved with masculine grace toward the kitchen door on the other side of the barn, not the one crawling with cats. His hands were full. He didn't haul a trash bag of castoffs, but carried a gumbo pot with a pie holder balanced on top of it. She rushed to open the door. Didn't want that pie to go splat. Apple, cherry, lemon meringue, she wondered, salivating like one of the shelter's dogs.

"I was just sitting down to dinner, but you are welcome to come in. Sorry about being so surly this morning." What kind of gumbo did he bear? Seafood, duck, rabbit, or her favorite, turkey-sausage? Leah showed him to her tiny table. "Please sit down. Can I offer you a cold drink? I used this fridge for extra storage." She flipped open the refrigerator door to reveal stacks of diet drink boxes, a bottle of white wine, and a six pack of beer. Leah shrugged. "I like to buy soft drinks when you get four for ten dollars."

"Very economical, but no thanks," he said as he lowered his height onto one of the small chairs. "I won't stay long. I'm on my dinner break since I have duty tonight, but I wanted to make sure you were okay, had a place to stay and food tonight no matter what you claimed. I cooked for my crew and had some leftover lentil soup. They didn't touch the spinach quiche." He presented the pie keeper to her.

"Oh, great." Disappointed, she accepted his offerings, shoved some of the cartons aside, and crammed them into the refrigerator.

"The soup is still warm. I puree the lentils and add a touch of garlic. Honestly, my crew loves it with a loaf of crusty French bread and a salad."

"I'll have it tomorrow. I bought dinner on the way home." Pointedly, Leah opened her sack and let the meaty, greasy aroma escape. She removed the paper container of fries and spread out the wrapper around her burger. Saying, "If you don't mind," she dug into her oversized burger. For a minute there, she'd been lured by his slim but toned body and those smoky eyes surrounded by thick, dark lashes. He wore his black hair short, almost military in style, but the start of a five o'clock shadow along his lean cheeks and jaw gave him a little edge. She'd forgotten about the food weirdness for a moment.

"Go ahead and eat," he answered with a slight smile on lips neither thin nor full but just right for a man. "You were right. I wouldn't mind living in a barn like this either."

His eyes roved, not to hers, but easily over Leah's

head to the large open space under the loft that served as a living area. Delta Savage had removed the rear barn door and replaced it with a huge window looking out on a row of oaks and at this time of year, the start of a blazing red sunset, the dynamic result of the burning of the fields. "Dangerous," he said as if reading her thoughts. "But all that debris in the air does make for a pretty sky at evening."

"Yes, dangerous," she babbled and quickly caught a dribble of juice and mayo sliding down her chin on a paper napkin.

He eyed the logo on her bag. "They make great shrimp po-boys and onion rings, too."

"Um, I thought you were a vegan."

"According to Chief Fontenot who doesn't know a lacto ovo from his big fat—behind."

"So you're this lacto ovo kind?" She ate a fry in his presence, couldn't help herself.

"No, I'm a pesco vegetarian. The seafood around here is too great to resist, and I'd be kicked out of the family crawfish boil if I didn't indulge in mudbugs."

"French fry?" she offered, shoving the container his way.

"Don't mind if I do." He took a few of the fresh cut fries and chewed them with relish. "My father died at age fifty-two from a heart attack. I'm doing all I can to prevent that. Mostly, I avoid fried foods, too, but every once in a while I get a craving. Nobody does fried better than Cajuns."

"True." Another kind of craving arose in Leah. No! Not the time to develop a yen for a firefighter, every woman's dream lover—not after her last romantic disaster with a stunning veterinarian who healed wounded animals. Did she only go for stereotypes? Before he had her lapping vegetarian vegetable soup from his helmet, Leah reached deep into her bag of defensive tricks and drew out rudeness and sarcasm. She planted her elbows on the table and leaned forward as if doing an inspection.

"So, you're the famous Ashton Blaise, savior of small creatures and beloved by their female owners. I dread to think what your mother might have named a brother."

"Cole," he replied, not at all offended. "She named my brother Cole Blaise. Our daddy was a fireman, too, and she had quite a sense of humor. We got used to the teasing at school. You have any siblings?"

Well, making fun of his name hadn't worked, and she had no smart retort. "A sister, Rachel." The answer came out plain and simple.

"Seems like your mom went Bibical. Wasn't Rachel the one favored over Leah?"

"Still is."

"Your sister must be something if she's better than you."

This wasn't going at all as planned. "You know what they call me around here?" Leah asked.

"Let me guess—the Cat Lady."

Ashton had such a charming smile, damn him. "That would be Miz Tweedy's name for me. I'm also known as the Cat Killer. I had to put down one-hundred twenty-one cats when I took over the shelter to stem an epidemic of distemper. The cats roamed free around the compound getting wilder and spreading disease. Only a few kittens were kept inside for adoption. No one wanted the rest."

"That must have been hard."

"I did what I had to do."

"I'll bet. I heard you've already gotten a cathouse built."

Did she note a hint of another smile? "That would be called a cattery, thank you. Yes, an anonymous donor stepped up to provide the funds."

"Sorry, wrong term. I guess you have no interest in hearing what happened to Bandit since you aren't sentimental about animals."

Let him think what he wanted, that she was tough and hard. "Did he survive?" Leah made sure to inject a note of indifference into her voice.

"My dog adopted him."

"Don't tell me—you have a Dalmatian."

Ash shook his head and helped himself to another French fry.

"A Rottweiler or a pit bull, some big, aggressive dog."

"Nope, Courage is a Jack Russell terrier mix. She's nursing four pups right now and just gave Bandit a sniff and a few licks and nudged him in with the rest of her brood. He went right for a tit. Now I have five animals that need homes."

Leah suppressed the "aww" that rose in her throat almost like a purr. Instead, she said, "You should have had the bitch fixed."

"Only got her a week ago. We were putting out a cane field fire pushed toward the road when the wind came up unexpectedly. It set the weeds ablaze. Out of the burning stubble comes this small dog with something in her mouth. She drops a puppy and goes right back into the flames, returns with another, and darts away again. I tried to follow her, but the smoke was too thick. One more time, she delivers a puppy to the side of the road and dashes back into the fire. We had the road blocked off, and those who didn't want to detour stood at the barricades and bet on how many times she'd return. I could see her fur beginning to singe, and she ran on tender paws when she made it out with the last of her babies. Those two were in a bad way. We took all of them to a nearby vet. He did what he could, then I took them home. I know the shelter is always overcrowded. I didn't want to dump them there."

"Good, we don't have room for more abandoned puppies. I would have turned them away." Leah took a deep suck on her Coke to cover the lump in her throat and the lie on her lips. Stories like this always made her choke up. Dang, she had to blink away the tears.

Ashton Blaise uplifted his fine body from the small chair. "I really need to get going. Give the lentil soup a chance. You might love it and the quiche." He considered her face for a moment. "You know, Leah Allain, I don't think you are as tough as you pretend to be. Finish your dinner. I'll see myself out."

Fortunately, he closed the kitchen door before she began to blubber into a burger-stained napkin. The whole day caught up with her all at once with the brave, little dog story turning on the waterworks. Now, she feared on top of it she would develop a taste for lentil soup.

Chapter Three

Leah parked under the porte-cochere that ran alongside the elegant small home in the oldest, leafiest area of Chapelle. Once the long narrow property ran all the way to a bayou dock for easy transport of goods, but through the years the land had been subdivided over and over again into town lots and bisected by much improved roads. The lazy brown river could no longer be viewed from the deep, gracious front porch with its slim, single story columns and clusters of white wicker furniture in need of repainting. Leah meant to take care of that one day, but for now, she hoisted two bags of carefully selected groceries, inserted her key, and entered by the side door where a short hallway intersected with a longer, lengthwise corridor.

Had she gone to the right, she'd have arrived at the darkened front parlor and an unused dining room full of heavy mahogany furniture after passing the closed doors to a study and a sitting room. Leah turned left and, ignoring the two bedrooms and a bath, arrived in the kitchen with its doorway and windows overlooking a small garden getting its second wind after the worst of the summer heat. Her grandmother sat asleep in a cypress lawn chair amid the second flowering of her Blaze roses and beds of snapdragons and pansies freshly planted by the yard service. No sense in waking her before she had to.

Leah filled the fruit bowl on the kitchen table and shelved the boxes of cereal and crackers. She put the pudding and yogurt cups into the refrigerator, the ice cream bars in the freezer on the bottom, so much easier to reach that way, and replaced a carton of slightly sour milk with a fresh quart. After placing small containers of soup and other foods that could be nuked in the microwave if her grandmother remembered how to use it, Leah ripped a paper towel off the roll on the counter and wiped her face. Once autumn officially arrived, Gran turned off the air-conditioning no matter what the temperature. In midsummer, she allowed it to run set at eighty degrees. No wonder her visitors were few.

Leah steeled herself for a brief visit. After all, the milk and frozen foods in her car wouldn't last long in this heat. She took the three back steps into the garden and noted one of the handrails wobbled. Despite being left with a sheet of people to call for repairs, Gran never used it, never picked up a phone for any reason unless the person on the other end was so determined they let it ring twenty times and she answered out of sheer annoyance. Leah added that to her to-do list: call the handyman.

She took a seat in the other lawn chair and for a moment breathed in the air scented by the old-fashioned roses. Hummingbirds sipped from the orange, tubular flowers of the trumpet creeper vine that engulfed a small structure in the yard said to have been slave quarters at one time. Certainly, Gran's household help, a married black couple and their son, had once lived there. Leah remembered them vaguely. Now, the building served as a storage and garden shed. The rapacious vine should really be pulled down before the house collapsed under its weight, but not before the hummingbirds left for Central America. They needed fuel for the journey, or so Gran always said. She planted plenty of flowers for them.

With that good memory in mind, she gently shook her grandmother's arm. The old woman startled. Her hand went to the emergency alert button hanging around her neck. Leah removed her fingers. "It's only me, Leah."

Gran stared for a moment, then withdrew recognition from the bank of her brain. "You're Sam's girl, the short one, the one with brains. What have you done to your hair? Why don't you ever wear a dress?"

Leah answered with patience. "I work with animals. I'm often outside. Dresses aren't practical, and short hair is cooler in this climate."

She'd told her this over and over. Maybe Gran detected the lie about her hair. Once nothing got by the former teacher. Truth be told, she'd whacked it off so short because Colton Dandridge, DVM, had loved it long. His wife, the one he was supposed to leave, said it made Leah look butch, but in her own opinion, the new haircut empowered her like a super heroine who would never fall for a falsehood again. So there.

Leah changed the subject. "I brought your groceries. Grapes, bananas, and Satsumas are in the fruit bowl. The Satsumas are local and really sweet. The pudding cups and yogurt you like are in the fridge along with your favorite ice cream. I know you get Meals on Wheels, but there's soup and cereal for you if you want it. Remember, your hot meal comes around eleven most days. Please answer the door. Raleigh is coming for you to take you for your dental appointment tomorrow since you wanted your teeth cleaned. You remember Raleigh, right?"

"Of course I do! Dot and Ira's boy. I helped raise him." Gran's eyes, green and sharp again since the cataract removal, zeroed in on the old cabin. "Where are Dot and Ira? Why, they've let that vine take over their house. I must speak to them about it."

If she insisted, Leah would have to drive her to the Mount Zion Baptist Cemetery out in the country where they lay at rest waiting for Kingdom Come. Instead, she said, "They've been gone a long time, but their son will see you tomorrow. How's that?"

"Good, I suppose."

"I have groceries in the car and have to get going. Anything I can do for you before I leave? Help you inside? Get something down from a shelf."

"I don't need any help! Leave, just leave."

Despite the gruff sendoff, Leah kissed Gran's cheek, its skin so thinned by age the bones poked out at sharp angles beneath it. The highly independent woman waved her away. She went directly to the porte-cochere by way of the garden gate and started for her home in the country. A bevy of accusatory cats waited on her arrival. Their staring eyes said she was late with the grub, but this time she parked by the kitchen door. Melting groceries came first.

A heap of black plastic garbage bags blocked her entry. She had two more in the back of her SUV thanks to the house fire being featured on the front page of today's *Clarion* complete with a photo of the charred remains and the caption *Survivor plans to live in barn.* Leah kicked two of the bags out of her way to get in the door with her groceries. She stowed a few sacks of frozen vegetables and a precious pint of chocolate-chocolate chip ice cream already going soft into her limited freezer, rammed the containers of milk and juice into the door racks, and started down the hall to feed the cats.

Delta had put in insulation and wallboard painted a neutral color, now dotted with nails where she'd once displayed her art. About time to get her own creative outlet, nature photography, hung on those walls. Thank heaven the boxes were stored in the loft. She could never recapture some of the sights, and somehow having them backed up on a computer wasn't the same as glossy, framed photos bedecking her home. The cats began to meow as they sensed her getting close to the feed sack. She armed herself with chow and opened the door. The wildest of the bunch leapt back, but Bonny all but jumped into her arms.

"Just so you know, Bandit is fine. He found another soft touch to feed him," Leah said as she poured out the kibble.

She'd gotten as far as rinsing the last of the water pans when the silver Prius turned into her road again. Ashton Blaise didn't drive like a fireman. He inched along protecting his car from the loose gravel, but he reached her nonetheless. Leah had the urge to wipe that bound-to-get-him-laid smile off his face with a squirt from the hose.

In fact, she did point the nozzle at him like a weapon. "If you come bearing another sack of used clothing, be on your way and take it with you."

His smokin' hot gray glance drifted to her breasts, then surged back to her face. "I don't think any of my duds would fit you."

"What, too long in the legs?"

"Yeah, that's what I was thinking. Put down the hose. I come bearing good news and a veggie pizza since you have the drinks to go with it."

Leah turned off the water. "I prefer pepperoni."

"You won't even notice the lack under the layer of double cheese on your side. I make a better one myself, but didn't have the time to prepare the whole wheat crust."

"Of course you do, along with saving kittens and giving homes to stray dogs."

Ash shrugged shoulders entirely capable of slinging her over them with very little effort. "It's what I do. Don't forget the good news. I'm not telling you out here in the middle of a cat frenzy."

"Okay, don't let any of them inside. The really wild ones go bonkers indoors." Leah edged through the door. Ash held off Bonny with his boot and followed her to the kitchen with the pizza box in hand. "Looks like I interrupted something other than the feeding of the horde."

"Just groceries and some other things I picked up at Walmart that will have to do for now."

"I'd be glad to help." He set the pie on the table.

"You don't know where anything goes. Besides, you'd have to handle meat." Leah opened a doubled plastic sack and shoved a pound of hamburger, two pork chops, and a single strip steak into the freezer on top of the vegetables.

"As long as I can't absorb it through my skin, I'm good. Where do the paper towels go?"

"Under the sink. Look, just open two beers while I take some things to the bathroom and slide the pizza onto the paper plates in that sack. My fine dinnerware melted in the fire."

By the time she returned from hiding tampons and stacking toilet paper rolls under that sink, Ash had uncorked the wine using one of the many corkscrews Miss Delta left behind in a drawer. "It was light beer. Sorry, not the fireman's choice. Wine okay?"

"Since I bought it, yes."

"I put the bags of salad in the vegetable keeper, but tomatoes should always be left out." He'd arranged them in a row along the window sill over the sink.

"I'll remember that." Leah raised the pizza to her lips—heavenly even without pepperoni.

"Basil, too. Put it in a cup of water on the sill."

"Great if I ever have fresh basil. I don't have time for gardening."

"Wine glasses?"

"We'll have to use the paper cups in the sack with the plates. I have six in a box somewhere. Could we just cut to the chase? What's the good news?"

Ash poured the wine first and raised his paper cup in a toast. "The fire marshal stopped by here today. Definitely a case of arson. Gasoline poured all around the back."

"That doesn't deserve a toast. Now I'll probably have insurance problems."

"There's more. You are no longer a suspect. Your volunteers swore you were at the shelter all morning."

Unable to resist, Leah cocked her head at her dinner partner. "I could have hired someone to torch the house," she said in her gruffest voice.

"Some people simply can't accept good fortune."

"Yeah, like having my house burn down."

"Without you or anyone else in it," he countered. "I have to go. Night shift again, then I'm off for four days unless we catch a big one. How about you?"

"I'm working Saturday. We're have an Adopt-a-Pet Day on the green in front of the church. There'll be plenty of people around for the Gumbo Festival."

"What about Sunday? You go to church or play golf?"

"I worship at the Cathedral of Nature. I'm taking my kayak out on Indian Lake."

"Great! I have a kayak. Where and when should I meet you?"

"Ah, seven a.m. at the boat ramp."

"I'll be there. Gotta boogie. Enjoy the rest of the pizza."

"Don't you dare leave me here with half a pizza, especially the part with greens poking through the cheese."

"I aim to please." Ashton slid his two remaining slices onto his plate and carried it out the door on his fingertips like waiter at a fine dining establishment. The pose flattered his biceps. The show-off. He gently nudged the door shut and left behind the glare of his grin in her imagination.

That man moved fast as a forest fire. Did she have a date Sunday morning or merely a day of kayaking with a new acquaintance? Actually, she'd prefer the solitude her life rarely offered and the chance to get some new photos of migrating birds not in residence the rest of the year. Sometime between now and Sunday, she'd call and let him know she didn't want company.

Leah placed the last of the heavy-on-the-cheese slices in the refrigerator wrapped in Saran like mummy food, wiped her fingers on a paper towel, and removed the precious pint of chocolate-chocolate chip ice cream from the freezer—still a little soft. Scraping the edges of the carton with a plastic spoon, she let the dessert melt in her mouth and promised she'd only eat half. Half disappeared terribly fast. Nope, Leah snapped on the lid and put it back into the freezer. If she didn't stop this "I deserve treats because my house burned down eating binge", she might actually fit into some of the XXL T-shirts in those trash bags. With her TV one of the casualties of the fire, what else did she have to do but sort through donated clothes tonight?

Dragging all the bags into the living area, Leah settled on the secondhand lipstick-red sofa left behind by Miss Delta who proclaimed she wanted to start afresh in New Orleans, the city of her soul. She plugged in her iPod earbuds, fortunately left in her car yesterday, and began to make piles. Other people's underwear—ugh, no! She'd picked up cheap but new at Walmart. Most slacks and jeans wouldn't fit her. She preferred khakis worn with a belt or anything with a drawstring—small waist, wide hips, short legs, and it was hell to take up jeans without a sewing machine so she rarely wore them. Aha! She excavated a trove of T-shirts XL, a size that wouldn't span across her chest, and bore designs and sayings neither provocative nor gross, but very patriotic or sports oriented in nature: American flag, Saints logo, camouflage. But infant clothes? Did Ashton Blaise really work that fast? Perhaps, he had a bevy of babies scattered around the parish, all with his smile, each born to a different woman. A man with four days off in a row could do plenty of damage in his spare time.

Holding that thought in her mind, she waded out of the piles of discards and the small mound of keepers to get her laptop. Sitting cross-legged on the sofa, Leah began a search for his phone number. Plenty of people named Blaise in Ste. Jeanne de Arc Parish, but none with the first name of Ashton. No Cole either. Maybe firemen didn't want to be bothered at home. She could call the firehouse, but that seemed wrong without having an emergency. Or she might stop by there tomorrow and try to catch him before he went off duty in the morning, an even worse idea since women probably tried to track him down all the time. Okay, come Sunday, she'd meet him at the boat landing and suggest he paddle one way, and she'd go the other. That should put out the last embers of any interest he might have in Leah Allain.

Leah went back to sorting. A particularly heavy sack placed in her SUV by one of her volunteers yielded an assortment of useful items: aqua-colored towels still possessing plenty of nap, miscellaneous pots and pans, an old-fashioned percolator, a cheap set of dinnerware with a floral swirl on the top once purchased long ago with Betty Crocker coupons, and in the very bottom, the best discovery yet—a well-seasoned cast iron frying pan heavy enough to brain a burglar. These she could use, but she had no room for romance.

Chapter Four

The village of Chapelle made up in festivals what it lacked in size. The town fathers and mothers celebrated hot peppers, okra, catfish, wooden boats, the arrival of the Acadians, zydeco music, and pig butchering, more delicately called a *boucherie*, with special weekends throughout the year designed to bring in the tourists that doubled the population. This particular mid-October day honored gumbo, though the temperature climbed to eighty-five, scarcely weather for spicy soup. Still, people came and all but licked the pots clean.

Leah and her volunteers set up the puppy pen and the kitten cage in the shade of one of the huge live oaks on the village green. She disbursed the teen volunteers to walk a few older dogs with good manners and winning personalities on leashes. Each one wore a bib with the words *Adopt Me Please!* around their necks— the dogs, not the teens—who were instructed to clean up after their canine companions with a pooper scooper and a paper bag. Nothing ruined a great cup of wild boar sausage gumbo faster than stepping in dog crap while eating it. Besides, the Gumbo Festival Committee would not have Safe Haven Animal Shelter back if that happened.

Leah slipped into the lovely, air-conditioned Catholic Church, a replica of an ancient structure that had burned some years ago, and hurried down the marble main aisle under the vaulted ceiling painted with golden stars. She made a sharp left at the communion rail and bypassed the famous Mary altar to pause before a small shrine on the opposite wall dedicated to St. Roch, patron saint of dogs and curer of skin rashes. A quick prayer never hurt no matter how many times she skipped Mass.

"St. Roch, I pray we will have many pet adoptions today because the shelter is overwhelmed. We could also use a cure for the ringworm on those kittens dumped on us yesterday, and a vet who will treat them for free. Amen."

Leah shelled out for a candle and left it burning in a nearby rack to get the saint's attention. She exited by a side door and doubled down with the same prayer at an outdoor statue of St. Francis tucked into the armpit of the cruciform church. From there, she hurried back to take a seat at the card table next to Mrs. Murphy, a lively and dear old widow who adored cats but frequently screwed up the paperwork for adoptions. Still, she acted as the shelter's secretary for free, and that said a lot about the woman's good intentions.

"Any action?" Leah asked.

"Lots of petters, no takers." Mrs. Murphy patted her perspiring face with an embroidered hankie. Some of her wrinkle concealing makeup rubbed off in the process. She wore it thick.

As usual, a ring of children surrounded the two pens. Hard to tell where their parents hid in the milling crowd swilling gumbo purchased from booths completely lining the square and boxing the children inside along with the animals. Towering over mere mortals, a crowned head moved their way. Bearing the official headgear, a twelve-inch tall edifice of rhinestones with a black pot made of jet emitting lines of red crystals to represent heat, the Gumbo Queen emerged into their little clearing. She wore a snug red dress, modest enough but fitting in all the right places. Leah only wished she could squeeze into something like that and look decent. The Queen also had Ashton Blaise hanging on her arm like a bracelet. The beauty must be a college student judging by her youth. No one Leah knew, but had to hate on principal for being tall, blonde, blue-eyed, and beautiful.

"Oh Ash, let's help the animal shelter. Pose with me while I hold a puppy," the Gumbo Queen cooed, adding a small moue of her scarlet lips. She delved into the pen to scoop out a fluffy, little white mutt and cradled it while the pimply tagalong photographer from the *Clarion* lined up the shot.

Leah jumped up. She waited until the shutter clicked to close in with another offering fished from the kitty cage. "Watch you don't scratch the pup with those acrylic nails. Here's the pet you truly need, a pure white cat with eyes exactly the same shade as yours. He's had all his shots and comes with a certificate for a free neutering. Better yet, take both. At this age, they can learn to get along."

The kitten didn't appear to agree as it arched its back when the puppy attempted to give it a tiny pink lick. Leah stroked until it calmed. The Gumbo Queen considered, though she couldn't really tilt her head with that mass of rhinestones atop it. "What's the adoption fee?"

Something they didn't put on the sign as it could be a deal breaker. "One hundred dollars each—free shots and neutering included."

"Steep and I don't have my purse on me. Unless you'd like to buy one for me, Ash?"

Of course, royalty never carried a purse. People bought things for queens. Ashton Blaise, looking very fine from the fitted black shirt sporting his badge and firefighting insignia to the soles of his shiny polished shoes, withdrew a wallet that appeared to be made of duct tape from the hip pocket of his dress slacks while Leah raced to justify the expense.

"The fee is high to prevent dogfighters from buying them to train their pit bulls. This way, we guarantee a good home—and you are saved all the early medical expenses of having a pet."

"I only have seventy-five on me and don't have my gumbo tickets yet," Ash said with a hint of embarrassment.

In a voice that cracked with unrequited adoration, the photographer chipped in. "I'll get the rest for Miss Jolie."

"Oh, thank you. Y'all are both so kind."

Leah hoped the Queen wouldn't get one of those fluttering false eyelashes stuck in her baby blues—or maybe she did. She kept a smile plastered on her face. "The puppy or the kitten?"

The puppy began to pee, but ever ready Ash grabbed it by the scruff and pointed it away from the stunning red dress, saving it from despoiling, a hero again. "Puppies do that when they get excited," Leah said. "Please forgive him." She thought the very young photographer might be on the verge of doing the same in his own state of ecstasy.

"Let me try out the kitten." The Queen cupped the

fur ball in her hands. Seemingly motivated to find a home, it began to purr on cue. "So sweet. I simply don't know. Could I get a BOGO because I'll give them a real good home?"

"A BOGO?" Leah asked as she relieved Ash of the squirming puppy.

"I guess you're not a girl who shops much. That's Buy One, Get One Free." The Queen fluttered her eyelashes Leah's way.

Did this *child* assume she was a lesbian? "I don't think…"

"Sounds good to me. Jolie, you need to get over to the gazebo for the gumbo judging. Chief Fontenot will meet you there and take over from me. I'll see to the paperwork for your pets," Ash offered.

The Queen's charming moue turned into a true pout. "I suppose judging gumbo is part of my duties, but you will join me after, Ash? I'll see you get some free gumbo since you spent all your money on me."

"Sure, see you later."

"And you, ma'am, you'll make certain no one else takes my babies?"

"I'm tagging them right now." Leah took another set of bibs from a box under the table. They read *Found my Forever Family!* The puppy accepted his with no problem, but the kitten immediately began to bat at his bib with a paw. Leah placed the cat back into the cage with the closed top to prevent kitten escapees. His fellow prisoners eyed the bib with suspicion.

"I'll escort you to the gazebo," the kid photographer said. "Let me break the way for you."

He set off into the crowd like a very slender icebreaker leading with his camera. Queen Jolie minced behind on her high heels, doling out regal waves along the way. Leah took some pleasure in the coating of white pet hair stuck to the front of the red dress. Dogs piddled, but cats shed when nervous. She'd worn her khaki shorts and a camouflage T-shirt designed for deer hunting in shades of green and brown, one of the donated items now in her wardrobe. Running shoes clad her feet in case one of the animals made a break for it. Her gaze following the Queen returned to a strong, tanned hand plunking down the accumulated cash for the adoptees.

"Nice wallet," Leah remarked about his duct tape creation.

"Bought it from a kid who has a booth with all things duct tape. Five dollars. I like to encourage enterprising youth."

Was there nothing she could say to insult this guy that wouldn't turn back and bite her? Leah stopped trying and got on with the deal. "I thought you were off the next few days?" she said as she filled in the necessary forms and added informational pamphlets on care, feeding, and when to have the pets neutered. "Would you happen to know Queen Jolie's last name?"

"Broussard, kin to the mayor. Got called up to be an escort since the chief can't stand the heat well anymore. Some of the other firemen are showing the side dishes around."

Yes, gray eyes could twinkle, Leah found. "Side dishes?"

"The runner-ups."

"Like rice, white bread, and potato salad? No nepotism or bribery involved?"

"Given the Queen's looks, none needed."

36

"She is very attractive—and young."

Ash shrugged. "A legal twenty-one and a senior at UL. Still lives with her mama and daddy though. Really, the animals will have a good home. This branch of Broussards don't lack for money."

"Yeah, like she needed a BOGO. Even if the vets offer us some free services, we still have to pay for the meds and those spay and neuter certificates."

"I'll see you get the rest after payday. She needed to move along, not dicker. So do I." Ash accepted the packet in a brown envelope. "See you tomorrow."

He broke into the crowd and showed her only the back of his dark head and tanned neck before Leah managed to sputter, "About that!"

"My, my, that young man could bring his fire hose by my house any day," commented Mrs. Murphy who had silently observed all as she often did.

"He's already done that at my place."

"Yes, when your house burned down. Not what I meant at all. You know, your cheeks turn a beautiful dusky rose when I embarrass you. You should wear some blush to bring out those cheekbones."

Mrs. Murphy's advice drowned beneath the happy voice belonging to teenage shelter volunteer Yancey Breaux, who led a black and tan Chihuahua mix with huge bat-like ears and dragged along an elderly man trying to stabilize himself with a cane. "Mr. Abner says his dog died last month, and he's lonely. He's going to adopt Bat."

"Abner, how long has it been since Elaine passed? And now your little pooch, Petey." Ethel Murphy knew everyone in town right down to the names of their pets, which made her an asset no matter how she muddled the papers or personally embarrassed Leah. Ethel stood and seized both of the elderly man's hands despite the cane in the way.

"Oh, the wife's been gone over a year now. Petey was mostly her dog, but we managed without her until he passed. Does this dog seem like a good idea to you?"

"You've mourned a respectable time, Ab, and deserve a dog of your own. Bat will make a good companion. Or, how about a cat?"

"Allergies, sorry. Okay, sign me up to take Bat home." He groped a hundred dollar bill from his front shirt pocket. "Won it at the casino and thought I'd blow it at the festival, just didn't figure on my splurge being a dog."

"A dog will last longer than any amount won at a casino, not that I have objections to a moderate amount of gambling. Call me next time you go, and we can get a good cheap dinner and play the slots. You know I'm in the book."

Abner removed an iPhone from his pocket. "Let me enter you in my contacts," he said a bit proudly. Ethel reeled off her number while Leah took care of the actual work of the adoption and fit Bat with a new bib.

The teen handed over the cheap nylon leash to the new pet owner. "Can I walk around with one of the puppies? They are so adorbs I think I can get a friend to take one," she said, using her favorite and frequent abbreviation for adorable.

Leah gave her the nod, and the girl selected one of the littermates of the Gumbo Queen's pick and scooted off, high pony tail wagging, to tempt another person into pet ownership. Good kid and not the problem some of the other volunteers could be.

She handed Abner Millet his owner's packet and said with a smile, "Bat has been neutered so not much chance of him roaming. He's two years old, and small dogs tend to live a long time. Have a happy life together."

"Yes, things are looking up for me. Next Friday for the casino, Ethel, or did you want to go when the place is quieter?"

"Oh, let's do Tuesday. You know where I live, and you have my number in your gadget to get the details. Enjoy the rest of the festival." As Abner walked away with Bat, Ethel remarked, "I do love a man with a full head of white hair. It compliments my own." She fluffed her short, curly do.

"You move fast, Ethel. Very slick," Leah said in a complimentary way.

"At my age, I haven't got time to spare. I played bridge with Elaine for years and years. I know everything about that man—except for the cat allergy, but he could just be saying that. Lots of people claim allergies to get out of adopting a cat." Ethel's blue eyes narrowed like a feline stalking prey. "Since I have three, I'll be able to tell if his eyes water and he sneezes when he picks me up. I can always build a cattery in my backyard if things develop. So, you and Ashton Blaise."

"It's nothing. He invited himself along to go kayaking on Indian Lake tomorrow."

"Hmmm, invited himself. He's been back in town about a year, and most local gals don't waste time getting to know a single man in this town. No one has brought him down yet. I wonder if anything is wrong with him?"

"Not on the surface if you can handle the fact that

he's a vegetarian."

"Chapelle isn't teeming with those. Could be a game stopper for some. I'll ask around."

"No need, really."

Leah saw Zola Sweat, who pronounced her name Sweet and attempted to make a living running an art gallery but sold mostly crafts, move majestically across the green in their direction. "I have a yen for a black cat," she said upon arrival, pointing at a yellow-eyed, half-grown kitten in the cage. The way she said it, a person might assume she wanted to devour it, but at one hundred dollars a pop for a few pounds that made cat more expensive than prime rib. Zola liked to shock people for the hell of it. She'd washed up in Chapelle along with Delta Savage after the levees broke in New Orleans, but did not plan to return. No matter how slim her business, she'd come with the money in hand.

"I had me a black cat in Naw Orlins. She disappeared in the flood. I'm gonna call this one Cleopatra after her."

With her explosion of frizzy black hair held back with a hot pink headband, a complexion that said mixed-race, and hoop earrings an elephant might leap through, Zola attracted rumors like metal filings to a magnet. Some claimed she'd been a voodoo priestess in the Crescent City. Leah doubted it, but owning a black cat would certainly add to that cachet. Zola gave Chapelle some color and fueled gossip. Leah liked her. She handed over the paperwork and the kitten.

"I can't leave here easily, but could you bring me that jam pot with the strawberries painted on the side I looked at the other day." Tit for tat. Zola had taken a cat and needed to recoup some of her money. Besides,

Leah had plans for that jam pot. Before she left today, she'd purchase two loaves of wheat bread from the bakery stand and a jar of homemade preserves to tempt Gran's appetite. A jam pot would be easier to manage than a jelly jar for an elderly woman with arthritis in her wrists though Gran wouldn't admit it.

Zola's broad, white smile spread across her face like butter on bread as she held the black kitten to her cheek. "I sure can. That Miss Rosemarie's work, the *traiteur*. I figure it come with good luck attached."

"That would be a bonus I could use right now."

"Be back shortly once I get Cleo settled." Zola swayed away with her puce and pink caftan tight about her wide hips.

Mrs. Murphy leaned a bony shoulder Leah's way and whispered, "I think she and Delta had something going on, but they split up over returning to New Orleans."

"Don't know. Don't care."

"Don't ask. Don't tell. If you aren't even a little bit interested in Ashton Blaise I'll wonder about you, too, girl."

"I have neither the time nor the inclination to get involved right now."

Ethel threw up her hands. "What are young women coming to these days? No interest in marriage and or even a little juicy sex on the side. I tell you that Jolie Broussard, she won't hesitate a minute to go after Blaise."

"More power to her."

Mrs. Murphy sniffed. "You deserve him more."

Leah refused to comment. The arrival of the lucky jam pot seemed to work magic. Following the example of their queen, the Gumbo Festival side dishes snapped up the other three puppies in the litter. Kittens went more slowly, but a few found homes. People seemed to feel dogs were worth more, especially with so many stray cats around town. At the end of the day, one Lab mix remained in the puppy pen, a classic plain black dog hard to place.

As Leah packed up the cages and put the little Lab into a carrier next to one containing the remaining kittens, she promised, "I'll find you a good home. Someone will want you."

"Better look out for yourself," Mrs. Murphy warned. "It's sad I have more going on than you, Leah."

Maybe so, maybe so.

Chapter Five

Ash waited by the boat ramp at Indian Lake. His fire engine red kayak already floated in the water. He'd arrived a full half hour early deciding if he came a second late, he'd find a note hanging from a nail on a piling saying Leah had gone ahead without him. Prickly as a cocklebur, but not at all clingy, that woman. He liked solving puzzles, loved reading mysteries. One day, he might look into becoming a fire marshal detecting the causes of questionable conflagrations. Figuring out what made Leah Allain tick appealed to him, too.

Generally, women were all over him—a fireman with a reputation for rescuing pets and family heirlooms, not bad looking, though his brother, Cole, had cornered the market on handsome in their family. He blamed his mother for some of his girl problems. He'd left a good job in Houston to return home and give her the help she needed. Immediately, Mom broadcasted the arrival of her fireman son to every single woman in town hoping to anchor him to Chapelle permanently with a local marriage—for his own happiness of course.

Ash always had a date sometime during his days off. On more than one occasion, the girls called him. He took them out. Some couldn't get past his vegetarian diet, though he wasn't all that strict. Others failed to

43

accept he'd be on duty some weekends all night long and not at their beck and call. A few believed he saw other women instead of the truth. He worked out, watched a game on TV, and slept in a single bunk while waiting for the fire bell to ring. They weren't meant to be a fireman's wife. He needed an independent woman to hold up the other end of his life when and if he married—or maybe the problem really was his mother.

Leah Allain arrived on the dot trailed by the dust her big SUV stirred up like a wake. She parked, got down by sliding to the running board and making a short hop to earth. She threw a curt nod Ash's way and proceeded to unstrap a small green kayak from the roof rack of her vehicle using a stepladder. Ash moved to help her, but she said, "I got it."

With a flourish, Leah unrolled a piece of carpet on the hood of her car and eased the watercraft to the ground. She turned the kayak on its side, squatted to raise the boat to her hip, then shoved her shoulder in the cockpit and hauled it to the water's edge. On the return trip to the SUV, she rolled up the carpet, packed the stepladder, and retrieved a small knapsack, a mighty professional-looking digital camera, her paddle, and a PDF exactly her size. "Where's your life jacket?" she said as she put hers on and secured the straps.

"I do have one," he answered since she appeared to imply he'd broken the rules already. Ash took it out of the trunk of the Prius and returned in time to be enveloped in the cloud of bug spray Leah shot from a can. "You want some?"

He figured they should call that stuff *Eau Don't Touch Me* it stank so bad, but better to reek than to be eaten alive by mosquitoes. Ash nodded. He'd worn a long-sleeved cotton tee and jeans in anticipation of blood suckers, but accepted a spritz on the back of his neck and across his hands. Great, now they smelled exactly the same, and it wasn't such a turnoff. Leah stowed her knapsack, lowered herself into the cockpit, and shoved the kayak into the shallow water off the boat ramp with her hands. "You ready? No talking once we're underway. I want to get some wildlife photos."

Following her orders early on, Ash nodded. He realized immediately he'd been a fool to tie his kayak to a piling instead of entering the water Leah's way. Casting off his line, he clambered aboard, not gracefully, but without dumping himself in the water. Leah watched, her green eyes amused at his awkwardness. Been a while since he'd taken the boat out, but his skills returned quickly. Quietly, they paddled from the dock along the shoreline but away from the reeds. At the slough where the big gators, still sluggish in the cool air of morning, sunned, she paused to take photos with the camera around her neck. It made a click. The alligators barely blinked their yellowish reptilian eyes.

They moved on to the huge bird rookery with Leah nosing her craft in close to get nearer to the egrets and herons, to capture a pair of pink spoonbills perched side by side. Ash let his gaze roam to the open part of the lake. He didn't know a great deal about birds, but one species he could identify for sure. "Eagle!" he shouted. Startled, Leah wobbled in her kayak as some of the birds in the rookery flushed, but she dug in her paddle and made a masterful turn in time to catch the great bird of prey as it sank its talons into a fish rising to the surface to feed. The eagle carried its prey to a big, sloppy aerie in the top of a vast cypress tree and tore apart its breakfast. She zeroed in on that, too.

"Thanks for the heads up, but no need to shout."

"Sorry."

They continued in the pale green light beneath the cypress trees not yet showing a hint of the rusty orange color their leaves would bear when the weather turned cooler. Leah spotted several small birds on their way to somewhere else that excited her as she zoomed in on them with her lens. Ash had no idea what they were. He'd only come along for the ride and had to say it beat sitting in a stuffy church on any Sunday morning.

They'd rounded more than half the lake by the time the sun rose high enough to cause a glare on the water and heated up the air to an uncomfortable degree. Leah signaled she'd decided to go ashore at a small, gator-free inlet and drove her boat part way up a low, muddy bank. Ash followed. They walked a bit inland to sit under a live oak that shaded out much of the brush. "Break time," she said.

"Is the cone of silence now lifted?"

That earned him a smile. "I guess so. Did you bring anything to eat?" He offered two energy bars from his shirt pocket and held up his stainless steel water bottle.

"That isn't real food, but thanks for not bringing plastic bottles to the lake." Leah opened the small knapsack and spread out a cloth. She deposited a few little oranges on it, three sandwiches, and a packet wrapped in foil. "Ham and cheese for me, your choice of peanut butter and jelly or three cheeses with mustard, all on brown bread—or you can have both of the last. You look like a two sandwich guy to me. If you take the PB&J, I'd suggest eating a Satsuma first. They're really sweet, but don't go well with strawberry preserves."

"Thanks for the warning. I had no idea this was a catered tour or I would have brought a better contribution. Did you like the soup and quiche?"

"Oh, yeah. Good thing real men don't eat quiche. I got to have it for breakfast *and* dinner. I ate the soup for lunch." She unwrapped her sandwich and took a bite, washed it down with a swig from her own water bottle. "I put provolone, Swiss, and cheddar in the cheese sandwich. Don't know if it will be good."

"It is. We'll share the PB&J after I eat the orange."

Leah delved into her own Satsuma. Its citrus scent sprayed into the air overcoming the odor of bug spray. She sucked on one section at a time, licking any escaping juice away with her tongue and blowing the little pips out through her puckered lips. Had she any idea how sexy eating an orange could be? Ash doubted it, but thoughts of Leah for dessert here on the Spanish moss fallen under the oak entered his mind.

"I feel like making a bed of moss and taking a nap right now," he hinted. "Mattresses used to be made out of this stuff."

Leah wrinkled a pretty cute nose at his suggestion. "Not that kind. The moss used in mattresses was soaked to get the outer layer off, then smoked over a fire. Fresh it's full of red bugs and spiders. We have brownies for dessert."

Had she read his mind or was he Captain Obvious? Leah opened the foil packet and offered him a brownie heavily iced with chocolate frosting, good as a candy bar and not as likely to melt. Butter cream bliss. He ate two.

"I have more back in the car along with your pie keeper and kettle. My grandma always said never to return a plate or a pot empty. I made them myself, not from a box." Why that statement made her cheeks color, he had no idea, but Ash liked it.

"Want to see the photos I took today?" She held up her camera. He came close beside her, leaning in to preview her pictures. She had a good eye and a steady hand for photography. The bald eagle pictures were particularly fine. He'd never had the patience to sit for a long time waiting for just the right moment.

Ash maneuvered an arm behind her, bent his head, and kissed her bare nape. Above that, the short hairs on her neck were soft and had a mild, clean scent unlike his own sweaty bristles. He sank his fingers into her thick topknot, and she jumped away like one of her feral cats afraid of a touch.

"I made you brownies. That's all you get for today."

He backed off, but couldn't help saying, "Real men do eat quiche and make it, too, in case you had any doubts."

"Your being a fireman cancels out the whole quiche thing when it comes to being masculine. Let's go. I like to get off the lake before all the pleasure boaters show up and churn the water."

On the way back to the boat landing, Leah paddled much faster with smooth, strong strokes like the devil might be on her tail. Nope, only a fireman, a slightly horny fireman. When they took their kayaks from the water, Ash heaved hers onto the carrier before she could go through the whole carpet, stepladder routine.

"I can do it myself," she chided.

"Yes, but you don't have to when I'm around. Remember that next time."

"Why do you think there will be a next time?" She removed the gumbo pot and pie carrier stacked with brownies from her backseat and thrust them his way.

Deep in his hip pocket, his cell buzzed like a rattler about to ruin his day. He took it out and read a text. "One of the condemned houses on Cinder Street caught fire. They think it could spread to the next. Lots of trash around there and the places are close together. Got to go. See you next weekend. I'll call." He strapped his kayak on the trailer he preferred to scratching the finish of his Prius and drove off like a house afire leaving a stunned Leah staring and still holding his kettle and those really great brownies.

Chapter Six

Leah's office phone rang. She pounced on it like one of the kittens Mrs. Murphy tempted with a string of yarn as she tamed them for the taking. Leah hoped every call to be a person who wanted to adopt a dog, cat, or one of the three rabbits turned in after they ceased to be Easter Bunny cute. They also had a parrot named Mr. Grey who appeared to be doomed to be her officemate forever. In a very short time, it had picked up her name and cried out, "Le-ah, Le-ah, baby, baby, please," whenever it desired a peanut or a grape. She hated to think where that bird might have dwelled before reaching Safe Haven.

Usually, the people on the other end of the line only wanted her to pick up some abandoned animal or get rid of one they owned. Mrs. Murphy's volunteer duties included answering the phone, but obviously she had a lap full of kittens. Leah injected cheer into her voice. "Good morning, Safe Haven Animal Shelter. How may we help you?"

"Hi, Leah. Ashton Blaise here. Sorry I had to run off without those brownies. Save them for me."

Why did his voice have to sound so creamy delicious? Shouldn't it be rough from inhaling smoke fumes? "The brownies are in my very small freezer as we speak. I'm not baking them from scratch again for you."

"As a decent cook, I respect the work that went into them. I apologize for running out on you at the lake. Two of those condemned houses went before we got the fire under control. Cliff Couvillon, one of our older volunteers, said too bad all those old cribs didn't burn down. They housed prostitutes way back when Chapelle had its own red light district, but only drug addicts and the homeless use them now as flops. I told him we put out all fires and couldn't pick and choose. Either arson or some careless heroin addict dropped a lighter heating his spoon. So, we leaving at seven again next Sunday?"

"No, I'll be out late Saturday night. I plan to sleep in Sunday."

"Really, that's disappointing. Would it be too bold of me to ask what you're doing Saturday night—some astronomy maybe?"

Not too bold, only too nosy and personal, but she answered with annoyance. "It's the night of the Doggone Delightful Ball at the casino, a fundraiser for the shelter. I put up posters all over town. It's on our web site. Even the *Clarion* gave us a free plug on the second page, and you didn't notice."

"Nobody reads the *Clarion*. Can't say I saw the posters, but I wasn't really looking. However, are tickets still available? I'd like two."

"Heck, you can buy them at the door. We hope some of the gamblers will stop by and bid at the silent and live auctions, and the casino hopes some of our guests will slip out and play blackjack when they get bored. Tickets are fifty dollars each, but the casino donates really great heavy hors d'ouvres. Cash bar, but a pretty good band. Are you thinking of taking the

Gumbo Queen?" Two people could be nosy and inappropriately personal.

"Jolie? No. I think she said she'd be at the Cattle Festival with the herd of other local queens. I hoped you'd go with me."

For a moment, Leah had no ready answer. The parrot squawked, "Oh, baby, baby!" No matter how much she might agree, the bird spoke up at the wrong time.

"What did you say?" Ash asked. "Because I think I'm flattered."

"That was a parrot we have in the office, not me."

"Oh yeah, the Bordello Bird. I carried him out of a black velvet bedroom when Madame Mystique's place went up in flames. Lots of interesting equipment lost in that fire. The ladies of the town thought good riddance, but she only relocated. I didn't know he ended up at the shelter."

Leah got a grip while he talked. "I, uh, don't need a ticket. I have to go really early to set up the silent auction tables and make sure everything is in place."

"No problem. I work Friday, but I have all day Saturday to help you out. What time should I pick you up?"

"I need to take my SUV to haul all the donations."

"Fine, I'll come over to your place and help you load. I have no problem with women drivers."

Leah felt her grip slipping. "Okay, I want to leave at six. The ball starts at eight. If that's too early for you…"

"I'll be there and pay you for the tickets then. Consider the second one a donation. Happy to help out. Bye."

Okay, she'd slid all the way to the bottom of the pole and had a second date or whatever with Ashton Blaise. Mrs. Murphy noted her stunned expression. "What's the matter, dear?"

"Nothing. I sold two more tickets to the ball, that's all."

"I know I wouldn't make brownies from scratch for just any man, but I might for Abner. He's my date."

Nothing wrong with the old lady's hearing. Leah came up with a solution to assuage Ethel's curiosity. "Ashton Blaise called. He volunteered to assist with the setup Saturday night and help with the heavy lifting."

"I'll bet he does that really well. Abner has a bad back," Ethel replied as if the two topics were intimately related in her mind.

"I'm sure a firefighter is in very good condition."

"Le-ah, baby, baby, please," Mr. Grey wheedled. Leah shoved a peanut through the bars of the big cage. The parrot gripped it delicately in its claw and proceeded to crack open the shell and pluck out the nuts with its black beak one by one before letting the husk drop to the floor.

"He's very taken with you," Ethel said as she rubbed a kitten's tummy. It latched its tiny claws around her bony finger.

"Ash, no, I don't think…"

"I meant Mr. Grey. He was pining before you came, plucking feathers, refusing to speak."

"He needed some stimulation, toys, ropes to climb, and more attention. I'm glad he's happier, but I could do without the chattiness. With his off-color vocabulary, we'll never find a home for him. Is it true he belonged to a bordello owner?"

"Absolutely. That Madame Mystique brought him here until she could find a new place to set up, but like so many, she didn't return to collect him. She's a sight to behold close up, nearly six feet tall, a mulatto gal, real light-skinned with a head full of these tiny blonde braids that go down to her waist."

"A weave," Leah suggested.

"A really good one that looks like her own hair. She flails them around like whips when she turns her head. I've never seen arms so toned on a woman. She's got some real muscle, but then, I've heard her place offers special services along with the usual. It's rumored a jealous wife burned her out." Nothing lit up Ethel's lightly wrinkled face like dispersing gossip with sexual content.

Leah sank her head into her hands. "This bird isn't named Mr. Grey because he's an African Grey Parrot then?"

"Of course not. Haven't you read that *Fifty Shades* book?"

"Didn't get around to it."

"Very enlightening, my dear, but people my age have thin skin and are often on blood thinners so those shenanigans are not for us. If I were younger…but I'd have to be the dominant. I'd never allow a man to hit me."

"Me neither." Leah wished could she wipe out the image of Mrs. Murphy tying Abner Millet to the bedposts and shoving a ball gag into his mouth. He'd probably have to take his dentures out first. She squeezed her eyes shut tight for a moment. "I'm going to take some pictures of the animals we want to feature at the silent auction. How about posing with these kittens? They'll be ready for homes soon." She took her camera from a drawer.

Ethel obliged by perching the two tiger-striped kits on either shoulder where they clung like Velcro and holding the orange one up close to her face. Leah took the picture. "I'm going out to photograph some of the dogs."

"Le-ah, give it to me, baby," Mr. Grey called out as she neared the door. He followed that up with some heavy panting.

"Give him a grape, Ethel. Maybe he'll transfer his affections to you."

"I don't think I have your sex appeal, but I'll try. You should save what you got for Ashton Blaise."

Leah shook her head. That remark deserved no answer. Now, if she could get a really sweet shot of the little black Lab mix, she might find her a home.

****

Saturday came all too fast. No calls from Ash thankfully, but Leah had enough to do rounding up the auction items and pumping the Doggone Delightful Ball. She carried tickets everywhere she went and had some success. Not her original idea, the ball was an annual event with committees well in place when she arrived. She added some of her own suggestions and let her volunteers run with the rest. Despite Ash's offer to help her load the SUV, she did that herself before going to take a shower in the barn's small, white-tiled bathroom, white everywhere with a long mirror on the back of the door opposite the clear glass box of the stall. At least, the donated aqua towels didn't clash with the décor, but she took no joy in seeing herself bathe as perhaps Delta had.

As she blew dry her short hair, Leah regretted for just a second chopping it off. An updo might have been nice for tonight. The current of hot air whisked the wedge of black hair out of her eyes. She turned toward the mirror and did a body assessment. Pits and legs shaved, but the dark bush between her legs unwaxed and a little too lush. Breasts still too large for her height, the hips to match. She'd seen it all before and couldn't do much about it.

However, Jolie Broussard wasn't the only one who owned a red dress. Hers didn't fit snugly, but it flattered. Like many of the clothes she rarely wore, the gown had survived the conflagration in a garment bag stored in the barn loft. Leah turned off the dyer, opened the door to the bathroom, and started across the living room to her bedroom. As soon as she noticed her naked reflection in the big window, she turned back and swathed herself in an aqua towel to make the crossing. Miss Delta had a penchant for walking around nude but none for curtains, and good curtains cost. Later, she had enough to worry about right now.

Leah shimmied into pantyhose to make her legs look sleeker and keep her feet from sticking to the practical black pumps with the two-inch heels. She had plenty of walking to do tonight and didn't possess a single pair of the ankle-breaking heels men found so sexy anyhow. The dress had a built-in shelf bra so no need for that. Checking her eyebrows in the little mirror on the bedroom wall, she plucked out a few strays. Dark as they were, they needed no color, but she separated her lashes with a wand and went for smoky eyes with shadow and liner. Red lipstick—definitely.

She dropped the dress over her head and fastened

the catch behind her neck. Two swathes of cloth across each breast helped hold them up and created a nice cleavage. Her back remained bare. She tied the sash that made a provocative bow just above her hips where the skirt flared out and dropped to just above her knees. So far so good. Opening a worn red velvet box, she lifted the diamond hair clip her Gran insisted she take along with two diamond stud earrings.

They'd had tea and been enjoying the brown bread with whipped butter and strawberry preserves served from the jam pot at the small kitchen table. As usual, Leah did most of the talking, chattering on about the animals at the shelter and the upcoming ball for lack of anything else to say. She'd never mentioned the fire for fear of upsetting her grandmother—and avoiding an invitation to live with her. She loved the woman, but no, that would not work.

Out of the blue, the usually silent Alene interrupted her. "Do you have a date for the ball?"

"Sort of. Not really. He's just this guy who wanted to help out."

"Wait here." Her grandmother rose entirely unaware of the glob of jam stuck in the corner of her mouth, which would have caused her major embarrassment in earlier years. The sounds of rummaging came from the bedroom where Alene had slept with her husband in the big mahogany four-poster all the days of their married life. Drawers crashed shut. Objects fell, but Leah knew she didn't dare interfere. The cleaning lady who came once a week would pick it all up without saying a word about the mess. In time, Gran returned with the jewelry box and held it out. "These might make you look more feminine."

Inside on black satin laid the earrings and a diamond hair clip shaped like a shooting star. "Grandpa gave you these when you had my father." Leah recalled seeing the jewels worn by her grandmother to any number of fancy social occasions. The Doggone Ball didn't seem worthy of them.

"Yes, I hid them away after he died, but had some difficulty recalling where. No matter. You should wear the clip over your ear since you have no hair left to speak of. It's thick like mine once was. A pity you are short and round. You can blame that on your mother because you certainly didn't get those short legs from me. The jewelry will draw the glance upward to your face and lovely green eyes."

"I'll take good care of the diamonds and bring them back as soon as I can."

"Keep them. I no longer go out where people stare and whisper about how feeble I've become."

"No one says that about you. Friends would like to visit if you'd let them inside."

"Take the diamonds and leave. I don't need this jam pot either. You think I haven't the strength to open a jelly jar anymore." Just like that their pleasant visit ended abruptly as it usually did with rancor over some imagined slight.

Imagining herself as tall and stately as Gran preparing for a magnificent evening, Leah placed the clip in her hair over one ear as directed. It shone like stars in a midnight sky. She put the earrings in just in time because a strong knock sounded on the outer door nearest her bedroom. Grabbing her evening bag and a short, dressy black jacket to cover her back, Leah went to confront Ashton Blaise.

Chapter Seven

Ashton watched Leah's eyes widen. His probably did the same. She quickly fastened the small buttons of her jacket and hid away the two stunning breasts wrapped in deep red like Christmas presents waiting to be opened. The diamonds in her hair and on her lobes distracted him for a moment, but the most eye catching parts of her face were the plump lips coated in vermilion—until she looked up at him with those cat-like green eyes. "You ready to go, James Bond?"

Shoot, he'd meant to impress when he got his dad's old tux out of the back of the closet and had it rush altered to fit his trimmer form. The elderly tailor, who once worked for the only department store in Chapelle before the malls in Lafayette put it out of business, called him dapper when Ash tried it on for a final fit in the little shop behind his home. "You don't see quality like this much anymore," he added, fingering the wide lapels. Leah failed to notice quality when she saw it.

His father bought the tuxedo for his wedding and wore it to Firemen's Balls year after year no matter how the styles changed, letting it out as needed. When Ash walked from his room tonight, he'd brought tears to his mother's always worried blue eyes. She cried harder when his granddad said from the depths of the recliner, "You and Hank going out, Linda? Don't worry. I'll take good care of the boys. No need to rush home. Sorry I couldn't do that when I was fire chief, but now I'm here to help." Better late than never—only Hank Blaise lay in his grave and the boys were full grown men.

Saying, "Don't leave yet," his mom rushed to kitchen. She stayed in there a long time, but returned with dry eyes, a smile on her face, and a corsage box in her hands. "I picked this up for your date at the grocery store."

Through the little cellophane window, he viewed tiny silver artificial roses with crystal dewdrops on a wristband corsage, every teenage girl's dream. Leah would laugh in his face. But if it made his mother smile, he'd suck that up. Ash kissed her cheek. "Thanks, that was thoughtful. She'll love it. Call if you have any trouble with Pop."

"Oh, I don't want to ruin your date. I can manage. He's quiet tonight watching LSU play. Stay out as long as you like." His mom applied that fake smile to her fragile face again and shooed him out the door.

Running late, he slapped the red siren on the roof of the Prius and broke laws both legal and ethical to get to Leah's place on time during Chapelle's miniscule rush hour. He knew she'd go without him given the chance. Dashing to her door on the stroke of six, he automatically picked up the corsage he'd intended to discard. Here he stood in front of Leah Allain with the box in his hand like a nervous high school boy, but he didn't know her all that well. Maybe she had a unicorn and rainbow spread on her bed and a case of arrested development. He doubted that as he offered her the fake flowers. "These are for you."

Oh, how those green eyes could roll. "We're going to the Doggone Ball, not the prom. You really expect me to wear that?"

Nope, she'd grown up a long time ago, but he might be able to turn the situation around as he so often did. He considered that one of his special talents. "You don't have to, but the sparkle matches the diamonds in your hair and the light in your eyes."

"Cheesiest compliment ever—but I can't remember the last time a guy brought me artificial flowers. Okay, put it on." She held out her wrist.

Ash held her fingertips, a little rough with short, clean clear-coated nails, as he slid the corsage onto her arm. He swore he felt an uptick in her pulse before he let go. Sad they couldn't skip the ball and stay here for the night. Too bad he had to squash the little bit of progress he'd made by saying, "I'll have to follow you in my car in case I'm needed elsewhere."

"Sure, I understand." She closed the door and marched straight for the SUV.

"Anything you need to pack before we go?" He rushed to beat her to the vehicle door and open it the second she hit the button on her key fob to release the locks. With his long legs, he won that race easily—and handed her up onto the high seat where he got to test her racing pulse again and note the blush on her cheeks wasn't all makeup.

"Nope, all loaded. You can help carry stuff inside. I'll lead the way."

"Let me know if you need a siren escort."

"Not likely."

Rather than driving out to the highway, she took the more direct back road to the casino, bypassing the sugar mill full of steam and noise this time of year, a few small towns where she slowed down for nonexistent traffic, and stately old plantation homes both rundown and restored. Knowing exactly where she went, Leah turned in at the impressive entrance to the casino sitting on Indian reservation land and drove directly to the doors closest to the reception room. She hopped out before Ash could park and opened the hatch on the SUV.

"Here." Leah loaded him down with boxes and stuck a few signs under his arm. She hung her camera around her neck, grabbed some bags, and held the door for him to enter. Apparently, the casino staff had done its job well because she smiled as she entered the room with the round tables covered in pristine white linen and long tables with drapes lined around the edge of the space. The cash bar stood ready with glass dishes of lemon and orange slices and olives plus plenty of liquor and a tip jar. Bandstand all set up, and a long line of catering dishes waiting to be filled. Beyond the reception room, the dim casino lurked, a place where day and night didn't exist, but in here the chandeliers shone brightly and the dinnerware gleamed. Leah removed the corsage and her jacket and went to work placing clipboards with the silent auction items listed on them, gradually disburdening Ash as she moved down the line. His eyes dwelled on the bare expanse of her back, tanned, no strap marks to mar the effect. Topless sunbathing, not a good time to think about it.

Leah centered a placard above a clipboard and removed a small duck effigy basket made of longleaf pine needles from Ash's stack of boxes. Trying to take his mind off of whether her hips were also evenly tanned, he leaned over slightly to glance at the starting bid. "Cute, but not cheap."

"The Tribal Council donated it. These figures are highly collectible and becoming rare since the younger people don't want to learn the craft. It will go for far more than that."

"Not to a fireman," he mumbled.

The next item, a beautiful sculpture of a Golden Retriever in a hunting stance so realistic the wind seemed to be feathering its fur, wasn't going to go cheap either. "By Ulee Boudreaux, one of the area's best decoy makers. Safe Haven does have great supporters."

"Again, out of my range."

Leah pulled a Victorian print of a basket of kittens heavily framed in gold from the next box. "From Zola Sweat's gallery, kind of sentimental, but someone will buy it."

"That I could afford. I'm certain the guys at the firehouse would love to have me hang it there. They could use it as dartboard."

"Not animal lovers like you?"

"They're okay with animals, but they're guys."

Leah shook her head in mock disapproval. She set up a picture next to the print of Mrs. Murphy covered in real kittens with a bid starting at one hundred dollars. "Take one or more of these fluffy bundles to a new forever home—your choice of the real thing," the descriptive card read.

"Does that include Ethel Murphy? She looks pretty fuzzy, too," Ash quipped.

"She'd surprise you if you spent any time with her. Here she comes now with the centerpieces."

Ethel had her own retinue consisting of Abner Millet in a proper suit and tie and Yancey Breaux, the teen volunteer, wearing a tight candy pink dress that older women would condemn on sight. Her slim, youthful body and apple-small breasts made the outfit more perky than bodacious. A high, blonde-streaked pony tail tied with a matching bow pushed her garb into the realm of cute. Yancey's boyfriend, undoubtedly a student athlete of some type by his build, trailed her.

All carried boxes containing miniature hay bales with various stuffed toy animals perched on them backed by fans of paper autumn leaves of the type never seen in Louisiana and with plastic pumpkins glued near their feet. They plunked one down on each table as Leah completed the silent auction table with a picture of the black pup. "We call her Sweetie because that's what she is," her sign read. "I hope she finds a home tonight," Leah confided to Ash.

"Don't look at me! Remember, a dog, four pups, and now Bandit. My mom will kill me if I bring any more home. Besides, I still owe you for Jolie's BOGO and tonight's tickets. I hope you take credit cards." He'd tried to make light of the situation, but watched Leah's face. Obviously, she was having an "Aha!" moment.

Her green eyes went wide and almost glowed as if she'd discovered radium or some other deadly substance. "I knew it! You aren't perfect. You live with your mother. Ashton Blaise is a mama's boy. That's why I couldn't find your number in the phone book to cancel the kayak trip."

The bow tie that went with the tux suddenly seemed too tight around his neck. "Come on, this is the South. Lots of guys still live at home if they aren't married. If you need the number, it's under Hank

Blaise. My mother didn't change it after my dad's death. But, I have my own cell. Here, I'll write the number down for you." Ash seized a pen attached to one of the clipboards, but not a single sheet of plain paper in sight and all the napkins were linen.

"I can write it on your palm!"

"Why not on my breast, oh most desired of all the firemen in Chapelle?" Leah smirked.

"That would work for me, but the competition isn't that tough. Most of the men are married. Look, I have extenuating circumstances. If you'd just give me a chance to…"

Some of the guests began to arrive early with the smoke of the casino clinging to their hair and clothes and graphite on their fingertips giving away the fact that they'd been killing time at the slots before the event. Chief Fontenot, wearing a huge white dress shirt and no jacket, but a red pepper patterned tie that seemed too small for his throat and rested on his big belly like child's fallen kite, made his way to the couple and immediately clapped Ash on the shoulder.

"Mind if I join you, Blaise? How's your granddaddy doing? Never was a better firefighter than Dalton."

Ash noticed Tank didn't say fire chief since he'd preceded Fontenot in that capacity, but he answered neutrally. "As well as can be expected at his age." No sense going into the rest.

The Chief assessed him from his head to his patent leather shoes. "Looking spiffy except for all the animal hair on your dad's tux. I can't recall how many times I saw him wear that. Me, I find those monkey suits damned uncomfortable."

Ash glanced down. He was indeed covered in dog fur and cat hair from carrying the boxes stored in Leah's SUV. Plucking a tiny feather from his lapel, he blew it into the air and watched it drift to the ground like his hopes of spending more time with Leah Allain.

Leah threw her head back and laughed, a good, throaty sound if it hadn't been directed at him. "Never fear. In my business, I'm always prepared." She found her black satin evening bag and took a lint roller from it. Standing close and starting with his lapels, she worked her way down his jacket, applying some real pressure and getting closer and closer to his crotch. Leah stopped at the bottom of the cummerbund and turned the roller over to him. "I can go no farther in public."

Fortunately, good tailoring covered the bulge growing in his elegant pants. Ash took the roller, turned his back and completed the job. He started to hand it back to Leah, but paused. "I think you have some on your backside."

She craned to see. "Darn, I put a blanket down on my car seat and still got some on me. Where?" She fluffed her skirt trying to get rid of the fur.

"It's down too low. I'll get it." Ash positioned the roller right under the pert bow on her butt and moved it slowly down to the very edge of the hem. He enjoyed watching her shiver.

"Need your jacket?"

"I'm fine!" She snatched the lint roller and returned it to her purse.

Oblivious to the byplay, Chief Fontenot said, "Mind if I sit with you two? I don't have a date tonight, but I'm on the prowl."

The entire town knew being on prowl had cost Tank Fontenot his first and second wives while the third grew tired of him as he aged and increased in girth. No takers so far to be number four. Leah took pity on him. "Certainly, we're right over there near the bandstand where Mrs. Murphy is sitting."

"She's a little long in the tooth for me, but why not?"

Not by much, Leah thought, but she replied, "Her date is Abner Millet right beside her."

"Okay, I'll behave myself, I swear." With a roguish smile on those blubbery lips that might once have been alluring to women, Tank waddled away to the table for eight where he took up two spaces.

"Leah, we need to talk about my situation," Ash said with a hint of pleading in his voice.

"Later. I have to greet the guests."

They poured in now, and Leah moved from group to group shaking hands and thanking them for their support of the shelter. Ash followed like the silent consort of a powerful queen. She greeted the famous retired quarterback, Joe Dean Billodeaux, his tiny wife, and as many of their twelve children as they could cajole into coming and filling out the table for eight. Even with iron gray hair, the football player still exuded a sexual mojo that made Ash a little jealous when the man held Leah's hand for a moment. That had his alpha male juices flowing.

He recognized the gamekeeper from Indian Lake, another man with an earlier reputation for womanizing, but he'd brought his strawberry blonde daughter, college age now. Zola Sweat showed up in a gold and silver-striped caftan, her wild hair wrapped in an

African-styled matching tignon and golden sandals on her expansive feet. The elderly village priest, Father Ardoin, arrived supported on all sides by some of his altar guild ladies. Councilman Tauzin must be working offshore this weekend because his environmentalist wife attended alone. Ash figured every character that inhabited Chapelle gathered here this evening, except for the billionaire Jonathan Hartz who sent regrets and a big check according to Mrs. Murphy.

Finally, some of his crowd showed up, Cliff Couvillon and his son, Cubby, and the three other professional firemen from his watch. They ragged him about the tuxedo. "Hey, we came to see you all decked out like a male model, Captain. I hear most of those pals are gay." One of the guys struck a pose and breathed, "Don't hate me because I'm so handsome." Simple Cubby might not have gotten the joke, but he laughed the hardest. Ash had to give Cliff credit. He took the kid everywhere and showed no shame over his slow wits.

"Okay, okay, I'll let you take a selfie with me in all my grandeur without charging. Now go find a table and put down some bids on the auction items. I know you need a kitten in your sad little lives."

His buds went off still snickering, and Ash sat down at his place next to Leah's chair. She'd climbed onto the bandstand and lowered the mic to her level.

"Thank y'all so much for coming tonight to support Safe Haven Animal Shelter. I won't keep you long because the food is coming out. I know people in Louisiana like to eat, then dance it all off. We have great music tonight with Chapelle's own Blue Bayou Band. They'll provide some dinner music first. Don't forget to check out the silent auction items. Bidding closes at nine-thirty when the live auction starts. Those items are in your program, which lists all of our wonderful sponsors, especially the Cypress Lake Casino, which donated the room and the delicious hors d'oeuvres. Smells wonderful. Feel free to help yourselves. Enjoy."

The light applause faded. The band struck up a moody jazz number, and the stampede to the buffet began before Leah got back to her place. Tank Fontenot already stood in line leaving a big, big gap at their table. He beckoned them to slip into a space he made in the line. No one objected. Ash found himself behind Cubby Couvillon who shoveled bacon-wrapped fried oysters onto his plate with gusto. "Leave some for others, son," his daddy prompted.

Cubby dropped the spoon and turned to Ash. "Hi, Captain Blaise. We like to come to the casino. Great cheap eats, right, Daddy?"

"That's right, boy, now move along. Look, tee-tiny crab cakes. Take no more than two, you hear?" Cliff Couvillon, a big man with a hard gut and his very decided opinions etched into the lines of his face, just shook his head at Ash. People knew Cubby loved to gorge whether on seafood or on a box of donuts left on the firehouse table for the whole crew. If Cubby showed up for a visit on his three-wheeled bike sporting an American flag on the basket, those donuts were gone. The overgrown kid skipped the next dish of slim asparagus bundles also wrapped in bacon.

Leah took one of each item and still filled her plate by the time they reached the end of the line where small pastries sat in individual ruffled cups near the coffee urn. "I'll have to come back for those," she told Ash. "I see you managed to find enough to eat and broke a few vegetarian rules along the way."

"I plan to give you my bacon. Everything seemed to be wrapped in it, even the veggies."

"Deal. Bacon makes everything better, even green stuff."

They settled in to eat. Leah had left the corsage on the table like an extra decoration and Yancey picked it up with admiration shining in her appealing brown eyes. "This is beautiful! Completely adorbs."

"I didn't know I was supposed to get you a corsage, Yance," her swain said. He started on his pyramid of food, second in height only to Fontenot's, by plucking the bone end of a chicken drumette from the pile.

"Oh, I didn't introduce y'all. This is Dirk Keene, Captain of the Flames football team." Yancey preened a little as she patted his youthfully muscular arm. "He said he'd buy a ticket if I'd go with him. I couldn't say no if it's for the good of the animals."

"I've seen you play. You're great. Gonna be another Joe Dean Billodeaux. He started out with the Flames in high school," the Chief said, pointing his own drumette at the boy as if they were about to duel with tiny chicken legs.

"Thanks. I hope so, sir. He's my idol."

"I know everyone in town. I'll introduce you later."

While the Chief's blather went on, Ash carefully unwrapped the bacon from his two asparagus bundles and the oysters and placed it on Leah's plate. He had plenty with double crab cakes and freshly baked wheat rolls, several fried mac and cheese balls, and eggplant planks topped with shrimp sauce. No way a man could get around fried or seafood in Cajun Country.

As he ate allowing the Chief to dominate the table, Ash considered the embarrassing corsage and formulated a solution. When Tank ran out of gas for a moment, he drove a wedge into the conversation. "I bought the corsage for Leah, but it's fine with me if you'd like to buy it from her for say, a twenty dollar donation to the shelter." He didn't want to shake down the boy for too much, but considering that Dirk went to the private parochial school, he probably had some cash in his wallet.

Yancey clapped her hands decorated for the evening with nails sporting little kitty faces. "I'd love that if Miss Leah can bear to part with something so pretty."

"For the good of the shelter, as you said." Leah handed over the corsage and collected the twenty from the boy. She sent Ash a sideways smile, maybe of appreciation, as Dirk, Yancey's romantic hero for the night, slid the corsage onto the girl's slender wrist.

As the plates cleared, the band struck up dance tunes. Yancey dragged Dirk from the remains of his meal and hit the floor. She held her hands above her head, letting the crystal dew drops catch the light. Dirk did ogle her small, bouncy breasts, but he showed some good moves of his own. Most of the elders stayed seated.

"Want to?" Ash asked Leah.

"Wait for a slow one."

His chance came two dances later. One of the band members did a surprisingly close imitation of Elvis singing *Can't Help Falling in Love with You.* Ash took advantage of a now crowded floor and slid his hands down Leah's back, clutching them right above that bow instead of assuming a traditional dance pose. That forced her to twine her arms around his neck. He leaned down, whispering in her ear, "If this were the prom that would become our song."

"And I'd save the awful corsage forever," she answered.

"Never fear. I can get you another one."

"No way!" She pulled back the second the music ended and the dancers thinned. "I have to make an announcement and check the silent auction. Off she went, butt bow bobbing, both cute and suggestive. Adorbs.

"It's nine-fifteen. Bids on the silent auction close at nine-thirty. Time to beat out your rivals for the best items. It's for the good of the Safe Haven Animal Shelter." Leah left the stage and marched down the line checking the bids. Ash tagged along. Most had at least the base bid with a rivalry going on for the duck basket, up to $1,000 now, between the gamekeeper and the famous football player.

"How can a gamekeeper afford that?" Ash questioned.

"Married to an executive at Hartz Technology. He might be bidding for Hartz, too, since he's also down for the retriever carving. Oh, no, not a single bid on Sweetie. She's nearly out of the puppy stage and getting gangling. They can tell by her big feet she'll be a large dog. Rats, even that drooling old bulldog got a bid."

"Georgia fan?"

"Maybe. No one is taking Mr. Grey, the parrot, either."

"He has a certain reputation for salty language. I'd say some of the men here are familiar with the bird and have passed the word. Cliff told me once he took Cubby to Madame Mystique's to keep him from bothering other women. Considering they were first on the scene when her place burned, I believe him. I wouldn't be surprised if the bird knows all the clients' names. Not a gift you take home to the wife."

"I suppose so. Those birds live to be sixty. I'll retire before he dies! They'll probably give him to me as a going away gift."

"Can't help you with the bird, but here." Ash boldly wrote his name on the first line of Sweetie's sheet.

"Your *mom* won't kill you?"

"The firehouse needs a dog. I'll keep her there."

"Both brave and kind of heart."

"Well, the tux didn't impress you. About living with my mother…"

"No need to explain. I must pick up the bids."

She did, calling off the winners and directing them to the cashier's table. The gamekeeper won the duck basket, the football star, the dog carving. Dirk Keene coughed up another fifty dollars for the kitten picture in the big gold frame. Yancey Breaux was no cheap date. Big-hearted Zola took another kitten, the orange one. Of course, Ash won the black puppy and wrote one whopping check for her, the tickets, and what he'd promised to pay for Jolie's BOGO dog.

Later, he bid at the live auction for a personally guided kayak tour of Indian Lake with Leah that included lunch on a float platform. His firehouse cohorts, snickering and belly-laughing, started showing interest as soon as he put up a hand. Bidding against him, they forced Ash to pay five hundred dollars for the pleasure of her company. At least one of them paid for use of a hunting camp, and Cliff Couvillon bought a pair of neon-colored four-wheelers to tool around his small ranch. Owner of many rent houses and commercial properties, he could well afford it.

As Leah threatened, she was the last to leave, picking up the signs, clipboards, the unsold items, and the centerpiece from their table which she'd won by having the birthday closest to the date of the Doggone Delightful Ball. The stuffed toy, a brightly colored parrot, bore no resemblance to Mr. Grey, but she swore she'd been set up. Mrs. Murphy knew she had an October birthday, and if any of the others at the table did, they kept their mouths shut.

"Would your mother like to have this?" Leah offered the centerpiece.

He seized his chance. "I don't think so. She needs my help at home, not stuffed toys. We're taking care of my grandfather because she promised my dad she'd care for his old man. He moved in before my father died and after I'd left for college. That went fine for a while, but Pop is starting to lose it mentally. He's nearly ninety, still a big man more powerful than my mom. Sometimes, he wanders off and shows up at fire stations all over the place because he used to be chief before Tank Fontenot. I can't tell you how many times I've been called to pick him up."

Ash raked a hand through his short-cropped dark hair. "I help with the heavy lifting, the bathing and shaving when I'm off, and keep an eye on him. I learned to cook to give my mother a break. We have a male aide for the days I'm on duty. Rod is a former Marine medic, big guy able to handle anything, but that gets expensive."

Leah held up a hand to stop him. "I know. I'm looking out for my grandmother, only she's become so reclusive she won't open the door to anyone. My folks set her up with a yardman, a cleaning lady, and on-line payments for her utilities, then they took off to retire in Florida."

"They abandoned her, and you have nobody else to help you?" Considering how close families were in Cajun country, he found that hard to believe.

"It's a small family, and Gran and my mom never got along well. My parents did buy a duplex and said she could live alongside them in Destin, but Gran refused to leave. My father had promised my mother a place in Florida, so Mom won their final battle. Once, I had a wonderful grandmother. We had real tea parties, and she taught us what she called deportment. We talked about books and nature. She's not the same anymore. Still, when I came to a breaking point at my old job, I returned here to watch over her. Ash, we both have too much on our plates right now to get involved."

Much as he didn't want to agree, he said, "I guess you're right for now, but things change." He mustered a grin. "You owe me a five hundred dollar kayak trip with lunch on a lake float, so we'll be seeing each other again regardless. I'll follow you home. Make sure you get in safely."

"No need. You should check on your grandfather."

Ash placed his hands on her shoulders, but didn't try to shake some sense into her. "There is a need. Leah, someone burned down your house on purpose either because you are a cat killer or a cat lover or maybe simply because they wanted to do it. I'd like to check the barn for fire safety before I leave you tonight." He hoped he'd made an offer she couldn't refuse, and she didn't.

"Fine. Follow me home and do your inspection."

Chapter Eight

Leah sat on the lipstick red couch and listened to Ash move around the barn. His tread, not as heavy as it would be in fireman's boots, sounded over her head as he inspected the loft. She gazed out her wide, bare windows and watched one of the feral cats, almost a shadow itself, skirt her yard in the moonlight. It paused to stare her way with yellow eyes glowing and a dead mouse in its teeth as if showing off its prey. She shivered at the thought that other eyes might be watching her right now and considering her fair game.

Ash came down the plain staircase that had replaced a traditional barn ladder and joined her on the sofa a fair distance apart. "Lots of cardboard boxes up there and only one small window. If a fire started below, you'd be lucky to get out."

"There's a chest under the window with an escape ladder in it. Delta left that for me. She spent a lot of time in the loft painting, but I only go up when I need something from one of my boxes. I'm not fully unpacked yet—and might never be at the rate I'm going," she admitted.

"Glad to hear someone thought about fire safety. Where's your extinguisher? In the kitchen?" He sounded the same way as she had when inquiring about his life vest on the kayaking trip, tit for tat. Only she didn't have a fire extinguisher.

Leah stared out the window again, avoiding the very serious gray eyes. "I promise I'll buy one tomorrow. I do have that hose already hooked up outside that might be a help in an emergency."

"Sure, but use it after you call the fire department. I don't see any smoke detectors. You need at least two in this space."

"I'll add them to my list."

"We have some we give away at the station. I'll bring them over and see they are installed correctly."

Leah wondered if putting up a smoke alarm could really be classified as difficult. Didn't you simply attach them to the wall? "I can manage. Just drop them at the shelter."

"Smoke rises. They should be mounted higher than you'll be able to reach." Ah, an insult to her height or a ploy to see her again?

Ash stood in front of her in his tux as if instructing a grade school class and held out his arms. "You have two escape routes in the front of the barn." He turned his back and pointed straight ahead. "I see two more on either side of the picture window."

"Yes, from the outside you can hardly tell they are there because they blend in with the barn timbers."

"Four emergency exits are good. Where is your bedroom—if a fire should start in the night?" he added immediately so deadly serious and dashing in his formal attire that he made her smile. James Bond indeed.

"The one on this end of the hall. It's a double stall so I have two windows. The other two are singles."

"I need to see it."

"Sure you do. It's nearly two a.m. I must get some

78

rest, and you need to go home to your mama." Leah added that little dig at the end to send him on his way.

"Fire safety is important, especially in your situation. By the way, you need to get drapes. This place might be out in the country, but anyone could spy on you from the tree line."

"Point taken. Now go home. I can climb out a bedroom window if need be."

As if he hadn't heard at all, Ash strode to the door of her room and opened it. "Interesting."

"Yes, a queen-sized, built-in box bed and not much else."

For lack of a dresser, her everyday clothes resided in black garbage bags, one for tops, one for bottoms, one for socks and underwear, all stashed in a closet across from the bed. She'd left the door open, and he could view her athletic shoes lined up in a row and her newly-purchased nightie and robe on hangers. Not that the nightie and matching robe were sexy or selected for seduction, but constructed of nylon in a pretty peach color, they would cling to her hips and the nipples becoming erect from just standing in a bedroom with Ashton Blaise.

He made no comment about her nightwear, but turned to two windows on either side of the large bed, opened and closed their latches, considered the space she'd have to wriggle through. Perhaps he thought with the size of her hips, she'd have difficulty. That's right, Leah, get mad and force him to leave. She started to voice the insult he'd never insinuated, but Ash spoke first.

"You should get a small bench to make exiting easier. I guess that's all for now."

A small coal burned in her heart about to die from lack of fanning. The nightie wasn't *that* homely. It had spaghetti straps easy to pull down and a kind of low dip in the front that on her would show cleavage and not be in the way of any lips that wandered into it. Where had her mind gone? She brought her imagination under control with a short tug on its leash. "Yes, you should go."

"Just one more thing."

The little coal kindled. "What?"

"I think this tux and that gorgeous corsage deserve a goodnight kiss."

"Maybe the tux does." She offered her cheek.

He took her mouth, biting down lightly on her lower lip as if it were ripe fruit so delicious that he sucked on it next. She opened for him and let his tongue explore. Her nipples pressed hard again the bodice of the red dress. One of his hands slipped inside and caressed, the other worked the clasp behind her neck until it opened and freed both breasts. He took his lips down there, and she wondered how much farther he would go if he untied the bow at her hips and loosened the dress—which he did. All the way, peeling the panty hose as he went. She regretted not getting that bikini wax. The thought dissolved as he plied his tongue between her legs, legs fast becoming liquid, so wobbly Ash easily tipped her onto the bed and finished stripping the hose and getting rid of her shoes.

She'd never gotten naked quicker. Even with…forget him. Leah managed to free the cummerbund and get into his pants with both hands, a move he appreciated with a groan as she cupped him and stroked his shaft. He fumbled in a pocket, withdrew a condom, ripped it open with his teeth, and let her do the honors of sheathing him from tip to root. He completely shed the trousers with the satin stripes, his underwear nesting inside, the shiny shoes and his dark socks, ripped off the bow tie, but seemed unable to cope with the intricacy of the studs on his dress shirt. With an I don't give a damn shrug, he mounted over Leah. She ran her hands under the shirt and climbed the ladder of his ribs with her fingers, found the patch of hair between the hard pecs, and stroked it like a furry pet. When she dug her fingernails into the muscles of his chest, he took the hint, stopped rubbing against her super-sensitive outside, and drove deep inside.

Embarrassing how fast she came—and came again because Ashton Blaise did not let up. Finally, he satisfied himself and rolled to the side, leaving her as limp as if he'd hosed her down. Ash gathered her against his chest, the shirt giving off a clean, starchy scent. "Rest if you want. You're safe. No one will set your house on fire tonight," he said. But, he'd already started a blaze.

****

Leah hadn't meant to fall asleep. She'd cuddle for a while as she never did with Colton, simply enjoy the moment, then send Ash on his way. He'd gone while she slept, as he should for a one-night stand, but had covered her carefully with a blanket. She appreciated the gesture nearly as much as a caress. Wary of the morning light shining in the living room window, she slipped on the thin robe and padded to the bathroom. The aroma of coffee and butter sizzling in a pan stopped her outside the door. Ash called from the kitchen, "Breakfast in ten minutes."

Slamming the bathroom door, Leah desperately checked herself in the full-length mirror. She'd planned to shower, but now left on her makeup, not too badly smudged, only the red lipstick gone. Instead, she washed between her legs, brushed her teeth, and replaced red lipstick with peach. Her hair required little care. In fact, the diamond clip remained in place. Okay, she'd go into breakfast like a Beverly Hills movie star. The robe did flatter, draping her breasts and hips almost elegantly with flimsy fabric. Holding her head high, Leah moved toward the kitchen and whatever waited there.

Ashton Blaise, his jaw and upper lip sporting dark stubble, grinned at her entry. His smile seemed amazingly bright against that background. "Just what I like to see in the morning, a beautiful woman in a sexy peignoir with diamonds in her hair."

Great, he was a person who woke up cheerful and ready to take on the day. "Cut it out," Leah croaked. "Coffee."

"My pleasure to pour you a cup." He filled a mug she'd finally liberated from the loft. It read, "Marry a man who loves animals—and is one in bed", the first part in bold red print, the second line in tiny black letters, a salacious going away gift from the women at the veterinary clinic. Leah accepted it and covered the motto with her hand as she took a sip. He made good coffee, darn it. Nothing she could complain about.

In her donated cast iron frying pan, a layer of eggs bubbled. Ash dumped handfuls of chopped green peppers, ripe tomatoes, broccoli florets, diced onions, and the mushrooms she'd intended to eat with the steak on top. He layered provolone over all of it and as the cheese began to melt, he folded a side of the omelet over, let it cook a while, split it in two with his spatula and slid the halves onto red paper plates. Handing her one of the Betty Crocker forks, he said, "Breakfast is served. I couldn't find a toaster, so I browned the French bread in the broiler." He removed the slices from the oven and placed two pieces each aside their omelets.

"The toaster went in the fire. I'll add it to my ever-growing list." She sampled the omelet. Her usual choice of fillings ran toward chopped ham and sausage, but this was good, too. "Great, thanks for cooking for me."

"I enjoy doing it."

"Try the strawberry preserves in the jam pot on the toast, homemade and delicious."

"Shouldn't they be refrigerated?' Ash asked as he slathered some of her real butter on the toast.

"Basically, preserves are fruit suspended in sugar. Like butter, it really doesn't spoil, and my fridge space is limited. Besides, Zola thinks the crock brings good luck because Rosemarie Leleux, the *traiteur*, decorated it. A nice selling point, but Madame Leleux never claims that."

"I don't know. Right now I feel pretty lucky." Still, he rubbed the jam pot's chubby sides with his long fingers.

Ash gave her one of his nerve-wracking seductive grins as if sitting across a tiny table from a luscious man, barefooted but dressed in formal trousers and a half-buttoned starched shirt weren't enough to give her alternative ideas on how to spend Sunday morning. "You really should take the advice of your buddies, give up being a firefighter, and become a male model," she grumbled.

"Can't. I'm the homely one in the family. You should see Cole. But you won't since I don't intend to introduce you. I can't begin to tell you how many women he's snatched from my grasp just by lifting an eyebrow and crooking his little finger."

"You don't have to worry about me. I'm not in your league or your brother's when it comes to looks. Besides, we both agreed we have too much going on in our lives right now—relatively new jobs, elderly people we have to care for. I think we needed to get away from it all and find a little relief last night. That's all it was. Great, but done." Leah rose to get herself more coffee and turn her back on Ash before she could see his reaction.

"Sure, you're right. However, I'd like to claim that kayak trip next Sunday while we still have great October weather. I'm working Saturday, so we can't do that."

Leah whipped around, sloshing the coffee in her mug. "You really want to do it? I've already shown you all the best spots on Indian Lake."

"Hell, yes. I paid five hundred dollars for the privilege. Nature changes every day, right? Then, there's the gourmet lunch on a lake float that's included. What do you plan to make for me?"

He had to be teasing. "I don't recall saying the meal would be gourmet."

"For five hundred dollars, it damn well should be."

Great, now she'd have to fret all week about what to prepare for a hunky vegetarian. His cell phone rang deep in a pocket of the trousers. Saved by the bell.

Ash answered, his turn to rise and move away. "I'll

be there as soon as I can."

"Fire?"

"Mom. Seems my grandfather heard a siren pass, and he wants to chase it in the car. His license was yanked a couple of years ago, and she keeps the keys hidden, but if he gets out, no telling where we'll find him." Ash bolted the last of his omelet and left a piece of toast. "Got to find the rest of my clothes. Sorry to leave this way, so sorry."

"No apologies needed. It's just one of those things we have to deal with that won't permit us to do this again."

"Whatever you say, gorgeous." He kissed her forehead near the diamond clip and dashed from the small kitchen to the bedroom. Within minutes, he left by what she called the cat door and revved the Prius down the drive.

Leah slathered the extra piece of toast with butter and jelly to eat with her second cup of coffee. She'd confess only to herself that his ready agreement about their mutual situations disappointed. Not one word to convince her otherwise, completely agreeable to the one-night stand concept. He probably did this all the time while she did not, despite her major lapse of judgment in Shreveport. Oh well, she had recipes to look up on her laptop and boxes to unpack, an anticlimax to how the day began.

****

Glad Leah couldn't see his face Ashton Blaise drove away with a huge smile on his face. He'd begun to figure out Leah Allain, learned they both had elderly grandparents to care for, a point in common. That she showed loyalty to a grandmother who could no longer reciprocate her feelings scored high with him. He liked the way she continually tried to fend him off. Nice to be the pursuer instead of the pursued for a change. Ash endured a ton of kidding from the guys at the firehouse about the increased number of pretty girls dropping off baked goods to show appreciation for their bravery since his arrival. The fellows on the other shift griped that none of the cookies and cakes were left over for them.

As he'd told Leah, most of the eight firemen making up the professional staff of the Ste. Jeanne d'Arc Parish Fire Department were married and older. Building a career here didn't exactly appeal to younger men, not with Chief Fontenot a big gobstopper in the way of promotion. Dangerous fires were rare. They spent more time cleaning up gas spills and extricating people from car wrecks, educating children about fire safety, and riding the trucks in various local parades than at their true jobs. Last week, they'd taken two pumper trucks out to refill the newly repaired fountain in front of the city courthouse.

Not exciting work, but lately fire calls had picked up—the brothel, Leah's house, the old cribs on Cinder Street, and several abandoned tenant houses on the periphery of cane fields. Often these last places were offered to the fire department to burn down for volunteer practice by planters who got tired of harrowing and harvesting around them, but at least three had burned all by themselves. People tended to blame vagrants or teenagers smoking pot. No harm done. No lives lost. Forget about it. Still, it niggled at Ash's mind, this uptick in arson frequency rather than the usual accidental fires from old wiring or rags and flammables stored next to gas water heaters.

Leah remained another mystery only partly unraveled. Why did she consider herself to be out of his league? Her body curved generously in all the right places. Ash liked her short, sassy hair. Most of the young women in Chapelle wore their locks long and constantly flipped them over their shoulders or raked them out of their eyes with pointy, polished nails, habits he found more annoying than sexy. Someone had done a job on Leah about her looks. He'd find out who and fix that because they weren't done no matter what she thought. For now, better to keep her off-balance by letting her believe he entirely agreed they should back off from any involvement.

Chapter Nine

Late getting home again, Leah pulled up to the barn to find the clutter of cats waiting to be fed and a silver Prius parked by the far door with Ashton Blaise inside, window rolled down to save energy. What did he want now? She'd stopped to buy the bench and home fire extinguisher he insisted she needed, even a toaster in case… Wasn't it enough that after finding the stuff and standing in a long checkout line, she'd arrived hungry and tired? The animals came first. Let him sweat while she filled the water pans and poured the chow into the dishes.

Sure enough, he came trotting over with two boxes in hand. "Too hot for you in the car, Smoky?" she asked.

"Yes, but I was afraid if I got out any sooner those ravenous cats would intentionally trip me up and eat my face off."

"Only if you died in the fall most likely."

"I brought the smoke alarms, and I have the time to install them right now."

"Well, I don't. All I want is dinner, a glass of wine, and a hot shower. I smell like dog pee." Ash on the other hand exuded a manly sweat full of sex hormones like pig perspiration was claimed to have.

"No, you don't." He sniffed her hair, practically burying his nose in her bangs. "Still smells great."

"That puppy didn't piss on my head." She should turn the hose on him and wash away the alarming pheromones in the air. Out of the corner of her eye she caught motion—Miz Tweedy staring through the sharp blades of her pampas grass, her hair like a white ball of yarn caught in the bushes.

"I have a vegetable lasagna in the car. I wasn't busy today so I cooked a big batch, one for home, one for the firehouse, and one for you."

"I planned on steak."

"This is all ready to go, still warm. Just shake some salad out a bag and you have a meal—tender noodles, a spinach and ricotta filling topped with cheese sauce and a layer of mozzarella."

Leah's mouth watered and not only for lasagna. Had she remembered to take the steak out of the freezer? No. Miz Tweedy aimed a pair of bird watching binoculars at them. Starving and fed up with her neighbor, Leah threw down the hose, wrapped her arms around Ash's neck, and whispered in his ear. "Kiss me, kiss me hard!"

He dropped the smoke detectors to the ground and cupped her face. Grinding his lips against hers, he added tongue, hollowing his cheeks in a way that even an elderly widow would know what he did. His erection grew, pressing against her cleft beneath the pee-stained scrubs. Out of the corner of her eye, Leah watched Miz Tweedy hotfoot back to her house. She broke the seal of their embrace.

"Okay, that's enough. We scandalized my old biddy neighbor enough to run her off."

"Not for me. I'd be willing to do it right here in the mud."

Ash, his dick prodding him in the belly, bent over to retrieve the smoke detectors as Leah turned off the water. The cats glared at them from the edge of the puddle formed around their food pans. Leah moved the dishes to firmer ground, and they crowded in for their dinner.

"Maybe some other time." Eyeing the now grubby boxes, she said, "I hope you didn't break anything."

"Only my heart. I hope you just made me a promise."

She declined to comment. "Come inside and be sure to wipe your feet."

"Yes, ma'am." They entered by the cat side door and crossed the long hallway to the small kitchen. Taking in the nature photographs she'd hung in a straight line, all in matching plain black frames, Ash walked slowly. "You're really good at this."

"Yeah, well, can't make a living at it, but I plan to leave a box of prints for sale at Zola's gallery. Nonprofits don't pay all that well." Leah took down two of the wine glasses she'd unearthed in the loft and poured from a half empty bottle of red sitting corked on the counter. "We both deserve this for driving away Miz Tweedy with our lust. Good performance."

"Who was acting? Say, do you think she set the fire? She hates your cats, but seems a little frail to be lugging gas cans over here." Ash carefully set the mud-splattered boxes on the drain board.

"Don't be fooled. I've seen that wiry old lady carry giant sacks of bird seed from her trunk all the way to her backyard. Still, I don't think she'd do it. Her grandmother once lived in the house, and she's very big on her family history."

"I'll get the casserole so we can eat."

"We?"

"I think I'm owed dinner with a pretty woman after that kiss if I'm not going to get anything else."

As Ash left for his car, Leah gave in with a wistful sigh over the pretty woman nonsense. She quickly shucked the odiferous scrubs in favor of a plain white tee and shorts. Racing back to the kitchen, she dumped packaged salad into wooden bowls from her attic stash, carved up one of the tomatoes ripening on the windowsill, and plunked them down along with an assortment of dressing bottles from her fridge. Grabbing the Betty Crocker dinnerware from a drawer, she set the table and shook her head at the paper plates. Better dishes, just another thing to buy.

Ash thumped his elbow against the outer door as he'd been doing for some time. Leah finally opened it. He entered holding a lasagna dish big enough to feed six and a shiny, stainless steel kitchen appliance tucked under his arm. She relieved him of the casserole and set it on the table crosswise. He made room on the counter for what was clearly the Cadillac of toasters, maybe even a Mercedes Benz—four slots wide enough to brown bagels and dual dials in case a person might want to do both bread and English muffins at the same time.

"Um, I bought a toaster today."

"Take it back and get some plates. Mine has been in storage since I returned home from Houston. Mom likes to use her own things. Someone should get some use out of this." Ash rummaged through her kitchen drawer and found a serving spoon and a metal spatula. "The lasagna is set. It should be easy to serve. Please, sit." He gestured to the cramped table as if he were the host.

Starving, Leah sat without argument and helped herself to a large square. Like everything Ash did, it was wonderful. "Compliments to the chef," she said and struggled to find more dinner conversation. "I guess you'll want that toaster back when you get married." Why had she said that instead of "when you get a place of your own?"

"Depends on what my bride wants. You never know with women."

But, men only wanted one thing, s-e-x. Both her mother and grandmother told her that, a topic of rare agreement between them, but only Gran spelled the word instead of saying it. She'd discovered they were mostly right, but a woman could want sex, too, very much. She finished eating in record time, better to get Ash on the road home. Still, she queried, "Coffee?"

"Dessert?" he questioned, making it sound like a whole lot more than a craving for sweets.

Lean turned and removed an icy, foil-wrapped package from her tiny freezer. "Your brownies. Be sure to take them with you this time."

He didn't take the hint. "Great, let a couple thaw while I hang the smoke detectors."

Leah placed the dinnerware, glasses, and salad bowls in the sink and threw out the paper plates while Ash opened the boxes and checked for any damage. "A-OK."

"You spent too much time in Houston."

"Maybe, but I think I came home at exactly the right moment. Stepladder?"

"I bought a sturdy bench today. It's in my car."

Ash hooked her keys from the peg where she'd hung them and started for the cat door. "You think they'll be gone by now?" he asked.

"The cats? Just shove them aside with your boot—no kicking though. They aren't vampires waiting to suck your blood."

"Cats and women, you never really know about either."

He went off with a smile on his face and returned with both the bench and the fire extinguisher. "I'll mount this for you, too. Lots of things around here need mounting."

"Better get to it, then. Here's a screw—driver." She slapped one into his hand like a surgical instrument—and immediately conjured up assisting Colton Dandridge at his clinic. Her zest in coming up with her own double entendre melted away.

"I've got a big drill—in my car." Ash waited for a comeback, but got no response. With a disappointed twitch of his shoulders, he went to get his toolbox.

Leah washed the dishes while he hung one smoke detector in the kitchen and scouted for another good place which turned out to be right outside her bedroom. He tested both, releasing a blast of shrieks that rose to the rafters and set her teeth on edge. Back in the kitchen, Ash searched for a spot to put the fire extinguisher and finally screwed the bracket to a sturdy upright post near the kitchen where a fire was most likely to start.

"I put the bench under your bedroom window." He slid into his kitchen chair seat again.

"Thanks." Lean placed a brownie on a paper napkin. "You want this to go? I have paper cups for the coffee. I put the rest of the brownies in your pie keeper for you to take home. One of these days, I'll figure out what to put in the soup pot."

"Don't forget the casserole dish."

His smirk told her she'd been set up again. "You brought enough for two more meals, so I shoved it in the fridge, but I will reciprocate, someway, somehow."

Ash took a huge bite of the brownie that left behind frosting smudges on his just right lips. "I'll eat mine here. Got nothing better to do. Since we have blocks of time off a lot of the guys have second jobs mowing lawns, painting houses, hanging wallpaper for extra income, but I haven't come up with anything yet."

"You can always volunteer at the shelter. I need a person to clean the kennels who isn't afraid of a pile of dog crap." Again, Leah questioned her motive and her choice of words. She'd meant to gross him out with the last part of her statement, but had she just issued an invitation for him to hang around her workplace?"

"A tempting offer, dog crap picker upper. I'll give it some thought. I know you want to relax, so go ahead and take that shower. I'll clean up when I've finished my coffee."

"You can let yourself out. The door will lock behind you."

"Sounds A-OK to me."

As was everything to always agreeable Ash. "Fine, then."

She went to her bedroom, shed her clothes, and put on the flimsy robe. Crossing to the bath, she noticed Ash still drinking coffee at the kitchen table. He failed to notice her passing. Leah shut the door loudly enough for him to hear. Turning on the taps in that clear glass box of a shower, she waited for the steam to build up and form on the mirror hung on the back of the door before stepping under the spray. With her head ducked under the stream of water, she did not hear his entrance, but a puff of cooler air alerted her. Leah whipped her long bangs out of her eyes and held the small aqua washcloth over her pubis.

"Want me to wash your back?"

"I—I..." She needed to say no very firmly, but then, had she issued an invitation by not locking herself in when she'd made a big deal over closing the door?

He took her stammering as a yes, peeled off another of those tight, dark T-shirts, and dropped his jeans, commando underneath. He must have left his boots in the kitchen for a quiet approach, yet Leah felt strongly if she told him to go to hell he would—and put out fires in Hades for her.

Ash stepped inside the chamber and lubed his hands with bath gel from a rack of toiletries. Moving behind her and turning her toward the mirror, he began not only washing her back but giving a fairly good muscle-relaxing massage as well. Something Colton never did. Women washed his back, not the other way around. Those strong fireman's hands slipped under her arms and covered her breasts with soapy liquid. Her nipples flushed and poked out through the foam. Leah couldn't turn her eyes away from the two of them in the looking glass, Ash bending over her, his fingers at work, now moving between her legs and giving that area a very thorough shampoo. She felt the pressure of his swollen shaft resting in the crevice of her hind cheeks, but he made a one-handed adjustment and placed his organ at the base of her cleft, rocking slightly against her, making no move to push inside.

"Say when you're ready for more."

"When," Leah answered.

She expected a rear entrance, but their heights weren't compatible to do this standing up. She didn't expect to be rotated and hoisted onto his erection while he cupped her buttocks in a way that made them feel lush and feminine, not out-sized. The turn left Leah peering over his shoulder watching their every move in the mirror, the tiles cool against her back, the shower warm and streaming between them everywhere but the place where they linked together. How fascinating to watch his slim thrusting hips as she grasped them in her hands. Then, her mind fogged over, unlike the mirror because he'd left the door wide ajar. All of her nerves seemed to coalesce in her pelvis, gathering force for one huge electric jolt not long in coming.

Ash lowered her feet to the floor tiles, turned toward the wall of the shower, and spent himself there. His seed washed away, circled the drain, and disappeared. A small sense of loss filled Leah, dumb but true. She should be glad he'd pulled out since he hadn't bothered with a condom and had no way of knowing if she took the pill. She decided not to tell him that she did. Instead, Leah laid her cheek against the expanse of his back and circled his waist. Weak in the knees and weak in other ways, she said, "Thank you. That was considerate."

"I thought you'd tell me to get out when I opened the door. Things went farther and faster than I expected, exactly like a lot of fires." Ash turned into the spray of the shower and rinsed thoroughly before touching her again. He placed a lingering kiss on her lips that grew hotter and deeper—until the warm water gave out and the shower doused them with cold. Being a gentleman, Ash let her bolt for a towel first, then noticed only one hung on the rack. He turned off the water and waited until she'd dried herself very thoroughly before putting on the thin peach-colored robe. Leah handed him the limp, damp toweling. He wrapped it around his shriveling balls.

"Got anymore of these?"

"In the cabinet under the sink, a matched set of six. Someone must have changed their bathroom décor. I thought I'd enjoy the view for a while." She could grin like a satisfied cat when she wanted. Leah shoved a dry towel his way and picked up a comb to swipe her bangs to the side. "Not much maintenance with this style."

"It suits you. I guess we both felt the need for a shower. Got sweaty sitting in the car waiting for you to arrive and fend off the cats. You might have noticed."

"Nope, not at all, but don't plan on showering here again." She cocked her head. "Is the big, brave firefighter really afraid of cats? You seemed fine with Bandit."

"Not one on one, but a mob like that makes you think of a feline version of *The Birds*. It's the way they stare." Ash dropped his towel and pulled on his jeans.

Leah tried very hard not to look. She concentrated on the patch of black hair on his chest until he covered that, too. Time to lead the way to the kitchen where she suddenly felt the need to become very formal.

"Thank you for the smoke detectors and hanging the fire extinguisher. Meet me at seven sharp by the boat ramp on Sunday with your kayak for the tour. See you then. Don't forget your brownies." Leah shoved the pie keeper into his hands while he still struggled to get his boots on and herded Ash outside. Locking and leaning against the door, she took several deep breaths to quiet her furiously beating heart. This could not keep happening. She simply must not get involved with another man sure to ditch her for someone better when he got done playing around.

****

Ash steered for his mother's house, passing cane fields glowing with embers on this still October night. Smoke from the burning of the debris penetrated the air vents of his car. Where there's smoke, there's fire. Leah certainly had fire. He'd expected to enjoy a quick glimpse of her naked body before she cursed him out and chucked a shampoo bottle his way. The way she'd allowed him to take her surprised and caught him unprepared. He needed to be more careful when playing with fire.

Ash decided to mull that over tonight as he watched a World Series game with his grandfather and shared brownies and beer and statistics. The old man remembered games he'd seen in the Fifties, but could not recall he hadn't been fire chief in decades. Maybe he'd run his suspicions about the frequency of fires in the parish past the once great fireman, Dalton Blaise, and see if anything shook free from the tangles in his brain. If not, Ash had Leah and Sunday to occupy his own mind.

Chapter Ten

Ashton Blaise did not call or show up at Leah's place of work to hose out the kennels. He didn't send flowers or a thanks for the shower note either. Good, they were on the same wave length about this quirky attraction between a gorgeous guy and a stubby girl with big boobs. Surely, it would die out now after a couple of copulations. Once she got past Sunday, she could put Ash into her past where Dr. Dandridge lurked.

Leah tried to concentrate on the press release about the success of the Doggone Delightful Ball since the *Clarion* hadn't sent a reporter. She'd managed to snap a few decent pictures of prominent guests enjoying the evening and paying up for auction items. The one she'd taken of Ash on the sly as he intently bid on the kayak trip, well, that belonged to her alone. The event brought in sixty-five thousand dollars thanks to the live auction and the ten thousand dollar check from the local billionaire. She had to deduct the cost of the band, centerpieces and other incidentals, but Safe Haven would have funds for kibble, cat food, and medical expenses for the next six months. Leah typed out an upbeat report, attached the photos, and sent it off to the *Clarion* where someone would rewrite it and put their own byline on the article. Not that she cared. Only the free publicity mattered.

Slow morning. Ethel Murphy went to the casino on Tuesdays, some kind of senior citizen day with a cheap lunch, and she'd probably dragged Abner along. A couple of retirees tended to cleaning the kennels, emptying litter trays in the cattery, and doling out food to the animals. Yep, only her and Mr. Grey in the office. The obstreperous bird had his head tucked under a wing, asleep and quiet for a change. Ash had at least one more day off. Maybe he'd stop by and claim Sweetie. No chance he'd make any moves here at the shelter, but her mind went fast forward to Sunday. Making good on her bid item, that was shelter work, right?

Leah typed in a search for vegetarian picnics, nothing too sexy like chocolate-dipped strawberries. Lots of bean recipes, the opposite of sexy, gassy instead. Vegetarian Italian Pasta Salad with artichoke hearts, that sounded good, and she could add ham chunks to her portion. She printed it out. Greek wraps on whole wheat tortillas full of feta cheese and veggies presented another possibility. Tofu dishes, ugh, she wasn't going in that direction. How about a Middle Eastern Orange Date Nut Bread guaranteed to pack well for dessert? If she went with Italian, Greek, and Middle Eastern, Leah figured she could call it a Mediterranean Feast and pass the whole thing off as gourmet if she threw in a bottle of wine. This meant a long shopping list and Saturday spent putting it together, but she could manage it. Her printer reeled off the recipes along with their brightly colored pictures.

The obnoxious roar of ATVs on the cane field access road near the shelter burst Leah's peaceful morning into shattered little pieces. How she hated the vehicles that disturbed the peace of natural settings. The dogs began to howl, yelp, and bark according to their breed. Mr. Grey awoke with a wild flap of wings and instantly demanded, "Give me some, Le-ah. Give me some." Worst of all, the off-road machines headed for their entry and arrived in a cloud of dust directly in front of her office.

She recognized the neon orange and green machines donated to the silent auction possibly because the dealer couldn't move them in a populace that preferred everything to be camo-patterned. Regardless, their sale made up a big chunk of that sixty-five thousand dollars. Leah placed a diplomatic smile on her face and opened the door to her guests as they shed their matching helmets. "Nice to see you again, Mr. Couvillon and Cubby. Enjoying your big auction win?"

"We sure are, Miss Leah!" Cubby spoke before his father, but Cliff nodded his silver buzz cut hair in agreement. "I don't need to ride my bicycle no more 'cause I got this."

"We thought we'd come out to see you about doing some volunteer work. Cubby fits in great at the firehouse, but I think he should diversify."

"Diversify," Cubby echoed as they stepped inside her sanctum.

"Maybe he could help out this morning while I check on some of my properties. Got a trailer park near here. Who knows? If he works out well maybe you might pay him a little for his time."

Leah jumped on that last sentence. What she did not need was a person who required constant supervision. She swore every ADHD kid in the parish had been dropped off at the shelter to help at one time or another and after frightening enough animals with their frenetic energy, she had to call the mothers to pick them up and ask them not to return. That wouldn't be the problem with Cubby, who appeared almost sluggish since he'd parted from the ATV. He dropped a ratty backpack to the floor with a clunk and homed in on the bowl of grapes she kept on her desk for Mr. Grey, helping himself to a handful.

"I'm so sorry but most staff consists of volunteers except for me and the vets we call in when needed who often donate their time. That's how we get by."

"Okay. He'll work for free. He loves animals, right Cubby?"

"Cub-bee, Cub-bee, give me some," the parrot mimicked from his cage in the corner.

Cubby's dull blue eyes suddenly brightened. "Mr. Grey! I'm happy Captain Blaise rescued you from the fire."

The parrot's beady black eyes sized up the boy and the grapes in his hand. "Give it to me, baby!"

Cubby shared with the bird. Leah seized her chance. "He's available for adoption. Look at how they've taken to each other."

"Oh, Mr. Grey and Cubby are old friends, but my wife wouldn't have that foul-mouthed creature in our house. I'll leave my son here, and you can show him the ropes. Be back around noon to fetch him." Mr. Couvillon didn't wait for Leah's agreement. He strapped on his helmet, made for the ATV, and was gone before she could protest.

Leah searched her mind for something to occupy Cubby. "Would you like to play with the cats and kittens? They need to be socialized before we can put them up for adoption."

"Huh?"

"We hold them and play with them so they'll make good pets."

"Nope, don't like cats. Miz Tweedy hates 'em. They eat her birds." Cubby sorted through a glass jar of unshelled nuts Leah also kept for the parrot. He picked up a Brazil nut and tested it with his teeth. "Hard."

"Yes, they take Mr. Grey longer to eat giving him something to do with his time." Besides harangue her, Leah failed to mention. Cubby offered the nut to the bird. Mr. Grey took it in one claw and began cracking through the tough shell, dropping the pieces to the bottom of his cage. He worked fragments of nut meat out with his smooth, blunt tongue and swallowed them down. Cubby shucked a peanut and tossed it into his own mouth.

"Cubby, how about walking some of the dogs around the compound? They need exercise."

"I'm skeered of dogs. Mama has a little dipshit poodle who nips me."

Leah raised her eyebrows at Cubby's use of a crude term to describe his mother's dog, but his round innocent face remained clueless about any impropriety. "We have some very nice dogs that don't bite. In fact, Captain Blaise has adopted one who is still here for the moment. Would you like to meet her?"

"Captain Blaise's dog? Sure."

Leah selected a leash from a peg and led him to the rows of kennels where Sweetie romped in a long run with several mixed-breed puppies half her size. She bowled over one of her companions with a big, friendly paw, but was still the first to reach the cage door when

Leah opened it. She clipped the leash to Sweetie's stretchy nylon collar and encouraged the pup to jump down.

"Now, Cubby, hold the leash fairly short and tell her to heel. That means to stay by your side. Give her a treat if she obeys well." Leah transferred some small nuggets from her pocket to his. She demonstrated a heel and a sit, giving Sweetie a treat at the end of the short lesson. "See what I mean?"

"I can do that. Easy-peasy." Cubby seized the leash and jerked Sweetie to his side.

"Not so hard, only a gentle tug."

Brought in close, Sweetie swiveled and planted her front paws on Cubby's knees. He kicked at her, dropped the leash, and backed away. "She wants to bite me!"

"No, she wants to play." The pup danced around Leah and chased the dragging lead. Leah held a hand over Sweetie's head and gave the sit command again along with a treat for a brief moment of obedience while she reclaimed the leash. She wished she could do the same with Cubby. He might learn to walk the dogs properly, but would need someone beside him constantly in the beginning. With his size and strength, he could injure a small dog unintentionally and clearly could not handle large dogs because of his fear. Leah put Sweetie back into the run and selected an older obese beagle/basset mix for a plod around the compound. No chance of this one being too exuberant for Cubby. Unfortunately, he soon grew bored with the task.

"Can I go back and see Mr. Grey again? Are there any games on your computer?"

"No games, only shelter business." A lie, but she didn't want to encourage Cubby to mess with her machine. "Sure, go back. I'll finish walking Waddles."

She took her time. The office area would seem crowded with Cubby's bulk taking up much of her space. Finally putting the panting part-basset back into his kennel where he stretched out in a shady spot groaning as if he'd just completed a death march, Leah forced herself to return to the office.

Cubby spun round and round in her swivel chair. The bowl of grapes stood empty, and all the peanuts had been plucked from the jar of nuts. Apparently sated, Mr. Grey took no interest in her arrival. "Hi, Miss Leah," he said. "You know you got poop in your little refrigerator."

"Yes, stool samples from the new arrivals still in quarantine to see if they have worms and other diseases. I'll check them under the microscope soon."

"Not stools, poop. You know, like shit." He lowered his voice on the last word and said it in a whisper.

"We call it a stool in veterinary language." Leah opened the mini-fridge sitting below the one that held the specimens and took out a bottle of water to glug. Warm day even this late in October. She noticed Ash's casserole dish sitting there with the foil folded back and one of the spoons from the coffee setup protruding from its plump, cheesy middle. "Cubby, did you eat some of my lunch?"

"Got hungry. It's good cold. Captain Blaise makes that for the firehouse guys sometimes."

"Next time ask permission before you take anything. You are welcome to a cold drink, but the volunteers often keep their lunches in there. The food isn't for everyone. Now if I could have my chair back..."

Reluctantly, Cubby removed his behind to the straight-backed wooden chair where clients sat when adopting a pet. "You're out of peanuts."

On her way to claim her rightful place, Leah tripped over the boy's dusty backpack and stubbed her toe on something hard. "What on earth have you got in there?"

"Pop bottles. I pick them up in the ditches to recycle. That's when you use them for something else," Cubby explained earnestly in case she didn't know about recycling. "It's a good thing to do, my daddy says."

More likely the contents of his pack consisted of beer and liquor bottles but those items needed to be recycled, too. Leah took her seat and noticed a distinct wobble in her nice, padded executive chair that hadn't been there before. It might never be the same again. In the distance an ATV buzzed like an aggravated hornet. Waddles roused himself to squeeze out a woo-woo-woo and set off all the other dogs. Dared she hope Mr. Couvillon had returned early? Oh, he had!

Leah rolled out her diplomatic skills and a bright smile again as she ushered Cubby outside to meet his father. "While I enjoyed your son's company, I'm afraid he's not going to work out as a volunteer. Cubby tells me he doesn't like cats and is frightened by dogs. He seemed bored with the task I gave him. But, he loves the parrot." Cubby's dad ignored the hint.

Cliff Couvillon reddened. "It's my wife's dipshit poodle he's scared of, not dogs in general. She sleeps with that pissant little beast. I can't even get near her at night without risking an ankle bite. No boy of mine is afraid of real dogs. Right, Cubby?"

Cubby's face turned the identical shade of red his father wore. "Right, Daddy."

"Of course he got bored if you put him to cleaning kennels with those old fossils you had hanging around here this morning. You need to give my boy another chance, missy."

Do not offend a big contributor, Leah prompted herself. "Maybe he could come back after school hours when our teen volunteers are here. He might enjoy their company, and they could train him."

"Now we're cookin'. Sounds good. What say we go get some overstuffed po-boys for lunch, son?"

"I'm hungry," Cubby stated as if he hadn't cleared out Leah's bird snacks and part of her lunch. He shrugged into his clinking backpack.

"*Bon appetit.*" She kept smiling as they mounted the ATVs and hit the road. At last, she relaxed her facial muscles and went inside to see how much of the casserole Cubby had left for her own lunch. Enough remained for her to have a hearty portion and still take some to her grandmother's house after work, but she wouldn't be having any grapes with it. As she ate Ash's lasagna reheated, Leah listened to the messages that had come in while she walked Waddles and continued her day.

****

"Did you have a nice lunch, Gran?" Leah busied herself reheating the lasagna in her grandmother's kitchen. Salad sat in the bowls and French bread sliced in a basket.

"I don't recall." Once straight and spare but beginning to bend, her grandmother took a place at the table and picked up a fork in one hand and knife in the other to indicate her readiness, a gesture she would formerly have called a breach of etiquette. No knife needed as Leah cut up the long planks of noodles to prevent any problem they might cause. Leah set the plate in front of her.

"You'll enjoy this. A friend of mine made it with lots of cheese."

"I don't like cheese."

"Yes, you do. When you had parties you always put out a lovely cheese tray."

Reassured, her grandmother began to eat without further delay. Leah rambled on about Ash. "My friend is a guy. He cooks really well, huh? He's a fireman, and he seems interested in me." She put it mildly. "But, I made this huge mistake in Shreveport and became involved with my boss, a married man, a married man with children. I wanted to believe he'd choose me over them. How wrong could I be in so many ways? I need to be careful and not so foolish again."

One thing about her grandmother's current mental state, she didn't interrupt Leah in mid-sentence to tell her not to talk with food in her mouth or how to hold her fork or what constituted proper dinner conversation. Gran offered stern advice on how Leah should live her life only rarely now. She listened uncritically or not at all, which made her a good sounding board.

Leah dropped her fork into the salad bowl when her grandmother announced very distinctly, "I was not a virgin."

"What?"

"I was not a virgin when I married your grandfather."

"Gran, no one cares anymore about being a virgin when you marry," Leah rushed to say, but her stomach clenched. She feared a terrible reveal that Alene might have been molested as a girl, the truth only now rising to the surface because she no longer had the will to keep it submerged.

"I also had an affair with a married man who had a family. People did not divorce in those days, not here, and teachers were held to a high moral standard. Many of them never married. They had a career. That was all. I needed more. I wanted to know passionate love."

"No need to tell me about it. I'm the last one to judge." Leah took a gulp of her iced tea and hoped her grandmother would do the same. She did not.

"His wife discovered our affair and threatened to have my job, to spread the truth all over town. I hastily accepted your grandfather's proposal, which put me in a position of unassailable social power. My lover and I no longer communicated with each other. Your grandfather, a good man, older, but not passionate. Gran ran a hand over the white braids that crowned her head, hair once as black as Leah's own. "He adored my eyes, my long, long hair."

Grandpa or her lover adored them? Leah did not ask. She remembered her paternal grandfather, always dressed in a three-piece suit, smelling of cherry pipe tobacco, not the kind of man who romped with children, but ever generous with money for movies and trips to the mall. He'd passed long before his wife.

"For years, I believed I remained childless because of my sin. Then, your father came along, and I felt I'd been forgiven." That momentary spark of light in Alene's green eyes winked out.

Leah reached across the table to cover her grandmother's trembling hand. "Everything worked out. No need to worry anymore."

Gran's lips moved as if she had to search for words after expending so many. "Move on. Go forward," she finally said. Was this advice she'd once given herself, or did she intend it for Leah?

Leah decided to take it to heart. "Thanks for the advice, Gran."

"What advice?" Alene pushed her half-eaten dinner aside. "Do we have ice cream for dessert? I want some." She spoke like a peevish child.

"We do. I'll get it for you." Leah discovered the carton still unopened. She softened the Rocky Road briefly in the microwave before giving a dish to her grandmother who attacked it as if it were her last treat before going to the electric chair. All of her refined manners fell away as she scraped the bowl and licked the spoon. "More."

Leah doled out another scoop. She'd lost her appetite for her own portion and let it melt. Move on. Go forward. That might be the last piece of lucid advice her grandmother ever gave.

Chapter Eleven

Ash sat cross-legged on the dock at the boat ramp. Fishermen out early this October dawn probably thought he watched the sunrise or practiced meditation. Wrong on both counts. He pondered a rare conversation with his grandfather and his next move with Leah because he really couldn't get enough of her. Technically after today he'd agreed they should keep their distance, but he'd think of something.

As for the unusual number of fires, Dalton Blaise agreed. He uttered one word after hearing Ash's story. "Pyromaniac." Taking a swig of his beer from a long-neck bottle, Dalton began to reminiscence.

"We had one of those right here in Chapelle. Old, deserted houses burning down, some of them historical, then a small fire at Chateau Camille."

"Where the botanical garden is now? Didn't the entire mansion burn down?"

"Not on my watch. Something fishy out there among the LeBlancs, old, rich family. Turned out the lady of the house, Vivienne LeBlanc, had a fascination with fire. They asked me to keep it quiet. Her people from New Orleans took her away and swore they'd have her committed. That's how things were handled back then. You didn't flaunt the wealthy and influential if you wanted to keep your job. But, she got out, burned down the church and her own house. Couple of people died. But, not on my watch."

"They caught her after you retired, then." Ash thought it might not hurt to remind the former fire chief he was no longer in charge since he tended to forget.

"Huh? I guess so. Not on my watch." Dalton turned his attention to the ballgame again and shook his head. "These guys with their beards and tattoos. Probably all on steroids." He reached into a bowl of Chex Mix his daughter-in-law had prepared for them and picked out the little pretzels he liked best with his thick fingers.

That ended the longest conversation he'd had recently with his grandfather, a man who'd inspired him to become a firefighter with rides in parades on the big red truck when he was very small and stories of personal valor later when he understood the cost of the job better. The Blaise family produced firemen like some raised sugar cane for generations back in time. His own father should have been the next chief, but his heart failed to outlast Tank Fontenot who looked like a coronary waiting to happen, but it never did.

Ash vaguely remembered the fuss when Dalton reached retirement age and showed a reluctance to quit. His sharp-tongued grandmother, Velma, nagged and nagged and nagged that her time had come. They'd buy a camper and see the great national parks, venture into Canada to peep at the autumn leaves, and go way down to Mexico to drink margaritas by the sea. Considering his grandmother never said a nice word about anyone or any place, Ash thought sharing a camper with her must have been a special fiery hell for his grandfather, but go they did. She'd died of throat cancer that spread to her brain after sucking down the nicotine of a two pack a day habit for years, a fireman's wife who always reeked of smoke. Ash's memories of her weren't fond, but she'd always gotten a kick out of his name.

Once, he'd asked his grandfather how he'd come to marry Velma and only once. "In my day, when you knocked a girl up you married her, and the Church told you it was until death do you part. That enough information for you?" He'd answered, "Yes, sir" and never asked again.

Ash used his last day off to research Vivienne LeBlanc at the library using their microfilm of the *Clarion*. The arson of one of the oldest churches in Louisiana held enough significance that the date was etched on the historical marker in front of the new church built from its original plans. He used the date to go right to the coverage of that event. Woman saved from the burning building along with the statue of the Virgin Mary, two dead in the Chateau Camille fire. Vivienne LeBlanc arrested and charged. Papers full of it for a while. What had become of the woman who was only around thirty at the time? He returned the film to the librarian, but had the sense to ask if they had other information on the LeBlanc family and the fate of Vivienne.

The fairly young woman staffing the reference desk smiled like he'd made her day. "Certainly. Our director, the second Mrs. LeBlanc, wrote a family history. It's in the Louisiana room." She consulted her computer and scribbled down a call number. "She didn't include Vivienne's death out of consideration for her step-daughter, but we do have a file on Chapelle's most famous arsonist. Comes up from time to time."

The librarian led the way to a file cabinet and extracted a folder. "Low-tech, but easy to use. Please make copies of anything you want to keep instead of just walking off with it."

"Do I look like a thief?"

"No, you look too good to be true, but I'll be watching." She pointed to a table near her work station. The hand bore a wedding ring, so only a slightly flirtatious remark meant to go nowhere or soften a warning. This woman wasn't on the prowl for the limited supply of single men in Chapelle.

Breathing easier, Ash settled down to sort through the clippings and copies of articles regarding Vivienne LeBlanc. Never went to trial by reason of insanity. Committed to an asylum—where she burned herself to death by setting her mattress on fire. A more circumspect *Clarion* obituary gave no cause of death, just the usual: age, education, hobbies (local history and genealogy, no mention of arson) and her survived bys—parents, siblings, and a lone daughter. What had happened to the only child? He doubted the librarian, no matter how coy, would give out personal information on her director's relative. He had a name, the internet, and his mother, as good a source on locals as any social media.

Trucks came and went after depositing boats into the water. The drivers carefully avoided Ash's red kayak stowed to one side of the ramp, but they could have driven right over it without his noticing he remained so deep in thought. A hand touched his shoulder, and he jumped.

"Meditating?" Leah asked.

"No, just thinking, why?"

"Sort of goes with the vegetarianism, I guess. Let's get this show on the road. We can both be home by one."

"I warn you, I tend to be a very leisurely eater." He said it with a drawl and a lewd glance to get a rise out of her, but unlike the fish in Indian Lake, she did not bite.

Leah turned on her heels and moved to her SUV to unstrap her kayak. Ash heaved it off the roof without being asked and got no thanks. Still playing hard to get though she'd been gotten—twice. Maybe three times was the charm. He carried the kayak to the water's edge simply to hear her aggravated voice say, "I can do that!"

"Can, but don't have to while I'm around," he reminded her.

Instead of answering, she opened her car door and removed his gumbo pot. They were having soup on a warm day while floating in a lake? Leah thrust it at him.

"Inside is an extra loaf of the orange date nut bread we're having for dessert. I consider us even for the lentil soup. Put it in your car now so you won't forget it if you have to run off."

Ash accepted the pot and locked it in his Prius, but said, "I was hoping for more brownies."

"Oh, you're one of those people who always wants chocolate for dessert?"

"Pretty much. Don't forget you haven't returned the lasagna pan yet. It's fine for making brownies."

"I'll keep that in mind." She shouldered her backpack, shoved her kayak into the water and sank into the cockpit. "You coming?" He'd like to, but figured she wasn't in the mood for another suggestive remark.

The paddle went about the same as the first time,

but she threw in some special thrills taking him down a narrow chute through the bird rookery where branches hung low and alligators lounged everywhere, more safari than recreation. Maybe she wanted to put him in his place or her place because she showed no fear. He'd rather walk into a burning building than be a reptile's lunch any day.

Leah led. Admiring her tanned, lightly muscled arms wielding the paddle, he followed. Occasionally, she paused and listened. "Hear that? A magnolia warbler." The tweet sounded like all other birds to Ash, but he nodded. Eagles plunging from the sky were more his thing.

They didn't return to the secluded live oak tree to picnic, more's the pity. Instead, Leah guided him to a rented platform anchored in the vicinity of the lone cypress bearing the eagle's nest. The float came complete with rings to tie up boats, a beach umbrella, and a short ladder for mounting after a swim in the lake, as if he'd do that considering the gator population. They climbed aboard. Nearly Halloween and they still had to adjust the umbrella for shade, not that it helped so close to noon.

Leah spread a cloth plucked from her knapsack on the deck and plunked down a wine bottle, plastic cups, forks, containers, and the Greek sandwiches tightly coiled inside of cling wrap. "Sorry about the twist cap wine, but I didn't want to tote a corkscrew out here. If you'd do the honors."

Ash broke the seal on the wine and poured. "What's for lunch?" He gave her a hungry glance, which she ignored as usual.

"I've prepared a Mediterranean Feast featuring an

Italian pasta salad, Greek wraps with feta cheese, and our orange date nut bread for dessert." Her voice held a note of pride.

"What, no Around the World Special?" he asked with a leer as he lowered himself cross-legged near the edge of the deck.

"You think I don't know what that means. Ugh!" Without a second of warning, she shoved him off the deck into the warm alligator infested waters of Indian Lake and warded him off with a sneaker to the chest.

Ash swam as fast as an Olympic freestyler around to the ladder on the far side of the float and climbed aboard. "Jeez, just joking. I didn't know what that was until I saw it on the Weekend Special Board the night Madame Mystique's whorehouse burnt down and I went in to save her parrot."

Leah gestured at him with a Greek wrap. "If you are really lucky, you might get numbers one and two, but never three from me. Sit down and eat."

"Sure, easy for you to say when I could have been a gator snack." Ash peeled off his soaked T-shirt, wrung it out, and spread it on the deck to dry in the sun. He dumped the water from his athletic shoes, and placed them next to the shirt. Leah eyed him as if she expected him to shuck his shorts as well. He shook his head. "Too many people on the lake today to go any further."

"I didn't ask you to." She handed him a plastic container. "Your pasta salad. Mine has ham in it." She studied the end of the wrap she'd used as a pointer. "This one's mine with some turkey added."

"Yeah, thanks for the consideration. Glad I lived to eat it."

"No need to be surly. The alligators mostly stay by the rookery. They're hardly ever out in the open water. Lots of people swim here. Besides, it's hot enough to take a tan." She proved her point by slowly unbuttoning her red, sleeveless blouse and taking it off. Underneath, Leah wore a black sports bra that did very little to suppress the fullness of her breasts bulging out at the sides and creating a chasm of a cleavage in the center.

Ash decided he needed some wine, finished the contents of his cup, and poured another. He tried the pasta, good, and gave her a nod. The wrap in its whole wheat tortilla satisfied. Leah placed a foil package of sliced orange date nut bread on the cloth. "Dessert," she said.

"I was almost afraid to ask for it."

"I can't believe you never went swimming here, being a local boy."

"Fishing, boating, yes, but I have more sense than to swim with gators." He nodded into the hazy distance across the lake where the two Indian mounds that gave the lake its name thrust out of the marshy ground. "The Twin Sisters, big make out spot the guys called the Two Tits back when I was in high school."

"Still do and still is according to Yancey Breaux."

"Ever go out there with a guy?"

"Not going to answer that." Leah poured herself a second glass of the not-too-bad-for-the-price wine as if she needed to wet her mouth immediately. "Do you want to brag about your exploits?"

"No, just trying to figure out how I missed noticing you back then. Did you go to Ste. Jeanne's?"

"Yes, but you had four years on me. Before I busted out, you left for college." Her green eyes flitted to her chest for a moment and rose again to meet his eyes. "I don't think you came home very much."

"No, my parents gave my room to my grandfather and put a bed for me into my brother's. Neither of us liked the arrangement very much. I usually found summer jobs on campus and stayed there. What about you?"

"I volunteered at the shelter which I now know was very poorly run, groomed horses at various stables since I wanted so badly to work with animals. Northwestern State offers an A.S. in Veterinary Medicine. After high school graduation, I headed there, studied, did a summer internship in Shreveport, took and passed both the state and national exams to become a registered veterinary technologist. The vet I worked with offered me a job right out of school. I stayed up north until my grandmother needed me. End of story." Leah gazed off into the distance, squinting at some incoming clouds.

There had to be more. Ash probed. "Why not get your DVM degree?"

Leah shrugged, making her breasts bunch together and causing him to be a little ashamed of noticing. "Takes a long time and incurs a lot of debt just like becoming a doctor, but a vet doesn't earn back the educational expenses as quickly. I wanted to dive into the profession and had a solid job offer with benefits. Seemed ideal at the time."

She was holding back. Maybe if he shared some of his concerns, she'd open up and reveal the source her hostility because he'd certainly taken some heat from her today. "I have a problem I'd like to run by you."

Her green eyes glittered at him. "Other than living

with your mother? If it's sexual, I don't want to hear it."

"Neither. I've noticed something at work, a high frequency of arson cases for an area this small, some shacks, those old cribs on Cinder Street, Madame's bordello, and your place. I mean we get space heater fires in the winter, trailers going up around chain smokers, and kids playing with lighters all the time, but not intentionally set fires. My grandfather thinks we have a pyromaniac on the loose. You ever hear of Vivienne LeBlanc?"

"Sure, the locally famous villainess who burned down our historic church. I went to school with her daughter, Angelle."

The wind picked up, rocking their float like a cradle, moving Leah closer to Ash's side, entirely fine with him. Best of all, no need to ask his mother if Leah knew the girl personally. "Do you know where she lives, and what she's doing now?"

"We weren't besties or anything. Really pretty girl but quiet, always drawing, didn't date much, covered up, no sexy clothes for her. I guess when the whole town knows about your crazy mother you can't wait to get away. She went to a fancy art school in Chicago on a Hartz scholarship after graduation. I think she stayed there. Comes home for holidays, Christmas, Easter, the Fourth. I run into her sometimes then. She came to the shelter with her stepmom after her old black cat died, and I helped her pick out a good one. She named him Picasso."

Ash topped off Leah's cup of wine. She sipped at it absently, still studying the sky. He asked, "Do you think she has the same obsession with fire as her mother?"

"Heck, no. At bonfires, she stayed way back in the crowd. My mom said the kids shouldn't make fun of her because she almost died when Domengeaux's sandwich shop burned down. It used to be right across from the church."

"I remember the place, great muffulettas and catfish po-boys. My dad used to eat there a lot since it was close to the firehouse. Domengeaux's probably contributed to his death."

Leah sat close enough now to give him an elbow in his bare ribs. "Don't judge if you don't know. Anyhow, I doubt Angelle LeBlanc sneaked back to town in October to set my house on fire or burned out Madame Mystique in January, sending all those girls outside in their scanty clothes."

"I suppose you're right. There goes my prime suspect."

"Speaking of going, we should get out of here. That black cloud over the Twin Sisters is dumping rain and coming our way." Leah grabbed containers, picnic trash, and the empty wine bottle threatening to roll off the float and into the lake, stuffing them into her backpack.

"It's only a popup storm and will be over fairly fast. Let's ride it out. Why take the chance of capsizing on the way back?"

"You're just scared the alligators will get you."

"Yep." Ash grabbed his still damp T-shirt about to take flight in the wind, not that it would make any difference if he got wet bare-chested or clothed. He saved his shoes from going overboard.

"The umbrella is catching the wind. That could tip

us over, too." Small whitecaps lapped the edge of the raft. Leah shoved her arms into her red shirt, but made no attempt to button it on the rocking float.

Ash reached under the umbrella and lowered it to make a tent over them, nice and cozy. The rain began to pelt down on the canvas. He drew Leah against his naked chest, felt the warmth of her breasts, the hardness of her nipples, and found his hands pushing the athletic bra out of his way to fondle them. He added a kiss, their breath tangy with wine. Her hands moved south, working at the zipper of his khaki shorts, a little stiff from having been soaked in the lake, but she would not be denied. Leah took him in hand and stoked his shaft with a maddening firmness. He wanted her so badly, but how in the middle of a lake filled with alligators?

First step, get into her pants, khaki shorts not much different from his own. He reluctantly left her breasts to attack her zipper. It moved downward more easily than his to reveal the top of black cotton bikini pants. He delved inside, found her already slick, and worked her with a finger and a well-placed thumb. She swirled the head of his penis in her palm while still stroking, stroking, stroking. Hard to say which of them came first or when the rain passed. They collapsed against each other breathing hard in their own private tent unaware of what went on in the rest of the lake until something poked the side of the collapsed umbrella. Alligator? Could he fend it off before it chomped on his tender exposed parts?

"Hey, hey, you two all right in dere?" Not an alligator.

"Who the hell is that?" Ash said as he wiped down his chest with the T-shirt.

"T-Coon Arton who runs the float, canoe, and kayak concession. Used to be a poacher. Mr. Landry, the gamekeeper, says it keeps him honest," Leah whispered as she repositioned her breasts in the sports bra and drew her zipper up in one swift stroke.

She crawled out of their shelter. Ash adjusted his shorts and balled the T-shirt into a wad. He put the umbrella up.

"Jus' leave it down. I come to give you a tow," said a wiry old man brown as a pecan husk and possessing an impressive expanse of gray walrus mustache across his upper lip. "You shoulda come in when dat storm blew up, no?" His thin, old shoulders heaved in a Gallic shrug. "But I been young once, too. T'ink you never gonna die. Got udder t'ings on your mind."

Leah's eyes went to her bra, making sure she was all tucked inside. Ash's hand double-checked his zipper. T-Coon laughed, showing his tobacco-stained teeth as he tied the float to his small inboard boat.

"*Bienvenue a Le Petit Canard.*" The elderly Cajun helped Leah aboard the boat he called his Little Duck and waited for Ash to gather the knapsack, his shoes, and make the transfer. Off they went with the float and two kayaks bobbing behind like ducklings. He dropped them off near the dock to complete a short paddle ashore and waved goodbye with a huge, knowing grin on his face.

Ash answered that grin and got a scolding from Leah. "That can never happen again!"

"I don't think we could ever duplicate the circumstances. What a wild ride with the float rocking and the rain pouring down and—alligators all around."

"There were no alligators!" She stamped her

perfectly dry sneakers.

His squished as he walked back to his car to load his kayak on the trailer. She followed.

"I mean we aren't compatible. We should both move on."

"Really?" He raised his brows to show his skepticism. "I think we couldn't be more compatible."

"In that way, yes, but not in the ways that count."

"Which are?"

"You're handsome and heroic. Every single woman in town wants you. I'm a stubby cat killer/cat lover someone wanted to drive out of town if the fire wasn't random. We're here in Chapelle because elderly grandparents need our help. When that responsibility ends, we'll probably both move elsewhere, go in different directions."

"Not me." Ash could read the doubt on her face. "I'm Tank Fontenot's heir apparent. The Council pushed him to hire a young professional deputy chief. They figure I might outlast him though no one else has. The older men waiting for years are near retirement and losing interest in the position."

Leah narrowed her cat-green eyes. "Then why does everyone call you captain and not chief," she said with suspicion.

"Well, Tank doesn't like to have anyone else called chief. He says it leads to confusion. Besides, I do serve as captain to my squad. In small departments like these, a guy often wears two hats. The fellow who heads up the other group is also training officer." While he had her mind engaged, he heaved her kayak on top of the SUV and started strapping it down without a hearing a peep of protest from her.

Instead, she leaned against the side of her vehicle and asked, "So what's the deal with Cubby? Is he really a volunteer fireman—because when his dad dropped him off at the shelter to help out he didn't have enough attention span to walk a dog—and cleaned out my snacks."

The change of subject surprised Ash, but he spilled what he knew. "He's more of a mascot, but Cliff brings him to all the training sessions, has for a long time. The kid got his certificate of completion from high school in May, and his family doesn't know what to do with him is my guess. The shelter is the next stop to getting him employed or occupied. Cubby worked at the library for a while, supposed to help the janitor but kept wandering off, usually to the fire station, which is nearby. I think he did a short stint at the pepper sauce factory, too, some problem there as well. Don't know what. I will say he's as sturdy as a fireplug with his bulk and good help with the hoses. He obeys his father's orders and doesn't get in the way. Of course in a bigger town, he wouldn't be allowed, but this is Chapelle, and Cliff and Tank are tight. That help you out any?"

Leah nodded. "Must be hard having a kid like that. Does he have any siblings?"

"An older sister who married away and rarely visits.

"Tough. I should show more charity and less concern that he ate all the grapes intended for me and the parrot. I'll see how he fits in with the teen volunteers who come after school. Maybe he'll do better in a group. Thanks for the info and the help with the kayak." Leah heaved herself into the SUV and slammed the door.

She'd thanked him. Progress. Ash rapped on her window as the engine roared to life. She opened it. "What are you doing on Halloween?"

"If you think I'm going to dress up in some idiotic costume and go to a party with you, forget it. Halloween is hard on black cats and pets that gobble down chocolate, which could kill them. I'll be standing by for emergency rescues."

"Me, too. We're all on duty that night. Mostly pranks gone wrong, but you never know. I just wanted to say stay safe if I don't see you again." He pressed a soggy business card into her hand. The front had the emblem of Ste. Jeanne d'Arc Parish, sugar cane stalks with a flame in their midst, his name, rank as deputy fire chief, and a public contact number. On the reverse, he'd scribbled his cell phone and home numbers written in water-washed ink but still legible. "Sorry, it was in my hip pocket when I went for my swim with the gators, but call if you need me for anything."

"This means you won't be getting in touch with me anymore, right? Because we aren't compatible."

Did he see disappointment in her green eyes? "If you say so. Take care of yourself—as I know you are capable of doing. But be safe."

"Damn right." Leah backed away, turned her SUV, and left him standing by the dock. She failed to notice her backpack at his feet. One of these days, he'd have to return it.

Chapter Twelve

Halloween night and here she stood spreading homemade butter cream frosting on a batch of from-scratch brownies baked in a lasagna pan. Leah shook her head at her sorry state. She'd had offers to go to a private party being held by one of her volunteers, accompany Ethel and Abner on some kind of big to-do at the casino, or dress up and hit the bar scene.

For a small place, Chapelle had more than its share of bars, the latest being an Irish pub in Cajun Country right on Main, not down the side streets or on the edge of town where most of them were situated. She did not care much for bars or casinos or Halloween in general, a night when bent folks felt free to torture animals or sacrifice a live chicken in a fake voodoo rite. So far, no emergency calls, but her first aid kit and confinement cages sat in her SUV ready to go.

During an afternoon visit to Gran, she'd made sure the porch light stayed off by taping it down as a reminder. No problem about keeping the blinds drawn. They always were. Leah reinforced to her grandmother about it being Halloween. People of all sizes would be roaming the neighborhood in costume. She shouldn't be afraid or bother to answer the door, not that Alene would anyhow.

Leah felt a little regret that she lived out in the country. No trick-or-treaters for her. She did like handing out candy to small children dressed as cartoon characters or traditional ghosts and mummies on the witchy holiday. But, not so much to teens big enough to extort treats or money from people like her grandmother.

Leah swirled the last of the dark chocolate frosting onto the brownies and inevitably thought of Ashton Blaise as she licked the spatula clean. Her grandmother advised her to move on, and she supposed that meant away from handsome, passionate men who only wanted sex. She'd drop the pan off at the fire station and flee. Then, they'd be even foodwise. No need to see each other anymore, easier said than done in a small town.

She positively had moved on from Dr. Colton Dandridge. During her internship at his emergency clinic, he'd heaped her with praise for her ability to calmly insert catheters into shivering Chihuahuas as well as tiny kittens and her willingness to do any task that needed doing without flinching. Colton allowed her to sit in on his amazingly skilled surgeries that put broken animals back together. How flattering when he'd offered her a position as soon as she graduated and passed her state and national exams.

Colton kept a private suite at the clinic with a shower and a very comfortable bed in case he wanted to stay overnight to keep an eye on a furry patient or was called in to do surgery during the night. The door to his suite locked. No one entered without knocking. He placed the photo of his perfect blonde wife and two handsome sons on his desk in the office, but not in his bedroom. No need to remind Leah of their existence as her admiration turned to love. Now that she thought about it, he'd only implied they had a future together, never promised her anything more real than frantic couplings in his suite which he particularly enjoyed while still on an adrenaline high from a difficult surgery. How he raved about her large, soft breasts, so unlike the fake boobs he'd bought for his spouse, her veil of dark hair that cloaked them when he placed her on top, her passion for him—and her work, of course.

Annika, his wife, owned none of these attributes. After the birth of their second son, she'd lost all interest in sex, he claimed. Leah wondered about that now. What the doctor failed to mention was his wife's fifty-one percent ownership of the clinic and her master key. She walked in on them one night and sent Leah scrambling for her underwear and green scrubs, even a scrunchie to bind up her loose hair.

Annika Dandridge placed her hands on bony hips worthy of a high fashion model and said, "Really, Dandy, such a short, dark, chubby girl this time. But, you always were a boob man, and she's got plenty on the top." With eyes of blue steel, the woman assessed Leah as she frantically stuffed her breasts into her D-cup bra. "Whatever your name is, you're fired."

The wife turned and left in a waft of cold air that might have come off a glacier. Probably just the AC blasting against the naked parts of Leah's body, but still she shivered. "Can she do that, fire me?"

Colton came up behind her and hugged her against his still nude body. "My in-laws paid for my degree and built this clinic. They made sure Annika got the greater share even if I do all the work. I'll be certain you get a great severance package and give you a fantastic reference along with a two week notice to make things look legit. We can still be together during that time and enjoy ourselves. She really doesn't care. With Annika, it's all about power and prestige. I could set you up…"

Leah drove her elbow forcefully into his solar plexus. He let her go as he doubled over. She drew up the bottom of her scrubs, pulled the drawstring tight and said, "I quit. I'm giving two weeks notice."

With no sexual benefits on the side, they played out the charade about her going to help her grandmother, which turned out to be true after Leah spent a sweltering weekend in her Gran's house and realized she was truly needed. The staff gave her a send off party and the salacious mug. One of the more motherly techs delivered a great big hug and whispered in her ear, "You aren't the first and won't be the last. Have a happy life." Easier said than done.

She'd lucked into the house since Delta Savage desired a quick sale. She declared, "When I am done with something, I am completely finished. I yearn for New Orleans, and there I shall return." Leah didn't need the details to appreciate the bargain she'd gotten with that generous severance package, guilt or hush money, whatever you wanted to call it, and her own small savings for a down payment. She found her new job online, its appeal being her own boss except for a charitable board, and making the shelter what it should be. Like Delta, she was completely finished with Colton Dandridge and being a fool. Gran would be proud if she remembered her advice.

Now, if only she could put another ridiculously handsome, sexy man she secretly admired and who only wanted sex behind her. Noble as Ash appeared on the surface he'd dump her for a superior model, someone tall, blonde and busty, when one sashayed by.

Stay strong, Leah, stay strong. Deliver the brownies and be done with it.

Outside in her yard, something shrieked—an owl attacking one of the feral kittens, a possum being run over on the road, or a Halloween prank? A long moan followed. Leah went to a window and peered into the darkness to see something white fluttering in the ruins of her old house. Another moan reached out and grabbed at her conscience with ghostly fingers. She should go out there and help. Yeah, right, like all those dumb blonde coeds in horror movies. Instead, she found the card she shouldn't have kept and called Ashton Blaise on his cell. He picked up immediately.

"Blaise here."

"Ash, someone is outside my place moaning and carrying on. I don't want to go out there alone. Can you come or shall I call the police?"

"I'm not far away, only over in the Belle Terre subdivision putting out a trashcan fire at Yancey Breaux's house. Some kid trying to impress her with his boldness, I guess, got away on an ATV. Her dad had it under control with a hose before we got here. We're just mopping up now. My men can handle it. I've got the Chief's vehicle. I'll be right there with the siren blasting. That should scare off any pranksters, but I'll check the grounds. Stay put."

"Help me! Help me!" a pitiful high voice cried.

Leah dug her fingernails into the door frame to keep herself from responding to a natural urge to assist. She heard the siren long before the pulsing red light turned up her drive. She opened her door a crack. The emergency vehicle came to a halt by the ruins of her house. Ash stepped out still in his turnout gear. The reflective horizontal stripes across the dark surface of his uniform glowed like skeleton bones on a costume as he stooped toward the white form. The sound of tearing cloth ripped through the night. He bundled the object in his arms and started for the barn.

Leah opened the door wide to give him some light and stepped out into the night. Pale, sinuous arms wrapped around Ash's neck. A waterfall of black curls cascaded over one sheltering arm while two long, slim legs dangled over the other. Part of a ragged white costume dragged along the ground threatening to make Ash trip over his boots. A ghastly face with hollowed cheeks and sunken eyes turned toward Leah. Blackened lips opened and said, "Happy Halloween, sis. How come you didn't help me? Not that I'm complaining about my rescuer. He's like a dream come true." The zombie's arms tightened around Ash's neck.

"Rachel, I didn't expect you tonight." Leah let them pass into the kitchen where Ash deposited her sister into a chair.

"Oh, I ran into some guys from Chapelle at a party in Baton Rouge who told me about the bash at the new Irish pub here. You know how you're always nagging me to visit Gran, so I said sure if I could stop by her house first. I thought she'd get a kick out of my costume, but she wouldn't come to the door. I had to get the key out of the garden shed and let myself inside. Gran was just sitting there in the dark with the TV on, and I snuck up on her and said, 'Boo!' "

"Oh, no!" Leah hid her face in her hands.

"Yes, no! She went right for that emergency button thingy. I had to rip it out of her hands. All the while, I'm saying, 'It's me, Rachel, your granddaughter.'

Finally, she quiets down and says, "You're the tall one with no brains." She totally got my zombie costume. Glad to see she isn't entirely senile."

Leah met Ash's eyes over her sister's curly head and shook her head sadly.

Rachel burbled on. "Anyhow, then we went to the pub and had a few drinks. I wasn't feeling so well and asked to go to your house. They dropped me off in front of what I thought was your place, but some bitchy old woman opened the door and said you'd burned down her grandmother's house and lived in the barn next door, to get off her property right now. I walked over here. Real creepy place, sis, all these golden eyes glowing in the dark, not much light out here."

"Those eyes belong to the feral cats I feed."

Rachel rolled her own green eyes made even more striking than usual ringed in black makeup. "Only you would do that. As a kid she always smelled like horses or whatever animal she petted last," she informed Ash. "They really spooked me."

"Yeah, they can be kind of intimidating," he agreed despite a glare sent his way by Leah.

"I started to run and tripped over something, turned my ankle and banged my head. I threw up, Leah, and you just let me lay there. The glowing eyes came closer and closer. I thought they were rats!" Rachel squeezed Ash's arm. "Then my hero arrived. Awesome costume by the way, right down to the snap-on siren on the top of your car."

"He's a real fireman, Rach," Leah said. "We're wasting his time. You can go now, Ash. Thanks a lot for coming."

"Oh, oh, I need a bucket!" Rachel clutched her flat

stomach strategically bared by the white, ragged gown she wore. Leah grabbed one from under the sink and shoved her sister's head into it. Her hand came away bloody.

"I have some EMT training. I should look at that wound. She did conk her head on a burnt timber, and her ankle was caught in some bedsprings. I had to tear her costume to get her out, not that it makes much difference to a zombie." Ash dampened a clean dish towel, parted Rachel's curls while she hurled into the bucket, and cleaned the area. "Only a bump and a small cut. She won't need stitches. You have an ice pack handy?"

Leah tossed him a bag of frozen peas from the refrigerator. Ash applied it to Rachel's head as she slowly removed her face from the bucket. "You have such gentle hands," she told her hero.

"Let's take a look at the ankle before I go." He knelt before the zombie sister and carefully probed her lower leg. "Only a slight sprain."

Before he could ask, Leah sacrificed a sack of corn from her freezer and produced an Ace bandage from a small first aid kit tucked in a cupboard. "You read my mind."

"R.I.C.E., right?"

"Yes, rest, ice, compression, elevation." He finished wrapping the bandage around Rachel's foot and ankle.

She peered down at him and released a gust of vomit-tainted breath. "I lost my ballet flats out there, but you carried me all the way to the house. I feel like Cinderella. Every Halloween as a kid, I dressed as a princess. Wouldn't have it any other way. Sometimes

Mom bought me store costumes, but the best ones Gran made. I got to wear her jewelry. Leah went with me as a frog one year and said, 'Ribbit' to everyone, really funny. Next year, she was my pea like the Princess and the Pea story, but nobody could figure out the big, green ball. She said, 'A pea, a pea!' People thought she had to, you know, go to the bathroom, but couldn't get her out of the costume. They were so panicked. What a riot!"

Ash stood up. "Did you ever get to be the princess, Leah?"

"Never," she answered short and curt. "Someone had a hissy fit at the idea there might be more than one princess in the house."

"I see. Where do you want her to lie down?"

"In one of the spare bedrooms. I guess she's here for the night."

Ash scooped Rachel into his arms. She murmured, "So strong" and wrapped her arms around him again with her head tucked so tightly against his ear she truly might have wanted to suck out his brains. That's how men became around Rachel, brainless.

Leah trailed them to the bedroom next to hers and watched as he placed one pillow tenderly behind her sister's head and one under her sprained ankle. Leah draped the bag of corn over the bandage and set the slop bucket next to the bed. "Don't puke on my floor, Rach. Get some rest. I'll drive you back to Baton Rouge in the morning."

Rachel's long lashes drifted down, but she kept talking. "I don't even know your name, my prince in fireman's gear."

"Ashton Blaise. I'm a friend of your sister's."

135

"Oh, I love it! Will you come see me in the morning to be certain I'm okay?"

"You should see a doctor, not me, to make sure you aren't concussed. Leah, wake her every few hours tonight to see if she's alert."

"Will do, fireman prince."

As they closed the door, he said, "I think the vomiting is from drinking too much, not the bump on the head, but have her checked."

"LSU has an infirmary. I'll take her there. Hey, before you go I've got something for you."

"What might that be? A reward for my heroism?"

For the first time that night, Leah noticed a hint of teasing in his voice. "Brownies."

Now she got the smile that could melt chocolate. The way he'd carried her sister around as if Rachel weighed nothing. Dang. She thrust the lasagna pan between them. "Now we're even, finished, done."

"Sure we are." Ash leaned forward as if he'd seal that statement with a kiss, but somewhere in his gear a phone buzzed. "Got to go."

Leah let him out into the night. She followed the glowing stripes on his uniform as he got into the chief's vehicle and turned on the siren. If he saw Rachel cleaned up and gorgeous, he'd be gone in more ways than one.

Chapter Thirteen

Ash ran on the station's treadmill while a pot of his vegetarian gumbo simmered on the stove in the kitchen. Good thing Leah returned his pot because the weather had finally chilled enough to raise the sugar in the stalks and make gumbo the meal of choice, not that Cajuns didn't eat it all year round anyhow. After his crew stopped ribbing him about making it with okra as a thickener instead of a roux, they'd shut up and chow down on his special mixture of black beans, tomatoes, peppers and onions, and quite a lot of spicy seasoning. The brown rice in his cooker should be ready soon. He'd clean up and have lunch shortly.

While mindlessly running up the miles, Ash thought of Leah. A piece of the puzzle dropped into place thanks to her blabbermouth sister. If a girl was always the frog and never the princess, maybe she couldn't think of herself in any other way. He'd have to work on that next time he saw her because there would be a next time. She intrigued with her resistance, her passion, her caring. Her sister made him want to run into the night with the feral cats for company.

One of the guys stuck his head into the inadequate gym area with its ancient stair climber, a set of weights, and a rowing machine mostly donated by people who'd given up on exercise like the Chief. The tax money tended to go for things like the bright red vehicle the

Chief drove and Ash sometimes got to use.

"Hey, we got a call for assistance."

"Traffic accident?"

"Nope, duck caught in a chimney."

"Why don't they call the animal shelter or Wildlife and Fisheries?"

"Chief said for *you* to handle it right away. Make the taxpayer happy."

Ash toweled off and put on his slacks and the black fire department shirt to make himself official. As far as he knew, ducks had no sense of smell and wouldn't be offended if he didn't shower. He gestured to one of his men, and they set out in the emergency vehicle where they kept the Jaws of Life to extract passengers from wrecked cars. Across the brown bayou from the station, families cleaned and decorated the graves in honor of All Saints Day. Some people got vacation for just that purpose, but not firefighters.

Their destination, a brick ranch style home set amid live oaks, sat on a high bank of the bayou not far from the landing for the little tourist steamboat named the Bayou Belle. A mixed flock of ducks consisting of mallards and abandoned Easter pets did hang out there thriving on the largesse of visitors and school children who fed them stale bread and the deep-fried pistolette rolls from restaurant meals.

The homeowner, a chubby middle-aged woman teary-eyed with distress, met them in her yard. "Thank God, you're here! I'm Beverly Labbe, the person who called. I came back from making my groceries, and there he was dangling head down in the fireplace. I called the fire department because I thought you might know more about chimneys than the animal shelter."

Logical, sort of.

She led them to a side door, through her laundry room, a kitchen with its counters cluttered with plastic grocery bags, and into a homey family room with a nice brick fireplace and the ugliest duck Ash had ever seen jammed in its damper. Its long, black neck ended in a large head with a pale beak surrounded by warty red bumps. It uttered not a single quack, but Ash could tell it hadn't died by the annoyed light in its black eyes.

"Okay, Lex, you pull on the damper hard as you can, and I'll try to squeeze the bird out."

No go. Bigger than the average duck, it showed its appreciation with a few feeble pecks to Ash's hands. "Pull again, and I'll see if I can make the gap wider with my hands." The duck shifted slightly exposing a shoulder, if ducks had shoulders, before the damper snapped back into place.

"We'll have to use the Jaws of Life on the damper. Don't worry, ma'am, we've got them with us."

"You can't do that! My husband is offshore and if he comes home to find the fireplace wrecked, he'll never let me feed the ducks again. I do enjoy that so much, watching their antics and such while I drink my coffee in the morning. They love my leftover cornbread muffins." She cocked her head at the duck. "I believe that's Putin. He's a Muscovy duck and leader of the flock, bigger than all the others. I've named them, you see. His mate is Empress, but he fools around on her with those French ducks, the hussies." Beverly took a picture with her phone of the hapless duck probably destined for Facebook. "I know you'll rescue him."

A duck with a name, the fire department would never live it down if the bird died in the chimney. Ash could imagine the *Clarion's* headline because this would surely make the front page—*Firemen fail to save Putin.* He suppressed a sigh. "We need a set of screwdrivers."

They put down tarps over the aging shag carpet and clothed themselves in the jackets worn for non-fire emergencies and black ball caps. Ash worked at the screws on one side of the fireplace insert while Lex did the other. All the metal parts seemed fused together by years of use. The ashes sat several inches deep in its bottom, and occasionally, the duck wiggled and dislodged soot onto their heads. Slowly, laboriously, they disassembled the fireplace and removed the entire damper. The duck plopped down amid the ashes and sent a storm of them into the air with a fanning of its wings. One didn't appear to be working quite right, but Putin marched directly to the French door Beverly held open and went outside. She dashed to get him a bowl of water and a muffin.

"You will clean up, won't you?" she asked.

An hour to take the fireplace apart, an hour to put it together, and still more time to roll up the tarps and clean the rug with a vacuum provided by the taxpayer. She had one last request. "I think you injured Putin's wing. You need to get him to a vet."

"Yes, ma'am." Ash didn't argue. He knew exactly where he'd take the duck for care. Putin, stuffed full of crumbled muffins, squatted on the edge of the patio near Beverly's Adirondack chair. Considering his size, Ash figured flying wasn't this duck's strong point. He scooped him up fairly easily and handed him to his partner to hold while he drove.

Beverly Labbe waved them off with a "Be sure he

has good care."

"You be sure to get that chimney capped so this doesn't happen again, and get it cleaned. You have a fire waiting to happen," Ash advised as he beat the soot from the ball cap and shook out his jacket.

Inside the emergency van, Lex grumbled, "Duck gets four muffins, and we ain't offered a cup of coffee."

"We live to serve. I'll drop you at the station. There's gumbo on the stove and rice in the cooker. I think some of the guys brought bread and potato salad. I'll drop Putin off at the shelter."

"I know you want me out the way, but you got a deal. My gut is growlin'. Say, was she worth five hundred dollars?" Lex, one of the prime instigators in driving up the price of the kayak tour, grinned ear to ear in his chocolate moon pie face.

Ash felt like punching him in the mouth and watching those Chiclet teeth fall, but he played it cool. "She certainly was."

"I mean for that price I could get me a big piece of the best ass Madame Mystique's girls supply for most of the night."

"She showed me some really big—gators."

"That supposed to mean something else 'cause I noticed that Leah is a lot top heavy."

"Nope. And then…"

"And then?" Lex stared at him bug-eyed, waiting for the details.

"We heard the sweet trill of the Magnolia warbler. She made a special vegetarian lunch for me, and we lay in the hot sun side by side on a floating platform, inches apart, the sweat running off our overheated bodies. We took off our shirts."

"Then?" Though they'd arrived at the station, Lex stayed in his seat waiting for the good part.

"A storm blew up, and we had to leave."

"You had me going for a while. You got nothing but lunch out of that babe. Here's your fuckin' duck." Lex set the Muscovy on the passenger seat and slammed the door.

"Save me a bowl of gumbo," Ash called after him. His excuse to see Leah again settled in and he watched the countryside roll by calm as a hen on a nest.

Ash arrived at the shelter around two-thirty and drove directly to the office amid the greeting chorus from the dogs. Securing Putin under one arm, he poked his head in the door to find his Leah hunched over a microscope on the work counter, her bodacious bottom putting on a nice show for him.

"Hey, I brought you something."

She straightened. "It better not be food since I am done cooking for you to return a favor."

"Nope, a duck in need." Ash offered her Putin with both hands as he were the goose that laid the golden egg. "We rescued him from a chimney. He might have a broken right wing."

"Let's see." She accepted the weighty duck and extended the wing in question, feeling along the structure of its bones. "I don't think it's broken. Probably just a sprain. We'll secure it with vet wrap for a while to keep the wing immobilized until it heals." Deftly, Leah held the big bird tucked like a football and taped the wing. "Here you go."

Ash put his hands behind his back. "I can't take him! I still have Courage, four pups, and a kitten, probably not a good environment for a duck. The puppies are ready for homes, and so is Bandit, only now he thinks he's a dog.

"Please don't bring them here. We are so crowded. I brought in Bandit's mom today for spaying. She's tame enough to make a good pet. Once I got her in a trap with a can of tuna, the kittens followed, but they need taming. I'm checking their stool samples for parasites right now before we release them from isolation. Worms in kittens are pretty much expected."

"Worms, please, I haven't had any lunch yet—and I cooked it. Couldn't you just put Putin in a cage here for a while?" His face must have shown his distaste because Leah laughed, which made the whole fiasco worthwhile.

"Putin?" She set the duck on the counter, and he waddled along its length.

"The homeowner named him. Said he's a Muscovy duck."

"Yes, mostly raised for meat. They can interbreed with mallards, but their offspring is sterile. We call them mulards. Got a few of those around the steamboat dock."

"He's most likely the duckling daddy." There, he'd made Leah smile again.

Putin reached the end of the long counter and came eye to eye with Mr. Grey in his tall cage. The parrot clacked his beak. Putin hissed and flapped his good wing. "I don't think they're going to be best buds," Leah said.

She scooped up the duck and gestured to Ash to follow. At a storage shed, she unlocked the door and asked him to remove a large wire cage they took along to any event where she thought they might find a home for a big dog. He carried it to the grassy area Leah indicated. She slipped Putin inside and fetched him a bowl of water.

"He can peck at the grass and eat whatever bugs come his way, but I'll get some duck pellets at the feed store. We wouldn't want the poor guy to starve."

"He's full of the corn muffins Miz Labbe fed him. No rush."

"Could be worse. Better than white bread. Tell her to buy some cracked corn instead."

"I hope I never see the woman again, two and a half hours getting that duck…" Ash paused in mid-sentence, a male reaction he couldn't control taking over his body, as a gorgeous woman emerged from the cattery clinging to the arm of Cubby Couvillon. Black curls rioted over her shoulders contrasting with a pale complexion and startling green eyes. She wore glittery flip-flops, khaki shorts not long enough for her endless legs, and a T-shirt with an American flag emblem that appeared to wave across her large chest as she hobbled along.

"Who's that?" he asked. He'd never been envious of Cubby before now.

"You should remember my sister Rachel. You rescued her, fireman prince."

Leah's tone was as dry as his mouth. Ash raised a hand in Rachel's direction. The anti-Leah waved merrily back and steered Cubby their way. He'd made a mistake, a big one. "Shouldn't she be in the infirmary at LSU?"

Leah stepped away from his side. "She refused to leave. It seems her midterms did not go well, and she wants to drop out for a semester and think about her future."

"Lots of people do that."

"Not when they've been in college for five years and had four different majors. She believes hanging out with me, eating my food, and wearing my donated clothes will help her come to a decision. Damn, why does everything I own look better on her?"

He started to say it doesn't, but the twosome arrived, and Rachel immediately shifted her weight onto Ash while simultaneously shaking off Cubby.

"Thanks for the help, Cub, but Ashton can take it from here." She glimmered at Ash and squeezed his bicep.

"Captain Blaise, we been taming kittens. The little ones ain't so bad, but I got some scratches." Cubby held out his arm for inspection.

"I'm scratched, too." Rachel stretched out the long, graceful limb she'd latched around his waist. "Can you take care of me?"

"I'm a firefighter, not a doctor, but glad you're feeling better than the last time I saw you." He couldn't shake off a woman with a sprained ankle, now could he, but Leah started to walk off briskly.

"For heaven's sake, come to the office and wash those scratches. I'll put some antibiotic cream on them. They aren't deep." They followed her like imprinted ducklings back to the office.

As Leah ministered to the wounded, she said, "Why don't you take Sweetie back to the station with you, Ash? I have her papers ready. In fact, they've been ready for a while."

"Ah, I haven't cleared her with the Chief yet." In fact, he thought he'd evade adding another dog to his life and consider the hundred dollar adoption fee a donation, but clearly, Leah wouldn't let him off the leash.

"You're getting a poor little rescue dog for the firehouse. That's wonderful!" Rachel cooed. She most likely would have slobbered over Ash some more, but a car drove up, a pretty slick red convertible bearing Yancey Breaux and Dirk Keene. Her attention passed to doing a calculating appraisal of the car and driver.

"Cubby, why don't you walk dogs with Yancey and Dirk. Stay with them and watch what they do," Leah suggested.

"I like Yancey! She's pretty." Cubby galumphed out the door and down the three steps in a hurry.

Leah shook her head. "I couldn't get him to go near the cattery, and he follows Rachel right in there. He'll do anything for Yancey, but not for me."

"You just don't have what it takes to influence men, sis. It's like my super power. If I'd been the one in Shreveport, that handsome married vet would be filing his divorce papers right now." Rachel regarded her nails, still covered in zombie black lacquer, with false modesty.

Ash noted the slight hitch of Leah's shoulders, the flush spreading under her tan. He knew he'd found another piece of the puzzle, a married man in her past.

Rachel raised her green eyes to Ash. "I can go to the firehouse with you and convince the Chief to let Sweetie stay. Maybe you could give me a tour. I'll bet it's changed since I went on a tour as a kid."

"Not that much." He hoped the short answer would put her off, but no.

"Leah, go get Sweetie, and we'll be on our way."

Leah did as if accustomed to obeying her younger sister. She returned with the dog on a leash and shoved the packet of information into Ash's hands. With lowered voice, she told him, "Take them both right now. This is Rachel's second good deed for the day, the other being keeping Cubby occupied. Her helpfulness won't last much longer, and I have those fecal smears to scan. Get her out of my hair."

"I like your hair better," he blurted, swinging his head to see if Rachel heard him. Fortunately, she was deep in conversation with Mr. Grey. "Who's your baby?" she coaxed, but the parrot, though accepting the peanut she offered, remained loyal to Leah and uttered not a word. Good for him. Feeling like a cheater, he helped Rachel to the emergency vehicle, told her to buckle up, and whisked her away like a princess in his red chariot to the palace of the Chapelle firehouse.

Chapter Fourteen

Leah stirred the vegetarian gumbo on the stove while she revived the brown rice in the microwave. Rachel sat with her foot propped on the opposite chair at the tiny kitchen table and chattered away as if making noise was her contribution to the meal Ash dropped off along with her sister. He didn't linger. Only said, "I thought you might not feel like cooking, and we had some leftovers." Leaving her sister in the chair and the food on the counter, he got the hell out of there before she managed to muster a "thanks" that sounded more like a curse word.

Oblivious, Rachel claimed, "See how I got him to provide dinner?"

"Not so hard with Ash. He loves to cook, but everything is vegetarian."

Rachel wrinkled her nose in that cute manner she had, a talent Leah never thought she'd mastered. "I'll bet I could convert him back to being a carnivore. I gave Uncle Tank a big hug and told him how great the station was giving a shelter dog a good home. He held me a tad too long, but in the end he agreed the firemen could keep Sweetie if he didn't have to walk her or clean up her poop."

"Uncle Tank?"

"He *was* a friend of Daddy's, and that uncle bit always works with older men. He felt like a huge cushion with a bone hidden in the lining." She regarded the industrial-sized vat of potato salad, mostly gone, and the French bread slices. "All starches. I'll be as big as the Chief if I don't get back to exercising soon. Darn ankle. Even if I wanted to get back to classes, I couldn't get around the campus."

"I'm sure I can borrow some crutches for you."

"No use. I've lost all interest in psychology. It didn't teach me anything."

"Do tell." Leah scooped rice into two jumbo, white coffee mugs that had taken precedence over buying dishes and ladled the gumbo over it. She stuck a soup spoon from her daffodil set in the side and handed one to Rachel who laconically buttered a piece of bread.

"The firemen were so much fun. First, they teased Ash about bringing them a dog named Sweetie and said she'd need a name change to stay at the firehouse. I suggested Ember, but Ash said he didn't want the dog to have a stripper name. They settled on Sparky since it's kind of unisex, and she jumps around like sparks. All this took place in their common room and kitchen area. Then this big, black guy named Lex, all muscle, threw me over his shoulder and carried me upstairs to their bunkroom, just beds in a row, no privacy whatsoever, and a bathroom with showers. Want to know how I got down?"

Not particularly, but Leah said, "On a great big pole?"

"No, even better. They have a sliding board right next to the stairs. The guys built it in their spare time for fun, but they can use it for emergencies, too. Ash took me down between his legs, and Lex caught me at the bottom because of my ankle. No salad?"

"Plenty of vegetables in the gumbo. You should make them something in thanks for the food and the tour. I'm sure they had better things to do." Leah tested her soup, spicy and interesting like Ash.

"I don't know about that. When we arrived, they had a card game going. All the vehicles had been washed that morning according to Lex. One is married, one newly divorced, and two single," Rachel recited.

"How could you tell?" Leah ate some potato salad directly from the vat, knowing it would go straight to her hips.

"Married guy wore a ring, newly divorced had one of those cheater's marks around his finger, and Lex told me he was available. The way Ash took me down that slide, I know he's single. I wish he'd made this with a roux instead of okra." Rachel pushed her half-finished mug aside.

"Maybe he's fooling around on his wife like Colton Dandridge, maybe he has a girlfriend." Why she wanted to plant seeds of doubt in her sister, Leah did not know or wouldn't admit.

"Is he, does he? I mean you've been living here. It's hard to keep a secret in Chapelle. If he were taken, everyone would know."

"He's not taken—but he lives with his mom." Leah played her ace for Ash's own good.

"Eeew! Give me some time with him, and he'll want to find a place of his own. Anyhow on Friday, he and Lex are taking me back to LSU to get my things. Lex has a truck. Ash said that way you wouldn't have to take any time off from work to help me."

"How nice of him. He drives a little Prius," Leah said, knowing that Rachel would consider that inadequate transportation. She liked both muscular cars and well-built men.

"He's not gay, is he? I didn't get that vibe off him. His reaction to me was like most guys."

The lie rested right on the tip of Leah's tongue. After all, she'd be saving Ash from Rachel and someday, he might thank her. But, considering the size of Chapelle, a falsehood like that could get around quick. Reluctantly, she said, "No, not gay," and finished her sister's rejected gumbo. The heat of the soup would cover her flush. Good thing Rachel was only observant when it came to men.

"Good, if I'm stuck here in the middle of nowhere for a while, I might need some recreation as well as rest."

"You can always stay in town with Gran or move to Florida with Mom and Dad."

Leah half-expected Rachel to emit another eeew, but she said, "No way with Gran. That house is so dark and close it's like living inside a coffin—and it used to be a fun place full of parties all seasons of the year. Remember that December, she turned up the air-conditioning so we could toast marshmallows over logs in the fireplace and not get too hot. I hate being around her when she's like this, all deranged and everything."

"She's not deranged, just forgetful and fearful, but she won't let me show her any assisted living homes."

"Then, it's on her. I used your phone to call the parents because I can't find mine. Some beach time would be good even in November, but they rented the other side of the duplex, and, eeew, I'm not going to live in the same house with them. It would cramp my style."

Definitely, as showing up drunk on their doorstep on any given night would not go down well with Dad nor her numerous boyfriends with Mom who had always wanted a popular daughter until she got one better than Leah. Their mother did not approve of hooking up, shacking up, or booty calls after midnight. Find the best man you can and settle down was her mantra. Ashton Blaise qualified, but he looked so much better with Rachel leaning on him than standing beside herself.

"Hey, help me to the bathroom, sis. I gotta pee and want to wash. I swear I still have zombie crud in all my cracks."

No, most of the black and gray zombie makeup streaked the bottom of Leah's once pristine shower, the one she'd shared with Ash. The ragged costume lay pooled directly in front of a perfectly good and partly empty hamper. A green plastic yard chair still sat inside the glass box from Rachel's morning sit down shower taken while Leah, bathed and dressed for the day, rummaged through her clothes for something her sister could wear. She helped Rachel to strip, get into the chair, and rubber-band a plastic bag over her ankle, no cast, but she didn't want to have to rewrap the bandage, too. Turning on and testing the temperature of the water, Leah handed over the soap and washcloth. "Call me when you want to get out."

"You would have made a good nurse," Rachel commented, quite a compliment since she'd washed out of the nursing program after one semester.

"Yeah, but animals don't complain the way people do."

She left her sister to it and went to make a strategic

call. "Hi, Ethel. Know anyone with a pair of crutches they aren't using at the moment?"

"Oh, *cher*, I can get you those, a walker, and a wheelchair if you want. My generation is falling apart, and we have closets full of medical aids. I know a widow who kept her husband's artificial leg for sentimental reasons."

"Just the crutches would be fine. Bring them to the shelter tomorrow when you come."

"You got 'em, honey."

"Thanks." No more leaning all over Ashton Blaise for Rachel Allain.

****

She needed peace. She needed quiet. She needed calm. Leah drove to Indian Lake with exactly that in mind. So what if she couldn't find her backpack. She threw two bottles of water and a couple of energy bars onto her front seat. The air had a nip to it this early in the morning with the mist barely lifted from the half-harvested fields. She would stuff the supplies in her hoodie. Most importantly, she'd get away from her whining sister and all thoughts of Ashton Blaise.

The last wasn't going to happen because there he stood by his kayak holding up her knapsack by its straps. Along with the smug smile on his face, he wore one of those tight, long-sleeved T-shirts that showed off his lean body and tight abs even if it covered his biceps, the ones put to use hauling Rachel's junk into the loft on Friday. If she hit the accelerator, she could run right over him and end the torment, but instead Leah braked and put down her window.

"What are you doing here?"

"Returning your backpack. You left it behind last

time."

"You couldn't just leave it at the barn when you infested my place with all of Rachel's stuff on Friday?" She put on her grumpy face to deflect his grin.

"Forgot to bring it along. She does have more clothes and pairs of shoes than most human beings use in a lifetime. Lex and I carted her boxes of textbooks upstairs, but left the bits and pieces of furniture down since the barn is fairly empty. Hey, she had a decent set of dishes. I put them in the cupboard for you. We mounted the flat screen on the wall, but you'll have to get the satellite TV people out to hook up service." Ash rested those strong, sinewy arms on the window ledge.

"So I noticed." If she raised the glass, maybe he'd get the point that she wanted to be left alone. Her finger wavered over the button.

"No thanks necessary. Glad to help. I brought your knapsack fully loaded."

"With what?"

"A veggie wrap for me, turkey for you. Two Honeycrisp apples, water, and a block of my mother's famous peanut butter fudge."

Leah glared down at her body. "Do you think I look like a person who needs peanut butter fudge? I'm fat enough."

"Not that I noticed. Everything you got seems to be in the right place and nicely abundant. A good paddle will work off those calories. Besides, Mom made the fudge with the crunchy kind. It has nut particles. Bound to be healthy. I thought we could take a break around noon and picnic under that live oak like we did before."

A most pestiferous man, Ashton Blaise, like a yellow jacket buzzing around sweets. There was way too much of him to call him annoying as a gnat. Deep inside, a little voice said, "Enjoy him one more time before Rachel steals him."

"Okay. The deal is this. No talking unless it's an emergency. I want to get some pictures. I lead. You follow." He'd begun unloading her kayak the second she'd given the okay. Whether he heard the rest, Leah couldn't tell. Additionally, he shouldered the backpack and refused to relinquish it.

"I'm protecting the fudge from the gators."

"They do eat pretty much anything thrown their way, but I think you're holding my backpack for ransom."

"Maybe I am. Lead on, Leah."

Ash kept to the rule of silence. She heard him mutter, "Magnolia warbler" once when the bird called, and more urgently, "Alligator on the left!" The small reptile hung in the water waiting for something toothsome to swim by its jaws, minding its own business, and not interested in kayaks. Leah simply shook her head and kept paddling. She refrained from steering him through alligator alley again. He stopped when she did to take pictures and once pointed out a pink spoonbill perched higher than usual. Behavior that good must be rewarded. She bumped lunch back to eleven and paddled toward the live oak rendezvous.

Ash removed more than lunch from the backpack. He spread a commodious blanket on the ground and set up a perimeter of insect and tick spray around it. When the air cleared, he handed out the wraps and apples. Leah ate, drank her bottle of water, and stretched out on the blanket listening to the breeze stir the leaves and the songs of birds who serenaded when nothing disturbed them. The turmoil of dealing with her grandmother, her job, the fire, and now Rachel faded away. She should add Ash to that list, but didn't. Her eyes closed.

They opened when she felt pressure on her lips, not a kiss, but sliver of peanut butter fudge being rubbed across them. Ash loomed over her gazing into her eyes. She sucked in the fudge and licked her lips. He took that as invitation to touch his tongue to hers and deepen the kiss. When they finished tangling tonsils, Ash took a breath and said, "You are not a frog."

"Is that supposed to be a compliment?"

"I meant you are a princess, too, in your own way, maybe Sleeping Beauty instead of Cinderella."

"Thanks, but I'd rather be a female superhero."

"Figures. You shouldn't feel inferior to Rachel in any way."

Leah failed to believe that statement. "Come on, she's beautiful and all feminine and clingy."

He leaned back on his elbows. "You don't think I've dated the type before—and held back their hair when they puke from too much drinking."

"You are quite the gentleman."

"It's not appealing." Ash unzipped her plain, gray hoodie, worked under her T-shirt and exposed her breasts. "These are appealing."

Leah's nipples puckered in the cool air and maybe because Ash stared at them so long. "It's not right to sleep with two sisters."

"These are the only sisters I'm interested in." He ran a firm hand over her large breasts and thumbed her nipples. "I haven't slept with Rachel and have no plans to do so." He sealed that promise with a kiss to each one.

"You will. She said she could change you."

"Into what"

"A carnivore with a place of his own to take her to and probably a bigger car."

"Not going to happen." Ash applied his lips and suckled.

Leah lost track of the conversation. One last time with Ash, one last time. She freed him from his jeans. He did the same to her. They went at it hard. The birds stopped singing and flew away from the moans, the groans, the sighs, and that short shriek Leah made when she came. The Indian Lake eagle answered her from high above the trees.

Ash simply expelled his breath in one great gust as he found his release. He pulled the blanket over their cooling bodies as they both recuperated and cuddled Leah against his chest.

"It's not always about a person's appearance," he said.

Great, she'd met one of the few men in the world who wanted to talk after sex. Colton surely hadn't. Nor did that man cuddle. Always, always get it done quickly before someone at the clinic discovered them. "You and Rachel look great as a couple. We are ridiculous together, me all stubby and just average; you all tall and so handsome."

"I don't think of myself that way, and you shouldn't put yourself down. Nothing wrong with your looks. The way you care about your grandmother and the animals you rescue, that's character, and it counts."

"Yeah, I have great character, so great I had an affair with a married man. I guess you caught that from Rachel's comments. The way I've let you have me, you must think I'm easy." Ashamed, Leah left the warn protection of his arms and lay on her side.

"I think you met a smooth guy, a serial cheater, who knew exactly what to say to get you in his bed. I'm guessing he praised your skill with animals because you're proud of that."

"You've just done the very same thing again." Leah pulled her hood over her head, hiding she knew.

"The difference is I'm single and sincere. As for the sex, we have a chemistry I can't begin to explain."

"Chemistry, that's an old line."

"Not if I mean it."

"You'd have the same chemistry with Rachel."

"No, I…"

Footsteps on the path! Leah pulled down her T-shirt, closed her jacket, had no time to fumble with the hooks of her bra. Men had it so easy. Ash simply drew up his jeans and zipped. Between the cool air and the buzzing mosquitoes, he hadn't taken off his shirt though Leah's hands had stroked beneath it. She worked her own zipper closed as T-Coon Arton appeared in the clearing.

"I was fishing nearby, me, and t'ink I hear a scream." The old man's grin creased his leathery face. "Everyt'ing all right here?"

"We're fine, Mr. Arton." Leah sat up to show how completely clothed she was—if a little soft and saggy in the bust. "Only taking a rest after our paddle and lunch."

"Musta been dat eagle. Lost his mate last year and looking for a new one."

"Thanks for checking. See you around." Leah gave him a cheery grin and a wave to move the man on his way. T-Coon took the hint.

"Is there anywhere that man isn't?" Ash groused.

"We're done here. Let's go. I left Rachel pouting at home because the TV isn't hooked up yet, and she's lost her phone. All she has left is her laptop to keep in touch with the world, poor baby, and she'll want to be fed like an injured bird."

"You have my sympathy. See, those dependent ones, not my type."

They returned to their kayaks and paddled back to the dock. Leah made sure she had her backpack this time. Ash stowed it in the backseat for her. Only when she got home did Leah find the pound of peanut butter fudge in its bottom. When would her food obligations end? Now she owed his mother.

Chapter Fifteen

Ash couldn't seem to catch Leah alone anymore. His schedule rotated in a way that he didn't have the next few Sundays off. If he went by the shelter under the guise of seeing how Putin fared, he found Rachel lounging in the office or the cattery, sometimes with Cubby, who had been showing up somewhat less at the firehouse. For the moment, neither were in sight as he stood talking to Leah by the Muscovy's cage.

Leah complained Cubby kept feeding the duck much in the same way he stuffed Mr. Grey. The parrot always squawked, "Cub-bee, Cub-bee," when the boy entered the room and received an immediate reward, though Ash knew they'd had a previous acquaintance. He bore a distinct memory of Cubby's flabby, white body shivering in nothing but boxers when Madame Mystique's bordello burned. Cliff managed to grab a white terry robe as the place evacuated, not the only upstanding citizen to be literally exposed that night, but Ash put out fires and did not care to light up Chapelle's gossip network.

"I think we'll keep Putin until after Thanksgiving. If we release him now, someone might mistake him for a turkey," Leah said.

"No more chimneys for him. I doubt he'd get off the ground," Ash agreed. "How's our lame duckling coming along?"

"If you mean Rachel, I took her to the doctor a couple of weeks ago. Said to use the crutches and keep it wrapped until she could put weight on the ankle again without pain. Her healing seems to be taking forever."

Ash seconded that because here she came from the cattery working her crutches like a stripper her pole and followed by her entourage of Cubby who kept his eyes on her gyrating hips. "Hi, Ash. I saw you drive up. I wish you'd give me a ride in that bright red van again. You should think of getting one like that for yourself."

"I'm happy with what I have." He looked at Leah hoping she'd get the point.

"I hate these darned ole crutches, so hard to get around, and see, my bandage is coming loose. Leah doesn't tie it as well as you do. Could you help me over to the office and wrap it again. Cubby, you carry these." Rachel tossed her crutches to the boy and collapsed against Ash full on and frontal.

He picked her up because that's what she wanted, and he might as well get it over with. Ash made short work of the bandage, too. Her slim ankle didn't appear swollen or bruised anymore. "Sure you can't put any weight on it yet? Because the Fireman's Ball is coming up next Saturday."

"Oh, I'd love to go. Let me see if I can manage." Putting her full weight on her foot, Rachel held out her arms. "Ta-da! I'm cured. Must be your special touch, Ash."

Leah's face read like a thunderstorm over the cane fields. She didn't follow where he was going with this. "Great," he said. "Tickets are forty bucks. I have some with me."

Rachel provided the rain. Her eyes filled and her

lips quivered in a manner she must have practiced since childhood. "Because I tripped over Leah's heap of trash, I haven't been able to work and my money is pretty tight." Her vulnerable shoulders shook.

"Should I give you a massage to make you feel better, Rachel? My mama likes when I rub her neck." Not waiting for permission, Cubby dug his pudgy fingers into Rachel's back muscles. "Cub-bee, Cub-bee," the parrot encouraged.

Rachel hopped right into Ash's arms to get away from the boy. "Stop touching me!"

Cubby whimpered like a hurt puppy. Leah turned him gently toward the door. "Recall what I told you about touching people without asking first?

Cubby nodded, but blubbered, "Some pretty ladies like to be touched."

"Oh, baby," sighed Mr. Grey from his cage.

"Only if they tell you it's okay. Your mom is due to pick you up soon. Why don't you go keep Putin company? Here, give him this cup of duck pellets." Leah doled out a small portion from a sack under the counter and sent Cubby off happily enough to stuff the Muscovy a little more.

Ash took it all in. Who's the frog now? Though if he recollected right, the princess in that story hadn't been very nice either.

Leah rolled her shoulders. "Not good for the duck, but I'm going for best outcome here. He tried to give me a back rub twice this week already. Do I look that tense?"

"Yes," both Ash and Rachel answered.

Leah gave them a glare that said she had two more people she wanted out of her office. She fished her purse from a deep desk drawer and withdrew two twenties. "Here, for Rachel's ticket. Now we're even for the Doggone Ball."

"I'm not keeping score. I experienced an outstanding kayak tour and picnic because of that auction. We'll have one of those, too. The guys conned me into offering a date with Ashton Blaise, and I'm hoping someone will bid. Just trying to improve my chances." Ash forked over two tickets. "My treat."

Leah narrowed her eyes, every bit as green as her sister's but not as enhanced by makeup. "Get real. All the single women in town will bid on time with you including Miss Ethel despite her ongoing fling with Abner Millet."

"Then, I'll go out with her. It's for a good cause. We really need some new bunker gear. The ball is formal, so get out your long gowns."

"I don't have one."

"Leah looks terrible in long gowns because she's so short and hippy," Rachel felt compelled to explain. "I own half a dozen from when I participated in beauty pageants."

"I can believe that," Ash said, pleasing her no end. Actually, he didn't mean it as a compliment. "No matter. They won't throw out anyone with a ticket. Who knows what Lex is going to wear? His taste is pretty sketchy."

"Lex is so much fun. He carried me up the stairs at the station over his shoulder. Did I tell you that, Leah?" Rachel gushed.

"I believe you did. Now, I need to draw some blood to test a new batch of kittens for FIV. That's feline HIV."

"Kittens can carry HIV? Oooh, I've been touching them all morning." Rachel dashed to the work station sink and started scrubbing her hands. A fresh coat of bright red nail polish flecked off like little drops of blood.

Ash realized he'd begun to understand Leah rather well. Her features remained serious, but her green eyes glittered with glee. He leaned down to whisper in her ear. "I'll bet people can't catch FIV?"

"Right."

"When are you going to tell her?"

"As soon as she sheds the nail polish she put on sitting at my desk all morning while I helped the volunteers scrub out the cat food dishes."

"Rachel doesn't do dishes, huh?"

"For cats or people. Ah, Rach, those kittens are still in isolation, and people can't catch it anyhow. You can stop washing." Leah appeared to be suppressing an unholy smirk.

"My manicure is ruined!"

"Hey, you've been here all morning. Take a break. I'm sure Ash will drive you back to the barn if he has the time."

That idea cheered Rachel no end. "We could stop for lunch and maybe watch a movie on the TV together this afternoon since Leah *finally* got the satellite dish hooked up. I'm so lonely out there." She attached herself to Ash again like a leach in a swimming hole.

"Um, Mom is expecting me for lunch—I live with her—something vegetarian because that's what I am, a vegetarian." Now, Leah grinned as he desperately rolled out the list of items making him less of a catch and added one more. "Staying with Mom saves money because firefighters aren't paid nearly as much as people think, especially in a place like Chapelle."

"That's so sad. A brave man like you should be able to afford a place of his own where he can entertain as he pleases. But, I'd love to meet your mother." Rachel ran one of her marred fingernails up the length of Ash's arm. He felt it clear to the base of his spine, but not in a good way.

The deep, hard blare of a horn sounded from an SUV on steroids that surged through the shelter gates. The dogs gave it their usual enthusiastic greeting regardless of vehicle size. Cubby came running, clambered aboard, and was carried away as quickly as if he'd been kidnapped. "Mrs. Couvillon," Leah explained. "I've never actually met her."

"Be glad. She's quite the battle-axe. You'll probably have the pleasure at the Firemen's Ball. Cliff bought three tickets this time after he got chewed out about only getting two for the Doggone Ball. She stayed home because Cubby had his heart set on going, I'm told." Ash felt his arm going numb under Rachel's tight grip.

"We should go, too, and not keep your mother waiting. See you later, Leah," the frog princess directed.

Ash bowed to the inevitable, led her to his car, buckled her in, and set out for home. On the way, Rachel worked on convincing him that a tall man like him really, really needed a bigger car. She suggested a few models he might want to consider. Probably, he could get a good trade-in on the Prius. The family home seemed as far away as New York or Los Angles instead of only fifteen minutes through the cane fields and into an older part of town marked by small, frame houses gone to vinyl siding and set in neatly kept yards framed by large crepe myrtles, their leaves painted dull yellow and vivid red by autumn.

His mom had vegetarian vegetable soup and toasted cheese sandwiches waiting. His grandfather slept in the recliner with Courage, the terrier, nestled in his lap. Curious about the new arrivals, her puppies and Bandit pressed against the baby gate that kept them in the laundry room blanketed with newspapers. One of them yapped incessantly, but Dalton Blaise didn't waken. Only the sound of a siren or a brisk shaking would do that.

Linda Blaise grew flustered about not having enough food—and the fact that he'd brought a girl home. Still, she held out her thin but welcoming arms to Rachel and said, "You must be Leah. I've heard so much about you, your work with animals, your talent as a photographer, the situation with your grandmother." Rachel frowned, grim as the reaper, until Linda Blaise added, "Such a beauty."

Then, she held out a hand and introduced herself. "I'm Rachel Allain, Leah's sister, visiting for a while."

Sponging off of Leah and making her miserable, Ash wanted to add so very badly. His mother's delighted face turned to puzzled, then concerned, but she said, "Sit down before the food gets cold. I'll make another sandwich for Dalton since he's sleeping."

Ash, well-trained, held out a chair at the round, maple dining room table in an area just off the living room and set with three places and glasses of sweating iced tea. He made sure he placed Rachel across from him and next to his mother, a safety perimeter of sorts.

The women kept up the conversation, mostly about the upcoming ball. His mother reminisced about past events she'd attended with her handsome husband. She got up to bring a pair of framed photos to the table, one showing the couple all dolled up and ten years out of date. The other portrayed three-generations of the Blaise men, Dalton and Hank, Ashton and Cole as teenagers, all with smoky gray eyes.

Rachel made a serious study of them before handing the photos back to Linda. "I can't wait to see Ash in a tux. He's so handsome like his father. Will you have your picture taken with me?" Rachel asked with a flirtatious tilt of her head. She ran her tongue over perfect teeth as if cleaning off the cheese and suggesting something more.

"Sure. Any of the firefighters will pose with you for five dollars. It is a fundraiser after all. Mom, you should go—with me as my date. It's been a long time since you attended. We'll get a sitter for Pop." By the displeased look Rachel shot at him over the glass pumpkin centerpiece, he gauged himself safe at last from her interest. He might get a reputation as a mama's boy since Rachel would be sure to spread the word, but cared less.

Totally engaged in their own tableau, they failed to notice Dalton Blaise rising, dumping Courage to the floor, and ambling to the table. "Lunch?" he asked in a voice still deep and full of authority.

"Right away, Chief." Linda hustled to the kitchen and back with a bowl of soup. "Sandwich coming right up."

Dalton took the empty seat and stared at Rachel until she squirmed a little in her seat and offered up a beauty queen's smile, obviously a remedy for discomfort that always worked. "I'm Rachel Allain. So pleased to meet you, Mr. Blaise."

"I know you. That's not your name! Why are you lying to me?" In his agitation, he overturned his soup, which spilled across the table like a miniature bayou teeming with vegetable fishes.

Rachel leapt up, agile enough on her bad ankle to get out of the way of the deluge. "I don't know what you mean!"

Ash grabbed a handful of turkey-imprinted paper napkins from a holder matching the glass pumpkin and mopped up the mess as his mother ran in with dishtowels to do the same. Courage helped out by lapping up the broth that cascaded to the tiled floor.

"He gets upset sometimes. We never know what will set him off so we seldom invite guests," Linda said, almost as distraught as the old man.

"We were finished eating anyhow, Mom. Aren't we, Rachel?"

"I guess." She'd barely touched the soup and picked at the sandwich as if it contained liverwurst and limburger instead of plain old American processed cheese.

"I'll take her to Leah's place. Pop will settle down once we're gone." He hoped. Steering Rachel out the front door, across the hospitable front porch with its rockers and pots of russet-colored mums, and down a couple of steps to the Prius in the driveway, he shoved her into the passenger seat and rounded the car to the driver's side.

His grandfather crashed the screen door back against the pale blue vinyl siding and shambled after them crying out, "Don't leave me, green-eyed lady," with his gait and outstretched arms doing a better zombie impersonation than Rachel at Halloween. Ash turned the man around and escorted him back into the house. Dalton craned his head back toward the car and its occupant who hit the door locks making an audible pop.

"That's a friend of mine, not her," he reassured, though he had no idea who the green-eyed lady might be. Granddad endured Velma by spending all his time at the firehouse. Could he have kept a woman on the side? No time to consider that now. They entered the first floor bedroom with its handicap bathroom and a recently installed new lock on the door. He encouraged the old man into a comfortable overstuffed chair by the window and got a bottle from the medicine cabinet.

His mom hovered nearby with a glass of water in hand. "I'm so sorry. I couldn't stop him from coming after you. He just pushed me aside."

Dalton stared out the window at the car in the drive. Ash turned his head and offered the pill. "Take it, Chief. Mom, put his lunch on a tray." He watched for the swallow that told him the tranquilizer went down. Ash stayed put until the cheese sandwich with a handful of chips and a pickle on the side arrived.

"I have to get Rachel out of here, but I'll come back as soon as I can. Come on, let me bolt the door."

"He'll get drowsy soon. If you want to visit with your friend I'll manage—but do you think it's a good idea to show interest in both sisters? That can lead to trouble, son."

He hated adding to his mother's worries, hated Rachel some in that moment though the ruckus hadn't been her fault except for inviting herself to lunch. "I'm only interested in Leah. This one is interested in me. I might have to ask Cole for help."

"I haven't seen him in so long. I know he's working his way through UNO, but do you think he'd come for a short visit?" That was hope glimmering in Mom's pale blue eyes.

"With enough incentive. I'll see what I can do." That plan in mind, Ash returned to his passenger.

"That was soooo scary. You live with outbursts like that all the time?" Before he could answer, she added, "You really, really need to get a place of your own."

Sure, and leave his mother to deal with the mess. Though Rachel had more suggestions for alternate housing than a real estate agent, Ash drove to the barn without responding. He didn't bother to get her door or help her out. Maybe she'd lose interest after today. But, no.

Before he could pull out, she leaned way into the front seat, lots of cleavage on view and said, "Leah found my phone in her ruins. It rang while she was feeding all those cats. Must have fallen out of my bra when I tripped that night. Still works!" Rachel delved her hand alongside one lush breast and withdrew a slim, pink and grubby cell phone, handed it over to him still warm from her body. "Now, you can put your number in there. No need to reach me through Leah anymore because that's soooo awkward. A girl never knows when she might need a firefighter to come to the rescue."

He gave her a number, the non-emergency one for the firehouse, and handed the cell back. Rachel replaced the phone as if she were giving herself a breast exam, making her nipples spring to life beneath the light, pink V-necked cotton sweater. "That's not an uncomfortable place to keep it?" He cursed himself for asking.

"Not if a girl is well-endowed. Want to come in and keep me entertained?"

"Not today. I need to get home and make sure my grandfather has calmed down." He failed to say, "Maybe later" because he'd mean "Never".

Finally, Rachel backed from the car and executed a long, feline stretch, saying "You do need a bigger car. We'd be so much more comfortable." She closed the door and gave him one of those cutesy goodbyes, a tiny wink of her hand.

Ash drove down the road a piece, past the bird lady's house and around a bend until safely out of sight. He found his own cell phone and called his brother who answered with the grouchy hello of a guy who still lay abed at noon.

"Cole, how about coming to the Firemen's Ball with me and mom?"

His sibling answered with a groan. "Only if you hogtie me to a ladder and transport me there on the pumper truck."

"I'll pay for your ticket and gas to and from New Orleans. Good band, great food."

"Got all that in the Big Easy." Cole filled the phone with an enormous yawn.

"Some beautiful women I want you to meet."

"If this is a ploy to get me married and settled down in Chapelle, forget it."

"Nope. I need you to take one of them off my hands for a while, that's all. And you need to visit Mom. She misses you. Don't know why, but she does."

If temptation didn't work, try guilt.

"When?"

"Saturday before Thanksgiving."

"Gets slow for the Macho Men around the holidays. Not much call for male strippers when the gals have pies to bake and turkeys to thaw. I'll see if I can take off, but you'll owe me my usual escort fee. Now let me get back to sleep."

"You got it. Thanks, bro."

No response, only a disconnect, not that it mattered. With the plan to divest himself of Rachel in place and time alone with Leah in the near future if it worked, Ash returned home to cope with his grandfather.

Chapter Sixteen

Why? Why? Why? Leah bumped her head softly against a full-length mirror in the commodious dressing room of the formal wear shop and left a small smudge on the glass at Chapelle's one and only Belles, Beaux and Brides. Why had she accepted two tickets for the Firemen's Ball from Ash? Why was she trying on an endless array of long gowns that failed to fit her bust and dragged on the floor? Why endure shopping with Rachel at all?

An entire rack of rejected dresses hung in a row to one side. Outside the cubicle, she heard Rachel and Regan, her friend from the pageant circuit, whom Leah always considered to be a blonde ditz, reminiscing about their past triumphs and trials, catching up on their current lives, approaching with another excruciating offering.

"I've found my dream job right here. All these gorgeous clothes. With my experience as a pageant queen, I can give such good advice to young women who need the perfect dress to catch the eye of the judges. That carries over to brides, too. They do want to look their best as well. Not to mention all the studly groomsmen you meet."

Regan, which one was she? Miss Yambilee, Miss Cracklin' Festival, or both? Meanwhile, Leah shivered in her bra and panties as cold air blasted from a vent overhead. She suspected a plot to keep customers from sweating in the dresses.

"This is the one, I'm sure. Even with your sister's odd build and darker coloring, this will flatter with a few adjustments. I have an eye for it, Miss Helen said, when I worked at her boutique during high school before she passed. That woman must have been ninety if a day, but she kept herself up until the end. She's my idol." Regan entered with a billowing gray cloud of a dress draped over her arm.

"Too poufy," Leah said immediately. She intended to make her escape from this agonizing situation that pointed out all her physical flaws in three-way mirrors by simply saying she'd wear her red dress. The end.

Rachel tossed her curls, the effect wasted on Leah. "You haven't tried it on yet. What a quitter. I was willing to try on dozens of gowns to get the right one when I competed. Of course, most of them flattered me. Really, it came down to which flattered the most. Up you go. Raise those arms."

Regan and Rachel each took an elbow and coerced her onto a low platform used for displaying and fitting wedding gowns to advantage. The skirt floated across her eyes like a heavy mist, then the bodice passed creating a blackout. Once Leah got her vision back, her attendants fussed with long, filmy sleeves and a black pearl button holding the netting of the bodice in place at her nape. Below that, her breasts filled out, but did not overflow, a strapless corset top of black satin encrusted with rhinestones that sent deep darts into a skirt as diaphanous as smoke swirling around her feet. She appeared to be standing in a dark cloud that allowed a few stars to be revealed in the form of tiny fake gems.

"A new shipment of Mardi Gras ball gowns just came in today. This time I went for the bra size and not the waist. We can alter that." Regan pinched the loose corset in the back to give an idea of the fit. "It's intended for an older woman with a big bosom, but I think it works. Rachel?"

Rachel plucked at Leah's bra strap and made her boobs wobble. "Lose this and yeah, it looks great. Whack off enough from the bottom to fit her height, and you've got a winner."

Leah stared into the mirrors that up until now had shown her to be short, hippy, and too big at the top. She envisioned her grandmother's hair clip resting above her ear, the diamond studs in her lobes. At that moment, she imagined she could have competed in a pageant and not come in first, but as second runner up to Regan and Rachel, the best she'd ever do.

"Waiting," Rachel prompted. "You saying yes to the dress?"

Leah managed a nod. "Price," she murmured.

"Seven hundred and worth every penny to look like that," Regan touted. "Fabulous, you'll wow every man in the place."

Leah gathered Regan worked on commission, but she found herself nodding like a bobble-head doll. Only one man, just one she wanted to impress, Ashton Blaise. Rachel had snatched away most of the guys Leah dated. Heck, though younger, Rach managed to snare a senior to escort her to Leah's prom. Her own date danced more with her sister than with her. She hadn't cared all that much at the time. He wasn't a steady or even close to it, simply a guy in her advanced biology class who wanted someone to go with him.

College, the same if she brought a young man home from Northwestern. Once they encountered Rachel, they flamed out as if burnt by napalm and began calling her at LSU. So what? Leah had her studies. If only Rachel had shown up in Colton Dandridge's office and prevented the affair. Where was her vamp of a sister when she needed her? A minute ago, she'd been called a quitter for her loathing of shopping. Now, she wanted to compete in the worst way. Save Ash from Rachel, save him for herself, she admitted to the woman in the mirror at last.

"Min, we need you in here," Regan bawled into the hallway, breaking the spell.

A tiny Laotian woman tottered in with her pins and chalk, dropped to her knees and began measuring the skirt from the waist to Leah's toes. She tucked pins in the back of the bodice, nodding her gray head with its topknot all the while. "I do very good job. You have Friday," and the seamstress was gone, returned to the back of the shop where the sewing machines resided out of sight like Min.

Rachel and Leah had moved on as well. "What are you wearing, Rach?"

"I think the emerald green from the Frog Festival."

"Stunning gown, got you first runner up, but they picked a local girl. That's the sad truth of the pageant biz. Another perk of working here, I can borrow any of the sample dresses in my size as long as I tell everyone where I got it."

Great, now she had Regan as competition, too. Regan resembled every beauty queen on TV—blonde, leggy, and busty, long nails, perfect teeth she'd probably smear with Vasoline for shine at the event. If

Ash asked her what she wanted, she'd probably reply world peace whether the answer made sense or not. Still, she divested Leah of the gown with careful, experienced hands and placed it reverently on a padded hanger. "I'll take this to Min right away."

"What do you want to do now? Get some crab cakes for lunch?" Rachel asked.

"I don't think I can afford to dine out for a long, long time once I pay for that dress."

"Why don't we try on wedding gowns for fun and pretend we're dieting to fit into them."

"Not my idea of a great time, Rach."

"And the local Firemen's Ball is?

"Gotta work with what I have, such as it is. The ball won't be too bad. Could be fun."

"In your dreams, sis, but better than sitting around at the barn.

Maybe.

Chapter Seventeen

Ash stood amid decorations that made him want to take a fire extinguisher to them. The Ladies Auxiliary had done their best on a very limited budget he supposed. They stayed with a black, red, and yellow color theme in plastic table cloths, cutlery, and paper plates. Black bag weights centered on each table anchored balloon bouquets of the same hues. The dropped ceiling of the town's Mardi Gras hall flickered with red twirly-whirlys and large, fluffy balls meant to catch the light. He sure hoped the stuff wasn't flammable and found himself checking for exits and the location of extinguishers. The Mardi Gras hall, no better than a large metal building dressed up on the inside to provide the town with recreational space, appeared to be up to code, and he knew ticket sales were limited to its legal capacity. Two of his fire trucks stood parked by the entrance making a corridor for the guests to enter between them. That should be enough to satisfy him.

What it lacked in ambiance, the hall made up for with a large bar along one side of the space, lots of room for dancing, and free usage for the fire department. No one in Chapelle would fault the food, all homemade, with a large ham, boudin sausage links donated by the local meat market, and several deep fried turkeys prepared by Chief Fontenot to provide the protein, the starchy dishes arrayed in between. With potato salad, crawfish fettuccini, rice dressing, baked beans, French bread rolls from Pommier's bakery, and thank heaven, a large tureen of fresh fruit salad and one bowl of salad greens, Ash had no fear of going hungry, maybe putting on five pounds, but not starving.

He did have hungry eyes—for Leah—and watched the entry draped with shredded sheets of red and yellow plastic cut jagged to resemble flames that guests needed to push through to enter from the lobby. Pretty much the same crowd as the Doggone Ball, but with more volunteer firefighters and their wives. He turned to glimpse his mother puttering around placing the favors, coiled blowouts that expanded into a little fire hose with a good breath exerted. He swore she wore the same black lace dress as the one in the picture taken with his dad at the last ball they'd attended before his death. Ash paid for his grandfather's aide to come early and allow her time get her hair done for the event, joking that he liked to treat his dates right. She'd returned with a blonde rinse over hair fast turning white with stress. Rod gave a low whistle, and Linda's pale face pinked up. That shook Ash a little, but if his mother enjoyed the new look, then fine.

He caught a flash of emerald out of the corner of his eye so out of sync with the color theme everyone in the hall turned toward the entrance. Rachel posed amid the plastic flames, holding them back with one long, white arm raised above her head of artfully piled black curls. A slim strapless gown draped her form in green sequins that moved like scales as she glided farther into the room. Ash knew the second she'd spotted him because she changed course from a table with empty seats toward him. He searched desperately for Leah again.

"Well, hello there. Don't you look fine in that tuxedo?" Rachel's hand possessed his arm.

"All the guys are wearing them. Look at Lex with his bright red vest. Even the Chief found one to fit him."

"Now that's a miracle. How Uncle Tank has let himself go." Disgust rippled over her perfect peachy lips.

"Women troubles. Too many exes in his life. Where's your sister?" Belatedly, he feared Leah had backed out. Knowing how she hated to be pushed, he hadn't offered her a ride or even double checked to make sure she'd attend.

"Parking that big, clunky SUV of hers. It smells of dog. We would have been here sooner but she insisted on stopping at Gran's house to show her our dresses and take pictures of the three of us even though Gran had on some ratty old robe."

"Sometimes you don't know when you'll see a person again. It doesn't matter what they're wearing." The picture of his mom and dad at their last ball flashed through his mind again.

"Do I smell of dog?" Rachel leaned in very close to his face, kissing close.

Ash took a quick sniff and stepped back. "No, gardenias."

"Gran had some of this old-fashioned perfume on her dresser so I helped myself to block out the animal odor. Oh, there's Leah. She cleaned up pretty good once Regan and I took her under our wings."

Leah parted the plastic flames and floated in

wearing a smoky cloud of a dress with rhinestones winking on it like tiny embers. Her hair remained the same, no elaborate up-do, but that diamond clip he remembered fondly twinkled in its darkness. Something different about her. Could it be confidence in her beauty? He planned to reinforce that over and over again tonight as far as his duties and Rachel let him. Where the hell was Cole?

"Excuse me." He left Rachel standing there, her eyes so enhanced by her sequins and eye shadow that he swore they shot green flames in his direction as he walked away.

She called after him. "I'll be sitting with my friend Regan. We'll save you a seat."

Ash failed to answer. He crossed the length of that room as if he had sirens screaming to tell people to get out of his way. No one dared stop him. "Leah."

"Ash. You look stunning as usual."

"I might say the same about you. Come meet my mother. Sit at our table."

He took her arm, a courtly escort through the thickening crowd. Linda Blaise sat hemmed in on one side by the bulk of Chief Fontenot. Cubby, Cliff Couvillon, and his large wife took up part of the table for eight. Ash held out the chair on the other side of his mother. "Someone special I want you to meet, Mom. Leah Allain." Nice to see the light in her blue eyes as she offered Leah a smile and a greeting. "I think you've met everyone else except Cliff's wife, Eunice."

"Oh, you come to pick up Cubby at the shelter very promptly, but don't get down. Nice to meet you in the fl…face to face," Leah said changing direction and putting her manners firmly in place. Mrs. Couvillon did have flesh, lots of it. Ash noted how Leah avoided mention of it. With Eunice's drab gray hair screwed into a knot atop her head and held in place with lethal looking combs and some kind of Oriental skewers, she gave off Dragon Lady vibes from the top of her high mandarin collar digging into her double chin to the bottom of a long black dress adorned with satin frogs its entire length, an ensemble also suitable for funerals.

Rachel slinked over and slid into the last remaining seat. Linda frowned. "Oh, we were saving that chair for my son, Cole. He promised to come," she told the interloper with lots less welcome in her voice.

"Maybe Leah could move to make room for me. I want so to sit with Uncle Tank," Rachel claimed. She flashed a brilliant smile at the rotund chief who answered it with a wide, salacious grin.

"And me, huh, Rachel!" Cubby said right beside her, moving his chair even closer.

"Sure, I guess."

"Mom, I don't think Cole is going to show. Let her sit there if she wants."

Unfortunately, that placed Ash between the sisters. Long evening ahead, but the Chief got up to start the food line and the Louisiana Red Hots played a little old-fashioned Dixieland jazz to move the people along. Leah took her usual spoonful of everything and robed a slice of ham in a roll. The Chief and the Couvillons returned with overflowing doubled paper plates to carry the weight. Rachel indulged in a slice of turkey, both salads, and a tiny dab of the fettuccini. Ash took a tablespoon of everything not meat and a lot of salad.

Seated again, Mrs. Couvillon examined Rachel's meal. "What's wrong with the potato salad?"

"Too much mayo. Potatoes are just big cubes of starch, you know."

"I made that potato salad from scratch, girlie. It's Cubby's favorite. My husband's, too." Mrs. Couvillon shoveled in a forkful and nodded her head in approval. "Nothing wrong with it."

Rachel made a diplomatic move to change the subject. "Cubby and I work together as volunteers at the animal shelter."

"I know. He talks about you and that slutty Yancey all the time. Wears her jeans too tight. And some women like to show off their bosoms to innocent boys." With large pupils black as cinders in her doughy face, Mrs. Couvillon eyed Rachel's décolletage shown off in her strapless gown and forced the young woman to tug up her top with her glare. A tiny smile escaped Leah's lips, and she shared it with Ash.

"We don't come here for the Mardi Gras Ball," Mrs. Couvillion continued, letting her hostile gaze roam free around the room as if judging a contest for the most immodest dress. She took a really good look at Regan from the bridal shop wearing a striking gold number undoubtedly destined for that holiday. Abandoned by Rachel, her table filled with single men of all ages. "Too much hanky-panky going on that night, drunkenness, and women nearly falling out of gowns like yours to tempt the men. This place promotes sin." Evidently, Rachel won first place because Mrs. Couvillion's stare returned blazing enough to burn a hole through her low cut bodice.

Her husband stood up abruptly. "I need a drink. Anyone else? What can I get you?"

"A beer for me," the chief said.

"Maybe a white wine?" Linda Blaise asked with hesitation.

"Anyone else?" The others shook their heads, and he stalked off dodging tables to cross the room.

"Cliff knows I'm a teetotaler, a Baptist dry as they come. He drinks to annoy me and thinks he can get away with it by being Catholic."

Linda Blaise stepped in with a change of subject. "Try the fettuccini, Rachel. I put a whole pound of Velveeta in it."

Wisely, Rachel ate her spoonful. "Delicious. Maybe I should have a tiny bite of the potato salad."

"I'll get it for you!" Cubby pushed away from the table in haste almost upsetting it, but the Chief's big belly kept it stable. He returned with a heaping plate of his mother's cooking about the time his dad set down the drinks, his own a double whiskey on the rocks. Rachel took a taste and declared it excellent. Ruffled feathers smoothed, everyone applied themselves to eating until the Chief signaled the band for a drum roll. He heaved from his chair and laboriously mounted the stage at the rear of the hall.

"Y'all can keep on eating. We still got plenty, but once you're done be sure to check out the silent auction items. We got some nice wrought-iron fireplace tools donated by the Home Depot and an honest to goodness Catahoula cur looking for a home from Safe Haven Animal Shelter. He's spotted enough to pass for a Dalmatian. Don't forget I made an extra fried turkey for some lucky person to buy. Show that turkey off, boys!"

Two of the volunteer firemen in their gear entered from the catering kitchen toting a huge turkey garnished with parsley on a silver platter and made a circuit of the room before placing it on the silent auction table. The Chief beamed over his culinary skill.

"Now, you can't keep the platter. Ethel Murphy loaned it to me along with parsley from her garden. Thank you, Miss Ethel. You know they say the male of the species always has the brightest plumage. For the live auction, three of our most eligible firefighters—Lexington Alexander, Ashton Blaise, and back on the market since his divorce, Neil Gondron—are available for date nights."

The other firefighters hooted, but the women gave a rousing cheer. The Chief might have resembled an obese penguin in his tux, but he excelled at patter, which probably helped explain his ability to keep his job. Who could fire the affable Tank Fontenot? Ash just shook his head.

"We're also offering a birthday party at the fire station for some lucky boy or girl. The Ladies Auxiliary will do all the work—and we'll throw in a ride on the engine. We got use of a condo in Destin for a week and a hunting camp on White Lake. Now's the time to get your geese and ducks. Let's start with those items."

The women, especially Ethel's bridge club who filled a table, put up a fuss. Ethel called out, "That's right, Tank, save the best for last. Make us wait." The elderly women appeared to be pooling their money in the center of the table like gamblers at a Texas hold 'em tournament. That worried Ash a little.

The birthday party went high and fast with eager grandparents flailing their hands in the air. Both the condo and the hunting camp brought in respectable amounts, but finally Tank got down to business. He beckoned Neil of the salt-and-pepper hair onto the floor to parade around in his tux if he were Mardi Gras royalty. Ash knew the guy had been working out since his wife dumped him for a man who had regular work hours and a bigger paycheck. It showed. He went for two hundred fifty dollars and seemed pleased to bring that much. In fact, Neil sat down gratefully at the table of the winning bidder, a woman about his age and not unattractive, with a bit of his confidence restored.

The Chief call up Lex next. The firefighter took off his jacket, opened his vest and showed off red suspenders straining against the rock hard abs under his starched shirt. He strutted around that hall with the light glinting off a shaved head so shiny it had to be waxed. The band threw in a little stripper music to add to the fun, but Lex kept most of his clothes on. He'd been sitting with Regan who put in a flattering bid, but she had competition. Lex passed Ash's table and encouraged Rachel with a wink.

"He's like the men the Kardashian sisters marry. Lend me some money, sis. I don't want Lex to feel bad," Rachel wheedled.

"I can't! I'm tapped out from buying this dress and replacing all the stuff that burned in the house fire. You'd think having a cousin in insurance would speed up the claims process, but he's moving as slow as cane syrup in January."

At Leah's refusal, Rachel stuck out her *boude'* lip like a child. "Then how am I going to bid on Ash? You don't want him to be embarrassed, do you? Bidding is up to four-fifty for Lex."

"That's your problem and his, not mine."

Leah's answer did not reassure Ash. If they still played tit-for-tat, she should be willing to offer five hundred for him as he had done for the kayak trip. Surely, she didn't want him to go to anyone else no matter what she said. He felt his ego bruising badly already. Regan ponied up four-seventy-five for a date with Lex who swung by their table to say, "See if you can beat that, brotha!"

"Now for the highlight of the evening. What would you ladies pay for a night with Chapelle's most eligible bachelor, firefighter and deputy chief, Captain Ashton Blaise? Another drum roll please!" The Chief gestured to his table. Feeling his cheeks burn under his olive complexion, Ash stood. He'd gotten out of this last year claiming to be too new in town after his long absence, but not now.

The plastic flame curtains billowed as a very latecomer entered the hall and headed straight for the center of the dance floor. Stunningly handsome, the new man in the tuxedo caused female jaws to drop and men to grind their teeth. "Cole Blaise here to help out a good cause and my firefighting brother. Some music please!" He segued directly into his act, hip grinding and pelvis thrusting around the room, easing off his jacket, letting it drop to the floor, loosening his tie.

Both relieved and embarrassed, Ash sat down and let his brother work the crowd. Even tough little Leah's mouth gaped. Rachel stared big-eyed and stammered, "He's exactly like you but—but more."

How true. Cole wore his hair shoulder-length long, a silky black mane that he shook as he moved. His eyes, large and so very dark gray, absorbed every female in the room. He flashed dimples in both cheeks. The tie went sailing over the crowd and nearly started a riot at the table where Yancey Breaux, pretty in pink, sat with her parents and several female teen friends. Cole ripped away his dress shirt to expose waxed and then oiled abs and pecs that put Lex Alexander's to shame.

Ethel Murphy dug into her bra, withdrew a wrinkled bill, and slapped another hundred into the pot on her table. With his mother in the audience, Cole stopped short of removing his pants and simply remained topless. Didn't seem to matter. He went for six hundred dollars to Ethel's bridge club and moved directly to their table to honor them with a gleaming smile and an offer to let their age-spotted hands pet his biceps and whatever else they wanted.

"Yes, that's my other son. He's working his way through college as an entertainer," Linda Blaise explained simply to her tablemates, though her cheeks turned red.

"For the last six years," Ash grumbled.

"A male stripper, cool!" Rachel exclaimed, her green eyes never wavering from a view of Cole.

"Disgusting, outrageous." Mrs. Couvillon expressed her disapproval without toning it down a notch.

The Chief still stood on the bandstand. "That performance made the evening. Don't y'all tell me you didn't get enough for your forty bucks. Ash, your turn. Let's see if you can outdo your brother. You're the one always saying we need new gear. He wants PBI instead of reliable old Nomex."

"Aaah," said a chorus of firefighters.

"Maybe even PBO."

The firefighters responded with, "Oooh,"

"Over two thousand dollars a pop, so get out there and earn it, boy!"

Reluctantly, Ash moved to the middle of the dance floor and held up his hands. "No, really, I think this group of great supporters for the Ste. Jeanne d'Arc Parish Fire Department is about out of cash. Mr. Hartz bid so high on that fried turkey he doesn't have funds for another one," he jested.

Ash had no idea what Hartz scribbled down for the turkey, but his charity donations tended to be generous and precluded any competition. The crowd laughed, and the blond, boyish local billionaire at a table with his Cajun wife and family smiled. He had no need for a condo or camp, and undoubtedly would donate the turkey to a soup kitchen. Ash started to move away from the center of attention.

"No, now a deal's a deal. What can you ladies offer for Captain Ashton Blaise, courageous firefighter even if he's not as great a looker as his brother?" The Chief just wouldn't let him leave gracefully. Ash should have kept his mouth shut about the state of the fire equipment.

The room went quiet. As Ash suspected, no one wanted second best now that they'd seen the alternative. He noticed Leah and his mother conferring. Leah rose in that cloud of a dress. "I bid six hundred."

"Sold!" the Chief declared.

She came to claim her prize right in the center of the dance floor. The band struck up a slow number, and Leah simply dissolved into his arms. They moved as one, as spontaneous as when they had sex together. He whispered in her ear just below that diamond clip in her hair. "I owe you a hundred.

"No, you owe your mother. She staked me. Didn't want your brother to upstage you."

"I'm crushed."

"I'm broke. This dress…"

"Is perfect on you. I've never seen a person so lovely inside and out."

"Not even Rachel, when she'd breathe down your neck?"

"Why can't you believe I prefer a woman of substance?"

"Are you saying I'm fat?"

Oh, Ash recognized this ploy, trying to start an argument to ward off his attention. "Nope, I'm saying you are perfect, the prettiest woman in the room."

"Sure." She rolled her green eyes under smoky lids.

"Besides, Rachel won't be a problem anymore." Ash turned her toward their table where Cole had taken over the seat next to their mother. He'd retrieved his tear-away shirt, but only put on his jacket over his bare chest. Rachel appeared riveted by the same sight close up that made Eunice Couvillon livid. Ash swung by their group with Leah in his arms as Cole stood and offered to dance with their mother.

"Not until you put your shirt back on, son. That body oil will ruin my dress."

"It won't bother my sequins, not at all." Rachel stood, and she and Cole stepped onto the dance floor practically on the hem of Leah's gown. Lex got into the action with Regan. Neil took the hint and asked his date to dance. Only Miss Ethel seemed a little miffed, but Abner Millet bowed over her hand like a courtly gentleman and led her out despite his arthritic hip. Others joined in. The Chief prompted everyone to take one last look at the silent auction items before clambering down from the podium and sweeping up Linda Blaise against his spongy belly. That left only the Couvillons at the table. Cliff showed no interest in taking his wife for a spin.

"Hard shell Baptist, probably doesn't dance," Ash whispered in Leah's ear.

"I'd feel sorry for her if she weren't so mean. When you said battle-axe I pictured someone taller. Eunice isn't much bigger than Cubby, but she sure has the attitude."

"They're a lot alike in build, but Cubby is nice as can be. Oh, there he goes to ask Yancey to dance. Good kid. She didn't turn him down."

The new couple made their awkward way around the floor with Cubby counting out a box step as they went. The song ended not long after, but by the look on the boy's face, he might have spent the whole evening with the pretty girl. The frown lines in Eunice's face grew deeper. The dancers returned to their table and came up one chair short for Cole.

Eagerly, Rachel said, "We can squeeze you in. Bring over a chair."

"I'll do that after I get my shirt back on and take Miss Ethel and her gang for a trot around the dance floor. It's good for my business. Don't you go anywhere, Rachel. I'll be back." Cole pressed a blunt fingertip tipped by a beautifully buffed nail against her chest exactly where her cleavage began and her heart should have been.

Mrs. Couvillon pushed back her chair with a screech against the wood. "We're leaving before Cubby is corrupted. Cliff, bring the car around back. I'm not walking the length of that gravel lot. Cubby, come with me to collect my pans and the leftover potato salad. I don't want it sitting out all night." Not waiting to see if either man obeyed because she knew they would, Eunice shoved off for the kitchen.

"Can't say as how I'll miss her company," the Chief said once all three were gone and Cole sauntered back to join them as the band took a break.

"Scary woman," Cole conceded.

Tank Fontenot sniffed the air, took a deep inhale. "I smell french fries. Is somebody cooking back there? More buildings in Chapelle been burned down by french fry fires than I can count. Blaise, go check out the situation."

The Chief might not have any get up and go left, but he did have a nose for fires. Ash followed orders immediately. A puff of smoke escaped into the hall as he cautiously cracked the swinging door to the catering area. He went no farther, but grabbed the fire extinguisher nearest the entry from its bracket and gave orders on the move. "Volunteers, evacuate the building, right side fire exits and through the lobby. Get a hose to the hydrant and run it to the back of the building."

Ash entered the kitchen where all the burners on the commercial gas stove shot flames toward the blackening ceiling tiles. He aimed the chemical foam at a flaming puddle of grease pooling at the base of the oven. The huge pot of peanut oil the Chief used to fry his turkeys lay overturned on the stove top, its contents still draining into the stove, turning it into a giant cauldron of fire. He emptied the extinguisher, tossed it aside, and ripped off his jacket as swiftly as Cole had his tear-away shirt. Hands covered by the coat, he turned off the burners one by one, hoping all the while that the fire hadn't spread into the ceiling space above the tiles. The old building had no sprinkler system. Few places in Chapelle did. He quelled his fears for Leah in her filmy dress, his terrified mother, for Yancey Breaux whose pretty young face could be permanently ruined by fire, even for vain Rachel who might not be able to move fast enough in that tight dress to escape. Help arrived, and he was proud of his volunteers for getting the hose line going so fast as the nozzle poked through the rear door, and he jumped out of the way of its pressurized spray.

Ash dashed back into the hall to view the last of the guests moving through the far exits propelled by directions from Neil and Lex. A few helium balloons near the kitchen popped and hurried the stragglers along. He moved through the lobby to gear up. The Chief had ordered the two engines farther from the building and unlocked the compartments where the helmets, boots, and old fire resistant Nomex trousers and jackets were stored. Wailing sirens approached. Ash searched for his loved ones as he drew up the bulky pants and latched the coat.

"Ambulance. One down with chest pains and a lady sprained her ankle running in high heels. We're damned lucky," Tank Fontenot reported as if Ash were his superior.

"Thanks to your sensitive nose, Chief," Ash said, but his eyes kept scanning the parking lot with its scanty lighting. There they were huddled near a sidewalk streetlamp. Cole had their mother and Rachel tucked under his substantial arms. Leah stood with them to one side but her eyes searched as well. Her hand went up when she saw him. He returned the gesture, the best he could do right now, and reassured her with a smile. Drawing on his gauntlets and helmet, he surveyed his volunteers, Cliff Couvillon and Cubby among them.

"We were turning out of the lot when we saw people leaving the building and returned to help. Left Eunice in the car."

"Suit up. We need to hose down the roof and make sure the fire isn't spreading in the ceiling." With that, Ash entered the vacant hall to do his job as well as he could, not the way he'd planned to end this evening— free of Rachel and with Leah in his arms.

Chapter Eighteen

Wearing her peachy robe and flip-flops, Leah trudged down her lane, clip-clop, past the burned out house, to the mailbox with its cracked, orange plastic receptacle attached for the *Chapelle Clarion*. Tired to the bone because she hadn't slept last night worrying about Ash's safety, she retrieved her Sunday paper. She caught Mrs. Tweedy in flannel nightgown and slippers doing the same and gave a friendly wave, always hopeful of overcoming the neighbor's hostility. Not getting a response, she unfurled the skinny newspaper that served as a wrapper for a giant wad of advertising. Outside of being a vehicle for ads, the *Clarion's* only purpose in the modern world seemed to be printing obituaries, birth announcements, local political stories, and human interest pieces. Still, the paper ran a Pet of the Week picture gratis for the shelter, and for this reason, she paid for a subscription.

Ash. Alongside Chief Fontenot and very nearly crowded out of the picture by his boss's bulk, he stood there safe and sound in all his gear under a banner headline somewhat reduced in size due to its length, *Firefighters fight fire at Fireman's Ball*. Give the *Clarion* some credit for alliteration. Obviously, Ash had come to no harm.

The article written by the society editor, who'd attended the bash, rather artfully combined the usual who was there with an account of the fire. She included both the french fry aroma that had tipped the Chief to the grease fire and the amount of money paid for a date with Ashton Blaise, hero of the evening, who had gotten the flames under control. No serious injuries. Destruction confined to the kitchen and some smoke damage to the hall. Forty-five thousand dollars raised, which might have been more if the silent auction hadn't come to an abrupt end. Winning bidders could pick up their goods and gift certificates at the downtown fire station. Chief Fontenot vowed to fry another turkey for Jonathan Hartz since the original had acquired a smoky odor, but remained edible. Leah smiled, her first of the day.

Nose in the paper, she returned to the barn, the very silent barn. No whining, demanding sister begging for breakfast like a starved hatchling filled the space. Rachel had not returned home with her last night. Instead, citing the doggie odor of Leah's vehicle, she'd gotten a ride from Cole in his silver Lincoln exactly like the one Matthew McConaughey drove on TV ads. Of course, they'd dropped Mrs. Blaise off first. By the time Leah reached home after lingering at the fire until the police asked everyone to leave, Rachel had her bags packed for a week's vacation in New Orleans courtesy of Cole who offered his apartment for her stay.

"I have to get out of this boring, boring place," her sister declared.

Boring—when she'd just attended a ball that ended with a fire? Let New Orleans top that. However, Leah hadn't tried to talk her out of the trip. Not on your life. She waved them off into the night, then fought an urge to call Ash for the rest of the evening. He'd be tired, worn out by his efforts, and not in the mood to hear from her.

Leah poured her coffee and put a bowl on the table for her cereal, but paused in dumping out Cheerios when the light sound of the Prius motor approached the barn. No, she wouldn't run to the door. She waited for the knock, walked calmly to the entry—and threw herself into the arms of Ashton Blaise.

"Best greeting I've ever gotten," he joked, holding her rather awkwardly since one of his arms hung onto a pet carrier.

He had his best smile in place amid an early morning black stubble. Maybe he didn't own a set of dimples in his cheeks. Perhaps his muscles were lean and not bulked up for show, and his chest had that little patch of hair. Not on any day of week would Leah trade him for Cole Blaise. One man was all for fancy; the other a true hero every day of his life. He deserved a reward, a big one. She heard the whimpering of puppies. Leah stopped in the midst of a kiss meant to promise more.

"You drove over here to dump abandoned animals on me? Did you find them at the Mardi Gras hall?"

"Absolutely not! These are special Jack Russell terrier mixed breeds, hand-raised, and paper-trained going to good homes only. They have their first shots, been wormed—and they aren't both for you, but you get pick of the litter. I'm also returning your kitten who is now a litter-trained housecat with all his shots because that's the kind of guy I am. Bandit does suffer from species confusion, I'll admit. He thinks he's a dog, but that's a good thing in my opinion. Gets along with all kinds."

Without further ado, Ash stepped around Leah, closed the door and opened the cage. Out bounded two pups and a tuxedo cat considerably larger than the last time she'd seen him cradled in the fireman's big gauntlet. Noses to the ground, the puppies began to explore. Bandit rubbed up against her leg as if she were his long-lost mother, now safely spayed and awaiting a home at the shelter. Leah would make sure Bonny found one. Ash slapped down a clean pee pad he'd tucked under his arm.

"That's where you go, guys. Bandit, got your litter tray in the car. We don't want to get off to a bad start with the lady."

"*You* already have." Leah's tone made it clear she didn't mean the pets.

"Hey, I saved a lot of lives last night. Give me a break."

"I worried about you all night. This isn't how I planned to thank you next time we got together."

"Not the way I wanted the evening to end either. What I wouldn't give to see you in that gown again and hold you in my arms for another dance."

His handsome face went serious, his gray eyes smoky, and she believed every word. No Colton Dandridge here with his false compliments and lies, but best and safer not to say anything except, "Want some breakfast? Coffee is on."

Ash eyed her empty bowl. "Dry cereal. No thanks. Why don't I whip up some scrambled eggs and see how my toaster is working out for you?

"Fine, I'll get dressed."

"No need. I like you just the way you are."

"Well, I don't. Excuse me."

Leah fled to the bedroom, the puppies who sensed a game at her heels, Bandit scampering along after them, but she shut them out. Ashton Blaise deserved to get exactly what he wanted. She'd showered early to shampoo away the greasy smoke smell of her hair. Last night's ball gown, beautiful as ever, hung carefully on the closet door. She found the scrap of black lace panties, the garter belt and dark hosiery, the silvery shoes she'd worn under it hoping for a better end to the evening and put them on. The dress proved to be a struggle without Rachel's beauty queen hands to help, but she dropped it over head and slid her arms in the filmy sleeves. Fastening the back required the skills of a contortionist, but she managed to pull the bodice tight. One more detail. Leah affixed the diamond clip in her hair. Taking a deep breath, she opened the door and moved quietly toward the kitchen.

The puppies alerted Ash with yaps to her presence as he shoveled scrambled eggs that looked nothing like the kind she produced, these all fluffy and showing signs that he'd raided her small supply of herbs, onto plates Rachel left behind. The toaster popped. He ignored it, set down the pan, and moved to take her in his arms again without a single word. They twirled down the hall and around the wide open living area with the pups and kitten chasing the billowing, cloudy skirt. Ash turned down the second hallway, spun Leah inside her bedroom, and kicked the door shut. "Sorry, guys, no voyeurs."

"Let's make that a rule. No pets in the bedroom."

"If we've gotten to the point where we're making rules about sleeping together, I agree. I wish I'd worn my tuxedo, but it's in pretty bad shape after last night."

"So, my gown smells a little like french fries." Leah followed her statement up with a kiss of the same nationality, long and deep.

When they parted, Ash said, a trifle out of breath, "Fried turkey oil, actually. That's what started the fire."

"Don't want to talk about it now." With two fingers to his chest, she pushed him across her bed.

"Me neither. Later. I want to make love to you still wearing that dress. You'll have to be on top."

He stretched into a more comfortable position, maybe relieving a little of the discomfort in his jeans. Leah took up a position at the foot of the bed and raised her skirts inch by inch until she'd revealed the scrap of black lace panties and the garter belt. She stepped out of the panties exposing the small patch of black hair between her legs.

"If I'd known what was under there at the ball, we would have danced right out of the hall to the Mobile Command Unit parked in back in case the Chief wanted to take a snooze and done it in his chair." Shoes kicked off, Ash freed himself from the jeans, hard and ready to receive her.

Leah daintily held up her diaphanous skirts and positioned herself on his erection. She worked her hands under his T-shirt and stripped it off. They moved slowly at first, caught in the cloud of the fabric, afraid to rend their fantasy. All too soon, Ash began digging his fingers into the edge of the mattress, thrusting up to meet her every move, holding back for her sake, she knew. Leah rode on, eyes closed now, her lips slightly open. She strove to stay upright as her orgasm built, pulled tight, and exploded throughout her body. Ash let go, sharing the moment. Leah stayed as she was, quivering and breathing as deeply as the tight corset top would allow.

"Let me help you out of that," Ash said.

She bowed over to let him unfasten the pearl button at the neck. His fingers played up and down her back until he figured out how the corset worked, then opened it skillfully. He raised the gown over her head with reverence. Reluctantly, she moved from his shaft gone soft and warm and gathered the skirts, hung the dress of dreams on its padded hanger again and returned to nestle by Ash wearing only the garter belt, stockings and diamond clip, her silver shoes long since fallen to the floor.

He kissed the top of her ear beneath the clip, worked his way down to suck on a lobe. "No diamond earrings in the way this time," he said.

"Didn't you notice? Rachel wore them to the ball. I said Gran had given me the set, and she accused me of wheedling the diamonds out of her. She wanted her share, so I gave her the earrings as long as she promised not to sell them."

"I barely noticed Rachel once you walked into the room. Sorry I can't afford to replace them." He kissed each of her ears.

"I don't mind. The hair clip is rare and unique."

"Like you." His tongue moved down her jaw line.

"I wasn't trying to set you up for a compliment."

"I know, another rare and unique thing about you. Rachel would have been fishing for one."

He ended his explorations with a light kiss to her lips, distracting Leah momentarily from her thoughts. "You called in Cole to take her away, right?"

"Yep. You catch on quick, too. She's sponged off

of you long enough. He'll show her a good time and convince her to return to college because he's as bright as he looks when it comes to women. See, I do know what it's like to be considered second best in a family. Even my mom is dazzled by him."

"Yet she paid six hundred for my date with you so you'd be equal."

"That's what moms do."

"Yet, I think if I plinked my fingers against Cole's pecs, the sound inside would be hollow." Leah moved her fingers against Ash's chest across that patch of dark hair as if she played a few notes on a piano.

"What do I sound like?"

She'd raised his curiosity, which was always considerable. "A steel beam, I think, in so many ways." That pleased him.

His smile expanded as did another part of him. "By the way, this isn't our six hundred dollar date."

"I think this morning was easily worth that much. Now, I'll have to repay your mom, especially if I get a BOGO as the Gumbo Queen would say." Her gaze came to rest between his legs.

"Don't believe him. He's willing but not yet able. We still have lots to talk about though." Ash playfully spanked her bare behind. "I'm starving. Let me wash up, get dressed, and start a new batch of eggs. The others are toast by now and well, the toast is only good for croutons."

He rolled from the bed with vigor. Leah felt only a lingering sexual languor and no desire at all for more talk over breakfast.

Chapter Nineteen

Ash had the second batch of eggs cooking and fresh bread in the toaster by the time Leah padded down the hall in her bare feet. She wouldn't want to talk about them or other serious issues. He'd get her in a good mood and start with some of the easier stuff.

On purpose, he kept his back turned and grabbed a broom and dustpan to clean up the havoc the pets wrought in their absence. One plate cracked cleanly in half and washed clean of cold eggs by puppy tongues lay on the floor. Bandit might have contributed to part of the action as he sat nonchalantly washing his face and paws in a corner while his co-conspirators napped nearby. Ash bent way over and twitched his ass a few times. Peering through his splayed legs at Leah's sheer peach polished toenails, he said, "See, I know a few of Cole's moves."

"Your butt is much leaner, the way I like center cut bacon." Leah took a step forward and pinched a butt cheek. Dropping the dustpan and broom with a clatter, Ash jolted upward. "See, it isn't easy being a sex object," she jeered.

"Move no farther. We might have broken glass on the floor, but so far it looks clean." He spun around, scooped her up, and settled her in a chair at the table in front of cups of orange juice and hot coffee. "Eggs up in a minute." The toast popped. He took the time to slather the bread with butter, slice it into triangles, and deliver the plate to the table.

With her chin cupped in her hands, Leah said, "Are you sure this isn't my dream date?"

"It might have been if I hadn't awakened the kids when I dropped the broom after you molested me." Ash served the eggs, piping hot and perfect, with the dogs panting for more by his feet and Bandit twining around his ankles. He took a moment to clean up the broken dish, now split in four and its shards, fending off the animals with his broom. "I don't think they swallowed any glass. No bleeding tongues or bloody whiskers."

"Jack Russells are good jumpers, and I'd say Bandit is no slouch at getting up on tables either. They probably ate first and destroyed later. You should never leave two of that breed alone together. They get into trouble." Leah smiled at him over the edge of her orange juice.

"So which one do you want? Let me present them. This is Yapper." Ash picked up one pup by its scruff. "Got good looks and lots of bark, a real little watchdog, which you could use out here." Indeed, Yapper appeared almost full-bred with his softly folded brown ears, stocky white body, and long curved tail. He wiggled his behind even better than Ash.

Ash set him down and presented the second pup. "This is Stubby, the last of the litter Courage carried out of the cane field fire. The vet did the best he could to fix up him after being burned."

Stubby wagged a tail no longer than a bulldog's appendage. His ears, both black, sat in perfectly clipped little triangles atop his head making him seem more akin to Bandit than Yapper. He yipped in a considerably softer tone as if the smoke might have caused some lung damage.

Leah shook her head. "You know I'll keep the homely one. The other reminds me too much of Cole. Rachel said he was you but more. I think Cole is just too much."

"Good news for me—that you like the homely one! I expected your choice. Actually, Bandit and Yapper don't get along too well, but he's best buds with Stubby. I'll sleep better knowing you have a dog." He held Stubby up to Leah's cheek for a puppy lick of gratitude. She laid him in her lap and allowed the dog a tiny bit of egg before setting him on the floor again.

"Yes, just what I needed—as if I don't have a hundred at the shelter to care for already. What will you do with Yapper? Leave him for me to find a home? What about the other two in the litter?"

"The rest have gone to my firemen buddies with lots of kids, and I know exactly where Yapper should end up. Finish your breakfast and get dressed."

Leah checked the stove clock. "More like brunch. Yes, I hear Mrs. Tweedy's car returning from ten o'clock Mass right on schedule. If this were really my dream date, you would have said finish your breakfast and get back into bed."

"We still have all afternoon ahead of us, but let's pay a call next door first."

"You know how to cook great eggs and ruin a day all at the same time. I mean I've tried to be friendly, but I don't even get a wave of the hand at the mailbox."

"All will be well. Dress for Sunday visiting."

****

For people like her grandmother and Miz Tweedy

that meant putting on a dress. Leah knew proper etiquette, but simply didn't apply it very often. She put on a simple, long-sleeved knit gown of deep hunter's green that had survived the fire while stored in the barn's attic with her winter clothes. She rummaged in Rachel's jewelry box for a few gold chains to hang around the turtleneck and shoved her feet into high tan leather dress boots that came up to its hem—good to go. Gran would have added a hat, gloves, and pumps, but Leah had no intention of traveling back in time fashion-wise to appease her hostile neighbor.

Ash whistled when he saw her. "Clings in all the right places."

"Then maybe I'd better change. Ernestine Tweedy is quite the prude."

"No, you're good. I'll carry Yapper. He sheds lots of white hairs."

They crossed the lawn and skirted the vicious pampas grass to get to Miz Tweedy's front door. All the while, Leah's mind churned trying to figure out what card Ash had up his tricky sleeve now. Surely an ace if she was getting to know him at all. He rang the bell, which emitted a cardinal's strong, aggressive mating chirp.

"Should be the caw of an old crow," Leah muttered.

Ernestine answered with a Styrofoam box in her hand. "What do you want? I was about to sit down to my dinner. I go out of my way to pick it up at Victor's Cafeteria next town over every Sunday. Why should I cook when there's no one to eat it?"

"We won't take much of your time, ma'am." Ash pushed all of his charm into a smile for the angry biddy.

"You're that fireman. What do you want with me?" Miz Tweedy stepped back defensively, and Leah noticed a slight tremor in the hand holding the box. Whatever for? Ash gave off strong vibes, but only good ones, no threats, no anger.

"May we come inside for a bit, Miz Tweedy? You told me about the conflict you have with Leah's feral cats attacking your birds, and I've brought you the perfect solution." Like a skilled telemarketer, he held up Yapper who wagged joyously and let loose a few barks twice his size.

Ernestine Tweedy did not budge an inch. "Only lonely old ladies keep yapping little dogs for company. I have my feathered friends." Her beaky nose rose into the air.

"Maybe you'd like to have a parrot," Leah barged in, hoping to ride on Ash's coattails and rid herself of Mr. Grey, another problem to solve.

Miz Tweedy now stared down her beak at Leah. "I disapprove of caged birds. The winged are meant to fly free." She emphasized this with a flutter of her free hand. Yapper took that as a sign for play and barked again.

Ash tagged in once more, fighting the good fight. "Why, just a second ago you guessed this little guy's name is Yapper. A feisty little terrier with a big bark will keep the cats out of your yard. I'd suggest you run a long line across your space to allow the pup to chase up and down or better yet, an electric fence to let him roam the whole area. That way, he keeps your space cat free, and Leah can still feed and manage the ferals." Yapper sniffed at the box in Ernestine's hands and licked one of her fingers hopefully. "He likes you," Ash said.

If Miz Tweedy fell for that line, a few others probably did, but pups tended to adore anyone with food in one hand and a kind touch in the other. Ernestine patted Yapper's head. Then, Leah heard words she never thought to hear again from her neighbor since their first meeting. "Won't you come inside and sit down? Let me put my dinner up. We'll talk."

They entered an old-fashioned parlor much like the one in Leah's destroyed house. Its tufted settee and two replica Victorian side chairs carefully covered in plastic squeaked as they sat on either side of a fireplace festooned with porcelain birds that also occupied several whatnot shelves and a large china cabinet. Miz Tweedy settled her bony rump on the settee behind a bow-legged coffee table.

"Quite a collection you have," Leah remarked. Must be a nightmare to dust, but she held in that comment.

"Oh, yes, I've been accumulating them for years. My husband, Harold, bought the very first one for our anniversary, that cardinal right in the middle of the mantel. We were childless, you see, no little fingers to break anything. I did teach school. Plenty of young ones passed through my hands. That had to do." Miz Tweedy gazed at the pup in Ashton's lap with a longing Leah feared she, herself, might show for the man holding him. "Let me pet him for a moment."

Her neighbor reached out her arms. Done deal. Leah had seen it happen often at the shelter. "There's no adoption fee, and I can throw in a certificate to have the dog neutered. I'll give you a care package and some food to get you started, too," she rushed to say.

"Oh, I wouldn't want to destroy his feistiness by having Yapper fixed. We're going to chase cats together, aren't we?" Yapper agreed by wriggling in Miz Tweedy's lap and depositing a number of white hairs on her funereal Sunday dress. The woman, enamored, did not appear to notice.

"He's an active dog and should be outside a lot, but remember to keep him on a line or get the electric collar. You don't want to lose him on the road," Leah cautioned lest Ernestine forget to keep the dog on her side of the pampas grass.

"No, I wouldn't want to lose you." She accepted a puppy kiss. "Where are my manners? Coffee and teacakes?"

Leah stood immediately. "Please don't put yourself out, Mrs. Tweedy. I need to go see to my grandmother and take her some lunch."

"Oh, yes, Alene Allain, the granddame of Chapelle. I hear she's not doing well."

"No, sadly, she's become very reclusive." Leah detected very little sympathy in Ernestine's tone.

"Well, bless her heart. Young man, if I might have a word in private before you leave."

"I'll go get some things for Yapper. I have a care kit and some puppy chow in my car."

By the time Leah returned, Ash stood on the small gingerbread work-encrusted porch, his face somber and thoughtful. Miz Tweedy accepted her offering with a curt thank you and shut the door. Something had destroyed his ebullient attitude. "What's wrong?"

"Miz Tweedy told me something that I can't share with you now, but soon. Oh, she also warned me you have that vixen's blood, and I must be careful of seduction. That warning came a little too late as I've been thoroughly seduced. So, we going back to bed now? I think I deserve another reward for what I accomplished back there." Ash steered her in the direction of the barn.

"Sure, that's going to work out until Yapper breaks some of her knickknacks or scares the birds away."

"She's in love even if she won't admit it and will forgive the little things that really don't matter." Ash gave her one of his meaningful gray stares, but went on to say, "Besides, I've observed if a person keeps filling the feeders, the birds will return after a little startle. They'll probably start perching on Yapper's line. Now about my reward…"

"Honestly, I could train you like a puppy with sex instead of treats."

"Works on most men."

Leah tripped over a tuft of brown winter grass. Ash steadied her with a grasp to her elbow. She swore his personal electricity shot straight to her heart. Time to clamp down on that. "Sorry, making me put on Sunday clothes reminded me of my responsibility to my grandmother. No Meals on Wheels today. I should take her some lunch, enough for supper, too. No more sex for you today." She acknowledged silently that she had cut herself off from her own desires as well.

"Why don't we do the Victor's deal? Eggs don't stay with you very long. By the time we get there and back, we'll be hungry and can have a late lunch with her."

"Okay. That's nice of you." In Leah's secret heart, she hoped there would be time for them to be together again today.

On the drive along the two-lane blacktop canopied by live oak trees, she made small talk. "Tofurkey for you on Thursday?"

"Nope, I'm working, giving the guys with children time off. It will be me, Lex, and Neil at the station, but the Ladies Auxiliary brings a spread with all the fixings. I'll have plenty to eat. My mom will make a dinner for my grandfather. He'll call her Velma and say she always was a good cook. Kind of depressing, but we'll have plenty of leftovers for the rest of the week. You?"

"Oh, cook for Gran, I suppose, with Rachel gone."

"If you miss your sister I can have Cole send her back."

"No, thanks. You working on Black Friday, too?"

"Yep, and the Saturday."

Ash passed a cane truck bearing a load of billeted stalks to the mill. Chaff pecked against his windshield. Nothing stopped the harvest, neither Sundays nor holidays, until all the fields were cleared. Big inroads left huge empty spaces in the landscape. He parked in the lot across the street from the family-run cafeteria, and they got in line with the last of the Sunday diners. Leah chose the thick pork loin in onion gravy over rice, greens studded with cubes of turnips, and carrot soufflé, as good as a dessert in its sweetness for her and Gran. Ash made up a vegetable plate and had the girl box a piece of coconut cream pie six inches high with its topping. Leah guessed he could get away with that since he ate only vegetables, but not her.

They retraced their journey, going to her grandmother's house instead of the barn. As Leah got out balancing four go-boxes under her chin, she warned, "I never know how I'll find her."

Ash divested her of her burden. "I understand—good days, bad days."

Leah opened the side door and followed the sound of scratchy old records playing songs of the Forties and Fifties to the front parlor. Gran had raised the blinds letting in the winter sunshine, but sat with her eyes closed, humming along to the music. She rested in a wing chair upholstered in a floral pattern that very nearly matched her dress. Her Sunday pearls adorned her crepey neck along with her emergency button.

"Leah and a handsome guest," Alene said as she raised her paper-thin lids and allowed her green eyes to show. A good day then and Leah was thankful.

"We brought you some lunch. Have you eaten yet?"

"I'm not sure. Father Ardoin brought the Eucharist today. That's about all he does now with the younger priest taking over. We had a nice chat."

Thank heaven Gran opened the door for the elderly man. "This is…"

"Captain Blaise. How nice of you to call." Alene pushed up on the arms of her chair and made her way to a matching loveseat. She patted the space next to her. "Do sit beside me. I don't know what the world would do without brave firemen like you."

Ash handed the boxes to Leah and accepted her grandmother's offer. "I guess I'll go into the kitchen and put the food on some plates." Alene paid no attention to her. How did Gran know Ash? From his picture in the paper, she supposed, and the long article praising his heroism at the hall.

Since the Lord provided a good day, Leah took the fine china from the heavy breakfront in the formal dining room and set out the silver from its flannel-lined drawers. She arranged the food on the plates—green, orange, and brown in a tempting array—even putting the dinner rolls on separate little dishes, and poured ice water into the fine crystal glasses. With a tweak of the dimmer switch, she turned up the lights on the chandelier and called the others to Sunday dinner.

"Nice. You have a lovely home, Mrs. Allain," Ash complimented as he held out the chair for the elderly woman. She sat with grace and proceeded to fixate on Leah's lover for the rest of the meal as she ate the roast her granddaughter had cut into small pieces. When Leah brought Ash his mountainous piece of pie, Alene fluttered her butterfly lids and begged for a small piece from his fork. He cut the piece in half and slid it onto her bread dish.

"Please bring us coffee and sherry in the parlor, Dot," she said as Leah began to remove the dishes. "After you clean up, you may have the afternoon off."

Despite being relegated to a servant, still a good day, Leah guessed as she hand washed the silver, crystal, and china and put it back in the breakfront. Chores done, she carried the coffee service and the tinkling sherry glasses to the parlor on a silver tray to find Ash gently dancing with Alene to the old tunes, their feet barely moving on the hardwood floor. Leah suppressed a wish to cut in and satisfied herself with a slug of sherry washed down with strong, dark coffee.

Eventually, her grandmother tired and took a seat, again next to Ash, relegating Leah to the wingchair. "I do believe I shall rest now."

"We should go. I put a plate with the leftovers in the refrigerator for you. Pop that in the microwave for your supper, okay, Gran?"

Head nearly resting on Ash's broad shoulder, Alene slept already, her chest and fallen breasts rising slightly with each breath. "We should go. She's likely to sleep the rest of the day and be up all night. Thanks for being so kind to her."

"Any time," Ash said, though she noted an odd tone in his voice.

Leah lowered the blinds again and let them out. In the safety of the car, she asked, "What did she say to you?"

"Don't take this wrong, but I think your granny hit on me. She made sure I knew she was a widow now. That if she stayed put in her house she knew I'd come to her. Maybe that's where you get your vixen genes."

Leah winced, remembering Colton. "She confessed to having an affair before her marriage, but I can't believe she cheated on my grandfather. They were a deal is a deal kind of couple and saw it through until death they did part. Do you think Gran hit on Harold Tweedy all those years ago, and that's another reason Ernestine hates me?"

"Miz Tweedy showed me a picture of her late husband while you were gone. Skinny little dude with a big mustache to make up for it, makes me think no way. Allie, she asked me to call her that, likes big men. By the way she patted my cheek I'd say she prefers clean-shaven."

Leah, glad she didn't have to drive, buried her burning face in her hands. "So sorry! I've heard those with dementia might engage in inappropriate sexual behavior, but did not see this coming."

"My grandfather went ape shit when Rachel came to the house, so we're even on that score. Forget about it. Only trouble is I've been truant too long. The aide doesn't come on Sundays. I need to go give my mom a break when I'm not working."

"I understand entirely."

Back at the barn, Ash walked her to her door and laid a lingering kiss on her lips, but did not enter. "Too tempting," he said.

Leah nodded. "Say, we're releasing Putin by the dock downtown on Friday at noon if you want to come to his launch party. I hope he doesn't sink the way Cubby keeps sneaking him food."

"It's a short walk from the station. Maybe we can grab lunch together."

"I'd like that."

A good but most peculiar day ended with a bloody red sunset over the fallow fields and the stellar warrior Orion catapulting into the night sky as Leah took Stubby out to pee and kept Bandit inside since the feral cats gathered for their dinner around six-thirty. Her new dog hardly bothered to yap at them, though she tied him up while filling the pans with food and fresh water. The clowder of cats viewed him with acute suspicion, but weren't about to give up their meal. She ended her evening on the sofa with both the cat and the dog in her lap watching Rachel's TV and thinking, thinking, thinking about her and Ash, and the little things—and some of the big ones—that didn't matter.

Chapter Twenty

Leah stuffed Putin into a pet carrier like a turkey into a small oven. She lacked Cubby's muscle today since he'd decided the fire station needed him more right after Thanksgiving. He probably counted on there being leftovers in the firehouse fridge. None here at the shelter. She'd relied on Walmart to provide a spread for four from the rolls to the pumpkin pie, more than enough for Gran and herself and Rachel if she showed. She took a share home and left the rest carefully labeled for Alene who fell asleep mid-afternoon as usual.

With a lift from the knees and a heave, Leah put the carrier in the rear of her SUV and headed for the steamboat dock by the little park along the bayou. A small gathering awaited her arrival: Beverly Labbe, Ash, Cubby, and Miz Tweedy, whom she'd invited in an attempt at friendship. Bev clutched a little basket covered with a checkered napkin. Cubby waved, but Ash hurried over to help her with the obese fowl that at first seemed reluctant to leave the refuge of the cage.

Beverly, who had come to visit the duck at the shelter, crouched down low. "Come out, Putin. Don't you see Empress and your other friends waiting for you by the water? I have something for you. Remember these?" She disrobed a corn muffin from the basket. Leah sighed. Hopefully, Putin would be able to swim from danger, because she doubted he'd get off the ground in his current condition. Bev crumbled a muffin and made a trail toward the stream.

"Here duckie, duckie, duckie," she coaxed.

"Oh for heaven's sake, he'll come out when he's ready," Miz Tweedy said. "However, I do appreciate the invitation to the release. I find it uplifting every time a bird is set free."

Glad Miz Tweedy found anything uplifting, Leah tilted the carrier, and Putin slid out like a butter-basted fowl. He waddled along, low to the ground, pecking at the trail of crumbs to Bev's delight. The other ducks caught on and crowded around him.

"How happy they are to see him again! I have to thank you and this young lady for saving him." Ash and Leah received big hugs tight to Mrs. Labbe's soft bosom. Cubby lined up for one and got it.

"Ah, Mrs. Labbe, I have to ask you to lay off the corn muffins when feeding the ducks. Here, take the remaining pellets. Use these. They are healthier, and the ducks really won't care. They'll still come to your yard. The ranch supply store on the edge of town carries them." Leah waited for a reaction and received backup from an unexpected source.

Miz Tweedy spoke up with great authority. "She's absolutely right, Beverly. You do that bird no favor by feeding him the wrong food. I use only the choicest natural seeds for my feathered friends, but a duck being more of a barnyard animal, I suppose the pellets are the best."

Mrs. Labbe pressed two pudgy fingers to her lips. "Oh my, I didn't mean to harm them. You take the rest of my muffins. Share them."

Leah found herself with a basket in her hand. "Um,

now that Putin is back in his natural habitat, I have some errands to run. I'm going to move my car to the little lot where Domengeaux's used to be, take some of my wildlife photos to the galley, then grab a sandwich at Subway." She glanced Ash's way and got a nod. Cubby eyed the muffins. "Here, take these to the station. Lex should get one since he helped free Putin from the chimney."

Knowing the contents would never reach the firehouse, she handed them off to Cubby who rooted in the pouch of his sagging gray hoodie, pulling out a Bic lighter, and a bunch of candy wrappers before unearthing a ten dollar bill. "Mama said she had other things to do, no time to pack my lunch. I want a twelve inch meatball sub with extra cheese and *no* veggies."

Ash took the money. "I have a list of sandwiches to get for the guys. I'll take care of it, Cubby. You go back to the firehouse." He sent the boy on his way with his backpack clattering as usual.

"Subway will never take the place of Domengeaux's, but they do make a decent sandwich," Miz Tweedy declared.

"No muffulettas, but I could *manger*," replied Beverly.

"You two go ahead. We'll catch up." Leah encouraged them to move along with a nod of her head. Miz Tweedy appeared pleased to have a companion interested in birds of at least one variety. The two set off for Main Street, heads bent together over the best seed to attract finches. She addressed Ash. "It might take a while to order all those sandwiches. Meet you there after I see Zola—when the crowd has cleared." She took another ten from her pocket. "A six-inch club on whole wheat with all the veggies, American cheese, light mayo, regular mustard."

Ash shoved her bill away. "My treat. Nice day, only a little chilly. We could eat in the park. Feed the ducks."

"Yeah, right. See you in fifteen." She got into her SUV and passed him as he walked the two blocks to the sandwich shop. He waved, not at all concerned that she didn't offer a lift. They were, after all, trying to kill time.

Leah parked in the small lot opposite the oak-canopied village green where a battered old farm truck parked in front of the statue of Ste. Jeanne d' Arc obscured the view. Not that anyone cared. Black Friday in Chapelle meant most of the populace had gone to shop in the malls of Lafayette. Main Street appeared deserted. Plenty of parking for a change. She removed the box with her photos all nicely encased in plastic sleeves from the rear of her car. Blowing away one of Putin's stray feathers, Leah carried it past the Subway, LeClerc's jewelry store, and into Zola Sweat's gallery. The bell rang. Two cats, one black, one pumpkin-colored, who lounged in the store window among the artwork on display, pricked their ears and stared.

From the spicy aroma, Leah gathered Zola heated gumbo for her lunch upstairs. She wasn't alone, however. A young woman around Leah's age, taller, slender and delicate, stood by the counter with her own box. Not a customer then, but a fellow artist. She possessed the large, dark eyes of so many Cajuns and the thick mop of curling black hair to go with it, but her complexion tended toward pale rather than olive. "Angelle LeBlanc, home for the holidays," Leah greeted.

"Leah—Leah Allain, right?"

"Absolutely. Nice to see you again. I've heard you're a big Chicago artist now."

"Hardly. I earn my living doing restoration work mostly and paint on the side." Angelle selected a few matted prints from her box and spread them out on the counter. "Sketches of the church, live oaks, Chateau Camille before it burned—stuff tourists and locals like to buy. I leave some for Zola each time I visit, and she sends me a check now and then. How about you?"

"Wildlife photography. Just a hobby. I'm running Safe Haven Animal Shelter now."

Angelle nodded. "Yes, I remember your fondness for animals and how outdoorsy you were."

Leah supposed she could have been remembered for worse things, like losing her prom date to her little sister. Before they could wander any further down a murky memory lane, Zola clomped downstairs in her clogs to see what they had to offer.

She sifted through the boxes. "Both of you bring your best. I like that. I'll get them in the inventory and out for Christmas sales soon's I eat—Naw Or'lins style okra-turkey gumbo. Want to stay for a bite?"

"Thanks, but I'm meeting someone for lunch," Leah said immediately.

Zola's thin-plucked eyebrows rose in her mocha moon of a face. "Valiant firefighter Ashton Blaise is my guess. He paid five hundred-dollars for a kayak trip with this gal," she informed Angelle. "How'd that go?"

"Memorable," was all she was willing to share.

Zola threw back her head in a hearty suggestive laugh. "I'll just bet. I think that be him lookin' for you

220

now."

Sure enough, Ash peered in through the front window trying to spot her inside, but the tinting to preserve the art made that difficult. Angelle also spoke her apologies. "Thank you, but I should get the truck back to the ranch. My younger brothers are home and have taken off in all the good vehicles. I should return it in case my dad wants to go somewhere."

The former classmates exited together. Leah made the introductions. "Ash, I want you to meet Angelle LeBlanc. Remember, I mentioned her." She really wished he wouldn't size up Angelle like a potential suspect, no charming smile on his face, his gray eyes intense. If possible, Angelle grew more pallid beneath his stare. Leah caught a flicker of light out of the corner of her eye that grew into a flare, followed by a shattering of glass, and a stupendous whoosh of flame rising from the bed of the old truck.

Angelle flattened herself against the gallery window as if she wanted to push herself through the glass. The flames reflected in the dark pupils of her eyes. "No, she's dead. This can't be happening again!" She slid to the ground and buried her face behind her knees.

"Does Zola have an extinguisher?" Ash asked.

"Behind the counter, I think."

"Call 911 and get the boys up here. Then take her inside and give her water, some Coke, whatever."

Phone already in hand, Leah did exactly as he asked. As she helped Angelle up and wound an arm around her narrow waist for support, Ash dashed past with Zola's extinguisher and began sweeping the truck with its foam. The fire siren sounded, bringing life to the street in the form of shop owners and ladies out to lunch come outside to gawk. The smallest of the fire trucks arrived on the scene. All traffic lights turned red, and Lex in full gear began directing the scanty traffic away from the area. Neil piled more foam on the burning truck already guttering out. His wide blue eyes avid with excitement, Cubby arrived panting on their heels.

"Stay back," Ash ordered. "Nothing you can do here."

"What about my sandwich?"

"Go get it in the shop. It's paid for. Stay there." He shouted to Leah sheltering with Angelle in the doorway. "Get inside, I said."

"She keeps collapsing on me. Harder than getting a kayak off a car top." Still, she had time to admire the way he took charge and gave orders. Zola, one big woman, came to her aid. They got the shivering Angelle inside and seated on the bottom step to Zola's quarters. The gallery owner pressed a bottle of water to Angelle's lips and wrapped one of the colorful hand-crocheted shawls the shop stocked around her thin shoulders.

The crisis flickered out in minutes. Except for having to maneuver around the orange cones set around the burned out truck, the piddling traffic resumed with drivers craning to see the wreckage at the feet of Ste. Jeanne, who continued to gaze toward heaven as if she had bigger problems of her own. Ash strode across the street and joined the women in the shop.

He knelt by Angelle, his gaze kinder now, his voice soothing. "Sorry to have to ask, but did you see who set your truck on fire?"

Angelle shook her head. "I was looking at you. Sorry I'm such a mess, but I have this sort of PTSD reaction to fire."

Leah gave him an "I told you so glare" and appreciated that he didn't press her friend further. Zola volunteered, "Saw someone run out from behind the statue. Thought he carried one of those big candles from the church at first, then boom! Man, I leave Naw Or'lins and still have to put up with crap like this, settin' cars on fire."

"Why would anyone torch my dad's old truck?" Angelle, doing a bit better, asked.

"Because kids now days got shit for brains, and nothing better to do. Too many video games, you ask me." Zola's earrings, today copper triangles dangling small alligator teeth, shook with her anger.

"Can you give me a description?" Ash persisted.

"White, stocky, gray hoodie. Couldn't see the face."

Leah met those smoky gray eyes over Zola's head. "Cubby," she mouthed. He nodded.

"Miss LeBlanc, can we call someone? Would you like to see a doctor?"

"No, not a doctor. My stepmother is director of the library. She's in town and knows how to deal with my episodes since I've had them most of my life. Dad would come, but he doesn't have transportation. I learned to drive in that old truck, and now it's gone, just like Chateau Camille." A shudder passed through her thin body.

Zola hugged Angelle tight. "I'll take care of her until Miz LeBlanc gets here."

"Thanks. I have to speak to someone." Ash rose

and started for the door.

Leah tailed him. "I need to hear this with Cubby hanging around the shelter. He could be a danger to the animals and the other volunteers."

Outside, Ash paused. "I told the Chief that Cubby might have a problem after the fire at the Mardi Gras hall. Someone turned up the gas and dumped the vat of peanut oil on the range. The Chief says he left the oil on a table clear across the room, nowhere near the stove. Cubby and his mother were the last to go into the kitchen as far as I know. I wanted to turn it over to the police, but Tank is Cliff's old friend, and Cubby almost a mascot. He said after the holiday weekend, we'd call the family in and have a talk with them."

"Maybe you'd better move that up before someone gets hurt,"

"So far we've been lucky with these arson cases, usually buildings no one cares enough about to investigate, lots of broken glass around the sites anyhow, but I'm thinking Molotov cocktails, crude but effective. All you need is a bottle, some gasoline, rags for a wick, and all hell breaks loose when it smashes."

"Cubby carries bottles around with him in that knapsack. You saw the lighter he had."

They entered the sandwich shop to find the boy in a booth by himself and Bev and Ernestine gone. He greeted them happily. "That was some fire, little but still good, Captain Blaise."

"Cubby, there are no good fires. People might have been hurt. Do you know what a Molotov cocktail is?"

The boy's blue eyes evaded Ash's stare. "Yep, I know. You make 'em with bottles and gas."

"That's right. Did you throw one of those into the

truck?"

Cubby's glance met his captain's. "Nope. But, those LeBlancs deserved it. A person in their family burned down the Cat'lic church over there. You can go to hell for burning any kind of church." His attention turned back to the meatball sub. He took a big bite, and the marinara sauce dribbled down his chin onto his gray hoodie.

"Where were you right before the fire?"

"At the station playing with Sparky. She's a nice dog, not like my mama's bitch." Cubby relished the word bitch for a moment before offering an open bag of chips. "Want some?"

Lex, still in full gear, walked over to the counter to claim the rest of the sandwiches and joined the conversation. "Nothing like a truck fire to whet the appetite," he said. "We got the cleanup done and sent for a truck to tow the hulk off Main Street before the mayor calls about eyesores in front of our scenic church. Cops are going over the scene now. Not much to find but a broken liquor bottle. Fire wipes out most everything."

"Have them check for footprints behind the statue. Zola said someone darted out from there."

"Will do."

"Wasn't I playing with Sparky when the siren went off, Mr. Lex?" Cubby asked.

"Sure was. Throwing sticks. She loves to retrieve." Lex dumped out Ash's twelve-inch cheese and veggie. "This short one must be yours, Leah. Glad I got the Subway B.M.T. The meatball would be soggy by now. Enjoy. See you back at the station, Captain."

"You gonna eat with me?" Cubby paused in eating

and took a big swig from a giant soft drink.

"No, Leah and I will take our lunch to the park. After that, I have a report to write. Don't forget our meeting at five on Monday. Remind your parents."

"Okay. Got my change? I want some cookies."

Ash doled out a few bills and led Leah away to get her unsweetened iced tea while he filled a cup with root beer. They left together and found a bench in the sunshine away from ducks.

"Do you think Cubby is lying?" Leah asked, catching a few escaped black olives from her sub on the wrapper in her lap as she bit into it.

"Doesn't seem to be. You can usually tell with him. What worries me is he's so suggestible, always does what he's told. If someone hinted that truck should be destroyed, he might go ahead and do it, but Lex did vouch for him. Cubby is eighteen, but I really shouldn't have questioned him without his parents present given his mental state. I could have messed up a case for the police. I guess we'll have them present for the interview on Monday."

"Do you believe it's safe to wait that long?"

"I don't think I can push it with the Chief. Be careful around Cubby until then, okay."

His concern showed in those gray eyes Leah had come to love and trust. "He's supposed to volunteer on Monday afternoon. I'll make sure he's not alone until his mother picks him up."

"Good. I don't want anything bad to happen to you." Ash leaned in, licked a dab of mayo from her lips, and laid on a kiss—in broad daylight on a public bench. In Chapelle, Louisiana, that amounted to commitment, especially if anyone noticed and passed the word.

When Leah opened her eyes again, she said, "Uh oh. Here comes Putin and his flock. I swear that duck can hear a crumb drop a block away."

"Give the guy a break. Leave him the rest of your bun. It is whole wheat."

"The things you make me do." Leah shredded the end of bread and tossed it as far as she could. "We both need to make our getaway."

Chapter Twenty-One

Tense, that described Leah on Monday when Mrs. Couvillon dumped Cubby at the shelter and sped away around three p.m. Yancey showed up with Dirk Keene, available for more good deeds now that the high school football season had ended. Mostly, he wanted to impress Yancey with his love of animals, Leah suspected. She put all three of them to work walking the dogs as usual and tried to get some paperwork done. Ethel took off for the cattery to play with the current occupants. The minutes dragged slowly toward five with only Mr. Grey muttering, "Give it to me, baby," from time to time. She did not expect the ruckus when it came.

A cacophony of voices headed toward the office: Ethel scolding, Dirk swearing, Yancey crying, and Cubby babbling. She went to meet them in the open. Ethel, a short bridge between two big pylons, grasped Dirk and Cubby by the ears, an old school punishment sometimes used by the nuns at Ste. Jeanne's. Leah held up her hands. "Everyone quiet. Ethel, tell me what happened."

"These two young bucks were rolling in the dirt, fighting over Yancey. I heard them shouting outside the cattery and went to see. There's Yancey weeping and pleading and the boys beating on each other. I mean Cubby is big, but Dirk here, knows how to pack a punch. Really, picking on a poor half-witted child." Ethel gave the captain of the football team an extra tweak of lobe. "I broke it up."

"But, but he…" Dirk said as he tried to escape the old woman's lethal pinch.

Leah folded her arms and put on her leader of the pack voice. "Okay. Now Yancey, what started all this?"

"Dirk went to put the dogs we were walking into the kennel and get the next bunch. Cubby and I waited near the cattery. All of a sudden, he pushed me against the wall and grabbed both my breasts. He said he loved me." Yancey whimpered a little, stopped herself, and went on. "Dirk saw him and pulled him off of me. Cubby pushed him. They started fighting and both went down. That's when Miss Ethel intervened."

"Cubby, is this true?"

Cubby turned as brilliant a red as Mr. Grey's tail. "Yancey likes me. She danced with me at the ball. When a girl likes you, she lets you touch her breasts."

"Not that way! I don't like you that way, Cubby," Yancey stated emphatically. "My dad won't let me work here again with him around." She began to snivel once more.

Miss Ethel's grip on the two young men weakened. Dirk broke free to put his arms around Yancey, and she snuggled against his chest. In the background, Leah became aware of loose dogs tearing around the compound in a delighted chase.

"Yancey, Dirk. Go catch those dogs and get them in their kennels. Cubby, inside with me. Ethel, you come, too. I need a witness." The three entered the office.

Mr. Grey set up a chant of Cub-bee, Cub-bee, and

the boy reached for the jar of nuts. "Mr. Grey will have to wait for a treat. What you did was very wrong, Cubby. You cannot touch a woman's breasts without permission."

"But she's my girlfriend. I set her trashcan on fire last Halloween because you do that to get a girl's attention some of the guys said."

Leah stored that statement away to give to Ash later. "Yancey is a girl and your friend, but not a girlfriend. I think she likes Dirk better."

Cubby began to cry. Bloody snot ran from his nose, and he wiped it on the sleeve of his navy blue jogging outfit with a white racing stripe up the side. Shoving pity aside, Leah continued to lay down the law. "Yancey has been a volunteer here for several years while you've only been working a few months. I'm afraid I'll have to ask you not to come here again. I'm going to call your mother and explain what happened. She needs to pick you up right now."

Cubby sank into the visitor's chair, folded his arms on Leah's desk, and cried his heart out, his whole blubbery body shaking hard, as she made the call. The reaction from the parent was not what she expected. As Mrs. Couvillon screamed at her about little whores and the innocence of her boy, Leah held the receiver away from her ear and waited for the tirade to end.

"I'm sorry you feel that way, but you need to come get your son. He can't work here again." She had no need to say more because the woman disconnected.

"Want me to stay with you?" Ethel Murphy asked.

"Yes, please. Cubby, wait for your mother outside," Leah answered, though she had the overwhelming urge to call Ash. Instead, she dealt with the Breaux and Keene families next. Mrs. Keene promised her husband would talk to their son. "It's just that he is so crazy about Yancey. Very protective." Mr. Breaux threatened a lawsuit for sexual assault and forbid his daughter from continuing to work at the shelter. Leah hoped he'd calm down and reconsider both statements.

The unmistakable roar of Mrs. Couvillon's huge vehicle approached. Leah braced herself for confrontation, and it came blasting into the office in the form of Eunice wearing a track suit identical to her son's and dragging Cubby by the hand.

"You bitch, taking the side of that slut of a girl and the kid who's probably banging her. They made up that story about my poor boy who wouldn't hurt anyone." Eunice leaned way over the desk, close enough to spray the spittle of her outrage in Leah's face.

Leah back pedaled in her chair. Ethel raised the telephone to her ear. Leah gave her the "wait" sign. "Regardless, Cubby cannot come here again. He has no impulse control. You need to watch him more closely."

"I've given my life to caring for Cubby. Cliff is well-connected in this town. He'll have your job." Mrs. Couvillon's plain face lit with sinister glee.

Leah mustered calmness. "You know we are a non-profit unconnected to the parish powers that be. The pay is nothing to tempt anyone, so you go right ahead if you want." She bluffed. Losing Cliff's support meant a big loss of donations for the shelter. Personally, losing this job might mean leaving Chapelle, her grandmother—and Ash.

"We'll get rid of you one way or the other." Cubby said nothing, just kept crying, as his mother dragged him from the office in the same way they'd entered. The Couvillons peeled out and were gone.

Leah exhaled. A timid knock sounded on the door. Dirk and Yancey entered. "The dogs are all rounded up. I guess we'll leave now. Dirk is driving me home."

"Be careful. Yancey, see if you can reason with your dad. We'd hate to lose you as a volunteer."

"I'll explain how I defended Yancey from that—that blob," Dirk asserted, winding an arm around Yancey's waist.

"I'd go lightly with Mr. Breaux. Good luck to you both." And to me, Leah thought.

Alone at last with Ethel, Leah noticed the clock had rapidly reached five. Right now, Ash and the Chief might be informing Cliff Couvillon about his son's problem with fire. What an afternoon. Leah raked her fingers through her short, thick hair. "Oh, Ethel, you can go. I'll lock up."

"Thought I'd have to call the police for a minute there."

"Me, too, but if we are lucky we won't see Mrs. Couvillon again. I do feel sorry for Cubby, but his troubles go way beyond the shelter."

"Well, the older female volunteers have been telling me for some time that Cubby hugs them a little too long," Ethel said a tad too avidly.

"You should have told me.

Ethel shrugged. "Maybe they like being felt up by a young man, but mostly I think they don't want to make trouble for the Couvillons. That Eunice is a nasty piece of work for all her church going, but Cliff does the best he can by them. But, I gather there's even more to it?"

No sense in winding up the gossip mill. "Maybe I can tell you later. Let's go home."

****

Dark fell so quickly in late November. Leah fed the ferals, herself, Stubby and Bandit. Again she wished she'd taken the time and spent the money to put up curtains over that wide back window. She took a glass of wine with her to the sofa, turned on the TV, and subdued another urge to call Ash. Only six-thirty. He might still be in conference with the Couvillons. Stubby and Bandit piled onto the couch with her, warming her feet. Diverting as *Wheel of Fortune* could be and not needing anymore puzzles in her life, Leah dozed after the stress of the day.

Stubby's weak little bark woke her. At the end of the couch, Bandit arched and bristled as he stared into the night. Groggy, Leah traced the arc of fire across her lawn, heard the thud against the back of the barn, before she registered Molotov cocktail. The adrenalin surge got her off the sofa and over to the fire extinguisher mounted near the kitchen. She ripped it from its wall socket and sprinted to the back door nearest the flames. Remembering the instructions to pull the pin and stand back, she swept the spray from side to side and prayed the contents would be enough to put out a conflagration far more serious than a grease fire on her stove.

"Help is on the way!" someone shouted—not Ash. If only it were.

Ernestine Tweedy arrived dragging the hose from the side of the barn just as the extinguisher emptied. She used the gentle shower setting for this emergency, putting out small pools of flaming gas that had escaped Leah's blast. "I've heard you shouldn't blast gas as that

233

might spread it. Just drown it, that nice young firefighter said."

The fire subsided, leaving both women side by side, night blind and breathing hard for a few minutes. "I went outside to give Yapper his potty break and heard one of those ATVs that tear up the land running along the back of my property and in the dark of all insane things to do. Yapper began barking. Before I could flag the ATV down and give the driver a piece of my mind, it passed onto your property and stopped. I tied up my dog and started the long way around to scold you and your guest, but when I saw fire, I tunneled through the pampas grass to get here quicker. Called 9-1-1 on the run." Ernestine patted an oversized cell phone meant for the aged that protruded from a pocket of her housecoat.

"That's the step I forgot. I thought I could handle it myself."

"We handled it. Yes, we did!" said Ernestine triumphant.

"Thanks for your help. Go inside and sit down. Catch your breath. I'll turn off the water."

When Leah returned, she noticed several shallow, bleeding cuts from the fiendish shrubbery on Miz Tweedy's aged face, her muddy slippers, damp housecoat—and the empty glass of wine that had been half full on the coffee table. The noses of her fearless dog and cat poked out from under the sofa.

"Sorry, I needed something to steady my nerves," Ernestine confessed.

"No problem. I'll bring both of us another glass. You're bleeding a little. Why don't you clean up in the bathroom? I have some antibiotic cream in the medicine cabinet."

Leah put some cheese and crackers on a plate, brought it, the bottle and an extra glass to the table. Ernestine returned with her face washed and small, greasy streaks of antiseptic cream on her face. The old woman seized the stem of her refilled glass and chugged down half.

"I was a sight, and I've muddied on your clean floors." Miz Tweedy's eyes tracked around the room. "Never been in here before. Nice place for a barn. This is very hospitable of you considering the way I've treated you." She held out her wine glass for a top off.

Leah obliged her. "Did you see who threw the bottle?"

"A person wearing dark clothes, but with a white stripe up the leg like the skunk he is. Didn't get a good look as he was running away, but I believe I know the culprit. I might have accidently encouraged him to burn down my own granny's house, your place, I mean, with my words." Shamefaced would have described Miz Tweedy's demeanor right this moment.

"Cubby?"

"Yes, I'm afraid so. His daddy has rent houses along this road and comes out to do maintenance always bringing Cubby with him. Poor addled boy, I invite him in for teacakes. He loves my teacakes."

Cubby loved all food as far as Leah could tell, but she didn't pass along the remark to the suddenly cooperative Miz Tweedy. "I had to fire him as a volunteer at the shelter today for fighting with another young man and harassing some of the women. I guess he wanted to get back at me."

"Maybe so, but the first time I complained and

complained about your feral cats to the boy. I don't get much company, you see. No one to listens to me. I said if you hadn't moved in and kept feeding them, they'd be gone by now. With him always hanging around the firehouse, Cubby is comfortable with fire. I told Captain Blaise all this when he brought me Yapper. Sorry about some of the other things I said to him. Times are different now. If an unmarried young woman wants to have an affair, what business is it of mine? Back in the day, though, standards were higher, especially among teachers." Ernestine's censure petered out.

Leah tried to stoke it with a bit more wine if the story concerned her grandmother. The sound of shrieking sirens approached, setting off Yapper next door, and shutting up Miz Tweedy who checked her watch, a mannish Timex with a big dial. "I called the fire department ten minutes ago. Seems like it took ages for them to get here."

"An eternity," Leah agreed. Knowing Ash to be off duty except for that appointment with Cubby and his family, still she counted on him to be with the firefighters. A knock, masterful and demanding, pounded on one of the front doors. She went to answer.

Ash stood there in his full gear much like the day she'd met him. "Where's the fire?"

"It was around the back of the barn, but it's out now."

Ash signaled to the team to check the rear. "Fire's out, but check for hot spots. Tell me what happened."

"Someone rode in on an ATV and threw a Molotov cocktail. Fortunately, it hit the window frame, not the glass, or I'd be burned out again. I used the extinguisher and my neighbor ran to my aid with a hose." Even under the shadow cast by his helmet, she noticed Ash's black brows shoot up.

"Miz Tweedy?"

"The same. She came clean about encouraging Cubby to burn my house, though I believe she never intended him to go so far. He might have been responsible for tonight's attempt. I had to dismiss him from the shelter for getting way too close to Yancey and inciting Dirk to defend her *mano a mano*. He admitted to setting the Breaux's trashcan on fire Halloween night. Cubby cried, Ash, but his mother got right in my face with threats and not a little spit. Damn scary. She might have put him up to this tonight—but didn't you and the Chief talk to him earlier?"

"The Couvillons failed to show. We'll have to ask for a warrant to bring him in for questioning. His confession about the trashcan isn't much, but it does provide a base for our suspicions."

Ash's co-captain reported in. "Looks clear back there, a little char on the wood, but no major damage."

"Look, head off any other volunteers answering the call. I'll stay and take down the report for you."

"Sure you will," the older man said. He gave Leah an appraising leer and an approving nod, but immediately switched back to professional and herded his men to their vehicles.

"Nothing stays cool at the firehouse for long. They all know how much I paid for that kayak trip and are curious if I got my money's worth. None of their damn business."

Holding herself up with one hand against the wall, Ernestine Tweedy tottered down the long hallway knocking some of Leah's framed photos askew. She waved the wine bottle clutched in her fingers. "Empty. My nerves need more calming."

"I'm afraid I'm all out. Should you be drinking so much with any meds you might be taking?" Leah asked.

Ernestine peered at her like an offended hen with feathers very ruffled. "I only take aspirin for the arthritis. I'm tough. Don't need anything else."

"Let's polish off the cheese and crackers then. I'm sure Captain Blaise will help you back to the sofa."

He did, shoring up the old woman with an arm around her waist and carrying his helmet. However, the cheese had been devoured. Bandit sat on the coffee table nonchalantly hooking the little cubes into Stubby's open mouth. Best buddies, indeed. Co-conspirators more likely. Ash managed to get a semi-coherent account from Miz Tweedy before seeing her home and letting Yapper into her house.

Back at Leah's, he took off the heavy jacket, listened to her story, and repeated Ernestine's tale. "I'll go over Miz Tweedy's account again tomorrow once she sobers up."

"When she talked to you, she added in the ATV being neon green like the one Cliff Couvillon bought at the auction."

"Details come to people even in her condition. More evidence for us. It bothers me that Cubby attacked your place knowing you were home. He's never threatened people before unless he took part in the bordello fire, but I don't like him for that. He loved going there and frequently told us all the details. But, this incident tonight makes it all the more important we find him. Want to lie down for a while? I'll keep watch."

"No, too wired, and Ernestine really did drink all my wine. Can you stay the night?"

"Since you asked me. No work tomorrow, but I have to call my mother. Yeah, I know how weak that sounds."

Leah shook her head. "It sounds caring to me considering your situation at home."

"Mom will feed my grandfather a sedative like she does when I'm working my shift to keep him quiet. I hate doing that, but we don't have much choice. She's not a strong woman. He could still overpower her easily enough and wander off." Ash placed the call. His mother made no objections.

"You know what would really relax me?" Leah asked, throwing in an impish smile.

"I'm hoping sex."

"I grant your wish, but I do have one desire of my own. Remember how you wanted to make love to me in my ball gown?"

"Best fantasy ever." Ash's smile went full blown like a fire fanned by the wind.

"For you. I can breathe a lot better when not laced up. Mine is to have a fireman in full gear."

"You just came up with that. Look, this outfit is heavy and hot. I'll sweat on you like it's raining."

"Put your on jacket and helmet right now or the deal is off."

He complied fairly fast. Leah hooked a finger into one of the latches of his jacket and led him to the bedroom. "Let it rain, let it pour," she said as she kicked the door shut in the faces in the faces of Bandit and Stubby who had tagged along. "No pets in the bedroom."

A light rain began to pelt the metal roof of the barn. Inside, Ash poured himself into Leah.

Chapter Twenty-Two

If Ash didn't have to work, Leah did. Reluctantly, she left for the shelter, the first to arrive as always. She unlocked the gates and drove into the compound, belatedly noticing a heap of broken bottles in the gravel as she rolled over them in the early morning light. The glass crackled beneath her tires. She parked and grabbed a broom and dustpan. No place for sharp edges with so many animals and people running around. Up close, she could see the glass lay in a ring of blackened dirt. Lucky a good, steady rain fell last night soaking the earth and maybe putting out the fire. Most of the shelter buildings were metal or cement block, not easily set afire, thank heaven.

Leah swept the shards into the dustpan and placed them in a garbage bag right before her volunteers started showing up to give the animals their breakfast. She patrolled the grounds and found a wine bottle still intact that had bounced off the office and landed in a puddle with its burnt wick still in place and the gasoline it contained floating inside its green walls. A chill ran down her spine as she considered that Mr. Grey, pest that he was, might have been nothing but a charred bundle of feathers this morning if the building caught fire. Going inside to call Ash, she uncovered the large bird cage and gave the parrot a heaping handful of nuts and a clump of grapes along with his regular food. "Leah, baby," he sighed in contentment. Seemed like Ash said about the same last night. With all her troubles, she smiled. Sometimes, men could be animals, and she loved animals.

Leah made the call to Ash and caught him still at her place. He'd been next door to confirm Miz Tweedy's testimony and enjoyed the second breakfast of her hot biscuits with homemade fig preserves while the old woman sipped a glass of tomato juice laced with hot sauce for her sore head. No changes in her story. Leah filled him in on what she'd found at the shelter.

"I'll take this report and my gear over to the firehouse, then stop by the shelter and investigate there. What kind of security do you have? Cameras, I hope."

"No money for that sort of thing. Who wants to break into a place to steal unwanted animals? We rely on a high fence and locked buildings in case someone thinks we have veterinary drugs or money on the property. There's a security light on a timer, but out here in the country, I doubt it is much of a deterrent."

"Did you leave the unbroken bottle where it was?"

"Yes, still in the puddle. I'll be glad when it's gone."

"Be there shortly."

As it turned out Ash's brief visit to photograph and bag the defunct cocktail turned out to be the highlight of her day. He filled in the puddle in case any of the gas had leaked into the water and took the bagged shards along as well. Before he left with the evidence, she seduced a kiss from his lips behind the office building, the only sweetness she'd experience for the next several hours.

Around noon, a woman called asking if the shelter

would take two large white rats her son left behind when he went to college. His dorm had a no pets policy. She did not like the rats, never had, but tolerated their presence in his bedroom as long as he took care of them. Feeding them these last few months simply gave her the creeps and cleaning their cage, ugh! If the shelter would not take them, she'd have them euthanized. Of course, Leah offered to pick up the rodents as the donor had no intention of traveling with them in her car any farther than the nearest vet.

Tuesday, Ethel's casino day, meant Leah had to deal with the phones and any prospective adopters. A family with small children stopped by to look at the puppies but left undecided. A single woman wanted a cat but couldn't choose among the many and said she had to think about it. Both took up chunks of her time, and before she knew it, the clock showed four-thirty. She still hadn't picked up the rats. Might as well wait until five, lock up, and swing by for the rodents on her way home.

Darn it, the phone rang and on the other end, Vernon LaBauve went into his usual screed. "Another god-damned dog dumped on my property, a big ole brute chasing my peacocks. I got him tied up, but if you don't come get him right now, I'm gonna shoot the beast, me!"

Leah tried to rub away the incipient headache a call from Mr. LaBauve always brought on by massaging her neck with one hand. Vernon LaBauve raised peacocks on his small farm waaay out in the country on the other side of town. Yes, people often dumped dogs in the area under the mistaken impression that some kindly farmer would take them in. Ha! Mostly the animals ended up shot if they disturbed the cattle, chased the chickens, or in this case, peacocks. It would help if Mr. LaBauve caged his birds, but he did not. He allowed them to forage as it saved on the turkey feed they ate and let them fend for themselves. Face it, peacocks were simply gorgeous turkeys with raucous cries and bad tempers they exposed when flashing those many-eyed tails.

"I'll get there in an hour or so, Mr. LaBauve. Don't hurt the animal, please."

"Hurt him? My wife been feeding him part of my dinner, good round steak she was gonna smother for me. He's tied up on da porch. Mind you don't run over no peacocks when you come down the lane."

"I'll be careful."

Leah followed the last of the volunteers from the shelter and locked the gate behind her. She drove into town and found the home of the rat lady in a cul-de-sac after wandering around a small subdivision for several minutes. The woman had the cage right inside her door. She thrust it at Leah along with a bag of their food and said, "Thanks for taking the vermin off my hands," before shutting the door. No donation forthcoming for the shelter evidently. She placed the rats on the back seat, saving the cargo area for the large dog and went on her way.

Darkness crept up on her as she drove along the two lane blacktop out of town. Leah slowed as she approached the area where infrequent farm roads mostly named for the people who lived at the end of them—Bob Lane, Theriot Lane, Our Lane—branched off from it. At last, Peacock Lane painted on a tilted white post that also held the dented mailbox appeared.

She turned up the dirt and gravel path made messy by deep puddles from last night's rain and drove very slowly. Sure enough, the first peacocks materialized in the lane illuminated by her headlights, the males grand and dragging their magnificent tails in the muck, the hens so plain as to be nearly invisible. They pecked at worms driven out of the ground by the soaking. Others, gone to roost for the night, perched on the lowest branches of the live oaks festooned with Spanish moss that lined the drive. The birds began screeching as she inched the vehicle past them. All in all, kind of eerie.

Alerted by the ungodly noise, Vernon LaBauve waited on the wide porch of his sagging, unpainted Cajun farmhouse. Dressed in coveralls, a green John Deere cap, and a gray stubble of several days growth, he waved away the mosquitoes that hatched with the rain and swatted at the moths circling the porch light. "About time you got here."

Leah hadn't expected cordial and didn't get it. She got down and mounted the porch. "I picked up some other animals on the way. Let's see what who we've got here."

The dog tied to the porch post with clothesline rose immediately to greet her. Long-legged and brindled, ribs showing, a shepherd mix with something even larger tossed into the gene pool, he wore a stout leather collar with the name Gargantua on a brass plate. Intimidating in size, but he had a kind eye and a nice doggy grin. Leah reached out a closed hand and let him have a good sniff. He ended the introduction with a lick of her knuckles. "Poor abandoned guy."

"Poor guy, my Cajun ass! He took one of my peahens. Shoulda shot him."

Leah suspected Vernon LaBauve of being a softie on the inside since he'd turned in two other strays during her tenure. Indeed, he could have shot and buried them with no one any wiser. For that reason, she put up with his gruff manner and replied mildly, "With the oil industry in a slump, a lot of families are turning out big dogs like this. They require large amounts of food and when it comes to feeding them or the family, the children win. Just yesterday, we had a Great Dane surrendered."

"Not my problem. You get him off my porch."

Leah untied the rope, and Gargantua went with her happily. She opened the back hatch of her SUV. He leapt in with ease. She tied the end of the rope to one of the hooks intended for dry cleaning or transporting clothing, not large dogs, but it would have to do.

Mr. Labauve paused as he opened his front door. The enticing aroma of smothered round steak destined to be served over rice filled the air. Gargantua hadn't gotten it all. Leah's stomach gurgled. She allowed herself a fleeting wish that Ash would show up at her place and cook one of his heartier vegetarian specialties. After all, she'd given him a key this morning while enjoying his superb French toast or *pain perdu,* lost bread as the locals called it. Her stomach rumbled as she wondered if he'd left any of Miz Tweedy's biscuits for her dinner.

"You be mindful of my peacocks, *cher.* Yourself, too. A fog is coming out da ground." LaBauve turned to go inside and tripped over an escaping cat. He caught it between his heavy boots and raised it by the scruff. The pretty seal point Siamese, white with chocolate markings, hung from his tight grip. Almost as quick as the cat, the farmer clomped down the wooden steps and tossed the animal into Leah's vehicle. Garguatua gave a surprised woof. The rats squeaked in panic as the Siamese vaulted over their cage and vanished under the driver's seat.

"Take dat aggravatin' cat wit' you. Yowls all da time and never caught a mouse, no."

Oh, no, not Pad Thai again. Leah had hoped to escape without adding another passenger. The cat, named after an oriental specialty food, belonged to Mrs. LaBauve. Her husband often expressed his opinion that cats belonged in the barn, not the house. Every time she journeyed out here, he shoved that cat into the car. Mrs. LaBauve always showed up at the shelter the next day and reclaimed her cat, leaving a nice donation behind for its overnight care.

"Sure," Leah said, wanting this whole evening over and done. "Enjoy your dinner."

She got into her SUV and inched down the lane. Most of the peacocks appeared to have gone to roost, but a sinister fog gathered in the ruts. She considered trying to coax Pad Thai from under the seat and leaving her in the lane, but she knew the cat. The last time, she'd gotten clawed across the back of her hand when trying to pry Paddy from her hiding place. Only a can of Fancy Feast would do that, and Leah had none handy. Looked liked she'd have to return to the shelter and drop off all her of traveling companions.

The fog rising from the damp earth grew thicker as she neared town, about knee-high now. Flashing red lights and a siren approaching in the other lane caused her to pull over like a good citizen. A fire truck tore through the thin fabric of the mist and headed for a crossroad that led to the interstate. Probably a traffic accident that needed cleanup. Ash would not be with them, not his shift. Gargantua went wild barking and somehow managed to vault halfway over the rear seat and plant his big paws atop the rat cage slowly caving beneath his weight.

Leah got out, removed the dog by grasping his hind quarters and hauling him back into the cargo area. She gave him a "down" command and was surprised when Gargantua cooperated, putting his huge head meekly on his large feet. Beneath the front seat, a pair of glowing blue Siamese eyes stared at the rats chittering in the undamaged part of their abode. She shut the rear door in a hurry. Not too far to go now. Back on the road again, she noticed her car pulling to the left and running kind of lopsided. On the dirt lane and oft-patched blacktop, she hadn't notice the rough ride until now. A flat coming up for sure. About a mile from town and she must make it to the first well-lit gas station as quickly as possible.

The fog reached waist high and out of it on the left side of the road shambled a large, old man wearing striped pajamas. He walked along zombie-like, not signaling any distress, his eyes fixed straight ahead. From what Ash told her, Leah witnessed Dalton Blaise in the flesh chasing another siren like an old dog that couldn't help itself from going after cars. She knew he might become violent if thwarted. Leah drove on, but winkled her cell phone from a pocket and punched in 9-1-1.

"I'd like to report an elderly man in pajamas walking north along Rt. 31 about a mile from town. He seems kind of out of it. I believe it's Dalton Blaise."

"Won't be the first time," the emergency operator replied. "We'll call his family or the police if they aren't home. Thank you for reporting this."

"Please get someone out here as soon as you can. The fog is getting worse, and a car might hit him." In fact, when Leah looked in her side view mirror, the mist had swallowed the man whole.

"Will do."

Not a quarter mile later along the edge of a cane field, her left front tire began thumping so ominously she parked on the verge again and got out. Not a great place to change a tire on the soft earth siding with a water-filled drainage ditch on the far side. How should she go about it? Leah racked her brain to recall driver's education information ten years old. Get out the jack, raise the vehicle. Pry off the hubcap. Remove the lug nuts. That would be a start, but this was south Louisiana where people still stopped to help drivers in distress.

Or as Ethel once said, "Honey, when you're young and built, just get the junk out of the trunk and stand there looking helpless. Some guy will come along and do it for you." Maybe, but on a weeknight like this traffic ran pretty thin while the fog grew thicker. A small car the color of the mist approached in the far lane and whizzed past before she could wave her arms in supplication. Okay, back to Plan B.

Leah put on her flashers, pocketed her keys, and made her way to the rear, pushing Gargantua aside to get at the spare and the tools. The jack had a crowbar to insert to pump it up and use later to remove the hub cap. The lug nut wrench lay across the spare. The tire looked big and heavy in the overhead light, but if she could haul a kayak, she could do this. Gargantua strained at his rope to get out. Issuing another down command to the dog, she gathered the tools and shut the hatch to keep the big mutt and Pad Thai in place, leaving the spare to wrangle with later.

Leah got the jack in place and worked on raising the vehicle. When she figured it was high enough, she popped off the hubcap. Easy up to this point—except the lug nuts would not budge. Now what? Too late to buy a membership in Triple A. With great relief, she heard a big-engined truck approach. Ethel often proved to be right.

Slewing a little in the dirt, the truck slid in tight behind her SUV. Two big fellows stumbled out of the cab so quickly she knew they hadn't bothered with seatbelts. A third vaulted over the side of the bed and saved himself from falling by gripping the edge of the box. None of them walked too steady, and she figured out all three were drunk before they got close enough to smell the alcohol on their breath.

"Lookee what we got here, a damsel in distress." Dark hair, short beard, brown eyes, tattoos of dragons on both forearms, Leah memorized in case she needed to identify him later. She labeled him Big Jerk Number One.

"Got a big rack for a little gal," Big Jerk Number Two said, though he was somewhat smaller than the first, had dirty blond hair and the kind of pale eyes you saw on wanted by the police for questioning ads.

"Mighty cold in the rear of that truck. I could use some warming up. Can't afford Madame Mystique's girls anymore," Big Jerk Number Three commented. Face pitted with old acne scars, shaved head, eyes too small and close to a big nose among his other crude features.

If anyone had asked her to guess their profession, she would have said roughnecks laid off from the oil patch, their state of origin—not south Louisiana. No kindly, helpful Cajuns, these guys, more likely rednecks from out of state and out of work.

Leah griped the lug nut wrench as if it were some exotic four-armed ninja weapon. She flexed her knees and picked the crowbar off the ground. "I can't get the lug nuts off. I'm going to call Triple A now, so no need for you to waste your time here." She had to drop the wrench to fumble for her phone and tried to thumb in 9-1-1 in a hurry.

"She said nuts." Big Jerk Number Two giggled like an adolescent. "I got some red hot nuts you can take in hand, baby."

Big Jerk Number One swatted the phone from her grip so fast she missed a chance to hit him with the crowbar. "Get in the truck. You can call from our trailer."

"No, thanks. Say, I'll bet three big guys like you could change this tire in a flash. Then, I'll follow you over to your place for a little party." Try flattery, try anything! She experimented with a wobbly smile and a provocative hip thrust, not that her khaki slacks and shelter shirt qualified as sexy.

"Not a bad idea. Nice SUV. We could get some money for it and have a good time to boot. Hand over the keys, doll. Flannery, get the spare. Onct we get it fixed, he'll drive it to our place." Big Jerk Number One appeared to be the brains of the operation. Number Three simply stood there drooling over the prospect of free intercourse.

Moving on to Plan C or was it D, Leah held onto her keys and the crowbar. "I wouldn't recommend that. I have a large, vicious dog travelling with me."

"Sure you do, honey. Haven't heard a single bark out of him. Throw me the keys."

Following orders, Flannery, the smallest one, moved to the rear of the SUV and waited. Gargantua must still be lying low obeying her last command. She knew of only one thing that would set him off—loud noises. All she had was a puny car alarm and a lot of hope. Leah squeezed the alarm button and popped the trunk. Honk—honk—honk. Bark—bark—bark! Flannery backed up to the bumper of the truck.

"She ain't lyin'. He's right atop that tire, Himes."

Himes, Big Jerk Number One, half-turned and ordered. "Git the gun out the glove box and shoot 'im. And turn that damned alarm off, bitch!"

By the time he faced Leah again, she had the crowbar positioned for a good, hard swing at his kneecaps and followed through like a major league hitter with her kayaking-strengthened muscles. With his bearded face in a rictus of pain, Himes folded. She should run into the fog and hide, but what about poor Gargantua all tied up, a sitting goose of a dog?

A siren sounded. Lights going round and round painted the fog red. The fire truck returning? Gargantua made a mighty leap and jerked the clothesline loose. By the sheer accident of his size, he vaulted on top of Flannery who covered his face and neck but banged his head fairly hard against the hood of the truck.

Big Jerk Number Three shouted, "The cops, she called the cops! They catch me with a gun and drugs, I'm back in the slammer."

Himes reached out a hand to him. "Help me up, Bundy. We gotta split."

"Yeah, I'll help you up. This time you ride in the back." Bundy dragged his buddy to the side of the truck and heaved him over the side. A yowl of pain added to the noise and chaos. Bundy got in the driver's seat and revved the engine. Flannery, shaking his head to clear it from the knock against the hood, backed away from the dog, staggered to the passenger side, and crawled in. The big truck rumbled onto the road, riding down the center line, and faded into the fog.

Gargantua continued to bark in the direction of the oncoming siren. Leah dropped her crowbar and grabbed his collar. "Settle down. That's a good boy."

The silver Prius with the flashing red light slapped onto its roof slid into the space vacated by the truck. Ashton Blaise jumped out and shut off the siren. "You okay? I saw you on the way to retrieve my grandfather and figured I'd come back to help with the tire once I got him before he drowned in a ditch or was hit by a car. He went out a window at home when the fire truck passed and escaped again."

"You're better late than never. Three of the wrong kind of guys decided to help me with the flat and have some fun as well." Leah hoped her snotty attitude might cover the tremor in her voice and the shaking of her body.

Ash put his hands on her shoulders. "You okay? Did they hurt you?"

"Threatened to, but I kneecapped one and Gargantua here nearly knocked another out when he jumped on him. The third decided he didn't want a run-in with the police."

"That's my Leah. You don't wait for the hero to arrive and save the day."

His Leah, the thought warmed her, but she kept her attitude. "Do you usually tear around in the fog with the emergency light on your puny car?"

"No, but my granddad insisted we had to get to the fire, and the light convinced him to get into the car."

A window on the Prius slid down. "Here King, here boy. Ash, it's King," a delighted but aged voice called.

"Who's King?"

"The German shepherd he used to keep around the firehouse. Let's get your tire changed."

"Aren't you afraid your grandfather will go out that window, too? "

"Nope, it's too small for him, and I've got the kiddie locks on. Take the dog over to visit him while I work. He's crazy about dogs. They calm him."

Loving pajama-clad arms reached out to hug Gargantua who returned the affection with broad, lavish licks of his tongue. Leah held onto the rope in case the immense mutt decided to take off, not that she'd be able to stop him if he did, but the mutual love fest continued. She leaned against the car and watched Ash deal with the lug nuts with ease, a trait in a man she could appreciate. Old tire off, new on, restore those nuts deposited in the hub cap for safe keeping, tighten them up, hub cap on, lower the SUV, job done. Ash replaced the tools and threw the flat tire into the trunk. He paused for a moment working on removing something from the treads. A moment later he presented his find to Leah on the flat of his palm as if it were a diamond engagement ring. The object did glitter in the light of his headlamps. "A piece of glass must have created a slow leak."

"I should have checked my tires after I ran over those bottles this morning, though heaven knows I could have picked it up anywhere along these roads. Sorry about saying you arrived too late. You came right on time really."

Ash caged Leah against the Prius by putting his arms on either side of her. "If you have car trouble again, call me."

"I thought I could manage alone."

"But, you don't have to any more. Do I get a reward for roadside repair? I'm thinking you put on the ball gown again, and we play bridesmaid and groomsman doing it in the bathroom."

"Why are you so obsessed with that dress?"

"I love it. I'd marry you in that dress."

That took her breath away for a moment. Why did he have to put love and marriage so close together in the same sentence as they stood on a deserted road in the fog? Leah pushed at his chest and Ash dropped his arms, letting her go where she would.

"I'll consider it. We better get going. You need to get your grandfather home, and I have a car full of animals to drop at the shelter. Oh, Jesus, Pad Thai!"

"You're hungry?"

"No! It's a cat that might have run off while we talked. She won't be able to find her way home from here." Leah handed Ash the dog's rope leash and rushed to the SUV to check on Paddy. She didn't have to search far. The Siamese had come from under the front seat and now crouched next to the rat cage, blue eyes in a predator's stare, chocolate-tipped tail flicking.

Nearly as big as the cat, the rats huddled perfectly still in the far corner of the bent cage as if to convey, "No one home, go away."

"Scat!" Leah waved her arms, and Paddy retreated under the seat again. Now, all she had to do was load Gargantua and get them all to the shelter. "Ash, would you bring the dog over here."

Ash tugged on the rope, and Gargantua dropped his front feet to the ground. Dalton Blaise howled. "Noooo! King always rides with us to the fires. You can't take him away from me." He kicked at the car door in an attempt to get out.

Ash shook his head. "This could get bad if he acts up while I'm driving. Okay if I take the dog home with us and return him to you tomorrow?"

"One less unwanted pet to unload at the shelter tonight," Leah agreed.

"Look, I don't want you to go out there tonight. We sent the sheriff to pick up Cubby. His whole family is gone. Cliff has a camp in the Atchafalaya Basin that can only be reached by water. They'll send a police boat out there in the morning to try to bring them in, but they could still be lurking around town. After all, someone assaulted the shelter last night, probably Cubby on his ATV. Can't you take the animals to your place?"

"He's tried to burn me out twice, but I believe Mrs. Tweedy will be on the watch now, so I won't be unguarded. We've become neighborly."

"Tough old bird. Just go home. I'll get there when I can."

"Remember, I have the dog and a cat you foisted off on me already."

"You love them. I know you do."

Those gray eyes, how they could speak to her without saying a word. "I kinda do. I guess I could put the rats in Rachel's room and cage Paddy for the night in one of the carriers I use to transport the ferals to the vet."

"A good plan that will relieve my mind." Ash stooped for a kiss and forgot about the rope in his hand. Gargantua pulled away and went back to the open window and Dalton Blaise who immediately quieted to pat his head. The kiss needed to be a brief one, and it was. Ash opened the back door of his small car.

Gargantua happily jumped inside and hung his head over the seat to rest on Dalton's shoulder. "No time for playing kissy-face, boy. Crank up that siren. We have a fire to put out!"

"Yes, sir, Chief. Leah, I'll lead the way in the fog and see you to the barn first."

"Fine with me," Leah said, knowing full well by now nothing would put out the fire between her and Ashton Blaise.

Chapter Twenty-Three

Leah heard Stubby's squeaky bark when Ash entered the barn using his key. Footsteps she'd come to recognize headed for her bedroom where she'd lain for hours unable to sleep after the events of the evening. Neither a dinner of soup and a toasted cheese sandwich nor a good slug from a new bottle of wine helped settle her nerves with Cubby on the loose and those three felonious guys possibly knowing who she was and where to find her, though she doubted that. They didn't appear to be animal lovers.

She and Ash argued about her filing a police report as they stood on her doorstep earlier in the night. What could she tell the cops? Three men stopped to help change her tire. She'd been the idiot who suggested she go to their place for a party. They hadn't touched her, only savaged her cell phone which now had a crack across the screen. Ash lost the fight mainly because he had Dalton and Gargantua waiting in his car and no time to draw it out.

The second he opened her bedroom door, she said, "You were right. I'll go to the police tomorrow. Shouldn't you be home taking care of your grandfather instead of here? Because I am serving notice that I might be awake, but I'm not putting on the ball gown at one a.m. to amuse you."

Ash toed Stubby back before closing the door and

sitting on the bed to remove his shoes and clothes. "You get a reprieve. I'm too tired to fully appreciate it." He slid in beside her, automatically slinging an arm around her shoulders and holding her close. "I gave my grandfather a sedative and let the big dog stay in his room. He's good until morning, but I told Mom we're going to have to do something soon about Pop. I hate the idea of putting bars on his windows. In Houston, an elderly woman burned to death because we couldn't get into her house in time since she had the place locked up like a jail. We need to take a look at putting him in Magnolia Villa."

Leah rolled to one side and hugged his chest. "That's a hard decision to make."

"Yeah, I couldn't rest worrying about that and Cubby maybe coming after you again. What if I hadn't arrived in time to scare off those thugs? Some hero I am."

"I could have run away if I hadn't hesitated about the dog being shot."

"Yeah, you don't need my help. You've said it often enough."

"No, but I—I need your love, your support, and you beside me in this bed." About time she admitted it. Ash went terribly still. He tucked his hands behind his head on the pillow. She'd blown it.

Finally, he spoke. "I'm still a vegetarian who lives with his mother. I'm not sure when that last part will change. Sure you can put up with it?"

Leah rose up on her elbows to gaze into those somber gray eyes by the light of the moon. "You are a firefighter who goes back into a building to save what he can and cares about his loved ones. You will always be my hero. And you can do all the cooking. If I crave a burger, I'll get one for lunch. Besides, I'm not perfect. Maybe you can't get over my past or the fact that my grandmother flirts with you and desires your body." She tried to make light of her affair by packaging it along with all the rest of her problems.

His lips quirked into a slight smile. "I believe I can fend off a ninety-year-old woman, and cooking is my pleasure. I only hope I'm not taking advantage of you, too, at a vulnerable moment in your life."

"No one takes advantage of me anymore!"

"Sure, that's why you have two rats and a cat you don't own staying with you tonight." When she started to protest that she was simply doing her job, Ash pressed a finger to her lips. "Hush. I love the way you care for animals and your grandmother. I love your independence. Leah, I love you. Now, I want to make love to you like a woman who will be in my bed for the rest of my life, slow and tender and in no rush because we have hundreds of nights ahead of us."

"No ball gown?" She melted back against his chest.

"None."

That's the way they did it—like two people with a whole lifetime to spend together.

****

Leah woke from a deep sleep to one of her favorite fantasies, Ash in the kitchen whipping up a sumptuous breakfast of his French toast or maybe waffles. No, she didn't have a waffle iron. Pancakes then, maybe with chocolate chips on the inside. She did have a large bag of those in her pantry destined to make rocky road fudge to repay his mother for the peanut butter candy—which she hadn't gotten around to making as yet. He'd find the mini-marshmallows next to the chips and maybe put them in hot chocolate. She sniffed the air and only scented coffee brewing. Good enough.

Even better when Ash backed into the bedroom with a tray holding a mug of coffee and a cereal bowl ornamented with a sprig of wild purple mist flower stuck in a clean hot sauce bottle. "I've been outside to feed your destruction of cats. I need to win them over if I'm going to be around a lot. The hot sauce only had a few drops left. You need to get more."

Leah sat up, the sheet slipping down her naked breasts. She tucked it in high under her arms. "No need to do that," he assured her. "I like the view, very lush."

"Won't be if I spill hot coffee on them. The only thing that could make this better is if you served me bare-chested with your fireman's pants held up by Lex's red suspenders." Leah poked at the contents of the bowl. "And if this were chocolate chip pancakes. What is it anyhow?"

"My own special mixture of oatmeal blended with chopped nuts, raisins, craisins, and cinnamon drizzled with honey. I brought along a sack of it last night in case I stayed over. This is better for you. Not every day can be pancakes, Leah, but every day we can have this." He placed the tray carefully on her lap and leaned in for a kiss.

The oatmeal wasn't so bad. Neither was the kiss. She finished every bite and swilled her coffee. "I have to get moving. I need to unlock the shelter and then assign the volunteers their tasks."

"I'll go home and help with my grandfather, get him shaved and bathed, but promise me you'll go by the police station and make a report about the men who threatened you."

"Okay, I will." He loved her, end of the argument, because when a person cared you gave them some slack.

Not her fault really that she couldn't shake free of the shelter until late morning. Mrs. LaBauve showed up early to reclaim Pad Thai and borrowed the carrier to take her home. She had a donation in hand and a can of Fancy Feast for Paddy to eat on the way. The cat had distained the dry chow offered in the cattery.

The family returned to choose their puppy, but while the papers were being filled out, the little boy became enamored by the two white rats in their slightly crushed cage. They tickled his fingers with their whiskers and inquisitive pink noses and made him laugh. Leah gave a quick speech about the high intelligence of rats and what little trouble they'd be, already hand tamed. Sold! Or at least taken to a new home since she threw them in free with the adoption fee for the pup. Good deal for everyone since Mr. Grey had begun beak clacking as soon as the rats arrived in the office.

An hour before lunch, she turned the office over to Ethel and shook free to go to the police department where she confessed her stupidity of offering to go with those men and why. Sheriff LeDoux stroked his full gray mustache with a finger and nodded. "You do what you gotta do in situations like that. Glad you made it out okay. You say the fellow named Bundy was on parole?"

Leah nodded. "I think so."

"Good, we can track him down easy enough and get a warrant to search for illegal weapons and drugs.

My guess is the guy you kneecapped will be in one of the local hospitals. Nothing hurts like a bum knee. Got one myself. We'll take care of this. Let them know they ain't welcome in our parish if we can't get them on anything else. Almost lunch break." The sheriff saw her to the door of his office.

A commotion broke out in the very small four desk bull pen shared by the staff. Two officers trailed through the building with the Couvillons in tow, all handcuffed. Cubby was crying again, but his mother cursed the police to hell, damnation, and back again. They wore identical gray hoodies, sweatpants, and running shoes as if the family had its own gang or exclusive club and lumbered along like a parade of elephants. Head hanging, Cliff said not a word. The procession entered a glass-walled interrogation room where the prisoners were uncuffed, offered uncomfortable plastic chairs and bottles of water. Leah heard Cubby say as the door shut, "I'm hungry. Can I have a candy bar?" It tore at her heart a little.

"Picked 'em up at their camp out in the swamp this morning. Can't hardly believe Cliff would get himself involved in arson. He donated a Kevlar vest for our drug dog." Sheriff LeDoux shook his grizzled head. "Regardless, I'm going to lunch. Let them sit there for a while."

The sheriff possessed a small paunch that said he didn't miss many meals, but his bulk was nothing compared to Tank Fontenot who nearly ran Leah down as he entered the station. Ash followed him like a lean, dark shadow of his younger self dressed in his black uniform. "Caught 'em, did you?" the Chief asked.

Sheriff LeDoux kissed his noon meal goodbye.

"Yeah, I guess we should question them first before they bring in a lawyer."

Leah caught his khaki-clad arm as he turned toward the interrogation room. "Since Cubby is accused of burning down my house, could I listen in?"

"I guess. Sit here and keep quiet." The sheriff gestured to another grim plastic chair outside the room and flipped a switch as he went inside with the fire chief following him like an oil tanker guided by a tug boat.

Leah stopped Ash. "Hold on a moment." She dashed to one of the two vending machines leaning against a wall and fed enough dollars into it to get a pack of peanuts, a chocolate bar, and a bag of M & M's. "Give these to Cubby."

"You'd feed the guy who burned you out and tried to do it a second time?"

"Cubby isn't responsible for his actions. He doesn't know when to stop unless someone tells him. What will happen to him?"

"No idea. I guess it depends on how many of the charges we can prove." Ash took the offerings and went to join the interrogation.

Leah settled herself on the hard plastic seat. The two arresting officers wheeled over rolling chairs from the desks. One of them said in a whisper, "It wasn't the kid that gave us a hard time. The mother took swings at both of us and bit Chauvin."

"For true." The other officer rolled up a sleeve to show a bruised impression of teeth on his forearm. "Cliff, he seemed resigned. Didn't give us trouble."

They quieted as the interview started. Sheriff LeDoux smoothed the harsh lines of his face with a grandfatherly smile. "Now Cubby, we have a long list of allegations against you. You are being accused of arson, that's setting fires."

"I know," Cubby answered around a mouthful of peanuts. "I work at the fire station."

"Okay, I'm going to read down this list, and you tell me if you set the fires."

"Don't you tell him nothing, son! We'll get a lawyer, a good one," Eunice Couvillon interrupted.

"I think we need to come clean," Cliff said. "What we did wasn't so bad. People will understand."

His blue eyes confused, Cubby looked back and forth between his parents. Sheriff LeDoux dove right in to take advantage of that. "You don't have to answer aloud, just nod if you did these things."

Cubby nodded, and the sheriff started down the list. "Setting aflame three deserted tenant cabins on separate occasions." He cited the dates, and Cubby nodded. "Let the record show the accused indicated in the affirmative," LeDoux said into a recorder he'd already set up with the date, time and those in attendance at the questioning.

"Wait, wait! This is my fault." Eager to explain, Cliff leaned over the table. "We don't have all that many fires in the parish, and the volunteers need practice. Sometimes a farmer will donate a shack we can set on fire, but it had been a while. I showed Cubby how to make Molotov cocktails from old bottles he scrounged, sort of a father-son project. We drove out in the country, picked some places that needed removal, and pitched our cocktails into them until they were burning good. Then, we went home and waited to be called. No one got hurt, and we did the farmers a favor since vermin and vagrants get into those places."

The sheriff glanced sharply at the big man in the community. "What if some homeless person had been sleeping there?"

"We checked real careful first, then we smashed those bottles of fire through the windows," Cubby said with excitement in his voice. His motion to show off his throwing arm sprayed M & M's from the newly opened bag across the top of the metal table that sat between the accused and the accuser. "We helped hose them down."

Thoughtfully, LeDoux picked up an M & M and popped into his mouth. Cubby immediately gathered the rest into a small pile right in front of himself and protected the heap like a goalie his net with cupped hands. "Let's move along. We can get the details later. Madame Mystique's House of Pleasure."

"No way! I wouldn't never burn up Miss Mystique or Mr. Grey."

"Mr. Grey?" the sheriff inquired.

From his place along the wall since the lawman and his chief took up the two chairs, Ash answered. "Mystique's parrot. I carried his cage from the burning house."

Cubby nodded enthusiastically. "Yeah! Me and Daddy were there having our night out because sex feels good and Mama don't like to do it with him. We put on our firefighting gear right over our underwear when the trucks come with the hoses. Nobody died 'cause we did a good job."

Mrs. Couvillon turned a burning stare on the sheriff. "That house of sin deserved to go up in flames. It corrupted my son. As for those fallen women, they got a taste of their future in a fiery Hell. The fire forced them to move out of this parish."

"Yep, it's a longer drive to fornicate now, but people keep right on doing it," the sheriff remarked. "That's a no from Cubby on the bordello crime. How about Leah Allain's home, the one next to Ernestine Tweedy?"

Cliff said nothing, nor did Eunice. Cubby hung his head, making double chins against his chest. He scarfed up more candy. The sheriff waited for an answer patiently as if it weren't his own lunchtime.

"Miz Tweedy always has teacakes. When Daddy and me go to work on the rent houses, I have teacakes and milk at her house. She hates cats. They eat her birds. She said if Miss Leah moved away, those cats would leave, too."

"Yes, son, but did you burn the Allain home?"

"Daddy sent me to get gas for the mower at the station down at the crossroad. On the way back, I splashed some around the back of Miss Leah's house and lit it with my Bic that I keep to light those cocktails. No one around. It didn't get called in too fast. A really big fire for us to put out, and we were the first volunteers to show up!" Cubby rummaged in the pouch of his gray hoodie and proudly withdrew his small cigarette lighter. "Whoosh!"

"Chauvin, get in here! Bag it and tag it and explain why you didn't search the suspect before you brought him here," the sheriff called out.

One of Leah's red-faced companions rose to carry out orders and give an explanation. "It wasn't like it was a gun, sir. His mom bit me on the arm, and I kind of forgot about the lighter."

"Out!" LeDoux waved him away with the evidence bag. "Okay, we're making progress here. Not much farther to go."

"I didn't know," Cliff said, knotting his big knuckles together on the cold table top almost as if praying for the ordeal to be over.

"Two abandoned buildings on Cinder Street."

"Nope." Cubby finished his pile of candy and unwrapped the chocolate bar.

Ash leaned forward. "Excuse me. Cliff, I recall you said it was a good thing those places burned because druggies hung out there. Are you sure you didn't encourage Cubby to set them on fire?"

"Cubby stayed home with me that day while Eunice went to her church service. We were watching the pre-game show when we got the call from the station. He's not guilty of that, I swear."

"We'll take your word for now. A trashcan fire set at the house of Yancey Breaux on Halloween," the sheriff intoned.

"Yeah!" Cubby's face lit like the flame of his Bic. "I wanted Yancey to know I loved her. I took my ATV over to her house and used my lighter to set some of the newspapers inside on fire. Her dad came out yelling, and I took off fast as I could before he got down their drive."

"Little slut!" Mrs. Couvillon muttered. "Leading boys astray."

Cubby rose half out of his chair. "You shouldn't call Yancey that. It's a bad word. Yancey danced with me because she liked me. You almost burned her up, Mama!"

Cliff pressed his son back into his chair. "Tell them

what your mother did at the Firemen's Ball."

"We was leaving through the kitchen while Daddy brought the car around back, and she says to pick up that big vat of oil Chief Fontenot used to fry the turkey and carry it over by the stove. I did because I'm strong." Cubby made a muscle with his arm. "She tipped it over and turned up the gas on all the burners. I said that's bad. Lots of people are in the hall. Daddy says never to set fire to anything where people could get hurt. Mama said Daddy could go to hell for all she cared and pushed me out the back door. We drove around front and by then the alarm sounded. Me and Dad helped put the fire out. Nobody died. That's a good thing, right?"

"Yes, it is," LeDoux agreed, but his savvy eyes stayed on Eunice. Leah noted that Ash and the Chief sized her up as well. "Only three more items on my list. A truck set on fire using a Molotov cocktail on Main Street."

"Nah. I told Captain Blaise that. I was just sitting in the sandwich place when that ole truck went up. But the family who owned it, they got bad blood, Mama said. Church burners go to perdition." Cubby crammed the last of the chocolate bar into his mouth, leaving behind dark smears on his innocent face and across the metal surface of the table.

"I see. Here's the last two. No one got hurt here either, but they might have been—a second attempt to burn out Leah Allain while she was in her barn, and an attack on the animal shelter, both done with Molotov cocktails."

Cubby shook his head hard. "No, no, no! Miss Leah was nice to me until I touched Yancey in the wrong places, and I never woulda burned up Mr. Grey. He likes me, too."

"Miz Tweedy says she saw a person of your build wearing a track suit with a white stripe on the leg run away from the barn after the fire was set. It's in the report Captain Blaise took down. Miss Leah says you wore an outfit like that on the day she had to let you go at the shelter for molesting Yancey Breaux. Why not confess it all, Cubby? You'll get a lighter sentence since no one was hurt." Sheriff LeDoux leaned across the table until he was nearly nose to nose with the boy.

Arms wrapped around his chubby body, Cubby shook from side to side. "No, no, no."

Leah shifted toward Officer Chavin and breathed, "It was her, the mother. She dresses them alike."

"Give the sheriff a minute. He comes across like a good ole boy, but he knows this town inside and out."

"With all these charges, we're talking twenty years or more hard time in Angola, Cubby. You won't be in the parish jail where your mama can visit every weekend, but maybe I could swing that if you fess up." Sheriff LeDoux kept his eyes, hard and pale, on the boy.

Watching the drama closely, Leah asked Chauvin, "Is that true?" The officer shrugged.

Cubby began to blubber. "I'm skeered, Mama. I didn't burn down no place with people in it. I'm never gonna see you again if they put me in a far away jail."

Eunice Couvillon shot out of her chair in a Mama Bear rage. "Let my boy alone! You think only a man knows how to look up the making of Molotov cocktails on the internet or splash a little gas around. I took their hobby up a notch and did some real good. I drove that

Whore of Babylon from our parish because you are soft on what they call victimless crime. Those girls taught my son to touch women and claimed they enjoyed it. Got him in trouble at the shelter and will get him in trouble again. As for those cribs on Cinder Street, they started out as places of sin and moved on to housing the drug addicts you don't arrest. I did your job for you."

Eunice poked the sheriff in the shoulder. LeDoux didn't move a muscle, but Officer Chauvin knocked over his chair as he sprinted into the room, cuffs at the ready, subdued the angry mother, and pushed her into her seat again. "That's assaulting an officer. You ought to see what she did to me, boss."

As if nothing had happened in the last few minutes, the sheriff glanced at the list of crimes committed again. "I gather you are also responsible for the truck fire and the second attack on Miss Allain's home and the animal shelter, Mrs. Couvillon."

Eunice licked the froth from her lips. "You bet I am. You don't treat my son that way, taking the word of the little whore who led him on and telling him he can't be on the property again. I couldn't let that go. I thought Leah would leave the parish like Madame Mystique with some encouragement. As for the truck fire, that was just a little reminder that no one has forgotten one of those LeBlancs burned down our historic church."

"What if Miss Allain had died in that barn?"

"Not my problem if the woman is too stupid to get out of a burning building."

The sheriff turned off the recorder. "It is now. Officer Chauvin, book Mr. Couvillon with simple arson, Cubby and Mrs. Couvillon with aggravated arson. Let Cliff call a lawyer. Me, I'm going to lunch." LeDoux rose and left the room without a backward glance while his officers took care of the details.

Chief Fontenot followed him. "My treat. Well done."

"You laid it all out for me, Tank. Nice report, well organized, dates, times, places—makes my job easier."

The Chief glanced over his shoulder at Ash and made a decision. "Captain Blaise is responsible for that. I didn't see it. Those old tenant cabins weren't worth investigating. I thought most likely set by kids of families I know goofing around. The Cinder street buildings, addicts probably. Condemned to be torn down. No real harm done in either case. Blaise made the connection between the burning of the bordello and Miss Leah's place, same M.O., set by people who had an agenda, but both of us suspected Cubby, not a whole family of arsonists living like a nest of copperheads in our midst, folks you see every day. Maybe I am getting too old for this job."

"Retirement looks mighty good to me right now. I have to admit Eunice Couvillon is right. I do go easy on women who have to earn their living on their backs and the druggies. Our parish jail can only hold so many, and I'd rather fill it with the pushers, the rapists, the crooks. Golden Dragon Buffet for Chinese or po-boys?"

"I think we both earned that buffet. Blaise, you coming?" The Chief turned to look at Ash and Leah locked tight together, his arm around her waist. "Your lady is invited."

"No, thanks. We've made other plans."

"Suit yourself. You know what I like best at the Golden Dragon? Their egg rolls and those triangles filled with cream cheese and fried. I could eat a whole bin of both."

"I'm sort of craving the chicken on a stick without the stick. At least, that's how they label it. It's good with noodles. I finish up with the upside down apple pie topped with frozen yogurt," LeDoux said.

"You know that's only a frozen pie they bake and flop over to slice. All the cakes are just Little Debbie's cut up in small pieces."

"Still good." Continuing to compare favorites in local Chinese cuisine, the two officers exited the station.

"We have plans?" Leah asked.

"Takeout at your place and a nooner."

"Past noon by now, but yes to both, a reward for a job well done and credit finally given. I think you are one step closer to being fire chief."

"After today, I'm not sure I want it. I'm only certain I want you."

Chapter Twenty-Four

Leaving a rumpled bed behind, Leah and Ash sat at the kitchen table and shared the fried rice and Chinese vegetables. Food can always be reheated if a couple has better things to do. Ash flipped Bandit a shrimp from his shrimp with lobster sauce. Stubby gazed at Leah with soulful eyes until she gave up a bit of meat from her pepper steak.

"We really shouldn't feed them from the table," she said. "They'll become obese little beggars."

"As long as they stay out of the bedroom, I don't care. Jasmine tea?" he asked.

"I had jasmine tea on hand?"

"No. I bought a box when I paid for the takeout." He got up, draped two teabags inside of mugs, and put the water on to boil. Returning, Ash fiddled with his chopsticks.

"I don't see how you can use those. I'm working with a fork, and I still spilled a piece of green pepper on my chest." Leah glanced down at the stain on her teal Safe Haven Animal Shelter knit shirt with its cute puppy and kitten logo.

"I don't mind. You have a big shelf. On other people it just drops into their laps and onto a napkin."

"Yeah, it's a special talent of mine, catching food on my boobs." Leah waited, but he didn't say he'd like to see that without the shirt. She sensed something off about him. How well she'd come to understand him over the last few months. "Considering all the exercise we had a few minutes ago and the satisfactory conclusion of the arson cases, you aren't eating very much. We're supposed to be celebrating."

As if trying to prove her wrong, Ash gathered a mouthful of rice and shrimp on his chopsticks and put it in his mouth. He didn't continue his meal, though, before speaking.

"When the Chief called and told me to get into uniform and come to the police station, I was having a serious talk about Dalton with my mother. We're taking him over to Magnolia Villa on Friday. They have a dementia wing there. It's pretty nice for a locked ward, individual rooms, a common area with its own dining room and a walled garden where the patients can sit in the sunshine or work with the plants. There are activities and crafts—though I can't imagine my grandfather cutting out snowflakes and valentines—and movie nights with popcorn. I've checked it out before, but Mom always said no, it's not time yet. This last incident scared her. He got farther than ever and could have been killed wandering in that fog."

"I'm sorry." Leah covered his hand with hers.

"Best thing about the place is it's out of town on country acreage and away from the interstate. He won't be able to hear the sirens from there. Anyhow, my mom wants his last few days at home to be pleasant. She's making all his favorite foods and plans to show the old movies and TV shows he loves. I can't invite you over considering how he reacted to Rachel. You both have those green eyes and dark hair even if…"

"I'm short and not pretty."

"Hey, you've met Cole. I'm not the pretty one in my family either, but you've always looked fine to me, Leah Allain. We're the ones who take care. Really, my mom likes you. She said the night of the fire in the Mardi Gras hall you stayed calm and herded as many people as you could outside while Rachel and some of the other twits became hysterical. It's just that she wants these last days to be only family my grandfather knows—or knew."

"I understand I'm not family." She couldn't stop herself from thinking—not yet.

"Can we keep the dog a little longer? Dalton still insists he's King and won't part with him."

She had sympathy for him, she really did, but hope ignited inside her. One of Ash's big problems would be solved on Friday. "You can keep the dog, maybe permanently? If Courage is about the size of Stubby, your mother might want a bigger watch dog around once you get your own place—or move in here." His face darkened as if veiled in smoke. She'd been bold and presumed too much, coming across as pushy as Rachel.

"It's more difficult than that. Magnolia Villa is crazy expensive. My grandfather sold his home when he moved in with us and still has that money socked away. He contributed his pension to the household. Now all that goes to the Villa. My mom lives on a widow's benefit, and I chip in, too. Her house is paid off thanks to a policy my dad had, one he said all firefighters should get, but if I move out I doubt she'll want to take my money anymore. Mom hasn't lived alone since she married my father practically right out of high school. I don't know how she'll do on her own.

She's fragile, not tough like you. She needs some time to work that out before I abandon her. Anyhow, I won't be seeing you tonight, maybe not for a week since I go back on duty Saturday. You understand, right?"

The teakettle emitted its shrill whistle, its puff of steam. Leah turned off the heat and poured the scalding hot water. She began to pack away the leftovers, the food she'd probably be dining on for the next two nights alone while the Blaise family ate Linda's fettuccini and watched a DVD of *Backdraft*. Ash placed his hands on her shoulders as she shoved the containers into her small refrigerator. She stood in its chilly draft to cool off before she spoke.

"I'm a grown woman. I can cope. Once you cut the cord, you become your own person."

"What's that supposed to mean?"

"Don't worry about it. After the last few days, I could use a few good nights' sleep without interruptions."

"So I'm an interruption now?"

"Of the best kind. You can interrupt me anytime."

Leah tried for a sexy leer, but all the while she gathered her defenses. She'd always be second to his mother as she'd spent a lifetime being second to Rachel. She liked Linda Blaise, a sweet woman who obviously loved both her sons and remained so devoted to her late husband she'd kept her father-in-law at home as long as she possibly could. The night of the Mardi Gras hall fire, she'd noticed Linda still wore her wedding and engagement rings on her left hand as if Hank Blaise hadn't died several years ago. Ash said his mother came in the exact dress as the last time she attended the ball with his dad. If Leah married Linda's son, would they have to live with her, do everything her way, walk softly because Linda wasn't strong? Leah had little respect for a person who couldn't stand on their own two feet and—move on.

"I really must get back to the shelter where I'm needed."

Ash kissed her nape since she'd turned her back on him. "We'll only be apart a few days. I promise."

Hadn't Colton Dandridge, DVM, promised on numerous occasions, they'd be together once he divorced his wife? "Sure." She hustled Ash out the door and headed for her SUV. The animals wouldn't care if she had a stain on her shirt, and Mr. Grey still found her sexy. Inside the barn, two cups of jasmine tea cooled off rapidly.

Chapter Twenty-Five

After a dinner of leftover Chinese food and two glasses of wine, Leah slept surprisingly well. Maybe she did need rest after the ordeals of the last few days. Maybe she wanted to hide in sleep the way depressed people did. She'd been tempted to allow Stubby and Bandit into the bed with her for the comfort of their warm, affectionate bodies, but Ash would be back if only for the sex. Her pets remained curled happily together in a single dog bed by the sofa, though she'd purchased two, while she considered if she'd be willing to settle for another purely sexual relationship.

While pondering, she'd drifted off and woke only when her phone began playing the ominous opening of Beethoven's Fifth beside her ear. Da-da-da—Dah!—the special dial tone of the emergency alert people whose button Gran wore around her neck. Had it been a shelter emergency, the sound of dogs barking would have wakened her. If Ash called, *Smoke Gets in your Eyes* sounded. Not good. She fumbled the phone from the night table and put it to her ear.

"Yes, this is Leah."

"Your grandmother is pushing her button over and over again, but either cannot pick up her phone or refuses to do so. Ambulance, fire, and police are en route. Do you want to come with a house key before they break in to deal with the situation?"

"I'll be right there!" Any old slacks, any T-shirt would do. She shoved her feet into sneakers, ran her fingers through her hair, and went out the door. Leah rammed her SUV through the silent night streets of Chapelle, ignoring red lights where no other vehicles waited, straight to her destination. Blinking lights of red and blue bathed Gran's house as if a Fourth of July celebration were in progress. She found the key and entered by the front door. One of the firemen followed her inside, but she paid no attention to him.

Gran stood naked in her darkened parlor pointing the alert button at her television, squeezing it over and over again. Leah flicked on a lamp that shone on her grandmother's sagging, pale posterior and loose white hair. A nightgown and a sopping Depends reeking of urine pooled at her feet.

"It won't turn on. I'm missing my shows. Dot, bring me a clean gown. I'm wet."

Leah gently pried the aged fingers from the button. "That's not the remote, Gran. Give me a second." She turned on the television and found the channel that seemed to play *The Golden Girls* twenty-four/seven. Her grandmother smiled and relaxed into her favorite chair unabashed by her nudity.

The fireman who hovered in the doorway backed off and called out, "Give them a second."

Leah brushed by him on her way to the bedroom to retrieve a fresh nightie and a dry diaper. "Ash? It's not your shift."

"I got the alert and turned out when I saw the address. Is she okay?"

"Just muddled. Mistook her alert button for the remote. It would be funny if it weren't so sad."

"I understand. Dalton made a couple of nude escapes. Fortunately, no one in this town pressed charges. At least, she stayed in the house."

Their conversation roused Alene from her seat. She moved toward them, long, skeletal fingers held out in welcome, her flattened and almost transparent breasts swaying, lank strands of her white hair providing her only cover like an elderly Lady Godiva. "You've come to call. How wonderful. Dot, do bring refreshments for Captain Blaise."

"Great, you she remembers. Sit down and watch your show, Gran. He can't stay."

Her grandmother's bereft expression culminated in tears funneling down the grooves by her mouth. Ash took her hand and gazed into her eyes. "I'll visit another time, Allie. Take care." He pressed a light kiss on the old woman's soft, lined skin. She beamed at him, her green eyes quite alert now.

"Would you tell the others they aren't needed? I'll stay the night with her and make sure it won't happen again. I'm just glad it was you who saw her this way and not a stranger. Please don't tell anyone."

"I wouldn't do that."

Leah pointed her grandmother back toward the chair and the blaring TV. By the time she got the clean gown over her grandmother's head, Ash had gone. Their lights extinguished, the emergency vehicles pulled out one by one and returned to their stations to await the next crisis.

Leah coaxed Alene to step into a dry diaper and picked up the wet items. She sprayed the floor with Febreze and hoped the odor hadn't seeped into the wood. Then, she made chamomile tea and brought it on a tray to the parlor.

"Thank you, Dot. Which Golden Girl do you think I'd be?"

"Dorothy, the sensible one."

"Really. I've always wanted to be Blanche and not care what anyone thought of me, have sex with whomever I pleased."

What you never wanted to know about your grandmother and wished you didn't know now! Leah sipped her tea and hoped it would help both of them to sleep. Then, she lay down on the sofa and propped some pillows under her head. The theme song of the show, *Thank you for Being a Friend*, woke her every half hour as sure as an alarm clock to check on Alene who had usually fallen asleep. If Leah turned off the TV, her grandmother woke immediately and reprimanded, "I was watching that."

Leah admitted to herself that come morning, she'd have to call her parents in Florida and tell them Gran needed nursing home care. She had a POA, power of attorney, in her name, being the closest kin in the area. She needed to be brave enough to use it. Dawn couldn't come soon enough to remedy this situation.

****

On Saturday, Leah brushed and braided her grandmother's long hair and pinned it up in the usual way. She picked out a pantsuit, not the fuzzy velour kind the more active residents of Magnolia Villa seemed to wear almost like a uniform, but one with style and dignity, pearl gray with small rhinestone buttons. Bring no jewelry, said the rules of the Villa. Her grandmother seemed as naked as last night without an accent pin, earrings, or pearls. The suitcase Leah packed contained mostly nightgowns, but a few dresses and other nice clothes. She hoped the staff would see that Alene dressed well. As a leader of local society, Gran had always taken pride in her appearance.

One of the more expensive suites had opened, and thank heaven, Gran had the money to pay for it until she turned one hundred and two and then some. She'd been left that well off by Grandpa. The suite—a bedroom, sitting area, and bath with a walk-in tub since Leah stressed how much her grandmother hated showers—had a window overlooking the walled garden. For this first day, Leah arranged for them to have lunch with old friends who roamed free in the assisted living area of the Villa, their brains unimpaired even if they got around with walkers and wheelchairs. Each one promised to look in on Alene and visit the dementia ward often after sharing a nice meal with so many selections that Leah had to order for both of them. Good, people hadn't forgotten her grandmother entirely.

Afterward, a soft-spoken attendant walked them to the dementia ward and punched in a code on the key pad to open the metal door. On the other side, the wing resembled the rest of the Villa with a cheerful common room and a small dining area with a more limited menu chalked on a board. No confusing decisions to make here. Rather than the spirited games of bouree or bridge on the other side of the door, some inmates viewed a game show on a large TV, but none shouted out the answers. A lone woman, back turned to them, industriously crocheted a brightly-colored afghan that spilled across her lap and onto the floor at her feet. A Christmas tree bearing store-bought ornaments and paper chains Leah figured the patients made filled a corner. The desk where the ward attendants watched over their patients blazed with red poinsettias.

Several people, one a tall, broad man standing up with a hand pressed to the window glass, simply stared outside at the courtyard cloaked in winter gray today. The December frost had blighted the garden, but white reindeer ornaments decked in lights occupied the central area. Leah understood the staff tried hard to provide a cheerful, stimulating atmosphere, but for him, it didn't seem to be working. Their escort, a champagne blonde woman old enough to have deep sympathy for the occupants, said quietly, "Alene's room is this way. Let's get her settled."

As they moved through the recreation area, their reflection rippled across the large window like ghosts of the past. The man turned and moved toward them, big hands held out. "Allie, Allie, my green-eyed lady!"

"Oh, dear, I hope we aren't about to have an incident. Sometimes the dementia patients mistake others for their deceased spouses. Mr. Blaise has only been here a couple of days, and we don't know what to expect. We should move along. I'll have one of the male aides deal with him," their guide said.

But Alene had ideas of her own. She stepped forward and welcomed the embrace. Resting her head on Dalton's shoulder, she said, "Oh, Dally, Dally, where have you been?"

"This isn't my home. I know that much. But, they say it is now."

"My friends invited me to stay at this resort with them. It's a nice place, nicer with you here."

Leah winced at the lie she'd told to get her

grandmother packed and into the car. The woman with the crochet project dropped her work and stood—Linda Blaise. She moved toward the couple as a young black man, brawny and bald, but soft spoken, came from the desk and tapped Dalton on the shoulder. "You need to let the lady go, Mr. Blaise."

Linda intervened. "He'll respond better if you call him Chief. I've never heard anyone call him Dally. He wouldn't stand for a nickname like that in the old days."

"Chief, please release this woman and sit down," the aide said, polite enough but insistent.

"I'm so sorry. This is your grandmother, isn't she, Leah?" Linda apologized. "Ash said you'd be bringing her here. He did want to help you, but…"

"I know. He's working. Better he didn't come since Gran gets, well, flirtatious when he's around." Exactly as it had at the police station, the pieces fell into place—the long ago lover who resembled Ash in his youth found again. "It's okay. They know each other. Gran, why don't you and the Chief sit down and catch up. I'll get your bag unpacked."

Never unclasping their hands, the couple took the suggestion and found seats on a sofa side by side. The male aide relaxed. "I'll keep an eye on them."

"This way," her guide said.

Linda trailed Leah along the corridor where each room had a cheerful wreath on the door decorated with a ribbon bearing the patient's name. They entered and crossed the sitting room which boasted a tiny kitchen area with a small refrigerator and microwave, but no stove to prevent accidental fires. Leah had long been afraid her grandmother might try her hand at cooking and set her house on fire, but having a cook most of her married life, Alene seemed content to heat food in the microwave when she remembered to eat and how to use it.

"I brought her TV and favorite chair in my SUV. I have a box of family pictures we can set around to help her remember. I'm parked right next to the last handicapped space."

"Good idea. I'll have someone bring those items in for you." The assistant took her car keys and left Leah alone with Linda Blaise.

"Ash would have carried those things for you if he were here. He moved the items he thought his grandfather would want just a couple of days ago. It's very hard, isn't it? Let me help you unpack." Linda unzipped the suitcase lying on the bed in the next room and began folding the nightgowns into a dresser drawer.

Really, Leah did not want her help—or her son's. Ash'd called the morning after the nude debacle. She let his message go to voice mail. Finally answering a text asking how she and her grandmother were doing, she told him Alene would be committed on Saturday. He expressed his regrets about not being available to help. She texted back, "I can handle it myself."

"Dalton isn't acclimating well at all. He won't talk or participate in any activities, hardly eats, they say. I'm going to try to visit a few hours every day until he gets used to the place. That afghan I'm crocheting is for his bed here, a touch of home, you know. He wants to see the dogs. I have a friend who trains therapy dogs in his spare time. Maybe I could get both Courage and King certified to visit hospitals and nursing homes, all the patients, not only Dalton."

Leah began hanging the dresses and pantsuits in the closet and tried to keep the conversation polite. "Yes, pets can soothe the trouble mind. Great if you are keeping Gargantua. Hard to find homes for dogs that big, though his appetite will put a hole in your budget."

"I don't mind feeding him. Are you upset that we changed his name?"

Linda must have sensed something in her tone. "Not at all. I'm glad he has a good home." With Ash and his mommy.

"I had no idea Dalton knew your grandmother. She was such a granddame in her day, the person who threw the beads at Mardi Gras, not the ones like us who caught them. Perhaps they met while planning those parades. The fire department always participates by bringing out the antique engine they call Old Smoky and tossing candy. A few lucky kids get to ride with them, usually the children and grandchildren of the firefighters."

Linda chattered on and on until Leah had enough and stopped her flat. "No, I believe they used to be lovers before Gran married. Rachel looks a great deal like a young Alene, much more than I do. That explains the scene when my sister forced herself on you at home, and why my grandmother seemed to—desire Ash. He does resemble his grandfather, especially the eyes."

"And his father, too. It's a strong family trait and both are tall, but Ash is more slender. Dalton was such a big bull of a man in his day. It's hard to conceive he'd appeal to a cultured lady like your grandmother. Though I can entirely believe Dalton cheated on his wife. Forgive me for saying so, but Velma was no prize as a wife, mother, or mother-in-law. I can't tell you how many times I asked her not to smoke in my house. She ignored me."

"Mother-in-laws, often a problem." Leah didn't think she'd put any special emphasis on the words, but Linda caught on quick.

"I wouldn't be. I promise you that. I don't want to stand in the way of my son's happiness. He gave up a good career in Houston to help me when Dalton became too hard to handle. I thought he'd be relieved when we brought his grandfather here. Frankly, I was. It's ugly, but now we have our lives back. Only Ash doesn't seem very elated. Troubled, really."

"I'm sure you'll both be very happy now." Together.

Linda wrinkled her brow. "Something has gone wrong between you and my son."

Saved by the arrival of the burly aide hefting her grandmother's chair and the blonde assistant carrying the box of personal pictures. Leah pointed to where she wanted the chair. She gratefully took the box and began sorting through it to evade answering.

Sweet Linda turned out to be as annoying as a horsefly buzzing around Leah as she placed the portrait of her grandparents taken on their wedding day on the dresser along with her father's high school graduation picture and another of Rachel and Leah as children. Others: her parents together on their last anniversary, Leah graduating from her vet tech program, Rachel being crowned queen of one of her many pageants, lives fading from Gran's memory.

"Won't you tell me what's the matter?" So this is where Ash learned his persistence—at his mother's knee.

"I think you should discuss that with your son. I'm fine. It has nothing to do with me."

The aide returned with the TV and hooked it to the cable. The assistant arrived with a tiny decorated Christmas tree, battery operated to light up, and set it on the bland, generic coffee table to make the room more festive. Gran had much better antique furniture, but far too massive for the suite. Leah directed her mind toward finding something better, away from Ash and his mommy issues.

"It's snack time," the assistant said. "Please join us for warm chocolate chip cookies and your choice of hot coffee, tea, or juice."

If snacking would get the persistent Linda off her tail, Leah gladly agreed. Besides, who didn't like warm chocolate chip cookies? She found a seat across from her grandmother who still held hands with Dalton, her Dally. Linda drew another chair over. The assistant took their beverage orders with Linda stressing that Dalton liked his coffee with half milk and Leah ordering tea for herself and Alene. A plate of cookies appeared on the low table sitting between them. The amorous couple, still clenched together, reached for the sweets with their free hands. When Alene smeared chocolate on her face, Leah moved to wipe it off with a napkin, but Dalton wet his thumb and scrubbed it away first. Adoration showed in her grandmother's green eyes.

"I don't think we're needed here right now." Linda rose and gathered her crochet work. "I'll be back to visit you tomorrow, Chief." Dalton failed to answer.

"Me, too, Gran, we'll have Sunday dinner together here at the—resort." Leah didn't rate so much as goodbye, but she noticed an expression she hadn't seen on Alene's face since Ash danced with her—happy. "Oh, I left my keys in the room. See you later, Linda."

Leah hid out until certain Ash's mother had left the premises. At the far end of the hallway, she noticed another locked metal door, the one leading to the ward where the worst cases no longer able to function waited to die. Life was so short. Had she squandered months of that precious commodity on two men unable to commit?

Chapter Twenty-Six

Ash walked in on his mother and Rod early Wednesday morning when the shift at the firehouse changed. He shouldn't think of it that way. They were merely having coffee together. A sliced loaf of Linda's excellent banana bread sat on the table between them, now appropriately decorated for Christmas with red candles sitting in small circlets of plastic holly. Both greeted him with a cordial welcome, and his mom hurried to pour a cup for her son. The early light of a sunny day glinted in Rod's silver buzz cut and illuminated the tattoo of the Marine insignia etched on one of his well-toned biceps. The man always seemed to wear short-sleeved, tight T-shirts like a trainer at a health club as if he were oblivious to changes in temperature. Never bothered Ash before, so why now?

Perhaps because as his mother's hands flitted over the coffee preparations, he noticed she no longer wore her wedding and engagement rings. With her hair still that light blonde shade she'd adopted for the Fireman's Ball and the burden of caring for Dalton lifted, Linda looked ten years younger. She had a glow about her, too, that Ash had seen on Leah's face post-coital. No, not his mom!

Ash took a seat, his coffee doctored exactly the way he liked it, and a slice of banana bread. "You here to pick up your last check, Rod?" he asked, trying for nonchalant.

"Nope. Linda asked me to come over. Man, that banana bread is the best. She always had something special for me when I came to help with the Chief. Gotta watch it at my age." Rod patted a stomach that appeared both flat and buff—for his age. "I'll miss the old guy. When I could jog his memory, he had some tales to tell."

"Why are you here again?"

"The dogs." Both Courage and King squatted at the man's feet hopeful of fallen crumbs. "Linda wants me to train them as therapy dogs to take to the nursing home. That way your grandpa gets to see them, and they'll bring joy to others. Mostly I train comfort dogs for Marines who have PTSD, but this is a good cause, too."

"How much is this going to cost?" Did this guy only want to continue collecting a paycheck? Ash hoped so.

"Nothing. I don't charge for my dog training, but your mother can always pay me in baked goods and fudge. That peanut butter fudge she makes is something else."

Yeah, Leah had liked it also on one of the days they'd had sex out at the lake. He recalled feeding her pouty mouth slivers of it and what followed. Ash shook his head. Rod misinterpreted.

"Really, no charge. I'll teach Linda how to handle them for free. We can start Saturday when I don't have any clients to attend. Speaking of which, I need to get going." Rod stood, leaned across the table to shake hands in farewell to Ash, but Linda received a pat of the fingers and a squeeze to her shoulders. She smiled like a happy little sunbeam, and the shine followed Rod all the way out the door.

Ash gulped his coffee. Ouch, too hot! He should have known better. His mom noticed and rushed to bring him a glass of cold water. As he took it from her hands, he asked, "When did you become Linda instead of Mrs. Blaise?"

"Ages ago. You were usually on duty when he came to help."

"For which we paid him a fortune—and you still felt you needed to bake bread for him?"

"Good work should always be rewarded beyond a paycheck." Linda raised her own cup in two hands and sipped. The gesture emphasized her naked fingers.

"Did you have to take off your rings to make banana bread?" She'd never taken them off, not when doing dishes or potting plants.

"No, I've removed them for good. I tried to do it once prior to your coming home from Houston, but that set Dalton off. He couldn't handle change of any kind and once accused me of cheating on your father as if Hank might walk into the room at any moment and notice. In your grandfather's mind, his son still lives riding those engines to the fires. Wearing them on my right hand didn't satisfy him either. It wasn't worth it to upset him."

"Okay, then." He felt as accusatory as his grandfather.

"I've been going to the Villa every day to visit. So far, he hasn't noticed the change in my jewelry though I do slip on the wedding ring when visiting. Dalton is too caught up with his lady love—Leah's grandmother. He called her Allie, not Alene. He's Dally to her. They were intimate many years ago before she married. Didn't Leah tell you?"

"No, she only said things were going fine when I texted her."

"I told her you would have liked to help move Alene into her room, but…"

"She didn't need my help."

"Yes, very self-reliant, a good trait in a fireman's wife."

That statement made Ash blink and cover his astounded expression with a more cautious sip from his coffee cup. His mother steamrollered right along unimpeded.

"We had Sunday dinner together at the Villa, the four of us, very pleasant."

"Did Leah talk about me?"

"Not a word. She changed the subject if I mentioned you. I simply knew you'd had a falling out. I certainly hope it had nothing to do with me. I know young men don't like to talk to their mothers about dating problems, but I might be able to help. After all, Leah and I worked out what to do about Dalton and Alene. We were called into the office on Tuesday. It seems your grandfather has been sneaking into Alene's room at night. An aide found them spooning together in bed when she arrived to help Alene dress in the morning."

Ash choked on his coffee and sputtered into a paper napkin adorned with a holly pattern. "Still too hot for you?" his mother asked with concern. He knocked his banana bread to the floor, and the dogs got it lickety-split. "They were having sex?

"We aren't sure. The supervisor asked if Leah

wanted her grandmother to be checked by a physician, and did we want Dalton placed in the other locked ward where he'd have no freedom to roam. Leah okayed the examination to be on the safe side, but we both said no to putting Dalton away as long as he didn't cause her any physical harm and they were happy together. We had to sign papers to that effect, but Leah and I felt good about our decision. Have another piece of banana bread. I know you love it."

That's how his mother softened people up, with food and relentless conversation. He might as well confess or she'd keep him here all morning revealing more stuff he didn't want to know—like if she'd slept with Rod. Ash scrubbed his hands over his stubble since he hadn't shaved or showered before coming home.

"I know this might shock you and make you think less of Leah, but she offered to let me move in with her since you don't need me to help with Pop anymore." He waited for Linda to call his girlfriend a slut as Mrs. Couvillon would, or at least show the stern disapproval of an Ernestine Tweedy.

She did neither, only nodded. "What did you say?"

"That I couldn't just abandon you as soon as we committed Dalton. You needed my financial support and help around…"

Now, he got the disapproval big time. "I'm not your wife, Ashton Blaise! Abandon me! For your information, I can take care of myself as I did for years when your father spent nights at the station. The house is paid for, and I might get a job since I am free of your grandfather's care. And where would you be?—only a phone call away if I needed you. Oh, I can't stand the thought of being like Velma who would come over here to swill coffee, blow smoke in my face, and complain about Dalton. Her number one fear was that he'd leave her because she'd tricked him into marriage by getting pregnant. I kept saying Dalton Blaise always kept his word and would do no such thing, not to mention his love for Hank. I am not and never will be like her, do you hear me?"

He heard, especially near the end when his usually mild mother began shouting in his face. "Abandoned was a poor choice of words. I thought you needed some time to adjust."

"Leah must have felt awful to be turned down when she put herself out there."

"Leah doesn't need me as she often says, and apparently neither do you." Ash chose to study the murky interior of his coffee cup rather than meet his mother's clear blue eyes.

"Love isn't about need, something Velma did not understand. It's about being with a person you want to spend the rest of your life with as partners supporting each other like your father and I did. Is that the kind of feeling you have for Leah?"

"Yes, I think so."

Linda left the table, whether to make more coffee or remove another loaf of banana bread from the freezer since Rod had eaten half of it, Ash did not know. He took the small dog he'd named Courage into his lap. Maybe some of her moxie would rub off on him as he scratched her back. King laid his head on Ash's knees and expected the same treatment. His mother returned with a small burgundy leather box in hand and plunked it down in front of her son. "Open it."

He did. His mom's engagement ring sparkled like a genie released from a dark bottle.

"It's a good stone, a half-carat. Your father always bought the best he could afford like that tuxedo he wore to our wedding and at every Fireman's Ball before his death. Take it over to LeClerc's, get it cleaned and reset if you want. When you are ready, give it to Leah."

"You sure?"

"Positive. I can tell Dalton that I'm getting the setting checked if he asks. He'll accept the same excuse day after day because he won't remember what I told him."

"Sad but true. Thanks, Mom. And sorry about Dad's tux being ruined in the Mardi Gras hall fire."

"He would understand the emergency."

"Now if only I can get Leah to speak to me again."

Linda considered the matter. "You didn't take her on the six hundred dollar date I paid for, did you? After the fire at the hall, I think it slipped all our minds."

"No."

Linda snapped the box shut putting the genie back in the bottle for the time being, but she folded her son's hands around it. "I'd say go big, Ash, go big. If you need help with the planning, call Cole."

No need to call his brother. He knew Leah and exactly what she'd like most.

Chapter Twenty-Seven

"I'm off duty Friday night. I'd like to stop by your place for a date." Ash could sense her hostility over the phone, but at least Leah had picked up his call.

"Sure, the sex is good. We both enjoy it, so why not?" Her voice came across dull and flat, not his contentious Leah at all. He knew Ashton Blaise had been relegated to the same category as her previous lover, men who only wanted her for one thing. All those weeks of trying to win her trust gone because he'd wanted to protect his mom.

"No, I mean a real date, the six hundred dollar date you won at the Firemen's Ball auction."

"Then you should take your mother. I haven't paid her back for putting up the money."

Ouch. "She doesn't want to go out with me either, but I promise, this will be special."

"You asked her first?"

"No!" Make a mental note never to reveal that Linda had reminded him of the unclaimed prize. "Wear the ball gown."

"Come on, Ash, the dress smells like smoke and sex. I can't go anywhere but here in it."

"Two of my favorite scents, but have it dry-cleaned. I'll pay the bill as part of the date."

She didn't answer immediately. A sign of weakening?

"Okay. What time?"

"Seven. All you have to do is be ready to go."

"Guess I can manage that. See you." She disconnected.

Now, to rent a tux, beg favors from Chief Fontenot, the game warden at Indian Lake, and get in touch with T-Coon Arton. The last said, "*Mais,* yeah, I got a white tent for rent, me. Peoples like to get married by the lake." The other two were onboard with his plans as well. All of them thought he was fulfilling his six hundred dollar date.

****

Leah dithered over her preparations for the big date, more than she had for the Firemen's Ball. You would have thought prom night had come again with all its adolescent insecurities. Without Ash around to lace her into the gown—or take her out of it, she called on an unusual source of help, Ernestine Tweedy.

Flattered, Miz Tweedy lowered the refurbished gown over Leah's head and pulled the laces with surprising strength for a woman of her age. "Oh my, I feel as if I'm preparing my own daughter for a wedding. I recall that diamond clip. Your grandmother wore it often to formal affairs, not that I attended many, but I noticed it in the newspaper plenty of times. Now, you'll need a wrap. It's chilly outside.

They raided the piles of clothes Rachel left behind when she took off for New Orleans with Cole Blaise. A black shawl shot through with silver threads emerged from a dresser drawer. Leah draped it over an arm.

"Perfect. We must take pictures," Ernestine declared.

"Oh, I don't think so. It's not that kind of date."

Leah hardly wanted a souvenir of what might amount to a booty call in another location, maybe a nice hotel in Lafayette with dinner in the room.

"No trouble. I'll run home and get my camera."

"Really, I have a good camera here if you feel you must."

"Of course, we must. Why, even your pets are agitated. Animals can sense when something big is about to happen."

Stubby and Bandit had picked up on Leah's own case of nerves more likely. Why she didn't know. She'd slept with Ash plenty of times, but somehow they seemed to be starting over again after their spat about his mother, blazing a new path across uncharted waters. A heavy-breathing engine approached the barn. Had he rented a limo? When the knock sounded on the door, Leah jumped, and Ernestine giggled as if she were a teenaged friend.

"I'll answer that. You make an entrance."

"He's seen me before in…."

But, Miz Tweedy was on her relentless way, camera in hand. "My, so handsome," she said as she let Ash inside.

Leah hung back only a moment. He clutched a clear plastic box with the same cheesy silver wrist corsage that he'd brought her for the Doggone Ball. She stepped from her hiding place right around the corner.

"Here is our Leah, so lovely tonight. Stand side by side now while I commemorate this event."

Ash drew her near and slipped the corsage over her wrist. "She is always beautiful, Miz Tweedy."

"I can't believe you found another corsage like the first one," Leah remarked with a quirk of her dark

300

brows.

"I knew it broke your heart to sell it to Yancey's boyfriend for the good of the animals, so I bought you another." Ash's grin was impish, daring her to say she hated it in front of her neighbor.

"Oh, many thanks," she managed.

"So sweet of him! I got a picture of him putting it on your wrist." Ernestine insisted on posing them together, Ash's arm around Leah's waist before allowing the couple to leave.

He helped her on with her wrap. Miz Tweedy captured that as well and followed them outside where a limo was not parked. Instead, a vintage fire engine, shiny red and appearing fully functional with its ladders and coiled hoses, awaited them. "Our ride for the night, Old Smoky."

Ash helped Leah into the high cab as Ernestine attempted to get the shot, muttering all the while about hoping she had enough light. Off they went, siren blaring. Ernestine waved goodbye.

Ash turned off the siren as they entered the city limits of Chapelle, passed by the string of bars heating up for the weekend on the edge of town, the firehouse, the quiet residential area, and zoomed out the other end where Main Street turned into a rural road again. He reinstated the siren, warning anything and everybody in his way to get out of it because he wanted to get where he was going fast. Cars going into town and trucks heading for the honkytonks out on the four-lane pulled over respectfully.

Leah, exhilarated, said, "This is more fun than riding in the Prius with a bubble on top—and possibly illegal."

"A little, maybe. I got clearance from the Chief." As they approached the estate of the billionaire and the home of his gamekeeper, Ash stilled the siren again. They turned onto the gravel road leading to Indian Lake. "I don't want to spook the wildlife or Mr. Hartz."

"Are we going moonlight kayaking?—because I'm really not dressed for it."

Ash stopped before the locked gate that gave access to the boat dock and the levee hiking paths. He produced a key, cleared the way, and drove the fire engine past the barrier, got down to close and lock it again before moving on. "Usually no one is allowed in here after six. They don't want night hunting or poaching going on, but I have an in with Pete Landry, the gamekeeper. We bring the fire trucks here to practice pumping water from a pond when no fire hydrants are available. I suspect Pete is a romantic at heart."

"Well, I've heard he has seven kids. It would take a lot of romance to convince me have that many."

"Rumor has it that a love potion was involved."

"No plans to roofie me tonight, I hope."

"Not that kind of love potion. Besides, we don't need one."

Ash flashed a smile at her as white as the egrets roosting in the trees—or the small tent glowing from within under a live oak near the dock. Leah hated to admit being both enchanted and intrigued by what might lay ahead, so she didn't. No ooohs or aaahs as he put his hands around her waist and swung her down from the cab of the engine. However, a little whoopee sounded in her heart.

Chilly air promised a thick layer of frost in the

morning, but the clear sky reflected every star on the calm surface of the water. The moon laid a silver path of light across the lake that seemed solid enough to walk upon. Leah shivered at the perfect beauty of the moment shared with Ash. He mistook her shudder for being cold. "We should go inside the tent."

What awaited there? A king-sized bed strewn with rose petals? No, two white wrought iron chairs and a table holding a bud vase with a single red rose sat in the center under the glow of a small crystal chandelier hung from the ceiling. Ash's fire engine red kayak sat along one side, its surface adorned with early camellias splotched red and white. The seat held a champagne cooler with a large green bottle and two crystal flutes. A table draped in linen offered baked brie served with fig preserves and crackers, an icy bowl of large shrimp and cocktail sauce, tiny spinach quiches, and a pyramid of fried brown balls. A tray of mini-pastries, obviously from Pommier's, suggested a choice of desserts: napoleons, pecan tarts, and petit fours topped with candied violets. Best of all, a portable space heater that resembled a torch warmed the area enough for her to leave the shawl draped over a chair.

Leah twirled around taking it all in. Her skirts gave a satisfying swish at her ankles. She gestured to the brown food. "Boudin sausage balls? Isn't that against your diet?"

"Actually, alligator boulettes. I don't think alligator counts as red meat, tastes like chicken. Or so the caterer said."

Leah elbowed him. "Does not! More like pork—or whatever sauce you cook it in. All this for me?"

"We can eat now or dance."

Leah half-expected a small combo to enter the tent, but instead Ash laid his iPhone on the kayak and summoned up a play list that opened with *Moonlight Serenade*, one of her grandmother's favorite songs, one that Gran had danced to with Ash. She held up her arms, and they began a slow circuit of the tent. She thought of Alene and Dalton together after so many years apart and tears came to her eyes, so she shut them. Ash kissed her closed lids, and moved his warm lips down her throat. When *Can't Help Falling in Love with You* came up, Leah said, "I think I'm getting dizzy."

"You need food and drink." They filled their plates and sat at the little table. Ash popped the champagne cork and poured. "To the extraordinary Leah Allain," he offered.

"To the brave and true Ashton Blaise," she countered. "This is the nicest thing anyone has ever done for me."

"Now you are going to force me to confess I got the flowers from my mother's garden, all except the rose, but the champagne is from Marcello's in Lafayette, top of the line stuff. Actually, I'm not feeling particularly brave this evening."

"Why not? This is definitely a six hundred dollar date. I owe your mother a check and that fudge I didn't make for her, plus a thanks for the camellias."

"More than that," he murmured. "However, we are only up to about four hundred dollars worth right now. Let me know when you're finished eating." He took a deep, deep breath.

"Nearly done. We should fill some plates for your mom and Ernestine. This is too good to waste."

"We'll do that afterwards."

"After what? Sex on the kayak in our formalwear? Because I am totally up for that."

"Me, too, but not right now. Let's take a stroll on the dock."

He offered his hand, and Leah found his palms sweaty. Valiant firefighter Ash nervous? Maybe ill. Perhaps the shrimp had turned. He'd downed more of it than she had along with a great deal of champagne. Concerned, she followed him into the moonlight out to the dock where they had launched their first kayak expedition together. Ash cleared his throat. She certainly hoped he wasn't about to throw up. So far, the night had been magical. It would be just her luck to have a bad shrimp ruin it. Could she manage to drive the fire engine back into town, or maybe just as far as the gamekeeper's cottage to get help?

Ash grasped both her shoulders, cold because she'd forgotten the shawl. Definitely clammy, his fingers. "Are you all right?" she asked. He nodded as if he couldn't speak. "Are you sure?"

His gray eyes gazed at her; his perfect lips finally moved. "Leah Allain, here in the Cathedral of Nature before God and all the saints, I am asking you to be my wife." He dropped to one knee and offered her a small leather box containing a solitaire diamond ring as bright as those stars above. "In the interest of honesty before you answer, you need to know this was my mother's engagement ring. She wanted you to have it. We can take it to LeClerc's and put the stone into one of those fancy settings with all the little diamonds if you accept it."

He truly believed she might turn him down. Her

heart said, "Yes, yes, yes!" Her mind said she'd only get engaged once. "In the natural course of things, a couple dates for a while, often moves in together to see how they'd get along, then considers marriage."

"I'm ready to move in any time."

"Your mother kick you out?"

"More or less. She said she didn't need me, and I know you don't either, but I should be with the woman I love. You know they say a man who treats his mother well will treat his wife the same." Ash remained in the same beseeching posture on his knees as if he wouldn't budge until he got a firm answer.

"I have heard that. Really, I like your mother, even more now. I was jealous, and that was petty of me."

"I don't think you have a petty bone in your body. I mean you are willing to go easy on Cubby for destroying your home."

Leah smiled upon him. "You know if it hadn't been for Cubby and his arsonist tendencies, we might never have met."

"Maybe, but I think I would have found you sooner or later. Um, am I going to get an answer tonight because T-Coon is coming to take down the tent at midnight. I promised him the leftovers."

"We still have time for sex on the kayak. Don't worry about it."

"Sex anywhere is the last thing on my mind right now. Yes or no?"

"We really should just live together first." Leah watched the disappointment cover his face like a pall of ashes. She had to stop teasing him. "But, yes, I will marry you, Ashton Blaise."

He placed the ring on her finger, a tight fit, and

stood. After a long overdue kiss, he said, "We can take it to the jewelry store and see about getting a new setting."

Leah held the diamond up to the moon as if offering it for the approval of its goddess. "No, I like the simplicity of this ring. We'll get it sized, that's all."

"One other thing." Ash's pallor had vanished and been replaced by his usual grin.

"Yes?"

"If I move into the barn with you, we're going to need a bigger kitchen."

"If you do the cooking, you've got it—as soon as my insurance check comes in as round and fat as a Muscovy duck."

"This calls for more champagne. Like you said, we have plenty of time for the kayak."

****

The headlights of the vintage fire engine scattered a gathering of feral cats at the barn and sent them ghosting into the shadows. Fortunately, plenty of time had remained for more food, more dancing, and sex that left both of its occupants weak in the knees to offset the champagne consumed. Still, they'd crept silently through Chapelle as if a local cop might stop a fire engine going anywhere.

"Ernestine must have left a light on for us. That's kind of sweet," Leah said as she noticed the illuminated kitchen window.

"I guess so. Don't get down. I'm coming around."

Leah prepared herself for another airy lift to the ground, but instead Ash gathered her in his arms and carried her to the door. "Aren't you supposed to save that for the honeymoon? I'm still quite a chunk, and I'd hate to have you injure your back."

"And I'm a firefighter who has carried two hundred pound men down a ladder on my shoulders. Besides, you aren't chunky, just one voluptuous package that I can handle easily."

Since Ash wouldn't put her down, Leah fumbled her door key from a tiny purse and turned the knob. They crossed the threshold like bride and groom to find Miz Tweedy, head down on the kitchen table with half a carafe of coffee at her elbow. She blinked awake when Stubby began to yip, and Ash kicked the door closed to keep Bandit from making a break.

"Back so soon. I waited up because I wanted to hear all about the fabulous six hundred dollar date."

Leah elbowed Ash, and he let her slip gently to the ground. "You know it's past midnight?"

"Is it? I must have dozed off." Ernestine touched the side of the coffee carafe. "Cold, I can make more."

"Don't bother," Leah hastened to say. "We're both pretty tired." She prayed Ernestine would take the hint.

"What was I thinking? I promised Beverly Labbe I'd take her out to Indian Lake for waterfowl observation in the morning. We won't have many more chances before duck and goose hunting season opens again on the nineteenth. Though I have thought I might rent a blind and take my air horn to scare the birds away."

Leah could tell Ash held in a grin by the compression of his lips. "I believe the gamekeeper would have a problem with that, Miz Tweedy. He believes in wildlife management and keeping the goose population in control."

"Pete Landry is a very attractive older man. I

wouldn't mind having him clap me in irons and carry me away the way Captain Blaise carried you inside, the perfect ending for your special date."

Yes, it would have been if the equivalent of her mother hadn't been waiting up in her home. Leah reached deep for her diplomacy skills once more. "We brought you a plate of food from our outing. It's still in the cab of the fire engine. Why doesn't Ash get it and walk you home. You know the birds are most active at dawn, and the gates at Indian Lake open at six a.m."

"Yes, yes, I told Bev no sleeping in for birdwatchers."

"Come over tomorrow when you get back. Tell me all about your observations, and I'll tell you about my date." Then Leah made the mistake of removing her left hand from the folds of her gown to brush the bangs out of her eyes.

"You're engaged! I knew this fine young man would make an honest woman of you someday." Ernestine popped from her seat to take a good look at the ring. "I'm so glad it's plain, not like those gaudy things most girls want these days. Plain and simple like you. When is the wedding?"

"We haven't discussed a date yet."

"Of course. So thrilling to be the first to know."

"Please keep it quiet until I can call my parents."

"Not a word." Ernestine zipped her wrinkled lips. "I'll come over tomorrow with teacakes. Now, if Captain Blaise would give me his arm so I won't fall into any holes getting home, I'll be going. Not everyone gets to ride on a fire engine."

Ash took the hint and escorted Miz Tweedy to the cab, lifted her avian-weight body into the air, and closed the door. He went back to where Leah waited in the doorway.

"I think I might have liked it better when Ernestine was my enemy, and she considered me a vixen," Leah grumbled. "Are you going straight home to tell your mother?"

"Nope. I think my mom wants her privacy. She and Rodney Salkowitz have something going on that I don't want to interrupt or think about."

"Rodney Salkowitz?"

"My grandfather's former aide. He loves her peanut better fudge among other things."

"It is good stuff."

"I won't be tempted to stay next door for teacakes, Leah, my love."

With that statement, he brushed her lips with his. So ended the six hundred dollar date, and worth every penny.

Chapter Twenty-Eight

Ash left the barn early to return Old Smoky to the bay of the firehouse. Leah made him swear to tell no one but his mother about their engagement. She had calls to make and fudge to concoct. With her phone held in the crook of her neck, she poured sweetened condensed milk over a bowl of chocolate chips and shoved it in the microwave. Her mother answered before it dinged.

"Leah, has something else gone wrong? You quit your last job, your house goes up in flames, then that fire at the Mardi Gras hall, and having to put your grandmother in Magnolia Villa. I can only ask what next?"

"Good news this time." Leah removed the bowl, stirred, put the melting chocolate in for another minute.

"Really. Let me put you on speaker phone. Rachel is right here, and your father is puttering around somewhere."

"What is Rachel doing in Florida?"

"Visiting before she returns to LSU to take her finals and see what she can salvage of the semester. A young man she met in New Orleans convinced her to finish in retailing this spring. He said that's where her talents lie. I confess I'd believe anything that came from his lips. She has pictures. The guy is gorgeous."

"Yes, I've met him—Cole Blaise." Male stripper.

Leah held that information back. "His brother and I are…"

"I told Rachel that would be a great name for a male stripper, but he's from Chapelle, a business major at UNO. Your daddy knew his daddy, so I'm certain he comes from a good family."

"Uh-huh." Ding! Rachel removed the chocolate mixture, beat the hell out of any lumps, and put it back for a few seconds more.

"I think Cole is interested in Rachel."

"What guy isn't?" Leah's sigh wafted over the airwaves all the way to the Florida panhandle. She tried again. "Actually, I'm dating his brother, Ashton."

"Yes, the firefighter. Rachel said they went out a couple of times before she met Cole."

No use in saying no they did not! She'd met the one man Rachel failed to enchant. Deep breath, Leah, deep breath. Let the previous statement go. "Ash and I got engaged last night."

"What!" That was Rachel's distinctive shriek. "I call maid of honor, and I get to pick my dress."

Then, her mother said the words Leah waited her whole life to hear. "Hush, Rachel. This is about Leah, not you. I admit I always thought Rachel would marry first, but this is wonderful. Have you discussed a date yet?"

Leah removed the bowl of fudge, added the vanilla, chopped pecans, and tiny marshmallows, folding the ingredients in gently. "I think in the spring, outdoors by Indian Lake. I have this great sort of smoky black dress I wore to the ball that Ash likes so much. I'll wear that." After she got it dry-cleaned again. "Only Rachel and Cole for attendants. I want to keep it simple."

"You can't do that, wear black to your own wedding!" Mom protested.

At sometime during the conversation, her father had shown up. "I don't know. If the boy likes the dress, it seems very economical to me. Leah always did have good sense. I remember how much we shelled out for Rachel's pageant dresses only worn a few times. She might have one that would do for maid of honor."

"I'll want a new gown if I'm going to be maid of honor. Let me call Regan at Belles, Beaux and Brides and see if Leah can get that same dress she loves in white," Rachel chipped in. "I'm dialing now."

"Are you sure about having it outdoors with the heat and mosquitoes and the possibility of rain, maybe even thunderstorms or tornadoes. We really should book St. Jeanne's if it isn't too late already. The repairs at the Mardi Gras hall might be done by then. Everything will be nice and new. Probably booked up already, but I'll try to get it," her mother nattered on.

Leah poured the fudge into an aluminum pan she'd bought for the purpose, no more having to exchange dishes. Linda Blaise could keep it. She jammed the candy into a space she'd made in her fridge to cool. Be cool, Leah, be cool. "May is one of our driest months and not too hot if you go out in the morning. Indian Lake is special to us," she explained so very rationally.

"Leah, baby, if you are worried about the expense, don't be. Whatever you want. I just don't understand women buying dresses they only wear once. Incidentally, has my cousin sent you a check for your house yet?" her father said.

"Not yet, but…"

"I knew he'd run that insurance agency into the

ground. People need their money to rebuild. He won't get new clients if he drags his feet in paying. Let me get on my phone and see what's what. The hell if he isn't in the office today. I know where he lives."

"Great! Leah, they have the dress in white. Regan knows your size. Should we put it on order? We can't waste any time if you want to go with a spring ceremony," Rachel contributed. "Oh, flash us a picture of your ring."

Leah splayed her left hand on the kitchen table, photographed the ring, and sent the picture. "Oh, kind of small and plain," Rachel commented as if she referred to Leah.

"It's beautiful," her mom said. "Don't listen to your sister."

Leah resolved she wouldn't anymore. "Look, Dad, before you ream out Cousin Brock about the settlement they had to close the arson case. Turned out to be Cubby Couvillon. His daddy taught him how to set fire to old buildings to give the volunteer firefighters practice. Cliff burned some old tenant cabins." She wasn't even going to try to explain crazy Eunice Couvillon to them.

"Cliff? I was in Rotary Club with Cliff. I can't believe it, but if it is so, Brock can get off his fat behind and settle your claim. Got him on the phone right now. Brock, you son of a…"

"Stop! Everyone stop! Listen up. I will be getting married in May at Indian Lake. Okay, if the dress comes in white, order it. We will be keeping this small. If you put any more pressure on me to do otherwise, we'll elope to Vegas. Got that?" Silence ensued, a quiet so deep she could hear Bandit purring under the kitchen table for no special reason at all other than that he now sat on her feet while Stubby snuffled around for fallen pecans.

"Sorry, honey, whatever you want." Her father became the first to relent.

"Don't do anything rash, Leah. We'll make this work," her mother said.

"I only wanted to help," whined Rachel.

"Yes, I know, but it is my way or the highway—to Vegas. We'll talk more later. I have fudge to deliver."

****

Leah stood on the Blaise front porch banked with greenery and red poinsettias waiting for Linda to answer the bell. She held the fudge before her like the Sunday offering plate at church. Seemed appropriate since she wanted to confess. When Ash's mother opened the door, the fudge nearly ended up smeared on Leah's chest, the casualty of a huge hug. "I guess Ash told you the news."

"He called first thing this morning, though I couldn't sleep last night wondering. It's a pity he's on duty for the next few days. We need to have a little family celebration, maybe if you don't mind, at the Villa. You were so sweet to donate the record player and those recordings for the old folks to dance. How they enjoyed that. Heavens, I'm keeping you on the doorstep like a stranger I'm afraid to let inside. Come have coffee."

"I loved seeing Gran and Dalton circling the room to *Tennessee Waltz*. They looked so right. Ah, I made some rocky road fudge to thank you for the peanut butter fudge you gave Ash for one of our picnics. Gran would say I'm way overdue to return the favor. Sorry,"

315

Leah said as she crossed the small living room, now minus Dalton's big recliner, and followed Linda to the dining area off the kitchen.

"Don't worry about it. There is only one thing I want from you—grandchildren."

"Oh, I'm not pregnant! That's not why…"

She'd never heard Linda really laugh. The tone came out warm, yet silvery like Christmas jingle bells. "When you and Ash get around to it."

A muscular man with a gleam in his light eyes when he looked at Linda and an awesome military tattoo rose from the table and offered a hand that could have held two of hers. "Rod Salkowitz. Linda calls this coffee, but let's be honest about it."

Oh please, don't say a booty call. No, people their age didn't use the term—love affair, having sex, hiding the sausage. Leah possessed no desire to confirm Ash's suspicions.

"This is brunch," Rod continued. "I come over for coffee, and this is what she puts out: fresh orange juice, cranberry muffins, this egg casserole with potatoes and other great stuff in it."

"It's Ash's recipe, but I added a layer of browned and drained sausages and topped it with bacon as well as cheese. Please help yourself."

Leah almost said she'd love to because Ash hadn't had the time to make her breakfast before his shift change. She quickly switched to, "I only had cereal this morning, and I'm on my way to the shelter from here. I'd love to have brunch with you." She took a place at the festive holiday table as Linda put a piece of the casserole on a plate for her. Might as well take a muffin, too. They looked very tasty. Leah bit into the pastry.

Linda appeared to have none of Leah's qualms. "I guess since Ash didn't come home last night, he has decided to move in with you."

Leah choked on the muffin crumbs, cleared her throat with a hastily poured glass of orange juice. "About that. I feel I might have pressured him too soon—and said some ugly words that I regret about him living with his mother. I apologize. We're thinking an early May wedding, and if he wants to stay here until then while you adjust to the idea, it's all right with me."

"Never mind all that. I will be quite fine on my own. Rod, Ash and Leah got engaged last night."

"Best wishes. Nice ring. Isn't that yours, Linda? I noticed you'd taken them off."

"Yes, new beginnings for all of us."

"Still, I'm going to have to look in on you more often if Ash has moved out. Make sure you're safe, and you have all you need." Rod waggled at finger the size of one of the sausages at Linda.

Leah figured they could reheat their coffee without taking it to the microwave considering the hot glance the two exchanged. She bolted the rest of her eggs and gulped down her juice. "I really have to get to the shelter. Saturdays this close to Christmas can be busy. We have to give the speech about not getting a dog or cat for a gift unless the recipient approves dozens of times. We hate to get returns. I have some fantastic volunteers who opened for me today, but I should join them." She pushed up from the table, but looked around missing something. "Say, where are Courage and King?"

"Out in the yard running off some of their energy.

Rod is going to start training them to be therapy dogs today."

"That's wonderful! All of it is wonderful. Linda, I love the ring. Thank you so much for everything."

Linda enveloped her again. "I've always wanted a daughter."

For a while at least, she would be the favorite daughter-in-law and vowed to be a good one. With that happy thought in mind, Leah headed for the shelter.

****

Busy, just as she thought. A half dozen cars and pickups filled the parking area. Families strolled among the runs and in and out of the cattery, all of them dogged by eager volunteers. Yancey Breaux caught Leah on the steps to the office and brought her up to date on adoptions. That girl certainly had a talent for matching animals with owners. Leah was glad her father relented about letting his daughter volunteer at the shelter. With Cubby gone, there should be no more problems in that area.

"The woman who has been here three times and couldn't make up her mind about which cat to take adopted Bandit's mother. I told her all about the poor thing being abandoned in the countryside because she got pregnant, and how she raised her kittens in a feral cat colony, a single mom all alone, before you brought her here."

"Very touching. You do have a knack, Yancey."

The teenager beamed, her high ponytail swaying with happiness like a dog's hindmost quarters. "Gets better. She took the calico kitten and the one who looks like Bandit for her nieces. Yes, before you ask, I gave her the Christmas present speech. She says if her sister objects, she'll keep them all. We're holding the kittens until the day before Christmas."

"Nice work, now try to find homes for some of the dogs." Leah opened the door to the office, and Mr. Grey greeted her, "Le-ah, baby. Give me some."

"Anyone want a parrot?" she asked Yancey before the closing door.

"No, ma'am. Sorry."

"Hi, Ethel, what are you doing here today?" Leah asked her volunteer secretary as she gave Mr. Grey what he wanted—a grape.

"I thought you'd need extra help, and I admit, I wanted to see the ring. You and that bodacious fireman getting married. I love it!"

"We've only been engaged for about twelve hours and most of that time people should have been asleep. How did you hear?"

"The Chapelle grapevine never closes down. I went to eight o'clock Mass and ran into Beverly Labbe. Poor thing. Ernestine Tweedy had her out at Spanish Lake by sunrise to observe waterfowl. Since she'd gotten up so early, Bev figured she'd get church out of the way for the weekend because she plans to sleep in tomorrow. A bunch of us went across the street to Pommier's Bakery for beignets afterwards. Bev said she heard from Ernestine who spilled the beans because she was too tired to stay out at the lake for more than two hours and offered you getting engaged last night as an explanation. Bev said, 'Thank God for that,' because her freezing behind wouldn't have lasted much longer squatting in the cattails. Well, you say something at Pommier's, and it will be all over town by the time church bells ring at noon. Which reminds me…" Ethel held out her hand, and Leah laid hers in the old woman's clutches.

"I like it. Not ostentatious. Suits you."

"Thanks," Leah said, so glad the words plain and simple did not enter into the conversation.

The door opened, hopefully another adopter ready to sign the papers and fork over the hundred dollar fee. Cliff Couvillon hesitated on the sill. "I guess I'm the last person you want to see."

Leah refrained from answering that. "How's Cubby doing?"

"Better than me. He's been ruled incompetent to stand trial. The judge remanded him to a group home out in the country where he'll be watched and taken care of while Eunice and I are serving our time. Two years for me. Forty for Eunice since she went down for two counts of aggravated arson by setting fire to buildings with people inside who might have been harmed. Could have been a life sentence if you or one of Madame Mystique's girls died. Since my wife confessed, the lesser charges for the truck and the cribs were dropped. Didn't help her much."

"Will she get out early for good behavior?" The thought of Mrs. Couvillon on the loose again chilled her.

"Eunice doesn't behave well, and she's up in years so I doubt it. Look, I'm here to make amends, both court-ordered and because I want to do it. The judge is giving me some time to get my affairs in order." Cliff held out a check written for an amount more generous than any he'd given to the shelter, twenty-five thousand dollars made out to Leah Allain.

"That's the fine Eunice owes for your house. I

hope it helps. I've already paid off Mystique. Got five hundred each to give Bob LeBlanc for his old truck and the farmers whose shacks I burned."

Speechless, Leah simply stared at the check in her hands.

"Hey, nice ring. I heard you and Ash are going to tie the knot. Good man."

"Yes, we are, but how did you know?"

"I wanted coffee and beignets at Pommier's one last time. You know how our baker gossips."

"I do now. Thank you for the money. It will help."

"It's asking a lot, but I need a couple of favors from you." Cliff took off his black volunteer firefighter's cap and crumpled it in his hands.

Leah appreciated the irony, and the fact that he'd given her the check first. Cliff Couvillon—always a shrewd business man. But why, oh why, did people assume she'd be a soft touch simply because she loved animals. People and their behavior came in a distant second in her opinion. "You can ask."

"Would you visit Cubby while I'm inside? Maybe take him some snacks. He's on a farm with a big garden and animals the residents take care of so it won't be like visiting a prison."

Okay, her heart softened a little. "I'd be glad to do that."

"And would you take my wife's dipshit poodle? I got it in a carrier out in the car. Maybe you can find a home for it with another old woman who hates sex."

"It's what we do, match animals to good new homes. Some forms need to be filled in for a surrender. We need its shot records, age, breed, any bad habits."

"Doesn't like men, that's for sure." Cliff sat down

to apply himself to the paperwork of getting rid of Eunice's pet.

"I'll get the dog while you're doing that." Leah stowed the large check in a drawer and went out to retrieve the carrier. At least, small animals were easier to place. As she lifted the crate from the rear of Cliff's SUV, another car entered the gates of Safe Haven Animal Shelter the likes of which she'd never seen.

The pimped out gold Cadillac came to a halt and parked in front of four other vehicles. Except for a few friendly welcoming yaps from the dogs, silence fell over the compound. Small children pointed, women frowned, and men goggled. The driver's side door opened to reveal mile long legs swinging to the side and rising up on six inch stiletto heels that matched the color of the car. The body that followed was toned as an athlete, curvaceous as stripper, and striking as a fashion model, all of it encased in pale, glowing yellow skin covered by a black spandex sheath. A fountain of tiny blonde braids flowed down the woman's body. She tossed them as if wielding a cat o' nine tails in a pirate movie. The copious gold bling around her neck swayed as she walked toward Leah.

"You in charge here?"

"Yes, I am."

"You have that air about you. I know when people are in charge." The extraordinary female held out a hand sporting red acrylic nails long and sharp enough to skin a muskrat. Leah accepted her firm handshake. "Mystique Bouvier. I've come for my parrot. I do hope I'm not too late to claim him. You see, I've lived in temporary quarters until renovations on my new place were finished. It took far longer than it should have, but doesn't it always? I bought the Spanish colonial on Indian Lake Road just across the parish line and way back in the pines for privacy. You know the place?"

Mystique's voice washed over Leah, soft and husky, almost mesmerizing. "I can't say that I do, but I hope you and Mr. Grey will be happily reunited there."

"Good answer." Madame Mystique's plump scarlet lips split into a smile. Her eyes, green as Leah's, turned up at the corners. "You still have him, then."

"Yes. Please step inside." Impressive how the woman managed the gravel and the concrete steps on those heels.

The moment they entered the office, Mr. Grey ceased grooming his feathers and squawked, "Mis-tee, Mis-tee!" His wings whirred as he plunged from his perch to cling to the side of the cage nearest his former mistress.

"May I?" asked Mystique. "I don't want him to hurt himself in his urgency. Not that the cage isn't nicely furnished. All of his toys were lost in the fire, and I did let him fly free quite a bit."

Leah nodded. Mystique opened the cage door and held out her arm as firmly muscled as a pro tennis player. Mr. Grey climbed aboard and walked its length to her shoulder. He rubbed his cheek against hers, billing and cooing. Mystique plucked a grape from Leah's bowl. She placed it between her lips. The parrot removed it delicately and gobbled it down.

"So good to see you again, my lover bird. May I take the cage as well?"

"I'm afraid I have to ask for the hundred dollar adoption fee since you left him here so long—and I'd have to charge you something for the cage since we added quite a bit to it to keep him from being bored," Leah managed to say.

"Mr. Grey was rarely bored at my place. He loved to watch. Cliff, darling, do you mind? I've endorsed your check over to the shelter. I really hated to take your money, and the cause is so good." Mystique's nails gently raked through his gray flat top. "I'll miss you and Cubby, sweet boy."

"Same here." All of Cliff's regret showed on his face, changing it from jovial Rotarian to future convict in seconds. "See you in two years, baby."

"Mis-tee, baby," Mr. Grey said, caressing Mystique's cheek again.

"Will this be enough?" The local madam turned over another twenty-five thousand dollar check. "You've taken such good care of him.

"Very generous. We'll put it to good use for the animals. If you'd fill in an adoption form to keep it legal," Leah said to the queen of the illegal. She managed not to choke on her words.

Cliff surrendered his seat as well as the dog. Mystique glimpsed the black button nose pressed against the bars of the carrier. "Perhaps I should adopt two animals today."

"No! Hates men," Cliff intervened.

"That wouldn't do at all at the House of Pleasure. Maybe another time." Mystique did the paperwork like a person used to getting things done. All the while, Mr. Grey perched on her shoulder. "Come, baby, back into your little palace for the ride home."

Cliff had loitered. "I'll help you with the cage. Maybe we should put it in my SUV, and I could follow you back to the house." He seemed hopeful of a reward better than hot beignets.

"Certainly, always a gentleman, Clifford." She turned her slanted green eyes on Leah. "I hear you are going to marry the firefighter who saved my parrot. Do thank him again for me." Mystique squeezed Leah's hand. "Best wishes to you both. Discount on couples services if you ever feel the urge."

"How did you hear... never mind. Goodbye, Mr. Grey."

"Bye-bye, Le-ah." Within a few minutes no sign of the parrot remained but a few floating down feathers and a circle on the floor made of nutshells, grape seeds, and a plop of parrot poop that had escaped the cage.

While these events unfolded, Ethel Murphy sat as quietly as a sack of dog chow at her desk taking it all in, probably for the consumption of her bridge club or casino buddies. "Bet you're going to miss that bird," she said.

"No, I'm not. He turned out to be very fickle. I don't want any of this discussed around town. People will find out soon enough about our family of arsonists, their sentences, and the location of Madame Mystique's new place without our help. We will formally thank Mystique Bouvier for her generous donation in the newsletter of course."

"You think that's her real name?"

"Absolutely not, but it doesn't matter"

"Well, my lips are sealed." Ethel made a zipping motion across a mouth bleeding red lipstick into her wrinkles, a gesture that too much resembled Ernestine Tweedy's oath.

Leah strongly suspected by the time she and Ash married in May, all of Chapelle would know the details down to the flowers selected for the boutonnieres and the filling chosen for the wedding cake. She didn't particularly care since everyone in town would wish them well.

Chapter Twenty-Nine

Leah peered nervously from behind a flap in a white tent four times the size of the one Ash rented with its three chandeliers and a much larger dance floor. Indian Lake put on its best demeanor for her, its calm blue face dotted with the reflection of puffy white clouds that shouldn't turn to thunderheads until her ten a.m. wedding was well over and the guests gone home. Behind her the wedding party, all but Ash and the priest, sat around tables waiting for the DJ hired for the affair to start the recording of the wedding march. Afterwards, the man agreed to play sweet old love songs, some Cajun, some contemporary music, and take requests like any of his ilk.

The caterers filled the tables for a mostly cold buffet immediately following the service with a menu much like the six hundred dollar date with the addition of pecan praline chicken nuggets and the ubiquitous chicken salad sandwiches no southern reception could be held without. They'd added beer and soft drinks along with champagne to the beverages, but not iced in a kayak this time as they'd sold Ash's boat. Small pastries surrounded the elegant three-tiered wedding cake (raspberry filling) with fondant wisteria blossoms cascading down its sides as if it had given birth to an unusually large litter of tiny mixed breed pups. Their father, no doubt, was the chocolate groom's cake shaped like a fire engine.

Thinking of fathers, the old priest Fr. Ardoin had been far more amenable to performing the rite of marriage outdoors beside a lake than his young replacement. He waited now beneath an arbor of purple silk wisteria vines. As Rachel insisted, the choice of flowers would compliment her slim, full length gown of off-the-shoulder lavender. Leah wore the white replica of her smoky black gown, but rebelled against a traditional veil. A sassy white hat with a short veil that brushed across her black bangs suited her so much more. She agreed to carry a cascade of white artificial wisteria blooms filled out with silver rosebuds from a certain prom corsage, ferns, trailing ivy, and touches of purple statice. As all of Chapelle knew, thanks to Beau Regard the florist, the boutonnieres were white rosebuds with a bit of fern and a soupcon of the statice with the ladies' corsages to match.

Leah found a formal gown of mauve with crystals sprinkled across the bodice in her grandmother's closet for Alene to wear, because of course she must be there along with Dalton, all protests from her mother ignored. At Magnolia Villa, Leah braided Gran's hair and put it up with the diamond clip at the back. Rod helped Dalton into his tux. Once Leah dressed, they headed for the lake followed by a mini-bus filled with the more able of their friends from assisted living.

That's what got out of hand—the reception. Leah held her ground about the date, place, and size of the wedding party, but the reception grew and grew like a four alarm fire. All of the firefighters and their wives had to be invited, her friends from vet tech school, her father's former business associates including the much reviled Cousin Brock who'd finally paid up for Leah's lost house, and the local friends of both mothers. Miz Tweedy wheedled an invitation adding Beverly Labbe as her plus one. Rachel and Cole wanted the Macho Men to attend. That's when Leah finally put her foot down and said no, stopping the rampage of guests. They had enough folding chairs set up for an outdoor BeauSoleil concert and still people stood in the rear. The crowd soon obliterated her view of the arbor, the priest, and any sign of Ashton Blaise, causing her a tee-tiny moment of panic.

"And a one and a two and a three, cue bridal march," the DJ announced from his platform by the dance floor. "Mothers, old folks, and dogs on the go."

Leah's mother took the lead somewhat flustered to be on Cole's arm. She walked down the aisle in front of Linda and Rod escorting Dalton and Alene along with two very well-behaved therapy dogs who patiently wore floral wreaths around their necks. Rachel began her bridesmaid's stutter step because that was Rachel. She couldn't merely walk like anyone else. Leah latched onto her father and simply floated along because that is how the gown made her feel, light as smoke, not short, not chunky—beautiful.

Ash waited, that ever persuasive smile on his face, as if he'd talked her into the greatest adventure of her life. He probably had. The ruckus broke out when Alene noticed the diamond earrings Rachel sported. Gran rose, pointed a finger, and said, "She stole those from me!" Leah's mother blurted, "I told you so."

Leah picked up speed reaching her grandmother, putting a soothing hand on her arm. "Rachel only borrowed them for my big day. I'm marrying Ash, remember, Dalton's grandson."

"Yes, I suppose you are right." Gran's sat again and took Dalton's hand for comfort.

The ceremony proceeded to its end with the kissing of the bride and another unexpected interruption. Dalton Blaise stood, bringing Alene along with him, and led them to the astounded priest. "We want to be married."

"Oh my, have you had your pre-marital counseling? I suppose at your age, that's not necessary. A license, is there a license, a ring?" Fr. Ardoin flustered.

"Please," said Leah. "They may not remember tomorrow, and we can do it all over again with the proper forms later. Let this be their day, too."

"I have a ring." Linda Blaise stood and removed the wedding ring from her right hand. Her left hand glittered with a new engagement ring as she made the transfer. She smiled at her ever-understanding Rodney. "Dalton, I want you to have the ring Hank gave to me. Let it be Alene's ring now."

He accepted the plain gold band. Both repeated their vows following the lead of the priest. Dalton put the ring on Alene's finger with some effort to get it over an arthritic swollen knuckle. It occurred to Leah that her grandmother had removed her own rings not long after her husband's death and had been waiting for Dalton to wed her ever since. Now he had.

The recessional blasted from the tent. The sudden noise flushed a pair of eagles from the trees. They soared together toward the aerie in the lone cypress. "He found a mate," Leah said.

"So did I," Ash answered, squeezing her hand.

After the food and the drink, the toasts and the cake, the opening dance to *Can't Help Falling Love with You* and more music, they planned to slip away for a brief three day honeymoon, all the time their professions would allow for now. Where, no one knew except for one person, T-Coon Arton, who'd set up a well-provisioned small white tent by a significant live oak on the other side of the lake. Their new red double kayak waited at his dock. Leah looked around at all the well-wishers applauding their union, and then deeply into her husband's smoky gray eyes. To think, all this love had risen from a pile of ashes.

A word about the author...

Once a librarian, now a writer of romance, Lynn Shurr grew up in Pennsylvania Dutch country. She attended a state college and earned a very impractical B.A. in English Literature. Her first job out of school really was working as a cashier in a burger joint. Moving from one humble job to another, she traveled to North Carolina, then Germany, then California where she buckled down and studied for an M.A. in Librarianship.

New degree in hand, she found her first reference job in the Heart of Cajun Country, Lafayette, Louisiana. For her, the old saying, "Once you've tasted bayou water, you will always stay here" came true. She raised three children not far from the Bayou Teche and lives there still with her astronomer husband.

When not writing, Lynn likes to paint, cheer for the New Orleans Saints and LSU Tigers, and take long road trips nearly anywhere. Her love of the bayou country, its history and customs, often shows in the background for her books.

You may contact Lynn at www.lynnshurr.com or visit her blog—lynnshurr.blogspot.com.

Thank you for purchasing
this publication of The Wild Rose Press, Inc.

If you enjoyed the story, we would appreciate your
letting others know by leaving a review.

For other wonderful stories,
please visit our on-line bookstore at
www.thewildrosepress.com.

For questions or more information
contact us at
info@thewildrosepress.com.

The Wild Rose Press, Inc.
www.thewildrosepress.com

Stay current with The Wild Rose Press, Inc.

Like us on Facebook

https://www.facebook.com/TheWildRosePress

And Follow us on Twitter
https://twitter.com/WildRosePress